"I'M GLAD TO HEAR YOU SLEPT IN, LESLIE."

Steve's provocative gaze slid down her red silk caftan, which revealed every curve. "I thought you were planning to wear that on the plane!"

Leslie blushed and pulled the collar tighter. "Why, I'm totally covered!"

"Umm, delectably. You're so tempting...." With a husky groan he pulled her into his arms. "You don't have anything on underneath, do you?"

Cradled comfortably against his chest, Leslie shook her head. His warm hands were stroking her back, her hips, mesmerizing her with his touch. He was saying something about getting dressed, but she couldn't concentrate on anything but the pleasurable feel of his body....

With a muttered curse he pushed her away. "Damn it, Leslie, move!" he snapped. "Before I don't let you...."

JUDITH DUNCAN
Is also the author of
SUPERROMANCE #51
TENDER RHAPSODY

Nightclub singer Jillian Lambert had a
special earthy quality to her voice that
excited critics and audiences alike. Her fans
didn't know that the deep emotion she
poured into her music was evoked by a man
in her past.

Jacob Holinski had been her passion, her
reason for living, her very soul. When a tragic
accident crippled him, he had left her rather
than become a burden....

Five years later the wounds were finally
healing. Life for Jillian was at least bearable.
And then Jacob came back, ripping open all
the painful memories....

JUDITH DUNCAN

HOLD BACK THE DAWN

A SUPERROMANCE FROM
WORLDWIDE

TORONTO · NEW YORK · LONDON

Published August 1983

First printing June 1983

ISBN 0-373-70077-6

Printed in Canada

CHAPTER ONE

THE ORNATE LUXURY of the richly appointed oak-paneled office was marred by a brittle tension that almost crackled. Leslie Kairns sat in the leather chair facing the large oaken desk, her fingers clenched tightly around the pencil she held, her face pale and taut. Apprehensively she studied her stepfather's face for some indication as to what kind of temper he was in.

She had never been adept at reading his moods. His aquiline features and hooded eyes gave him a predatory air that had always unsettled her. His dark hair, brushed back from his forehead, made him look like an eagle that was ready to strike.

Leslie sighed softly. His expression was enigmatic, controlled—like a plastic mask, she thought.

Her eyes strayed to the blue-bound report that was lying on the corner of his desk. She wished he would say something—anything—that would end this silent ordeal. But Luther Denver totally ignored his step-daughter as he made notations in another document that lay on the desk before him.

Leslie forced herself to take deep even breaths in an attempt to ease the tension within her. He would be annoyed with her over the report; of that she was certain. But then, he always was annoyed with her.

She had learned a long time ago that Luther resented her, that her existence was a source of irritation to him.

She had been five years old when he married her mother, and for a number of years she'd tried every trick in the book to worm her way into his affections. All of her efforts had been appalling failures. Luther consistently treated her like some piece of objectionable trash that the dog had dragged in. Consequently, Leslie had developed into an uncertain child who had often escaped from reality into a world of fantasy.

It wasn't until her adolescent years that she finally realized Luther detested children, all children. Especially her.

As she grew older, his loathing turned into a less frightening, but still painful, attitude of bored disdain. He made no effort to conceal his feelings from her, or from anyone else who happened to be around. That he recognized her at all was because, unfortunately, she happened to be the daughter of his beautiful remote wife, whom he adored.

Accepting his rejection of her had been a major and very agonizing hurdle in Leslie's life. Once she struggled through the painful realization that he would have disliked her no matter what, she was able to finally come to terms with the unpleasant situation. From then on she made a point of staying out of his way.

During her high-school years there had been a cold guarded lull in their difficult relationship, but that shattered when she enrolled in university. Leslie still could not fathom why he should be so deadly opposed to her career selection. If anything, she'd expected that for once he would extend grudging approval.

Since Luther was the president and major stockholder of Denver Oil Company, Leslie had been indirectly exposed to the oil industry for most of her life. Through this exposure she had developed a fascination for the science of geology. When as a child she'd discovered that rock formations could tell the story of what had happened to the earth aeons ago, the doors of her imaginative and clever mind had opened wide. Her interest had continued to grow, until it felt only natural that she major in the subject.

Instead of being pleased, or even slightly flattered by her choice, Luther had been enraged. There had been a horrible scene, with the result that Leslie left Calgary and attended a university in the east.

When she graduated with first-class standings, she had received numerous job offers—partly because of her marks, and partly, Leslie was realistic enough to realize, because she was a woman. Industries were looking for their token females.

She had just made up her mind to accept a position with one of the major oil companies when she received a very stiff letter from Luther. Her mother had cancer, he'd written. And although her doctors felt very positive about the treatment, Vivian Denver was faced with a complete mastectomy and several months of chemotherapy. Luther wanted Leslie to move back home to be with her mother during the ordeal. If she returned to Calgary, he would guarantee her a position in the geological department of Denver Oil.

It was an out-and-out bribe, and Leslie recognized it as such...and she knew why he had done it. Beneath Vivian's cool elegant exterior, there was an emotional fragility that could very easily shatter under stress. Luther would go to any lengths to insulate his wife from the fear and uncertainty of the trail she faced, and if that meant tolerating his stepdaughter in his home, he would do so, as long as having her there would give Vivian some measure of comfort and support.

Leslie was caught in a nightmare of a trap. Her conscience dictated that she must go, while her need for independence bade her not to.

Leaving Alberta in the first place had been a frightening ordeal for Leslie. She was extremely shy, and surviving the impersonality of a huge university had been a challenging experience. But she had learned to cope, and her tenuous grip on independence was something she valued above all else.

But her sense of duty won out, and with a certain amount of dread, Leslie reluctantly returned to the stifling inhospitable existence.

The only respite from the pressure at home was her job. Granted, she was low man on the totem pole in the geological department, but she was gaining valuable experience, and she loved the work. No one in the company had any idea that she was the boss's stepdaughter, and she cautiously protected that anonymity. She promised herself that as soon as Vivian was able to cope, she would find a job with a different company.

She had been at Denver Oil for only a few months when Ted McAllister came to work for the company as exploration manager. Ted had worked for one of the major oil companies for many years and had reached a high management level. He was approaching retirement age when he decided, like a bolt out of the blue, that he was tired of "flying a desk." The search for oil was his first love; he wanted to be back in exploration.

He had been a close friend of Leslie's grandfather, so he knew what her home life had been like. But he was also shrewd enough to realize that she had tremendous potential. He had taken her under his wing and had made her responsible for the lab analysis of core samples taken from promising formations at the drilling sites.

This unexpected opportunity presented Leslie with a challenge that elated her. She was a disciplined worker who thrived on the precise research that was required. And during two years of working under Ted, she developed an uncanny sixth sense when it came to playing hunches.

It was because of a hunch, some extensive lab work and her intense analysis of old seismic data that she was sitting in Luther's plush office now, her palms clammy, her nerves vibrating like high tension wires. If she had to sit there much longer, waiting for Luther to say something, she would come unglued, she decided. She grasped the pencil tighter in her hands and twisted it nervously.

"Don't do that."

Leslie nearly flew out of her chair at Luther's curt command. She swallowed with difficulty as he stared at her chillingly.

Picking up the document from the corner of his

desk, he dropped it with disdain in front of her. "Well, Leslie, this is quite a report. Needless to say, your portion of it sounds somewhat like those fairy tales you used to fabricate when you were a child."

Leslie could feel a flush scald her cheeks, and she experienced the same feeling of humiliation Luther's sneering comments usually aroused in her. He had found her whimsical streak totally repulsive, and he still used every opportunity he could to belittle her over it. His one derisive comment shattered any small hope she had of her stepfather giving her report an iota of consideration.

Luther was still staring at her, his arms folded rigidly across his chest, his pale gray eyes boring holes into her. A thought flashed absently through Leslie's mind: he had the same look of revulsion on his face as her mother would if she discovered mouse droppings in the pantry. Suddenly Leslie had the most awful desire to laugh. She somehow managed to quell the urge, however, and forced herself to meet Luther's unwavering gaze. He might scare the daylights out of her, but she was determined he would never know it.

"Well, Leslie?"

"I'll explain what happened—"

"I don't want to hear your half-witted explanation. This piece of fantasy that you refer to as a report has been circulated throughout the entire production department. I have been forced to call a meeting of the board of directors this morning as a result. Some members of our staff have been duped by it, it seems. You will be at that meeting, where you will explain your theory to my satisfaction."

Leslie's chin was set with a hint of defiance. "First of all, Luther, I had no intention of circulating my theory. The studies I documented were for Ted's—"

"I hope you don't expect me to believe that. I think you deliberately included your 'studies,' as you refer to them, in the geological report of the Redwillow area. Now, *you* are the one who must be accountable for your rashness."

"Luther, I can support—"

"You can support nothing." He rose from his chair and strode angrily toward the door. "You are dismissed for now, but you'll be in the boardroom in exactly one half hour, and as I warned you, you will answer all questions to my satisfaction." He yanked open the door, stomped out and slammed it shut behind him.

A feeling of impending disaster flooded through Leslie in a sickening rush. Luther had reacted even worse than she'd expected, and she was realistic enough to know she would pay heavily for rousing his anger. At that moment she wished she had never heard of Redwillow. It was turning into a nightmare of gigantic proportions.

An isolated area in northwestern Alberta, Redwillow was named after the river that ran through it. Denver Oil had carried out an intensive seismic program that revealed some very promising geological anomalies. Based on that information, Luther had acquired large landholdings for further exploration. In fact, he had gambled heavily on the prospect of locating a major oil field. He had had three exploration wells drilled there, at a cost of two million dollars each. Two had been dry wells, or dusters, while the third had hit a low-volume find of natural gas.

At this point, Luther had overextended the company's financial resources. As a last ditch effort, he had drilled one more well in Redwillow. Nothing. There was no oil, or very little, at Redwillow.

Leslie had pored over the seismic charts and had painstakingly analyzed the core samples from all four Redwillow wells. The more research she did, the more convinced she was that she was onto something. She had told Ted McAllister about it, and he had given her the green light to intensify her research.

As far as Leslie was concerned, her theory was no longer a theory but cold hard fact. Denver Oil had been looking specifically for oil. Her amazing discovery was that, true there was no oil; but Denver Oil's leases were sitting on top of a vast basin of natural gas.

She had written a detailed report describing what she had found, and Ted had nearly gone through the roof with excitement. A discovery like that would be a boost to the entire industry.

But then everything started to get complicated. Because of the financial situation the company was in, Luther needed to recover some of its losses. He had instructed Ted to prepare a report on Redwillow for the board of directors. The purpose—to gain approval to sell the massive landholdings Denver held in that area. Ted had tried to reason with him, but when Luther discovered Leslie had been involved, he refused to even look at the report.

Ted had taken the matter into his own hands and had included Leslie's report with his own, circulating it within the production department. Since one of the petroleum engineers was a nephew of one of the senior directors, he knew the board would find out about the report and likely force Luther's hand on the issue. And that was exactly what had happened....

Uncertainty curled within Leslie's belly as she pushed herself out of the chair and stood staring at the floor. She sighed heavily and turned to leave the room. At the door she hesitated for an instant, then turned and walked back to the desk. She hesitated again, then with a burst of bravado picked up the confidential report and tucked it under her arm. What she was doing was professionally unethical, but she was going to keep a copy. Her assessment of Redwillow was correct, she was certain, and somehow, sometime, she would prove it.

She left the office quietly and slipped past Luther's secretary unobserved. Stella was typing furiously, her back to the door. Leslie walked quickly to the elevators, heaving a shaky sigh of relief when the door slid open to reveal an empty compartment.

The elevator stopped at the second floor. Leslie stepped out and walked rapidly down the corridor to the ladies' powder room. Again Lady Luck was with her; the room was empty. She located her coat among the others hanging on the rack. Rolling up the report, she stuffed it into the sleeve, then shook the coat vigorously until she was satisfied that the bulkiness of the manual would prevent if from slipping out. Smoothing her hair with trembling hands, she took a deep breath to steady her nerves, then left the room.

The next half hour went by far too rapidly for
Leslie. As she made notes from her research file, she
tried to convince herself that she had no reason to
feel as terrified as she did. She was certain that the
data she had compiled would more than support her
theory. It was not an idle farfetched daydream, but a
theory that was supported by very technical and
detailed facts. After all, geology was a science as well
as an art.

She finally quit trying to convince herself, and instead went to the window and stood staring out, her
arms wrapped around herself. She was in a rotten
situation. No amount of rationalization was going to
change that. Luther had pushed the company to the
brink of financial collapse, and his only remaining
maneuver was to sell the leases at Redwillow. He
would use any incident, or any employee, as cannon
fodder to draw the fire of his board of directors.
What he definitely did not want at this time was the
board eyeing Redwillow as the pot of gold at the end
of a rather battered rainbow. What a mess.

"Les, are you okay?"

Leslie sighed heavily as she dropped her arms and
turned around. Ted McAllister was standing by her
desk, his face lined with concern. Poor Ted. She
trusted this man not only because of his close friendship with her grandfather but also because of his
sound judgment. He had been involved in the Alberta oil industry for years, and what he didn't know
about drilling wasn't worth knowing. Now he had
stuck his neck in a noose for a green, untried geologist. Damn! Damn! Damn!

"Leslie?"

She grinned up at him weakly and waved him into the chair beside her desk. "I'll survive, Ted. Don't worry about me, please."

"Well, I do worry, damn it. Luther's out for blood, and I think he's being totally unreasonable about it."

Leslie raised her hands in a gesture of hopelessness. "Luther's like a cornered rat right now. He thinks my theory on Redwillow is a fairy tale. He's not about to reconsider the possibility of drilling in that area—*especially* when it's based on research I did."

Ted pulled a package of cigarettes out of his shirt pocket, lit one and stared at Leslie through a haze of swirling blue smoke. "I know, I know. But damn it, Leslie, I would bet my life on that big basin of gas. I wouldn't have included your research in that report if I didn't feel it had merit. Damn it, now you're in hot water up to your neck."

Leslie studied the lined weathered face, the thatch of unruly gray hair and the steely gray eyes that reflected such concern and worry. Knowing that he believed in her meant so very much. She sat down on the corner of the desk and took one of Ted's massive hands in both of hers, her face reflective.

Ted returned the pressure. "It's too bad the old man isn't still alive, Les. He would never've tolerated you being walked on by Luther—or by anyone else, for that matter."

Leslie swallowed to try and ease the painful constriction in her throat as a wave of acute loneliness washed through her. She had adored her grandfather. He had been the only person in her life who had genuinely cared about her, the only person with whom she felt secure.

"Perhaps, but grandfather would expect me to deal with my own problems." She looked at him, a message in her eyes. "And Ted, this is *my* problem. I should have left Denver Oil as soon as mother was finished her chemotherapy. It was bad judgment on my part."

"Yeah, it was, girl. You would have been better off somewhere else, but ain't hindsight wonderful?"

Leslie grinned and nodded. She glanced at her watch, her stomach lurching as a feeling of apprehension settled upon her. It was time to go.

Ted glanced at his own watch, sighed deeply, then ran his hands through his rumpled hair. He slumped in his chair for a moment, then heaved his huge muscled frame to an upright stance. "Come on, girl. I guess we may as well get this show on the road." He took Leslie's hand and tucked it through the crook of his arm in a fatherly gesture as she stood up. "You aren't going to be alone in this, Les. I want you to know that. It was my decision to include your assessment in my report, and I truly believe you did a terrific piece of detective work. It could be worth millions of dollars to this company if Luther would only use his head."

They walked to the row of elevators and stood watching the flashing numbers in ominous silence. She squeezed his arm as she looked up at him. "Ted, please don't say anything that will jeopardize your position with the company. It really isn't worth it...."

Ted looked down at her, his face unreadable. "We'll see, girl. We'll see."

They rode up to the twenty-second floor in silence. Leslie was glad, for it gave her some time to deal with the icy knot of dread that was beginning to curl and snake in the pit of her stomach. She was terrified, but she had learned a long time ago that she must not reveal her fear, especially in front of Luther. He loved to bully anyone who would cringe and tremble.

She was jolted sharply back to reality as the elevator jarred to a halt. She glanced up apprehensively at Ted and experienced a new surge of uneasiness at the set, grim look on his face. That look was an open call to battle. Ted could be intractable in a situation like this, and above all else, Leslie did not want to see him endanger his job because of a misplaced sense of responsibility toward her.

"Ted—"

He ignored her beseeching eyes as he swung open the ornate door to the boardroom and propelled her inside. "I'm an old street fighter from a way back, girl, and I'll be damned if Luther is going to use you for target practice."

"Ted, don't—"

He patted her hand reassuringly as he seated her in one of the leather sofas at the back of the immense ostentatious room. "Stop stewing. This is going to be one battle that I wouldn't miss for the world! I'll get in a few good licks before I go down."

It was hopeless. There was no point in arguing with him when he was in that frame of mind. In a supreme effort to blot out the tension that was building inside her, Leslie clenched her hands together and forced herself to concentrate on her surroundings.

"Leslie."

She looked up at Ted questioningly. He nodded toward the head of the table, and Leslie took a long, shaky breath. The board of directors were filing in through the double doors at the opposite end of the room. Zero hour.

If Leslie had a shred of hope left, it withered and died when Luther entered the room. One look at his rigid face told her more clearly than words what was in store for her.

Ted shook his head ruefully as he watched her small elfin face grow pale, her doe eyes become dark and wide. He took her clenched hands in his. "Don't worry, girl. We're going through this together. Luther's making a big mistake—I feel it in my bones. And we'll prove it, somehow." Leslie couldn't unclench her teeth to answer him.

Luther cast Leslie a slicing icy glance that carried a warning. Then, as chairman of the board, he took his place at the head of the table. With a cursory nod to all those present, he brought the meeting to order.

Leslie's head began to ache as the items on the agenda were dealt with, one after the other, with tedious thoroughness. It was taking so long.

"The next item on the agenda is the report concerning the evaluation of the Redwillow area. As many of you know, a theory from one of our new geologists was inadvertantly published in that document. That theory has caused some concern among you, so it is my intention to discuss this issue now. Here to answer any questions is Ted McAllister, senior exploration manager, and Leslie Kairns, the geologist who drafted the report. Ted and Leslie, would you join us please?"

Ted squeezed Leslie's hand as he helped her to her feet. She lifted her chin, her dark eyes cool and calm as she approached the table and slipped into the chair Luther indicated. Leslie couldn't suppress a small wry smile as Luther waved Ted into a chair on the opposite side of the table. Split the ranks. Divide and conquer. Yes, Luther was well versed in strategies and tactics.

"As you know, gentlemen, we experienced little success in the Redwillow area with, I may add, sizable capital expenditures. It is my personal opinion that any further exploration in that particular area would be futile. However, some of you on the board feel that Miss Kairns's report bears some consideration. Because of that factor, I feel it is essential that we determine immediately what Denver Oil is prepared to do at Redwillow. May I point out that if you gentlemen decide that the logical action is to dispose of our lease holdings there, we could recover several million dollars by the sale of those leases. Are there any questions?"

Leslie unclenched her hands and concentrated on relaxing her muscles. Determination grew like a flame within her. No matter what, she was going to walk out of here with her head held high. Luther might upset her, but he would never have the satisfaction of knowing it.

"Miss Kairns?"

Leslie lifted her head, her face composed. "Yes, Mr. Cahill?"

"Would you please explain your theory in less technical terms? I'm afraid I'm not too well versed on the jargonese of a geologist."

Leslie smiled and nodded at the elderly gentleman. Mr. Cahill was the uncle of an engineer on staff with Denver, and she knew full well that the "jargonese" had been thoroughly explained to him.

"Certainly. In the core samples extracted from the Denver Oil wells, there was a formation of rock known as a conglomerate. To describe this formation in simplistic terms, one could compare it to gravel that has been cemented together by extreme pressure."

"What's the significance of this type of formation?"

"This type of sample usually identifies an underground river channel. These channels may contain large pockets of oil and natural gas. However, the recovery rate is not too successful, for it is nearly impossible, even with today's technology, to map the subterranean routes of these river channels."

Luther squinted his eyes, his manner suddenly patronizing. "Well, Miss Kairns, I feel very gratified to hear you represent your profession with such integrity. I'm sure these gentlemen understand that your report was speculative, rather than factual. Now gentlemen, I think it's clear that we must cut our losses and dispose of the Redwillow landholdings."

Ted's eyes flashed in anger, his weathered face turning red with fury as he slammed his hand on the table. "Now just one minute. There's more to Leslie's theory than a river channel and you know it!"

Leslie knew she was doomed anyway. There was no reason to bring Ted down with her. "I'll explain,

Ted—please.'' She looked at him, silently imploring him not to get involved. Ted gazed back for a moment, then wearily shook his head as he slouched in his chair. "All right, Les. It's your show.''

Leslie didn't dare look at Luther. "Gentlemen, I said that type of formation is *usually* a river conglomerate. However, the core samples taken from Redwillow were not of a river conglomerate but rather of a beach conglomerate.''

A loud babble of excited conversation broke out around the table, and Luther had to use his gavel several times before order was restored.

Leslie pushed on before her stepfather had a chance to intervene. "A beach conglomerate is very significant in that it identifies an old seabed—and that means an extensive underground basin. Denver Oil was exploring for oil, not natural gas. Consequently, no testing for natural gas was done. My research indicates the presence of a massive natural gas field.''

One of Luther's prime supporters raised his voice above the clamor, his face flushed with annoyance. "If that basin is really there, I don't see how that much gas could go undetected. Other companies have been drilling in that area for years!''

Nervousness pressed the air from Leslie's lungs, but somehow she managed to take a deep enough breath to answer him calmly. "The reason it went undetected was because of the type of formation that exists. Although the reservoir has a high-porosity factor, there is very little permeability. That explains—''

"It doesn't explain anything to me! Porosity and

permeability...I'm a banker, not a geologist!"

Leslie glanced at Ted, and had all she could do to smother a grin as he rolled his eyes heavenward in an exaggerated expression of disbelief. She managed to keep her face solemn as she explained. "Rock formations have tiny pores that contain hydrocarbons—like a sponge holds water. That determines porosity. If the pores in the rock are connected, allowing oil and gas to move through the formation, they are permeable. This rock reservoir is extremely porous, but it isn't permeable. Consequently the formation would have to be fractured before the hydrocarbons could be recovered."

"And how is an underground formation fractured?"

"A special fluid is pumped into the hole under extreme pressure. The pressure is so intense that the formation eventually cracks open. Then proppants are mixed into the fracturing fluid—proppants can be walnut shells or aluminum pellets—and these enter the cracks in the rock and 'prop' the fractures open, allowing the gas or oil to flow out when the pressure is removed."

"And you analyzed the core samples from the four wells that Denver drilled and found evidence of natural gas?"

"I found evidence of the beach conglomerate in three of the wells. The well that produced a low-volume find was several miles east of the basin location."

A babble of angry, agitated voices erupted, and as the volume increased, so did Leslie's feeling of futility. She looked across the table and felt slightly reassured as Ted nodded his head in approval, a broad grin on his face.

What little confidence she had died abruptly when she glanced at Luther. He was glaring at her, his face contorted with rage.

It was the first time in her entire life that she had ever publicly defied him, and she realized that he had never expected her to do so now. He thought he had her under his thumb, but for once she had out-maneuvered him and made him look extremely bad in front of his board of directors. By openly challenging his authority, however, Leslie had left herself wide open to the most viperous retaliation. And Luther would retaliate, she had no doubt about that.

The thought of withstanding yet another of her stepfather's confrontations left Leslie feeling drained and very weary. It was so hopeless; nothing would ever change. She couldn't accept Luther any more than he could overcome his aversion to her. She wanted to live her own life, to be herself without fear of his hostile censorship. And she sensed intuitively that if she *was* to survive as an individual, she was going to have to assume the responsibility for her own destiny without delay.

She stared at her hands for a moment as she considered her only course of action. Her only ace in the hole was to act before Luther had an opportunity to do so. He would never expect her to do anything now.

With a swift solid conviction that she had only one avenue open to her, Leslie slipped out of her chair and stood up.

Luther shot an angry glance at her, his voice brittle. "Sit down, Leslie. I haven't dismissed you yet."

She ignored him. "Gentlemen, excuse me please." All heads turned and a hollow hush fell upon the group. "I'm convinced that Denver Oil is sitting on one of the largest gas fields in Canada. I also realize that debating this issue is a futile formality. When the board puts the question of Redwillow to the vote, the decision will be to sell the landholdings." Leslie clasped her hands together so no one could see that they were trembling. "Because of this negative attitude, my only recourse is to resign from my position with Denver Oil."

Her glance swept around the table. Ted's face registered stunned admiration and delight. Luther's, on the other hand, registered speechless wrath. She had caught him completely off guard. She managed to smile and tip her head in acknowledgement. "Good day, gentlemen."

She never gave anyone a chance to respond or comment. With rigid control she turned and walked quickly out of the room.

Somehow she managed to retain her facade of composure all the way back to her desk. Her resolve was further reinforced when she found Luther's secretary already there, obviously waiting for her. Without acknowledging her presence or purpose, Leslie gathered together her few personal belongings and stuffed them into her attaché case. She was well aware that Luther had dispatched Stella immediately to make certain his stepdaughter departed from Denver Oil with no company documents or files.

"Are you to escort me out of the building, Stella?" she asked finally.

The woman reddened and fidgeted uncomfortably as she nodded her head. "Those were my instructions." Her eyes fell away from Leslie's level stare and she cleared her throat. "You'll have to turn over your company identification card to me. Security reasons, you know," she explained unnecessarily.

Leslie studied her for a moment, then sighed heavily as she unclipped the plasticized card from her lapel. "Yes, I know." She handed the card to Stella. "I'll have to pick up my coat on the way out."

It wasn't until Leslie was standing outside the office building in the bright autumn sunshine that the enormity of what she had done really struck home. She shivered as she stood staring at the sidewalk, her thoughts a confused jumble. Yes, she had definitely burned her bridges and there would be no turning back. It was over. She had severed any ties that she had with Luther and with her mother. She could never go back again....

Suddenly it was as though the door to her cage had swung open. An oppressive weight that had held her immobile was gone, vanished. With a sense of freedom, Leslie turned and walked briskly down the street toward the car parkade.

CHAPTER TWO

LESLIE SLIPPED ON HER SUNGLASSES and waited for the lights to change. The streets of downtown Calgary were so congested it felt like rush hour instead of midmorning.

The traffic light changed and she swung up Fifth Street. There was a more direct route home than along Elbow Drive, but she preferred to travel the winding picturesque road, especially this time of year. The park that nestled comfortably against the banks of the meandering Elbow River was beginning to parade the colors of autumn. The wide-spreading branches of huge poplar trees reached for the sky as their leaves fluttered gold and yellow in the sunlight.

There was a carpet of brilliantly colored leaves strewn across the lush green grass. A variety of shrubs scattered throughout the park had donned their autumn hues, ranging from deep magentas to bright reds to vivid oranges. The colors were so intense that they seemed to have been touched by magic.

The parade of colors continued when Leslie turned her car off Elbow Drive and started weaving her way through the residential streets of Mount Royal. The stately old district had an air of dignified luxury that in a subdued, refined manner indicated the presence of enormous wealth. There had always been a certain aura about the exclusive area that Leslie had often jokingly referred to as the "snob-quality factor." Vivian and Luther had never found the reference amusing, but Leslie's grandfather could see the humor in it. He had been disgusted by his daughter's assuming attitude about his own vast wealth, and that of her husband. He had found his granddaughter's unaffected manner refreshing.

A feeling of reluctance settled upon Leslie as a picture of her mother flashed through her mind. Cool elegant Vivian. Leslie sighed and eased her foot off the accelerator. She truly dreaded a confrontation with Vivian Denver.

They had never enjoyed a very close relationship. Her mother had never been abusive or deliberately unkind—rather, withdrawn and disinterested. But she had always made Leslie feel guilty for reminding her of a past she preferred to forget. There had been a distance between them that was unbridgeable.

Leslie had never been told anything about her natural father, and her illegitimacy was a strictly forbidden topic as well. On one or two occasions, Leslie had tried to ferret the information out of her Grandfather Kairns, but he, too, had refused to discuss it. It wasn't until just before he died that he told Leslie the one and only condition Luther had ever imposed upon him—that if he ever told her anything about the man who had fathered her, he would not be permitted to see his only grandchild again.

Leslie turned into a long sweeping driveway and parked, then sat staring at the English-style manor that had been her home for most of the last twenty years. It wasn't really a home, but rather an expensively furnished showplace that was Vivian's great pride. Leslie had never been permitted to display posters of her teenage idols in her own suite of rooms, or to have stuffed animals on her bed—unless, of course, they matched the decor. Consequently she had never felt that it was really hers. Her real haven had been at grandfather's—*that* had been hers.

Leslie grimaced and forced herself to get out of the car. Putting it off solved nothing. She might as well go in and have the awful scene with her mother over and done with. She would have given anything to simply avoid the issue, but there wasn't much chance of that.

She walked unenthusiastically up the wide steps. At the door she hesitated, then sighed as she slowly dug her keys out of her bag and entered the foyer. She had an impulsive urge to dash up the stairs to her suite and lock herself in, but knew she would have to face Vivian sooner or later.

"Mother?" Her voice quavered. The only answering sound was the mournful chiming of the antique grandfather clock in the library.

"Mother?" Still no answer. Leslie checked the downstairs rooms, but Vivian wasn't there. She entered the kitchen just as Bertha, the stout German housekeeper, waddled in from outside.

"Ach, child. You're home."

"Hello, Bertha. Do you know where mother is?"

"She's gone downtown to shop, then to meet Mrs. Martin for lunch. She said she'd be home around three o'clock. You need her?"

"Oh no. I was just curious." Leslie felt weak with relief. That meant she had four hours before her mother returned.

Bertha bustled over to the sink and rinsed her hands under the tap, then dried them. "I go for groceries, then run some errands. Do you want to come?"

Leslie jumped guiltily and smiled. "Ah, no...no thanks, Bertha. I have some things I'd like to do here. But thanks for asking." Her smile turned into a genuine expression of amusement. Bertha's tactics were so obvious! The main reason the housekeeper had invited her along was to find out why Leslie was home at eleven o'clock in the morning. Bertha always knew exactly what was going on.

The woman gathered up her coat and purse from the table. "Oh, well then. I will see you later, child."

The door had barely closed on her heels when Leslie, with a sense of urgency, sprinted up the stairs two at a time. If she hurried, she could be out of the house before her mother returned. She hesitated at the top of the stairs, then dashed down the long hallway to the storage room at the end of the corridor. There she got out a large steamer trunk and dragged it down the hallway.

She was taking the coward's way out, but she had to leave and she would prefer to do it without involving everyone in an ugly scene. And it would be an ugly scene!

Three hours later she had packed everything that she wanted to take. She had even wrestled two trunks and her matching set of luggage down the stairs, and now they were stacked in the front hall.

Her knees nearly buckled beneath her in panic when

there was a loud knocking on the front door. Vivian! No, it couldn't be. Her mother would have rung the doorbell if she didn't have her key. Besides, it was only two o'clock—she wouldn't even have finished lunch yet.

Still, Leslie's heart was beating a trip-hammer tattoo as she opened the door.

"Hello, girl."

She could have collapsed with relief. Ted McAllister was standing there, a half grin on his face.

"Ted! What are you doing here?"

"Can I come in?"

"Of course!" She opened the door wide and motioned him in.

Ted looked from her to the pile of luggage, then back again, his face solemn. He ran his hand through his hair as he sat down heavily on one of the trunks. "Does this mean what I think it means?"

Leslie's face was sober, her voice quiet with distress. "Yes, it does, Ted. I can't continue to stay in this house any longer. My being here has always created a strain, and it will be absolutely intolerable now that I've publicly defied Luther." She smiled abjectly. "He never expected that from me."

Ted shook his head, his eyes gleaming with humor and admiration. "To be quite frank about it, neither did I." He bowed his head and stared at the parquet floor for a long time as the cloistered silence of the house settled heavily upon them. "Where are you going to go?"

"I've called a delivery service to pick up my things. I was going to check into a hotel until I could find a place of my own."

"You're sure this is what you want?"

Leslie swallowed against the lump in her throat and nodded weakly. "Yes. There's no other way. You know that, Ted." Her voice was barely audible.

Ted looked at her, his face set with concern. "Leslie, I went home before I came over here. I told Maggie what happened this morning. She wants you to move in with us—in fact, she sent me over here to get you."

"Oh, Ted! I can't impose—"

"Now listen here, girl. Your grandfather and I were friends for a good many years. Besides, I'd like to think that this is my opportunity to repay him for the many times he helped me out." Ted held up his hand when Leslie opened her mouth to speak. "Maggie and I have wanted to do this for a long time, but we didn't want to interfere. Besides, you know that Maggie is really fond of you, and she's been feeling pretty lost ever since the kids left home. No argument, girl. I'm taking you home with me!"

Leslie couldn't speak. She put her arms around Ted's neck and hugged him as she tried to smother the mixed feelings of overwhelming gratitude and an undefinable grief that choked her.

Ted patted her back, then ruffled her hair as he stood up. "So let's get this show on the road. Is this all you want to take?"

"Well, there's my ski equipment and things like that. I really would like to keep them but—"

"Where are they? I'll load them up."

"Out in the garage. Come on. I'll show you."

Ted smiled knowingly. "I think Maggie knew what she was talking about when she told me to bring the half-ton truck. We'll end up with a full load."

Leslie grinned at him as she led him into the garage. "You had it all planned out, didn't you?"

"Sure did. Say, Les, you'd better give that express company a call before their van gets here."

"Oh, damn. Right."

Ted caught her by the shoulder as she turned to go. "Are you going to leave your mother a letter?"

Leslie's smile faded and was replaced with a look of despair. "Yes."

"Are you going to tell her where you're going?"

Leslie shook her head as she stared blindly at the ground. "No," she whispered.

Ted sighed, then raked his fingers through his hair. "Perhaps that's best." He paused as he mulled the situation over in his mind, then shrugged. He patted her affectionately on the cheek. "Now show me what you want to take from out here, then make that call."

The letter hadn't been easy to write. In fact, there had been several painful attempts before Leslie managed to convey what she wanted. After making her call she propped the envelope on the mantel of the library fireplace, then hitched the strap of her handbag over her shoulder, walking out of the house without a backward glance.

She found Ted loading the last of her things into the back of the truck. He looked at her, his face solemn. "Ready?"

"Yes, I'm ready." She slipped on her sunglasses, then called to Ted. "Don't close the garage door."

He threw her a questioning look. "Is there something else?"

"No. I'm just going to put my car in the garage."

His eyebrows shot up in surprise. "Aren't you going to take it with you?"

Leslie looked at the sleek powerful Mercedes that her mother had given her. "No, I don't want it. I never did."

Ted wisely said nothing. There wasn't much he could say anyway. Vivian had always tried to force her daughter into the mold of a cool, sophisticated socialite. And Leslie didn't fit.

An awful ache engulfed Leslie as she climbed into the truck. She leaned her head back against the headrest and closed her eyes. It would be better for everyone this way. She would build her own life, in her own way. Somehow. After all, loneliness was not something unknown; it had been a grim silent companion all her life.

IT WASN'T UNTIL MUCH LATER that evening that Leslie found out what had happened in the board meeting after she'd left. Ted, Maggie and she were sitting around the table in the McAllisters' spotless kitchen, indulging in a bedtime treat—steaming mugs of hot chocolate and massive wedges of sponge cake. Ted finally relented to her persistence and told her what had happened.

There had been a very heated debate after she had left. A few members of the board had felt that they should consider the possibility of reopening Redwillow. But Luther had managed to bring the dissenters under his unyielding control, as usual. The fiasco had then developed into an imbroglio between Ted and Luther. The whole nasty incident had ended with Ted tendering his resignation and storming out.

Leslie felt terrible. She grasped the heavy hot mug with both her hands as a surge of remorse swamped her. She had not wanted to entangle Ted in her problems.

He was watching her pale solemn face. "Hey, girl, don't get yourself in a twist over what's happened."

Leslie felt so guilty, so responsible, for the situation that she had great difficulty in meeting his gaze. He reached out and patted her shoulder reassuringly. His weathered face creased into a big grin as the corners of his eyes crinkled into familiar laugh lines.

Her voice wobbled treacherously. "Ted, I didn't want to drag you into this—"

Maggie snorted as she refilled the mugs. "Leslie, dear, my Ted has always enjoyed a good fight, be it barroom or boardroom. So don't spoil his fun!"

"But—"

Ted chuckled, his eyes merry. "Damn it, Les, Maggie and I are well enough off that I don't have to work another day in my life. Your grandfather saw to that. But neither Maggie nor I are the type who can sit in one spot and go all mildewy. I love the oil patch—yes I do—but I was getting fed up with Luther's attitude. He's in the business for the big money, the prestige, the recognition. I'm in it because I like the challenge of drilling, the excitement. I was getting bored. I needed a change."

Leslie's expressive face mirrored her misgivings as she groped for words. "Oh, Ted, I just wish it hadn't been over me—"

"Now, girl, don't think like that. Your being involved made the whole nasty business worthwhile.

Besides, your grandfather would have enjoyed every minute of it!''

Leslie tipped back her head and laughed. She had a sudden vision of her grandfather hovering over the conference table, angel wings flapping leisurely, a broad grin on his face as he nursed his beloved pipe. Yes, grandfather would have enjoyed every minute. He had always felt that Luther was an overbearing pompous ass who needed to be taken down a peg or two. It would have delighted him to no end that his granddaughter had done it.

Leslie sighed, then grinned at her friends. "Well, Mr. McAllister, what do we do now? Start our own exploration company?"

It was not an idle suggestion. Leslie had inherited the bulk of her grandfather's immense fortune. The old man had astutely camouflaged her wealth with various trust funds and vast corporate holdings, so that only a select and trusted few were aware that Leslie was probably one of the wealthiest women in Canada. Ted, as an executor of her estate, was one of them.

He stroked his chin and chuckled as he winked at his wife. "Well, we might have to, girl, if we really want to try out our deep-basin theory. But before we do that, there's one possibility I'd like to explore first."

Leslie looked questioningly from Ted to Maggie. Obviously they had discussed this already, but he wasn't prepared to tell her about it just yet.

He took Leslie's hand in his big one, his expression one of sincerity. "Whatever happens, Les, we're in this together. I want you to know that."

She fought down the tide of emotion that once again threatened to strangle her and rapidly blinked away the burning sensation in her eyes. "That's good enough for me," she managed to grin at him.

Ted stood up and stretched. "I sure wish I could have scoffed one of those Redwillow reports before I left, but I was very considerately ushered out of the building by the security guard."

Leslie's eyes widened as her hands flew to her face. She had completely forgotten about the report! It was still tucked in the sleeve of her coat. She bounced out of her chair and darted from the room.

The couple exchanged looks of bewilderment at their guest's unexplained behavior. Ted shrugged. "She must have forgotten something."

Maggie nodded as she started to clear away the table. "Poor little thing. She's been bullied in one way or another all her life. She's never had anyone. except Mac, and he kept her so isolated."

"He had to, Maggie. He had to keep Leslie's existence a secret. She would have been a prime candidate for abduction if it was public knowledge she was Mac Kairns's granddaughter."

"I know. Luther detested her, and Mac isolated her. She never even had any close friends. A child shouldn't have to grow up like that. I feel so much happier now she's here with us."

Ted hugged his wife affectionately. "So do I, Maggie. So do I!"

"You've set up an appointment with Steve McRory for tomorrow, haven't you?" she asked him.

"Yeah. That was Steve who called just before supper."

"He isn't going to be too thrilled when he finds out Leslie is a girl, you know."

Ted looked at his wife, an amused look on his face as he considered some private thought. "Well, there'll be sparks, all right, of one kind or another."

Just then Leslie came dancing back into the kitchen, her hands tucked behind her, an impish grin on her face. "Which hand do you want?"

Ted shook his head. "What are you up to, Leslie Jordan Kairns? I know that look."

"Which hand to you want?" she persisted.

He scrutinized her face, his eyes narrowing speculatively before a look of disbelief dawned on his face. "You didn't!"

Leslie's brown eyes were dancing with glee as she stood before him, barely able to contain her excitement.

"Leslie Kairns, you didn't!"

With an exaggerated flourish, she handed Ted the blue manual. "I did! I pinched it off Luther's desk."

A loud shout of laughter exploded from Ted as he caught her up in a bear hug and swung her around the kitchen. "We're going to make Luther Denver eat crow, girl, and I don't think it's a dinner he's going to enjoy!"

LESLIE WASN'T FEELING QUITE SO CONFIDENT the next day as she stood before the mirror in the front hall, halfheartedly studying her appearance. She was experiencing the same doubts she had the first time she'd tried to fly a kite—would it really fly or would it crash?

Ted had left the house early that morning before

she was up. He had stuck a message on the fridge door, informing her he had gone downtown to meet with someone about Redwillow, and that he would give her a call around ten.

He had phoned as he'd promised and told her she was to meet him downtown for lunch at one o'clock. He had been very businesslike on the phone, but Leslie could tell from the tone of his voice he had good news. She assumed that he was calling from someone's office, and that he couldn't elaborate on the details then. He had, however, stressed that it was a "business lunch," so Leslie had dressed accordingly. Now she stood before the mirror, trying to see herself through a stranger's eyes.

She wasn't impressed. A wisp of a girl stared back at her, with solemn dark eyes that overwhelmed her elfin face. Her thick sweeping lashes and gently arching brows accentuated the enormous eyes that dominated her face. For some reason, it all left her looking like a lonely street urchin.

Her thick dark hair hung to her shoulders, making her face seem even smaller. The style didn't particularly suit Leslie, but Vivian had been adamantly opposed to a "fadish cut." Leslie had given in to her mother rather than fight over it.

She sighed heavily. Why couldn't she have been tall and elegant like Vivian? She grinned weakly at herself and groaned. She must remember *not* to smile. When she did, a deep dimple appeared in either cheek, and her age was immediately reduced by half. Why did she have to look like such a baby, she bemoaned inwardly.

The suit was perfect, though. It was a sleekly

tailored pearl gray wool outfit, with a mandarin collar and a slim-cut skirt. She had on plain gray suede boots, and carried a matching gray suede clutch purse.

She analyzed her reflection a moment longer. No, the hairstyle would *not* do. She whirled and ran lightly up the stairs to her room, where she grabbed her shoulder bag off the dresser and dumped its contents unceremoniously in the middle of the bed. Rummaging through the pile, she found a handful of pins, then she snatched up her brush. The cab would be here any moment, but she had to change her hairdo.

She brushed her hair straight back from her face and twisted it into a chignon at the back of her head. She had just finished pinning it securely when there was a blast from a car horn outside. Picking up her purse again, she dashed down the stairs. She hesitated for a moment before the mirror. That was better, but not much. Now she looked like a melancholy ballerina.

During the drive Leslie concentrated on organizing her thoughts, trying to predict some of the questions she would be expected to answer. There was a flutter of nervousness that she tried to ignore as she mentally went over the data concerning Redwillow. She had an excellent memory, and seldom needed to refer back to source material. She was definitely grateful for that ability now.

By the time the cab pulled up in front of the restaurant, she felt prepared and reasonably composed. She paid the driver and stepped out into the bright September day, pausing to take a long slow breath, and savoring the clean crisp smell of autumn. It was a day to play hooky, a day for walking through a park and letting her imagination soar like a kite on beams of sunshine.

She grimaced guiltily and shook her head. She was dawdling again. She took another deep breath of resignation, squared her shoulders and walked briskly into the restaurant.

After the brightness of the clear autumn sunshine, the dim interior seemed to smother her. She paused for a moment to allow her eyes to adjust to the artificial light, then approached the reservation desk.

She smiled warmly at the woman behind the desk. "I'm to meet Mr. McAllister for lunch. Could you show me to his table, please?"

The hostess returned the smile and nodded. "Certainly. Follow me, please."

Leslie smoothed back a stray tendril of hair as she followed the woman into the dining lounge. Ted looked up as they approached the table, and Leslie flashed him a brilliant smile, completely forgetting her resolution about not smiling.

Ted stood up, a broad grin on his face. "Hello, girl."

The other man seated at the table rose as well, and Leslie turned to smile at him, certain that he was the person who was interested in Redwillow.

But as she looked up, she experienced the most unbelievable sensation. She was suddenly unable to breath, and it seemed like the room was going into a lazy spin as her gaze collided with the most piercing blue eyes she had ever seen. She felt as though she was being drawn into their blue depths by the sheer magnetic power that surrounded the man.

He was tall and very ruggedly built, with virile chiseled features that radiated an almost frightening inner strength. His thick, sunstreaked, tawny hair reminded her of a lion's mane; in fact there was a certain grace about him that made her think of a jungle cat. Their eyes held as a chill of apprehension, and some other emotion she couldn't define, flooded through her with a force that left her feeling weak. Nothing, absolutely nothing, could be concealed from those eyes.

Leslie caught her breath as he smiled slowly at her, his eyes suddenly warm. The odd paralysis that had suspended time disappeared, and she smiled back at him.

"Girl, I'd like you to meet Steve McRory of Ramco Exploration. I've known Steve and his family for a good many years."

Leslie took the hand that was offered to her, unable to suppress a peculiar feeling of awe. It was almost as though a strange spell was being cast on her.

Steve McRory continued to hold her hand as he seated her at the table, then sat back down himself. His smile deepened provocatively. "I know who I am, Ted, but who is the bewitching lady?"

Ted grinned, a wicked gleam in his eyes. "She's the granddaughter of a very old friend of mine."

Leslie felt as though she had no will of her own as she sat there, mesmerized by his eyes. Intuitively she knew that Steve McRory was as dangerous as he was attractive.

"And I presume she has a name?"

Leslie couldn't help but laugh. Steve sounded like

someone who was very patiently trying to pry information out of an exasperating child.

She glanced at Ted, then smiled at Steve. "I think Ted has either forgotten my name, or he's stalling for time."

Steve tipped his head back and laughed, a deep musical laugh that was a genuine delight to hear.

Ted didn't laugh. In fact, he looked guilty. He refused to meet Leslie's eyes as he cleared his throat and toyed with the silverware beside his plate. He *was* stalling. Leslie braced herself as his uneasiness created a foreboding lull. She turned to face Steve McRory and found him studying Ted's reaction with a tight set look that was most definitely suspicious.

Leslie removed her hand from Steve's, her face sober. "I'm Leslie Kairns, Mr. McRory. I'm the geologist who was with Denver Oil—I think perhaps Ted has mentioned me."

The relaxed warmth evaporated abruptly and was replaced with strained silence. "I see." The friendly blue eyes became shafts of steel as McRory leaned back in his chair and surveyed Ted with cool reserve. "Why did you deliberately let me assume your geologist was a man, Ted? You know what my policy is concerning women in the field."

Ted set his jaw stubbornly and stared at Steve, his own eyes flashing metal. Steel against steel, Leslie thought.

"The reason I led you down the garden path was because I *did* know your policy. That research for the deep basin was *all* done by Les, and I think she's onto something big. I hoped you would at least have the decency to hear what she has to say."

Steve leaned forward and rested his arms on the table in a gesture of finality. "No doubt her work is brilliant; I won't deny that. However, I will not employ women in field operations, *especially* not Miss Kairns. My God, man, she wouldn't have the stamina of a butterfly!"

Leslie's head jerked up as her temper flared. Of all the nerve! Who did he think he was, making idiotic comparisons like that—and acting as if she wasn't even there? Her voice was quiet, but clipped with ice as she stuck out her chin with determination. "I think the analogy of a butterfly is an apt one, Mr. McRory. A monarch butterfly appears to be frail, but it migrates thousands of miles in its lifetime." Her fixed smile was pure saccharine. "Didn't your mother ever tell you not to judge a package by it's size?"

His face was calm and controlled as she stared at him. If he thought for one moment that he could intimidate her by his high-handed arrogance, he was sadly mistaken. The absolute insolence of the man!

Steve McRory returned her stare, his face as hard as granite though a muscle twitched menacingly in his jaw. Ted unobtrusively relaxed in his chair and made a conscious effort to keep his face expressionless. He had predicted sparks, and they were flying. He hadn't realized until this whole mess developed that Leslie had such a strong streak of the old man in her. Mac Kairns had been a scrapper, and Ted was beginning to realize that so was she, in her own quiet way. What she lacked in size she most certainly made up in determination. Yes, this was going to be interesting, if nothing else.

Steve was watching Leslie through narrowed eyes. "There really isn't much point in discussing this, Miss Kairns. Our company had one experience with a woman engineer that was a disaster. Never again will I leave Ramco vulnerable to that kind of unprofessionalism."

The anger in his voice was like a razor. One didn't have to be particularly bright to realize that Steve McRory had suffered through a very bad experience that had tainted him for life. The anger was one thing, but there was also an underlying impression that the episode had left other deeper, more painful scars. For some strange reason, Leslie was oddly unsettled by the feeling of intense regret that gripped her.

Steve shifted his gaze to Ted. There was no doubt about the sincerity in his voice. "I would very much like to take you on staff, Ted. Frankly, I desperately need someone of your calibre—someone who's dependable, knowledgeable, experienced. But I can't buy the package you're selling. I'm sorry."

Leslie shrugged off the despondency that had settled on her and studied both men intently. Something was going on that she couldn't quite fathom. She chewed her lip, her face puzzled. Ted was watching Steve closely, assessing the situation, assessing the man. What exactly had he said to this man? A disturbing possibility developed in Leslie's mind. Ted wouldn't have done that, would he?

Leslie looked at Steve, the anger gone from her voice. "Mr. McRory, you referred to a 'package' that you wouldn't 'buy.' What exactly is Ted merchandising? It wouldn't happen to be me, would it?"

Ted opened his mouth to speak, but Leslie silenced him with a challenging glance. There was just a glimmer of amusement in Steve's eyes when he answered. "As a matter of fact, it was. Ted has given me a brief outline about your findings. He also told me what happened at Denver Oil because of it."

He looked at Ted, a droll grin on his face, his voice tinged with reluctant admiration. "What he *didn't* tell me was where the basin is located. Of course, I'm particularly interested in that piece of information. Ted has been very specific concerning the terms though." His gaze leveled on Leslie again. "In a nutshell, it's you and Ted—or no one."

It took a brief moment before the words registered and Leslie was able to digest their meaning. Once again, Ted was jeopardizing his chances because of her. That changed everything. She could not let him throw a golden opportunity out the window.

She took a deep breath as she looked at Steve. "I'm sorry, I hadn't realized that Ted had made such a stipulation."

"Leslie—"

"Ted, don't—please." She laid her hand on his arm in a gesture that implored him not to be stubborn, to listen to reason. Her expressive wide eyes spoke silently, but more eloquently than any words. She shifted her gaze to meet the steady appraisal of Steve McRory. "I think perhaps I owe you an apology, and an explanation. Yes, I would like to have an opportunity to be involved in this project. However, I'm not prepared to be part of a negotiation, under any circumstances." Leslie swallowed her disappointment, her eyes downcast.

"Leslie, damn it, we agreed last night that we'd stick together on this thing. It was your detective work that uncovered all this—"

"Ted, don't try and stampede me into anything! I don't want to be rammed down someone's throat. The deep basin is the number-one priority for me, you know that."

Ted sighed heavily and stroked his chin as he considered what she had said. Steve McRory was watching the byplay with an intensity Leslie could feel, and she also sensed that he didn't like it very much when she made the comment about being rammed down his throat. She fervently wished that he was not so disturbing, so overwhelming.

She squeezed Ted's arm, her eyes pleading as she grinned lopsidedly up at him. "I may have found it on paper, but you, Ted McAllister, are going to have the responsibility of finding it in the ground."

Ted looked at her for a long time, then his leathery face creased into a smile. He patted her hand with clumsy affection. "All right, girl, if that's what you want." He opened the briefcase beside him, pulled out the familiar blue manual and handed it to Steve. "It's all here, Steve. Have a look and see if you're still interested."

Leslie had a queer sensation in the pit of her stomach as Steve McRory took the report. He wasn't looking at the manual, but instead was looking directly and deliberately at her. "I'm very interested."

Her eyes dropped in discomfiture. This man rattled her. He made her feel like she was in the middle of a lake in a leaky canoe. She stared at her hands, her head bent. She didn't want anyone to be able to see her face. Steve flustered her—and that would show. She was also feeling disappointed—and that would show as well. She had so much wanted to be a part of the exploration team that tackled Redwillow. She would have to leave before Ted detected that disappointment, or he would refuse to change his terms.

With all the poise she could muster, she rose from her chair. Ted looked at her, his bushy eyebrows shooting up in surprise. "You're not going now, are you? At least stay and have some lunch."

She patted his arm. "No, I don't think so. It would be best if you and Mr. McRory discussed this privately." With a great deal of difficulty, she forced herself to meet Steve McRory's gaze. She wished he hadn't stood up; he was more overpowering than ever when he did so. "I'm really sorry I caused you concern, Mr. McRory, and I do sincerely wish you the best of luck in this venture."

"I appreciate your perception, Leslie." The low husky tone of his voice feathered down her spine and left her breathless. Leslie desperately did not want to take the hand he offered her, but she knew she must, if only for appearance sake. Her nerves tingled with a warning as her small hand disappeared in his. A quiver of trepidation shot through her as he stared down at her with those eyes that could see everything.

"Won't you change your mind and stay for lunch? We can leave the business discussion until later." His voice was warm and engaging.

Leslie shook her head mutely. She could feel herself slipping under the magic of his disarming manner. She eased her hand out of his. She had to get out of there—his closeness was doing strange things to her.

She picked up her purse and smiled mischieviously at Ted. "Since you're now among the employed, I suppose I had better start pounding on doors before the rent is due."

The twinkle in his eyes belied his solemn expression. "You'd better hustle, girl, before the landlord tosses you out."

Leslie pulled an impudent face, then turned to leave. She glanced up at Steve. His jaw was set in a hard angry line, and she had the feeling that he would dearly love to shake her. She felt really confused. Why was he so angry with her? She had made it possible for him to hire Ted without any conditions, and that was what he wanted. Wasn't it? She didn't understand.

With a small uncertain gesture of farewell, she turned abruptly and fled from the hypnotizing riddle of Steve McRory.

CHAPTER THREE

LESLIE PACED BACK AND FORTH in the living room, her forehead creased with a frown. Her insides churned with such a muddle of emotions that she had given up trying to sort them out.

What was taking Ted so long? What was happening? Would Ramco be interested enough in the report to speculate on it, or would Steve McRory view it with skepticism? Would Ted follow through? The suspense was driving her crazy!

She tried to concentrate on other things, but Steve McRory's smile kept intruding on her thoughts with unrelenting persistence. She chewed nervously on her bottom lip; she didn't want to think about him, or about why he affected her the way he did.

"Leslie!"

She nearly jumped out of her skin when Ted's voice boomed out right behind her.

"Well, girl, I suppose you've nearly worn a hole in Maggie's new carpet."

"Good grief, Ted—you nearly gave me a stroke!"

Ted laughed, tossed his suit jacket on the sofa and sat down. Only Ted never really *sat* down—he more or less dropped his body into whatever was there to accommodate his massive frame. The sofa groaned in protest as he settled himself in and patted the space beside him.

"Give your legs a rest from all that pacing and I'll tell you what's happened."

Leslie stepped over the coffee table and sat cross-legged on the chesterfield, her elbows propped on her knees, her face cradled in her hands. She had changed into faded blue jeans and a bright pink sweater. Wisps of her fine hair had escaped from the severe bun to curl alluringly around her face. She looked about seventeen years old, and very removed from the crisp professional woman she had portrayed earlier that afternoon.

"Be merciful and tell me what happened. The suspense has been killing me."

Ted lit a cigarette and tossed the package on the coffee table as he inhaled deeply. "Well, I have a job—I signed on this afternoon as a matter of fact. And—" he took another deep deliberate drag and exhaled slowly "—if your research can stand the test of Steve's scrutiny, we're going into Redwillow."

Leslie let out a shout of jubilation and hugged him, her eyes sparking with elation. Ted barely had time to hug her back before she bounced off the sofa and did a crazy little reel in the middle of the room. "That's marvelous! I can't believe it!"

"Hang on to your shirt, girl. We aren't moving a rig in tomorrow, you know."

Leslie grinned as she flopped into the armchair. "Oh, I know. It's just that everything seemed so horrible and bleak this time yesterday, and now there's a light at the end of the tunnel." She sighed contentedly and curled up in the chair. "What happens now?"

"Well, Steve would like to pull all the information together and map it, then he would like to do some aerial reconnaissance to see if he can locate an outcrop, or some surface evidence of an old ocean bed."

"That makes sense. I think you really should have that kind of supporting evidence before you make a final decision."

"If we can find it, we'll map out our strategies and start buying up Denver leases as soon as they hit the market. Steve stressed the need for tight security now. Ramco should be able to purchase those holdings at a good price, as no other company seems to be remotely interested in that area. He was really dumbfounded when I told him the location."

Leslie's face was radiant. Maybe dreams really did come true...sometimes.

"Leslie?"

"Yes, Ted?"

Ted's voice was serious as he leaned forward and reached for the ashtray. "I think I had better fill you in on some information I just found out about. I had heard a few rumors years ago, but I put it all down to oil-patch backbiting, and didn't give it much thought."

Leslie settled herself deeper into the chair and studied him, her eyes questioning. "Okay."

"About ten years ago, Luther pulled off a couple of unscrupulous deals that very nearly ruined Ramco."

A sickening sensation flattened the elation instantly. "What did he do?"

"Basically, it all boiled down to a case of underhanded industrial theft. He bought off an engineer who was in charge of a classified exploration project Ramco was pulling together. By obtaining, in advance, the technical information Ramco had assembled, Denver got the jump. That's how Luther made such a killing in the South American project. Denver was able to make the big strike based on an exploration plan that was actually developed by Ramco.''

Leslie felt as though the bottom of her world had dropped out from under her as the grim reality of what Ted was telling her penetrated. The conversation at the restaurant echoed ominously in her head, and suddenly everything became crystal clear. "It was the woman engineer, wasn't it?''

Ted roughly butted his cigarette in the ashtray. "Yeah, it was, Les.''

She shivered with a sudden coldness. No wonder Steve was so vehement about women in the oil patch. Leslie knew that Denver Oil had made a fortune in South America. In fact, it was the discovery of that field that had put Denver Oil on it's feet financially. She really did feel sick. Luther Denver had done it at another company's expense.

Another cold horrible thought struck her. "Ted, what we're doing is the same thing that Luther did, isn't it?''

Ted shook his head, stood up and started pacing. Maggie's poor carpet was undergoing a trial today. "No, it isn't. Actually, Steve and I spent most of the morning with a top-notch corporate lawyer hashing that out. McRory didn't want any part of anything remotely unethical, and neither did I.''

He continued pacing, his head bent in thought. "This thing with professional ownership is really under scrutiny now. If we sold the information to Ramco while we were still in Denver's employment— yes, it would be the same thing. However, the subject was discussed before the board of directors and Luther dumped it as so much nonsense. He discounted the research openly and publicly, and we both quit over it. Everyone in that room would testify to the fact. We left that company with the information in our heads.''

''But the report?''

''The only thing in that folder now is the paper you put together, the geological report on Redwillow. I burned the rest.'' Ted leaned against the mantel on the fireplace and stroked his chin. Then he chuckled. ''Before I stomped out in a temper yesterday, I made a very loud declaration that I would find natural gas at Redwillow even if I had to dig the damned well with my bare hands. Luther shot back that he would lend me the shovel, but that's all the help I'd get from him. The lawyer said that was certainly a statement of intent on my behalf, and a declaration of discharge on Luther's.'' He pushed himself away from the fireplace and ambled over to Leslie, patting her on the shoulder. ''So don't worry, girl. We're well within the law.''

Leslie wasn't worried. Above all else, Ted valued his integrity. He continued his pacing as she slipped into deep thought. This was becoming much more involved than she had expected, and there were ramifications that she hadn't even considered until now.

''Ted, there's obviously no love lost between Ramco and Denver Oil, right?''

''Right.''

"Will Luther be able to foul up Ramco when they start selling the leases?"

"Not unless they find out whose buying them and refuse to sell. That land will probably hit the market in about three weeks' time. Steve will use various land brokers to purchase it, just to be on the safe side. The important thing is that nothing leaks out before then."

"That makes sense." Leslie toyed with the gold ring on her little finger abstractedly. "Does Steve know I'm Luther Denver's stepdaughter?"

"No."

"Promise me that you won't tell him."

"Why?"

"How would you feel if you were about to sink millions of dollars into a program that had been researched by the stepdaughter of an unscrupulous rival?"

"Steve's not like that, Les."

"Perhaps, but I don't want him to know who I am until you find that basin."

"I don't think knowing or not knowing is that important, but if that's what you want, I won't tell him." Ted squinted his eyes, his mouth puckered with thought. "Leslie, I think Steve's going to change his mind about hiring you."

Leslie snorted. "I don't."

"Would you consider hiring on as a preliminary consultant?"

"You know I would consider it, but what makes you think Steve McRory would?"

"Two reasons."

"And they are?"

"First of all, he's eventually going to realize that you're the logical person for the preliminary work. He's going to realize that the fewer people who know about this, the better. Until Ramco has its hands on that property and has secured the drilling licenses, this operation has to be kept under tight wraps. He doesn't dare risk having any information leaked to industry. It would drive the prices out of sight on those holdings. Let's face it, Les, only you and I and Steve would need to know until we're ready to move into Redwillow.''

Leslie hated to admit it, but she could understand the reason for Steve McRory's attitude. She couldn't help feeling resentful about his narrow-mindedness, however. One bad apple.... Suddenly she chuckled to herself. Here she was, the stepdaughter of the man Steve McRory least trusted in the world, feeling resentful about his attitude. Oh, well.

She shook her head ruefully and turned her attention back to Ted. He was pacing again. "What's the second reason for Steve hiring me? Personally, I don't think he'd touch me with a ten-foot pole.''

"Les, don't forget that you were dropped on him very unexpectedly.''

"Oh, very.''

Ted smiled at her dry tone, then his face became serious. "I'm not saying he'll completely relent and hire you on for the duration of the project, but I do think he'll see the logic of hiring you on as an initial consultant.''

"And you are going to do all you can to encourage that rationale?''

"Yeah.''

"What was the second reason?"

Ted looked at her, a curious blank look on his face that hid the gleam of speculation in his eyes. "Oh, Steve will begin to realize. . . he'll just start seeing you in a different light."

It sounded like a very feeble reason to Leslie, but she didn't give it much thought. She was too busy trying to stamp out the little flame of hope that fluttered in her breast. She did so want to be involved in a part, any part, of the project.

Ted picked up his cigarettes, lit one, and tucked the package back in his shirt pocket. Leslie's brow creased in consternation as she was plagued with another doubt. "Do you think Steve will find out about my personal connection with Luther?"

"I doubt it very much. Luther and Steve certainly don't travel in the same social circles. And let's face it, Luther hasn't exactly announced from the highest building that you're his daughter. Besides that, Luther has kept his personal life very private. I know there are only two or three of his closest associates who are even vaguely aware that your mother was Mac Kairns's only daughter."

Leslie knew that was true. Leslie's grandfather had made his fortune in timber and the pulp-and-paper industry, and had refused to be involved in any way with Denver Oil. In fact, he had refused to back Luther financially on several occasions. There had never been any love lost between Luther Denver and Mac Kairns.

Ted looked at his watch, then slipped on his jacket. "I told Maggie I'd pick her up at the hospital after she finished her volunteer work today. We're going

to shop for some groceries, then she's going to drag
me around to look at new furniture for the study.
Would you like to come along?''

"No thanks, Ted. Shopping is not my thing."

"It isn't mine either, but I guess it won't kill me."

"I doubt it," answered Leslie unsympathetically.

Ted made a mock threatening gesture and Leslie
grinned. "Tell Maggie I'll have dinner ready."

"Don't bother. We'll eat out. We'll likely be home
about seven."

Leslie followed Ted to the door, where he looked
down at her, his face woeful. "You will have the coffee on when we get back, won't you? I'll need something to soothe my soul."

Leslie laughed as she pushed him out the door.
Poor Ted. He was really suffering—she could tell.

Leslie spent the remainder of the afternoon tidying
the house and vacuuming for Maggie, then she finished her own unpacking.

Finally she made a delicious-looking cherry cheesecake for Ted. It was a special favorite of his, so she
had made it to "soothe his soul" when he and Maggie returned from shopping.

She was putting the final touches on it when the
front doorbell chimed. She popped the dessert into
the fridge and glanced at the clock on the stove.
Seven o'clock. She hadn't realized it was so late.

She glanced at herself in the hallway mirror as she
went to answer the door. More of her hair had
escaped its chignon and was framing her face in a riot
of soft curls. She made a grimace of disgust, then
switched on the hall light and opened the door.

Her first instinct was to slam the door and run; her

second was to scream in frustration. One small consolation was that Steve McRory seemed to be as
astonished to find her there as she was to find him.
She felt like she was suspended in a vacuum as she
stared up at him, her muscles stunned into immobility.

Steve was the first to regain his composure, and
Leslie could tell by the glimmer in his eyes that her
astonishment was giving him some satisfaction.
"Good evening, Leslie. Is Ted home?"

She had to mentally shake herself to dispel the
state of shock she was in. "No...no, he and Maggie
went shopping, but they should be back anytime."
She stepped aside and motioned to him. "Won't you
come in?"

Steve entered and Leslie closed the door behind
him. She resolutely quelled an impulse to sweep her
hair into some semblance of tidiness. "Let me take
your coat."

Steve handed her his leather jacket and leaned
casually against the newel post of the staircase as he
watched her hang it up in the hall closet. "I must
admit, I didn't recognize you for a second."

Leslie cursed herself silently as she felt a telltale
warmth stain her cheeks. She really wished she would
quit blushing; it was so adolescent. She glanced up at
him, aware that the top of her head didn't even reach
his shoulder.

He was studying her, a strange look on his face.
"You really aren't very big, are you?" As he spoke,
he smiled down at her in such a way that Leslie's
pulse did a flustered double beat.

She smiled back at him with a touch of wariness

and a certain amount of shyness. "It's because I'm a dwarf, you see," she blurted out.

He raised his eyebrows quizzically. "Really?"

"Well, I don't know if it's 'really' or not. I'm not quite five feet tall, and someone told me once that anyone under that is classified as a dwarf by the provincial government." She blushed again. "I never bothered to check it out."

He seemed nonplussed for a split second, then he tipped his head back and laughed, the reserved look on his face dissolving instantly.

Leslie smiled up at him, quietly returning the perusal he had subjected her to. She had never seen such long, thick eyelashes on a man before, but for some reason they only added to the masculinity of the chiseled features and the square jaw. Strange how something like that should be out of place, yet wasn't.

"And what do you see, Leslie Kairns?"

Leslie felt herself flush yet again as he caught her off guard. He knew she had been studying him. Thank heavens she had the ability for quick recovery. She dimpled up at him, her eyes dancing. "I see a man who looks like he missed his dinner and would give a king's ransom for a cup of coffee."

He tipped his head to one side, almost as though he was trying to see her from a different perspective. "How very astute. Right on both counts."

For some strange reason she had known she was. She pushed the closet door shut. "Do you mind sitting in the kitchen? I'll raid Maggie's fridge and see if I can find something before you get surly." As soon as she said it, she wished she hadn't. It really sounded petty.

He caught her chin with his finger, a spark of dry humor in his eyes. "Ah, Miss Kairns, I think perhaps that was a pointed reference to my behavior at lunch today."

Her eyes fell away from his as his touch ignited a warmth within her. "No...not really—"

He forced her chin up, willing her to look at him. "I don't particularly enjoy being taken unawares." His face revealed a hint of anger.

Leslie's gaze was honest and direct. "I don't blame you. Neither do I." She certainly didn't like being caught unawares—and here she was, feeling like someone had just tossed her out of a window.

He dropped his hand and grinned down at her knowingly. "No, I know you don't." He watched her for a moment, then smiled engagingly. "Now please tell me you were serious about making me a coffee."

Leslie silently blessed all the hours she had willingly spent in the kitchen under Bertha's expert tutelage. She quickly and efficiently prepared a bacon-and-mushroom omelet and a salad while the coffee brewed.

They chatted casually about the state of the petroleum industry and the general exploration that was taking place. Both of them deliberately avoided mentioning Redwillow—that was off limits.

Steve had just finished eating when Maggie and Ted came in, their arms loaded with bags of groceries. Leslie jumped up to relieve Maggie of part of her load.

Ted set the bags he was carrying on the counter, then turned to face Steve. "Sorry we're late, but once you turn Maggie loose with a handful of money, she refuses to leave the store until it's all gone."

Leslie nearly let the parcels slip through her arms. Ted had known that Steve was coming and he had deliberately not told her! Damn him! She shot him a look of irritation. His only acknowledgement was a broad grin and a hint of a wink.

Leslie glared at him, then turned to help put the foodstuff away.

"Leave it, Leslie," Maggie said. "We can do that later. All I want is a cup of coffee and a chair. My feet are killing me."

Leslie patted her on the shoulder. "You sit, Maggie. It'll only take me a minute." She had everything cleared away in no time, silently grateful that she had something to do to occupy her hands. Steve McRory's presence made her feel like a gangly schoolgirl.

Finally she retrieved the cheesecake from the fridge and cut it into servings. As she lifted the pieces onto plates she scooped up a blob of cake with one finger to sample it, flushing guiltily when she realized Steve was watching her old childhood trick with amusement. Damn those eyes!

She served everyone at the table, but set Ted's portion in front of him with more force than necessary. "Not that you deserve this, Ted McAllister." She ignored his wide-eyed look of innocence. "Let's say this is for all your sins, never mind the soothing of your soul."

Ted laughed as his wife looked at him questioningly. "I tried to pull a shady today, Mag, and I got caught in my own trap. I didn't tell Steve that 'Les

Kairns' wasn't a man. Needless to say, it caused a wee bit of a rumpus when Leslie walked in.''

You didn't tell me he was coming here tonight, either, fumed Leslie silently.

"You didn't tell me Leslie was living with you and Maggie, Ted." Leslie's glance flew to Steve. He was watching her, a wry grin on his face. He was reading her thoughts perfectly.

Ted continued to look innocent. "Didn't I?"

Leslie reached out and twisted one of Ted's ears firmly, her voice trembling with suppressed laughter as she tried to glare sternly at him. "No more of your scheming, Ted McAllister, or I'll feed the rest of your cheesecake to the dog."

Ted seemed only slightly penitent. "Well, now Les...."

Maggie shook her head knowingly, then continued to refill the coffee cups. "Don't trust him, Leslie. You can bet when he has that look on his face that he's determined to get his own way."

"Don't worry, Maggie. Ted can't very well play his game when no one will play it with him," Leslie said.

"My life is going to be hell with the two of you ganging up on me!"

"Poor thing." There wasn't an ounce of compassion in Maggie's voice.

Leslie finished her dessert and coffee, then picked up her dishes and loaded them in the dishwasher. Maggie followed her. "Thank you for doing all the housework today, Les. It's such a treat to come home and have everything done."

"You're very welcome, Maggie."

The older woman sighed wearily. "I think I'll go pamper myself with a long soak in the tub."

"You go ahead. I'll clean up here." Leslie tidied up the clutter on the counter, studiously avoiding looking at Steve. Then she slipped quietly out of the kitchen and down the stairs to the family room. She switched on the light by the piano and sat down. Playing the piano helped her to unwind, to clear away the jumble of thoughts in her mind.

She forced herself to concentrate on Chopin for a long time, but then, as usual, she began to drift from one piece to another. Her mood became pensive as she drifted into "Nadia's theme." The music was poetic, flowing with a haunting beauty. She was aware only of the touching refrain until a shadow moved across the piano. She looked up to find Steve leaning against a corner of the piano, quietly watching her.

"That was very beautiful." His voice was evocative and low.

"Thank you." She wondered why he was here. Steve McRory wouldn't come downstairs just to listen to her play. She looked up at him, her eyes questioning.

"I wondered if you would mind coming upstairs and clarifying a few details concerning the deep-basin theory."

Leslie's eyes widened with surprise at his request. "But I thought—"

He didn't give her the opportunity to continue. Instead he sat down beside her on the piano bench and took one of her hands in his. Leslie suddenly felt as though she had indulged in too much wine, for a warm heady feeling enveloped her.

"I think perhaps I owe you an explanation, Leslie." He looked at her, his manner forthright and slightly apologetic. "There's a very specific reason why I have the attitude I do about women in the field. But that doesn't mean I think women are incapable, or unknowledgeable about the technology involved in exploration. One very bad experience makes one wary about certain situations, that's all."

Leslie, by nature, was a direct and honest person. Because of her sensitivity, she learned very early in life to put herself in someone else's position. She could understand Steve's concern. She didn't agree with him, but she could understand how he felt.

"Steve, Ted told me a little about what happened between Denver Oil and Ramco a few years back. I can understand your concern. I meant what I said— what's most important to me is proving the deep-basin theory. Don't let Ted push you into something you'll be uncomfortable with."

"Your research has been very thorough, Leslie. I know the discovery of that potential basin came more from hard work than from luck." He leaned forward slightly and began to trace idle patterns on the back of her hand. His shadowed profile was unreadable, but Leslie could tell by the hunch of his shoulders that he was deep in thought. After a long silence he sighed, then looked at her. "How much did Ted tell you about the incident between Ramco and Denver?"

"Very little. He told me Denver bought off the woman engineer who was working on a very confidential project for Ramco, and that Ramco suffered heavy financial losses because of it."

Steve frowned slightly. "There was more to it than just the money. My uncle is actually the president of Ramco Exploration. About ten years ago, he hired Nora to develop the technology for a very innovative kind of exploration program in South America. Over a period of time, John and Nora developed a very close working relationship, which blossomed into something very special for both of them.

"Luther Denver managed to dig up some old dirty linen about Nora and blackmailed her with it. With the information she was able to provide, Denver got the competitive edge and secured the landholdings we had identified for exploration. When the dust finally settled and Nora realized what damage her sellout had done to John personally and to Ramco corporately, she drove her car off a cliff. She left a letter for John explaining everything. If it hadn't been for that, we would never have known for certain what had happened."

Leslie could sense Steve's distress. She gripped his hand firmly and he returned the pressure. Inwardly, she felt sickened by what he had told her. She had always known that her stepfather was callous and grasping, but she had never realized how far he would go to attain his goals.

She closed her eyes briefly, then looked at Steve. "That's tragic!"

He released her hand and stood up. Ramming his hands into his pockets, he began pacing the floor. "Yeah, it was. It destroyed Nora, and it damn near destroyed Uncle John."

So Luther had actually sacrificed a person's life to satisfy his ruthless greed. Leslie felt chilled by the icy reality. She doubted if Luther had been affected by the tragedy at all. Not Luther.

"Why are you telling me this, Steve?" she asked finally.

He didn't answer her for a moment, then he turned to face her. "I don't know, really. I just don't want you to think my prejudice is based on some triviality."

"Your prejudice, if you want to call it that, is based on an awful tragedy."

Steve rested his elbow on the top of the piano and faced her squarely. "Look, Les, Ted and I have been going over the Redwillow material for the last hour. I'm very impressed with the calibre of research you've done. Since you've done the basic groundwork, it would be senseless and risky to bring in another geologist to finish the investigation."

Leslie tried to ignore the swell of hope that was growing in her.

Steve continued. "I'm quite prepared to go with you until the preliminary study is completed." He was watching her closely, his eyes hooded. "This means a great deal to you, doesn't it?"

Leslie didn't answer immediately. For the first time in her life she was experiencing the bitter taste of venom. Luther Denver was a detestable human being. He had ruined the lives of others, and had very nearly ruined her life, too. It was time for her to even an old score, not only for Ramco Exploration, but for herself. It was time Luther Denver learned the meaning of defeat—a defeat he would understand. If the big-basin theory was sound, the company who tapped it could make millions. Luther would understand that—the loss of money.

Her voice was nearly unrecognizable even to herself when she finally answered. There was an implacability in it that had never been there before. "Yes, it's important to me. I need to know if I'm right or wrong." She didn't realize her face was set with rigid determination as she remembered her confrontation with Luther. "For my own credibility within my profession, I need to know."

"That's so very important to you?"

It was important to her only because she wanted desperately to rub Luther's nose in defeat. "Yes," she replied.

"Very well, as long as my own position is perfectly clear and there are no misconceptions."

"There are no misconceptions." Leslie's voice was low and controlled. The thought of Luther Denver filled her with loathing.

"Nor are there any on my part."

Leslie was jolted out of her intense state by the raw anger in Steve's voice. He was very angry with her, and once again, she didn't understand why. Neither did she understand why she suddenly felt so empty and so very much alone.

CHAPTER FOUR

THE NEXT FEW DAYS were the most demanding and confusing Leslie had ever spent in her entire life. The pressure was on for the development of the project plan for Redwillow. Steve could only estimate when Denver Oil would release their landholdings in that area, but he wanted Ramco to be ready to roll when they did.

He had come up with a brainstorm—to dig up the geological records on every well that had been drilled in that area in the last twenty years. The records turned out to be a gold mine of information. Leslie's primary job was to transpose all the information available onto various maps, and to color code the data to give a comprehensive visual picture of what lay beneath the heavily treed, undulating topography of the district. It was fascinating work, but painstakingly slow, for it had to be precisely transferred latitudinally and longitudinally. There was no margin for error.

Then a huge cross-section map of the geologic structure had to be drafted, to present a picture of the various rock formations and their locations. It was intense nerve-racking work, because everything had to be checked and double-checked.

What Leslie found even harder to cope with was

Steve's cool detached attitude toward her. He wasn't unpleasant or overly demanding, and he certainly didn't expect anything more from his employees than he was prepared to give himself. She didn't understand why his conduct should unsettle her the way it did, but it was making her feel edgy and uncomfortable. The more uncomfortable she felt, the harder she worked to overcome the feeling of inadequacy. She was caught in a vicious circle, and the strain was beginning to show.

He unsettled her with every impersonal glance, with every word, with every touch, and no matter how hard she tried to rationalize her own strained behavior, she could find no answer. She couldn't understand what was happening to her.

Here was someone she hadn't even known until a few days ago, and for some reason, it was essential that he approve of her. The odd time he bestowed a nod or a warm smile, Leslie felt as though she had been given the world. Yet he frightened her, too. He threatened her with his air of casual confidence, his magnetism, his intensity. He made her acutely aware of how insignificant she was, how vulnerable, and that also frightened her. She didn't understand. Nothing made sense.

She would wake up at night, her soul aching with an emptiness that was alien to her, almost as though a vital part of her had been stripped away. She became more and more solemn as the inner turmoil gnawed away at her. Why this peculiar haunting dissatisfaction? Why this sensation that her life hung suspended in some gray void?

Every time she tried to identify the source of her

misery, an image of Steve McRory would develop in her mind. When it did, she would clamp her mind shut on that Pandora's box and throw herself into her work in an attempt to drive the confusion from her mind.

Ted's attitude didn't help either. He seemed to have a perpetual air of restrained amusement that was a further irritating factor. Leslie didn't understand his amusement. She didn't understand anything.

The more confused she became, the more she withdrew behind her professional facade. Before long she felt like an overextended rubber band.

Leslie rubbed the back of her neck wearily in an attempt to ease the tension. They had been working in some unused office space attached to a warehouse that belonged to Ramco. The lighting wasn't the best and it was stuffy; that didn't help either.

She forced herself to concentrate on the huge topographical map of northern Alberta that was rolled out on the table before them. The parcels of land that Denver Oil and other companies held were marked in various colored blocks. The unclaimed land remained untouched.

Ted and Steve were discussing the strategy for acquiring the property they wanted without tipping their hand to other oil companies.

"One thing Ramco has going for it, Steve, is that you're a relatively small company. The majors are going to pretty well ignore what you're doing."

Steve straightened up and stretched, then ran his hands through his thick hair with a tired sigh. "Yeah, I hope so." He gave Ted a rueful look, his voice heavy with irony. "Just tell me again that this whole damned thing is a marvelous challenge and that we're thriving on every minute of it."

Ted snorted and shook his head. Leslie felt so frustrated and so drained that she could have happily torn the map to shreds. She couldn't stand the tension one second longer. "Well, I don't know about you two," she said, "but if I could get my hands on one of those big, fat, wax kindergarten crayons, I'd take the black one and scribble all over this damned map."

Steve's eyes widened slightly, but his voice was devoid of any expression. "Really?"

"Yes, really! I'm sick to death of this thing."

Steve's smile was cool and slightly sardonic. "But wouldn't that be unprofessional, Leslie?"

She stared back at him, her voice tinged with petulance. "It might be unprofessional, but it would be so...so...so *satisfying*."

He flipped open his briefcase and handed her a large black-felt marking pen. "Will this do?"

It was an open challenge. Leslie looked at the pen—it was so damned tempting! But she couldn't. She thought of the hours and hours it had taken her to transpose the lease boundaries onto that map. If she ruined it, she would just have to do it all over again. She felt like throwing a massive temper tantrum, and knew she had to get out of there before she exploded.

Without looking at either one of them, she picked up her bag and jacket, then headed for the door. "I'm going home!"

Ted called something after her as she flew down

the stairs, but she didn't hesitate. She had to escape.

It wasn't until she was back at the McAllisters' that a feeling of panic really hit her. She had to get outside for a while and burn off some of the awful nervous energy that was building like a mighty river of water behind a very shaky dam. She had never experienced anything like this before. Even more alarming, she was afraid of finding out why.

Instinctively she knew she had to do something physically exhausting. Otherwise she would go mad. She raced up the stairs and ripped off her clothes, ramming her legs into an old pair of jeans and pulling on a sweat shirt that had Rocks Make Great Pets emblazoned on the front. She shoved her feet into her old track shoes, then raced back downstairs, where she scribbled out a note for Maggie and stuck it on the front of the fridge with a magnetic butterfly. She couldn't get out of the house fast enough.

Once on the sidewalk, she broke into a full run. There was a beautiful park half a block from the McAllisters' where she jogged every day. This afternoon it was going to be no easy lope, but a hard fast pace that would absolutely exhaust her.

And that's exactly what she did. She ran until the perspiration soaked her whole body, until the muscles in her legs felt like sharp knives. She ran until she simply couldn't take another step. Then she collapsed on the grass, her whole body heaving as she fought for breath. She shouldn't have run like that without warming up first, but she'd just had to. Everything had felt like it was pushing in on her, smothering her, trapping her.

She stretched out in the warm sun, her body now

heavy and relaxed. Through half-closed eyes she watched the fat, fluffy, white clouds float lazily across the brilliant blue sky. A peaceful serenity settled gently on her, and she drifted into a relaxed slumber.

She awoke with a start much later, blinking against the brightness. Rolling over, she squinted at her watch. Four o'clock. Maggie and Ted would soon be home for dinner. She hauled herself to her feet and stretched lazily, her body free of the tension and edginess that had plagued her all week.

She broke into an easy lope as she headed toward home. Her route took her past the empty swings, which looked forlorn and forgotten in the October sun. On impulse she stopped and turned around, a smile on her face as she trotted back to them.

Sitting down in one, she pushed off with her feet and started pumping. In no time she was soaring, her spirits flying free as a sense of well-being bubbled within her. She breathed deeply, relishing the smell of autumn, which sort of reminded her of pipe tobacco. She hummed to herself as she hooked her arms around the sturdy chains and leaned back to let the momentum carry her along. It was then that, from the corner of her eye, she caught a flash of color.

Leslie's head snapped around, her eyes wide with alarm as her lips mouthed a silent, "Oh, no!"

Steve McRory stood leaning against a tree, puffing on a pipe, a wry grin on his face as he watched her swing. Leslie sat up abruptly, her knees suddenly shaky as she continued to stare at him, her cheeks red with embarrassment. He rapped the dottle from his pipe and stuck it in his sweater pocket, then pushed himself away from the tree and sauntered over to the swing.

When the swing arched toward him, he swept her up in his arms, then, stood there holding her, a lazy smile on his face as he studied her expression. Leslie was suddenly filled with a sense of harmony. She was caught in the hypnotic spell of his magnetism as she stared up at him.

"Well, well. So you do let Leslie out to play once in a while." His voice was as seductive as a gentle caress, and a strange warmth spread through her as he continued to hold her.

His eyes crinkled at the corners as he smiled, captivating her with his masculine charm. "What's the matter, Leslie, has the cat got your tongue, or are you getting yourself all geared up to claw my eyes out?" His voice was tinged with laughter.

The spell was broken, but the harmony remained. She finally returned the smile, her eyes dancing. "Well, it's hard to think of a slicing rebuttal when you've played hooky and have been literally caught in the act by your boss." She stared pointedly at his strong arms, which were holding her so easily.

He tipped his head back and laughed, then he set her down to face him, his arms draped across her shoulders. "And what did you do while you played hooky—swing for three hours?"

She shrugged her shoulders sheepishly as she slanted a glance up at him. "No, I...I came out here to try and run off my frustrations."

He brushed back a tendril of hair that blew across her face. "Sounds like good therapy. How far did you go?"

"I . . . I'm not sure. Maybe three miles."

Steve raised his eyebrows. "Really? Do you do that often?"

Leslie felt her cheeks color with embarrassment and she bent her head.

"Leslie?"

She looked up at him and grimaced. "I run nearly every day, but I don't usually go that distance."

His voice was gentle but probing. "And why so far today?"

She didn't answer him; what could she say? How could she explain without sounding like an idiot?

"Have I been driving you too hard at work?"

Her head shot up and she stared at him. "Oh, no! No, it isn't that. Sometimes it seems like everything is closing in on me, and—"

"And that's how you deal with it?"

"Yes." She stuck her hands in her pockets, keenly aware of the weight of his arms across her shoulders. "I'm sorry I created a scene at work today, Steve. I didn't plan to have a snit just so I had an excuse to come home."

He laughed softly. "I'm glad to hear that." With one arm still draped across her shoulders, he pulled her alongside of him. They started strolling leisurely toward the road. "After the distance you did, I don't suppose you feel like doing another circuit with me?" There was an odd timbre to his voice. It sounded as though he expected her to say no, and he wished she wouldn't.

Leslie's sense of well-being suddenly soared to a new plateau. With supreme effort she managed to keep her face expressionless as she studied him up and down, her eyes assessing. He had on an old sweat-suit top that had definitely seen better days and a pair of blue jeans that were in worse shape than hers. But he had on an expensive pair of joggers. She studied his feet, then stuck out one of hers in comparison, her face set in mock concern.

With laughing eyes she asked, "Do you suppose my track shoes will actually run in company like that, or will they sit here and sulk?"

His face relaxed into a broad grin. "They don't look like sulky sneakers to me, but then maybe they're sneaky sulkers."

Leslie groaned loudly, then laughed. "That's a rotten pun, Steve McRory—but I guess we'll take you on anyway." She grimaced as she looked at his long muscular legs. "Well, maybe you're on. You can probably walk faster than I can run." She looked up at him, her face alive and full of laughter.

His expression suddenly became serious, and he slowly traced her jaw with his finger. His voice was so low it was almost a whisper. "Leslie, I have this feeling that I'll never quite catch you, no matter how hard I run."

Her breath stopped as she looked up at him. Their eyes met for a spellbinding moment, and Leslie tried to quell the bubble of warm excitement that swelled within her.

Steve's mood was suddenly light as he slipped his arm from her shoulder and caught her hand, pulling her along with him as he started off in an easy jog.

There was something strangely intimate about running beside him, their arms occasionally brushing together as they ran through the park. The grass was

richly carpeted with a brilliant red-and-gold mosaic
of fallen autumn leaves, the wild grasses like amber
and bronze touches on a canvas. The mountain ash
trees were gloriously dressed in their magenta leaves
and jeweled with the bright red of their autumn ber-
ries. It was all like a glorious tapestry, embroidered
with golden sunshine and the bright blue sky.

They ran an easy mile in companionable silence,
the only sound their heavy regular breathing and the
crunch of dried leaves beneath their feet. Finally
Leslie turned her head and grinned up at him, her
eyes sparkling with high spirits, her face flushed with
exertion and good health. She indicated her feet with
a wave of her hand. "You know...they won't...
stop unless...yours do. It's a case of...keeping
up...with the Joneses."

Steve threw his head back and laughed as he sharply checked his long stride. Leslie staggered to a halt
beside him and wiped the beads of perspiration from
her face with the sleeve of her sweater. She bent over
at the waist, letting her arms hang limp until her
breathing returned to normal.

When she straightened up, she felt suddenly shy
and discomposed. Steve was sitting on the grass, his
arms draped across his flexed knees. He was watching her intently.

She sprawled out on the grass and tried to think of
something to say to break the silence. He was probably staring at her like that because she looked like
such a wreck.

"You'll likely slap my face for saying this, but you
look marvelous right now, Leslie."

She rolled up into a sitting position and crossed her

legs Indian fashion. Her voice was imperious and stilted. "But, of course." She ran her hands through her damp tousled hair and lifted her chin regally. "Coiffured by Grizelda Gruesome, makeup by Sarah Sweat!"

Steve laughed and tossed a handful of dried leaves at her. "Miss Kairns, weren't you ever told that ladies do not sweat—they glow."

"Ladies may not sweat, Mr. McRory, but dwarfs definitely do!"

He laughed again as he leaned forward and ruffled her hair, then caught her chin with his thumb and forefinger and lifted her face. "Feeling better?" The question was a gentle query that spoke clearly of his concern.

She grimaced, her face pink with embarrassment. She nodded, her voice contrite as she met his level gaze. "Yes, I feel better. To cop a term of Ted's, I get in a 'twist' now and again, and I've often been told that I resort to childish tactics when I do."

He took both of her hands in his, his eyes twinkling with suppressed laughter. "The important thing is, are you feeling properly untwisted now?"

She grinned at him and made a face. "I'm so untwisted I think I'm unravelling."

He chuckled and pulled her to her feet as he stood up. "Just hang together until I get you home. Maggie sent me out to get you with a warning look in her eye, so I'm not keen on facing her if I bring you home looking too frayed!"

They started ambling toward the street hand in hand, and Leslie was acutely aware of his touch. Her voice was hopeful as she asked, ''Are you staying for dinner?''

"You wouldn't mind if I did?''

Her heart gave an odd little jump when she realized he had been studying her. ''No, I wouldn't mind at all, unless—'' she slanted an impish look up at him ''—you brought that damned map or the file on Redwillow!''

He shook his head as he reached out and tucked a strand of hair behind her ear, his fingers lingering. ''Not a chance. I've more sense than that—I don't bring the competition to dinner.''

She frowned, her eyes puzzled. ''What did you mean by that?''

He grinned and squeezed her hand. ''Never mind, Dwarf. I don't want you getting into another 'twist.' ''

She pulled a face and laughed. ''Didn't anyone ever tell you, Mr. McRory, that it's impossible to twist jelly?''

They arrived back at the house to find that Ted and Maggie had slipped over to the neighbor's for coffee. Leslie showed Steve where the downstairs bath was so he could shower and change, then she ran upstairs for her own shower.

She had donned a very casual but very feminine peasant dress that emphasized her petiteness, the soft burgundy color highlighting her flawless complexion and the natural flush of her cheeks. She was standing at the kitchen counter making a salad and enjoying the late-afternoon sunshine that was streaming through the window when she experienced a tingling sensation along her spine.

She turned to find Steve leaning against the door-frame, his face reflective as he watched her through hooded eyes. He had changed into the dark brown slacks and shirt he'd had on at the office that morning. It made Leslie ache inside to look at him.

"Would you like a drink, Steve?" Her voice was so husky it was only a whisper.

He didn't answer her but continued to watch her with a smoldering gaze that shattered her already shaken composure. She was mesmerized as he came toward her. "Do you know that there are little beams of sunshine caught in your hair?" His voice was low, seductive. He cradled her face in his hands for a moment, then ran his fingers slowly through her hair, sweeping back the slightly damp tendrils. "I like to be able to see your face, Leslie."

She felt her knees grow weak as a warmth wreathed within her. She laid her hands on his broad chest, partly to steady herself and partly because something growing inside her needed to experience the feel of him. His grasp tightened and he tilted her face up toward his. She breathed his name as he lowered his head, and his mouth closed softly over hers. Then his arms came around her, molding her tightly against his hard muscular body.

Nothing that Leslie had ever experienced had prepared her for the explosion of raw emotion she now felt, an explosion that sent shock waves shuddering through her. Nor was she prepared for the unleashed passion in her response. A fervent desire erupted in her with a force that sent her senses reeling. She was aware of nothing but Steve's hot demanding mouth on hers, his strong masculine body contoured against her own. Red hot hunger welded them together, and Leslie was lost to the virile charisma of Steve McRory. She buried her hands in his thick hair as he trailed his moist warm mouth down her neck, his tongue leaving an agonizing trail of fire. His hands caressed her body with a tormenting slowness that was inflaming her to a fever pitch.

She uttered a low ragged moan of protest when he raised his head and pressed her face against his heaving chest. His heart was racing, his breathing hoarse and labored as he held her firmly against him. He bent his head and dropped a gentle kiss on the throbbing pulse of her temple, then nestled her trembling body closer to his. He caressed her back with comforting strokes in a way that was protective and possessive.

Leslie leaned against him, spent and powerless as she fought to control her own ragged breathing and galloping heart. He held her for long, golden moments, his hands soothing as he continued to stroke her back. She buried her face tighter against his chest when he tried to lift her face.

"Leslie?" Without warning, he picked her up and seated her on the kitchen counter, his arms wrapped around her shoulders, his forehead resting against hers.

She sat unmoving, her head bowed, her hands clasped tightly in her lap as a cloud of dismay settled upon her. What had happened to her that made her respond so wildly?

"Leslie, what's the matter?" He forced her head up, his jaw set as he studied her face.

"I never—I don't—" How could she explain to

someone like Steve McRory that she was relatively innocent when it came to men? How could she explain that her reaction was like a bolt of lightning out of the blue? Her expressive eyes mirrored her bewilderment, her confusion, as she reluctantly raised her eyes to meet his. "Steve, I don't know what...."

His expression softened, and she noticed a warmth in his eyes that was as potent as brandy when he brushed her hair back from her face. "I think you're trying to tell me that not only did you surprise the hell out of me, you shocked yourself as well."

She blushed at his accurate insight. Steve laughed softly. "So.... The efficient collected Miss Kairns who's been coming to work all week is only a clever cover-up."

There was a wicked gleam in his eye as he watched Leslie's eyes widen with bemusement. "How did you know...?"

"Ah, I'm just beginning to realize that there is much more to Leslie Kairns than her professional exterior."

Leslie lowered her gaze. He could see too damned much with those eyes of his.

He immediately tipped her head back and kissed her, his warm moist mouth soft and undemanding. Her lips were instantly pliant under his, and her world slipped into a long slow spin.

Steve took a deep shaky breath. His arms tightened around her, and he nestled his face in her hair. "Miss Kairns, I wonder if you have any idea what a very tempting morsel you are?"

Leslie felt slightly intoxicated as she slipped her fingers into his hair and kissed the corner of his mouth. She smiled at him softly, her eyes shining with a touch of mischief. "That comment tells me I'm faced with a starving man who's obviously hinting that it's time for dinner." She brushed a lock of hair off his forehead. "Talking about morsels when really what he wants is a big steak."

Grinning, he ran his fingers slowly across her lips. "Well, no, that isn't exactly what I want, but I guess I'll have to settle for second best, won't I?"

She caught his hand and laced her fingers through his. "Are you going to let me off the cupboard, or am I going to have to climb over you?"

He contemplated the question for a moment, then sighed in capitulation. "I guess I'll have to let you off, although the other option could present an interesting exercise." His smile deepened, his eyes crinkling appealingly at the corners when she blushed. "But Leslie, I want you to know that I'm going with option number one *only* because Maggie and Ted are coming up the back walk."

Steve laughed at the look of confused alarm that swept across her face. He lifted her off the counter and planted a firm kiss on her mouth.

When Ted and Maggie entered the kitchen, Leslie was busily finishing the salad, and Steve was nonchalantly leaning against the cupboard, his eyes gleaming with devilry as he casually munched a carrot stick.

No one noticed Ted's eyes narrow slightly, or the smug knowing look that flitted across his face. "What! Don't you have dinner ready, Leslie? I thought for sure I'd come in to the aroma of burning steaks!"

Leslie threw him a warning look as she finished tossing the salad. "You can scorch them yourself, Ted McAllister!"

Laughter rumbled from Ted as he opened the fridge, lifted out the tray of marinating steaks and set them on the counter. Then he went into the front hall to hang up his jacket.

"That's the way. Don't let him bully you, Leslie," said Maggie. She patted Leslie on the back as she, too, walked past on her way to the front hall.

Steve leaned over, his breath warm against Leslie's ear as he murmured softly, "You could have told him the heat was on, and I can certainly testify that it was scorching." He laughed when Leslie colored beautifully, then bent her head to let her hair obscure her flushed face. Steve reached out and tucked a strand behind her ear. The provocative touch sent her blood rushing heatedly through her veins.

"Ah, Dwarf, there you go again—hiding behind your hair. You can't use that ploy on me anymore because I know exactly what you're doing."

Leslie was about to retort, but she closed her mouth and glared instead as Maggie and Ted entered the kitchen.

Ted caught the look and sighed exaggeratedly. "Jeez, I hope you two aren't going to be in full battle tonight."

Steve looked at Leslie and winked, a wicked glint in his eyes. "No, we've agreed to a kind of truce, haven't we, Dwarf?"

Leslie looked up at him, her eyes dark with the heady recollection of those unbelievable moments she had spent in his arms. His eyes grew lambent, and she knew that he was reading her like a book. Their gazes met and locked as a current coursed between them.

Then Leslie grinned, her dimples flashing. "A truce perhaps, but never a surrender!"

She heard the sharp intake of Steve's breath, then he laughed huskily, his voice audible only to Leslie. "That sounds very much like a challenge to me—and you know that I love challenges!"

After dinner they all retired to the cozy family room downstairs, where they sat before a crackling fire. It was such an ordinary scene, yet for Leslie, it was very special. This was the homey informal setting she had always longed for. Maggie was sitting in her favorite chair, busily knitting, and Ted was comfortably sprawled out in his big reclining chair enjoying a brandy. Steve lounged at one end of the sofa, his feet propped up on an old-fashioned hassock. His pipe was cradled in one hand, a drink in the other. Leslie was curled up on the opposite end of the sofa, watching the flickering fire through half-closed eyes. Yes, this was how it should be—no stiff formality or stilted conversation.

She turned her head slightly and let her gaze rest on Steve. She had never met anyone like him before. She had been so intimidated by him during the past few days, but in spite of that she had come to respect his integrity, his intelligence, his perspicacity. Today, though, she had seen another facet of his personality, one that left her feeling more than a little lightheaded. She had never expected to find him the easygoing cordial companion he had been that afternoon. For the first time she realized he was a very casual, open person who not only possessed a keen sense of humor and a great deal of charm but was also very empathetic. She liked him; she liked him very much. He was so easy to be with. For Leslie, that alone was unusual, for she was basically very shy. But she hadn't felt tongue-tied or dull around him. Anything but shy, she thought, when she remembered the unbridled passion he had unleashed in her.

She studied him unobtrusively. No one could deny his rugged good looks, but there was more to his masculine appeal than that. There was an aura of restrained animal power and cunning about him that could be released in a flash. Still, his most fascinating feature was his eyes. They were such an unusual shade of blue. They reminded her of deep blue mountain lakes that could become a cold steel gray when a storm was raging.

Steve shifted his position slightly, and his eyes glinted as he grinned at her. He had been well aware for some time that she had been watching him, and he was making her squirm for it now.

Ted came to the rescue. "Say, how about a game of crib, Steve. As I recall, you play a pretty mean game. But I think I could skunk you."

"As much as I'd like to take you up on that challenge—" Steve paused and shot a pointed look at Leslie, his grin broadening as she dropped her eyes, her cheeks pink "—I'm afraid I can't. I have to go to Edmonton for a few days, and I'd like to make the 8:45 airbus."

"Well, you don't have to rush off, man. You don't have to leave here until about quarter after eight to make that flight."

Steve glanced at his watch. "No, I'm going to have to leave now. I have a couple of errands to run, and I have to stop by the office for a few minutes."

"When do you think you'll be back?"

"Probably by Thursday, if all goes well."

Leslie couldn't smother the empty feeling of disappointment that washed over her. It was going to seem very strange not having him around.

"Well, Leslie and I should have all the loose ends tied up by then."

Steve stood up and nodded his head. "That would be great." When Maggie laid down her knitting and started to rise, he said, "Don't bother seeing me out, Maggie. You wouldn't want to spoil Leslie's fun in shoving me out the front door, would you?"

"No, I certainly wouldn't. I don't know how she puts up with you two. I really don't."

"Now Maggie, do you really think we'd give the dwarf a bad time?"

"I have absolutely no doubt about it."

Steve looked at Leslie, his eyes sparkling. "Hmm. Perhaps I'd better change my methods of dealing with her, then." He studied Leslie for a moment, then bent over and kissed Maggie on the cheek. "Thanks for dinner. It was terrific."

"You're welcome anytime, Steve."

"See you in a few days, Ted."

"Right, Steve. Have a good trip."

Leslie was halfway up the stairs before she heard Steve follow her. She was enveloped in a mood of despondency that could best be defined as dismal. Knowing that he was going to be gone was affecting her far more than she would have expected, and it didn't make much sense.

She was leaning against the newel post, her hands tucked behind her back when Steve set his canvas gym bag on the floor and tossed his jacket on top of it.

"Come here, Leslie."

She looked up at him, her small face overwhelmed by her dark vulnerable eyes.

"Leslie?"

Without a word she walked into his arms. He gathered her against him and held her close, somehow sensing how very fragile she was at that moment. Her arms went around his waist as she nestled her head against the broad expanse of his chest. She had to fight to swallow the hard lump in her throat. What was happening to her? Why did this man have such a potent effect on her?

She felt his cheek resting on top of her head as he caressed her back with strong yet gentle hands. When she felt him smile against her temple, she tipped her head back to look at him. He didn't say anything, but lifted her up and stood her on the bottom step of the staircase.

He continued to hold her against him as he laughed softly and ran his fingers through her hair. "I keep forgetting you're a dwarf. I'll have to get you a box to stand on."

Her mood lightened with his gentle teasing, and she was able to smile. "You could always stand in a hole, you know."

He laughed again, then whispered huskily, "There's another solution, Leslie, but I don't think you're quite ready for that one."

Leslie shivered. The thought of lying beside Steve left her breathless and shaky. Her eyes darkened and her mouth trembled as his face sobered, and he lowered his head. "Steve—" It was a low husky plea.

"Shh."

His mouth covered her parted lips with a tenderness that sapped her strength. His own lips moved slowly against hers as his tongue explored the sweetness of her mouth. Leslie melted against him as she yielded to his touch, her body responding to his seductive caresses. A throbbing ache grew within her as the kiss intensified and Steve's arms crushed her against him. Leslie lost touch with reality as she clung to him, submitting to him. She whispered his name when, eventually, he trailed his mouth across her face and kissed her eyes, then nestled her head against his neck.

"Oh, Leslie, you are definitely high voltage." His voice was hoarse with emotion as he whispered softly against her ear.

Her own voice wobbled treacherously as she whispered back, "Does that mean I'll short circuit if I come in contact with another high voltage?"

He laughed softly, then lifted her face and kissed the tip of her nose. "Either that or there will be the most spectacular fireworks ever witnessed." He held her face in his hands, his thumbs caressing her ears. "Leslie Kairns, I think you are a potentially dangerous package. I've been warned more than once that dynamite comes in small bundles."

Leslie raised her eyebrows in mock surprise, her eyes wide. "But you can't mean that, Mr. McRory. As I recall, you made the comment that I wouldn't have the stamina of a butterfly."

Steve grinned as he tapped the end of her nose with his forefinger. "Ah, yes, Miss Kairns, but I was imperiously informed by an expert that I shouldn't judge a package by its size."

The wicked gleam in his eyes challenged her to deny it. She had no quick retort to his comment, but she knew that five minutes after he left, a perfect response would pop into her head.

Steve chuckled. "You're spinning your wheels, Leslie."

She looked up at him, a smile tugging at the corner of her mouth. He was doing it again—reading her thoughts. But as he gathered her against him and covered her mouth with his, it no longer disturbed her that he could.

CHAPTER FIVE

LESLIE'S ENTHUSIASM for the Redwillow project had been rekindled, and she entered the office the next morning with a determined, cheerful attitude. Much of the work she had yet to do was basically unrelated to her training as a geologist, but it was the type of groundwork she had done at Denver Oil. It was tedious and boring, but very essential.

She tossed her jacket on a chair and walked over to the massive table, frowning slightly. A note in Steve's bold handwriting was clipped to the map, and a box wrapped in brown paper was beside it. She leaned over to read the note.

To: Miss Kairns, Geologist
I expect all the pertinent information to be transposed onto this map by the time I return.

McRory

Leslie felt as though someone had just thrown a pail of cold water in her face. He was letting her know very bluntly that their relationship on the job was to be strictly professional. Her temper flared. Why had she been so quick to let her defenses down yesterday?

She stood glaring at the note, her mind in turmoil.

She didn't want to acknowledge the hurt that that terse note had inflicted, so she let her anger build up enough to block the injured pride and the sinking feeling of disappointment. She set her chin with determination. If that's how he wanted the game played, that's exactly how she would play it.

She snatched the parcel, which was addressed to her, off the table. It probably contained a nest of vipers. She lifted the lid and unfolded the piece of paper that was lying on top of the tissue-paper-wrapped contents. She sat down abruptly, her knees suddenly weak, as she blinked rapidly against the burning sensation in her eyes.

To: Leslie, Dwarf
I wanted to get you something special to say thank you for sharing your day with me. Somehow this seemed especially appropriate.

Steve

Leslie folded back the tissue paper and laughed with genuine delight. Inside was a pair of jogging shoes, identical to the ones he had been wearing. She kicked off her high heels impatiently, then slipped her feet into them. They fit perfectly. Lacing them up, she did a little dance around the room to test the fit, her face beaming with pleasure.

It wasn't until she picked up the box to throw it in the garbage that she realized there was another note inside.

Miss Kairns, do you realize how difficult it is to find shoes that are dwarf sized in this city? The salesclerk in the sports store informed me (with a peculiar smile on his face) that they didn't have much demand for dwarf shoes, but perhaps a child's size might do.

Oh, yes—may I recommend that you keep the box. It's just about the right height and it may come in handy for...things.

S

Leslie was overcome with a muddle of emotions—delight, loneliness, relief and a haunting ache. Steve McRory had exploded her world with a force that left her bewildered and breathless. She felt as though she was riding on a roller coaster in total blackness, unable to determine what lay before her, unable to prepare herself for the sharp curves, the paralyzing drops, the steep climbs.

She read the three notes again, then looked down at the bright blue-and-white joggers on her feet. Her eyes filled with tears as she finally faced a truth that was both frightening and beautiful: she was in love with Steve McRory. She had been from the first time she'd lost herself in the spellbinding blue of his eyes. He had annihilated her barriers, leaving her defenseless against his heart-stopping charisma.

Leslie was still sitting transfixed at the table, as motionless as a fragile statuette, when Ted walked into the room. "Something wrong, Les?"

She gave a start and fumbled with the box in her hand. "Yes— No— No, I was just off in another world for a minute." She carefully tucked the notes inside the box, then turned and looked up at Ted, a disconcerted expression on her face. "You just caught me daydreaming, that's all." She stood up, walked over to the chair where she had laid her coat and set the box down beside it.

"It must have been one hell of a daydream. You were as white as a ghost."

Leslie felt at a loss for words. But before she could answer, Ted went on, "Where did you get those running shoes, girl? They don't do a whole lot for the outfit you're wearing!"

Leslie laughed, her eyes sparkling. "That's one way of looking at it, I suppose. Maybe the truth of the matter is that the outfit doesn't do a whole lot for these joggers!" She laughed again at the puzzled look on Ted's face as she picked up the shoes she had been wearing and tossed them on top of her coat. "Come on, Ted McAllister, we have a stack of work to wade through before the boss gets back."

He shrugged and shook his head as he settled his massive frame behind the desk. "Okay, slave driver, let's finish these lease possibilities."

It was midafternoon when Ted tossed his pen on the desk, leaned back in his chair and flexed his arms to ease the tense muscles across his shoulders. "I don't know about you, girl, but if I don't get out of here for a while, I think I'll lose my mind."

Leslie stood up and stretched. "I need some fresh air myself. Want to walk over to the coffee shop for some lunch?"

"No, I have to go downtown to the bank, and I promised Maggie I would pick up the cleaning today."

"What time will you be back?"

"Oh, an hour, an hour and a half."

"Would you mind dropping me off downtown? I'd like to pick up a few things."

"Sure. No problem. Do you want to arrange a time to meet so I can give you a lift back?"

"No, I don't know how long I'll be. I'll just grab a cab when I'm finished."

"Better change your shoes, girl. I still think running shoes look peculiar with a dress."

Leslie pulled a face and laughed.

Half an hour later she had completed her shopping and was contemplating what to do next. The sky was dismal and overcast, and there was an unpleasant bite in the wind. She shivered and changed her mind about going for a walk. It was too cold and miserable to really enjoy being outside. She started strolling idly down the street. There was one very exclusive shop that she wouldn't mind spending an hour in, but it was one of Vivian's haunts. Leslie didn't want to risk a chance meeting.

She sighed heavily and wondered how long it would take before the hurt faded. Had Vivian been concerned about the welfare of her daughter, she would have contacted Ted, Leslie knew. She hadn't, nor had Leslie really expected her to, but the child in her had hoped that perhaps Vivian cared enough to make sure she was all right. A familiar wave of loneliness swept over Leslie; she knew she didn't dare dwell on what had happened, however. It was in the past, and she had to keep it there.

Leslie resolutely squared her shoulders and quickened her step. Down the street was a small shopping plaza that had always been a favorite of hers. She would spend some time wandering through the shops there.

Her hair blew across her face and tangled in her earrings as she walked into the wind eddy in front of the revolving door. When she'd entered the building, she glanced at her watch. If she could get an appointment immediately, she'd have time to get her hair cut and styled. She really was tired of wearing it long.

Leslie made a halfhearted effort to convince herself her decision had nothing to do with Steve McRory or his teasing comments about her hiding behind her long locks. But she knew she was lying through her teeth.

Ted had already returned to the office and was absorbed in sorting through a stack of files when Leslie blew in, her cheeks pink with cold, the clean smell of fresh air clinging to her.

He looked up and whistled. "Well, well, don't you look spiffy!"

"Do you like it, Mr. McAllister?"

Ted nodded in approval. She'd had her hair styled very short and swept back off her face, the natural curl giving it body and bounce. She looked very much like an attractive, saucy Peter Pan.

Ted squinted through the blue haze of smoke as he lit a cigarette, then leaned back in his chair. "Well, I'm not a fashion editor by a long shot, but yes, I like it very much. It's not so severe."

Leslie curtsied prettily. "Thank you, kind sir!" She combed her fingers through it as she grinned at Ted. "Now I can do what you do when you get frustrated, right?"

"Right!" Ted tossed her a drafting pencil and mo-

tioned toward the roll of land maps on the table.
"And all those should be frustrating enough to test
your hairdo!"

Leslie grimaced and wrinkled her nose. "By the
time I finish that, I'll have it all pulled out by the
roots."

BY WEDNESDAY AFTERNOON Leslie was indeed ready
to pull her hair out by the roots. The map work was
so tedious and boring! But it had to be precise, for it
was crucial that Ramco Exploration know exactly
what leases were available, which ones were held by
other companies, and which of those leases held by
other companies were about to expire. Leslie had
completed all the drafting and was now color coding
them so they could tell at a glance the status of each
section.

She had, out of desperation, resorted to climbing
on top of the table so she could reach from one side
of the map to the other. She was sitting cross-legged
in the middle of the table, shading in the last of the
segments when one leg developed a painful cramp.
To ease the muscle she stood up and stretched, then
stared down at the map beneath her feet. It had been
a terrific amount of work, but it would be worth it.

She heard Ted chuckle behind her. "Leslie Jordan
Kairns, what exactly are you doing?"

"What every smart geologist should be doing. I'm
looking for the big X that says drill here."

"Well, that's one method that's never been tried
by Ramco!"

Leslie whirled around. Steve stood leaning against
the doorjamb, his thumbs hooked through the belt

loops of his jeans, a wicked grin on his face. There was an older man with him, who was staring at Leslie with a look that could best be described as dumb-founded. Her face turned scarlet.

"Leslie, I'd like you to meet the president of Ramco, John McRory. Uncle John, this is Leslie Kairns, the geologist I was telling you about."

As Leslie scrambled off the table, John McRory continued to stare at her with the oddest expression on his face. "My God, Steve, she's a girl—she's a *child*!"

"Only sometimes, Uncle John. Only sometimes."

Leslie had never felt so embarrassed. Here she was, in slacks and a sweater, no makeup on, Steve's joggers on her feet—she knew she must look about fifteen years old! And the president of Ramco had found her standing on a table making ridiculous statements. To top it off, he, too, had assumed the geologist would be a man.

She wished the floor would open up and swallow her. She threw Steve a desperate glance, and found him watching her with an expression that clearly said, "How are you going to get yourself out of this one, Leslie Kairns?" It didn't help when she saw that his eyes were gleaming with suppressed laughter.

She turned to face John McRory. "How do you do, Mr. McRory." Her dimples flashed as she smiled up at him, her face pink and sheepish. John McRory took her outstretched hand, his eyes still slightly dazed. "Your nephew is thoroughly enjoying your reaction, I'm afraid. He didn't think I looked like much of a geologist, either."

John McRory retained her hand in his big one as

his brow knitted for a brief moment. Then his eyes crinkled and his face relaxed into a disarming grin. "Then my nephew is a sap, Leslie. It is indeed my pleasure to meet you." He pursed his lips, his eyes still dancing. "But you aren't very big, are you?"

Leslie could feel herself flush again, especially when Steve said, "She's a dwarf, Uncle John." His voice was rich with amusement. Leslie tried to glare at him, but she could feel a smile coming on.

John patted her on the shoulder as he winked at her. "Of course she is—she's one of the enchantresses. Anyone can see that." He was as matter-of-fact about it as if he was stating the time of day. Leslie turned to grin triumphantly at Steve, and found him watching his uncle in total disbelief.

John McRory led Leslie over to the table. "Now, Leslie, Steve tells me you have done some extensive analysis concerning Redwillow. I understand you have a very sound theory on the possibility of a large gas field there. I'd like to ask you a few questions, if you don't mind."

For the next three hours, Leslie was subjected to the most intense interrogation she had ever experienced. It didn't take her long to realize that John McRory was an authority on the petroleum industry, and that he was as tough a taskmaster as his nephew. All the preliminary studies and preparations they had labored on the past few days were now paying dividends. Steve had left not one item to chance. The information was all there, and Leslie could tell that John McRory was more than a little impressed.

Steve said hardly a word during the interview, leaving Leslie, and sometimes Ted, to field the rapid-fire questions from his uncle. Leslie was quietly confident during the entire session. She was well prepared, thanks to Steve, and the simple fact that he was in the room with her was reassuring.

At last John McRory leaned back in his chair and squinted at Leslie as he lit another cigarette. She knew he was mentally evaluating both herself and the facts she had presented. She was beginning to develop a severe headache, partly from the tension that was gnawing at her nerves and partly from the heavy blue haze of stale smoke that hung in the room.

"So, Leslie, you feel that if this particular type of geological outcrop can be located on the western periphery, it would be the final supporting evidence we need?"

"Yes, sir."

"Have you any recommendations about where we should begin the search?"

"Yes. If you look at this topographical map, you can see there's a very definite ridge that runs just east of the Alberta–British Columbia border. That would be the most obvious area to check with an aerial survey."

"What if nothing shows there?"

"I think the area farther west should be explored."

John studied the map, his brows knitted. "What do you think, Ted?"

"I'm not a geologist, John, I'm a drilling engineer. But Leslie's recommended approach appears to be a very sensible one."

"Steve?"

Leslie held her breath and tucked her hands behind her back, furtively crossing her fingers. Steve came over and stood beside her to study the map. Unobtrusively he slipped his hand behind her, his eyes narrowing with a knowing, amused look when he caught her hands and felt her crossed fingers. She glanced up at him and grimaced ruefully. He laced his fingers through hers and gave her hand a reassuring squeeze.

"I think we should locate that outcrop before we make a final decision."

"Sounds like you plan on finding it."

Steve's hand tightened around Leslie's. "I'm going to give it a damned good try."

John pressed the tips of his fingers together and tapped his chin reflectively with his forefingers. After what seemed to be a never-ending silence, he leaned back in his chair and slammed his hands down on the table. "If you can find that formation, I think Ramco should move on the Redwillow project immediately."

Leslie's feeling of light-headed elation was short-lived. A moment later the impact of the awesome responsibility she had undertaken slammed into her. A company was prepared to spend millions of dollars on an exploration program based on her research, on her theory. It was terrifying. Here she was, a young untried geologist with the minimum of field experience, accountable for a massive development.

She eased her hand out of Steve's and moved over to the window as panic snaked within her, arousing a multitude of misgivings. She felt as though she had inadvertently stepped out onto a tightrope, and her only means of escape was to walk across it.

Leaning her face against the windowpane, Leslie closed her eyes as the coldness of the glass soothed the throbbing in her temples. Some of the rigidity eased from her body as she felt the weight of Steve's hands on her shoulders.

"Headache?"

She nodded weakly.

His strong fingers began massaging the taut muscles across her shoulders and up the back of her neck. "What's the matter, Les?"

She shrugged her shoulders. How did you tell your employer that the magnitude of a project they were about to embark on terrified you?

He grasped her shoulders and turned her to face him. "I have to drive Uncle John back to the airport. Why don't you come with me? We could stop off for dinner somewhere afterward."

Most of the gut-twisting apprehension she had been experiencing oozed out of her as she looked up at him. His strength and self-confidence radiated from him, surrounding her with a warm security.

She smiled at him. "I'd like that, Steve. Thank you." Her eyes began to sparkle with mischief. "I also want to thank you for the dwarf shoes—they even fit!"

He laughed softly and squeezed her shoulders. "I noticed. I also noticed your hair. I like it like that, Leslie—it suits you."

Leslie lowered her eyes, feeling suddenly very shy. It was almost as though he knew she'd had it cut because of him.

"Steve, we'd better go. I don't want to miss that Toronto flight."

Steve eased his hands off her shoulders, picking up his jacket and Leslie's as he turned to face his uncle.

"Right, Uncle John. The dwarf is coming with me, Ted, so she won't be home for dinner. I think perhaps it's time someone explained to her that selecting drilling locations by looking for X's on maps is not a geologist's usual method."

Everyone laughed as Leslie colored beautifully.

LESLIE TRIED TO IGNORE her terrible doubts about the project, but they kept eating away at her for the remainder of the afternoon. She was relieved that Steve had accepted her excuse about having a headache. He didn't attempt to draw her into the conversation, and she was more than content just to listen to him and John.

It wasn't until after dinner that she realized she hadn't fooled him for one minute. They had finished dinner and were lingering over their coffee.

"Leslie, what's been bothering you all afternoon?"

Steve's voice was very quiet, but Leslie was aware of the unyielding metal in it. She took a deep breath as she tried to shrug off his question. "It was just an off day, Steve. Developing the different profile maps was nerve-racking, and I was feeling really frustrated by it."

Steve absently stirred his coffee, his face reflective. After a long silence he looked at her, his face unreadable. "I know that's not the whole truth, Les." He continued to watch her with a penetrating gaze that made her feel uneasy. How could she explain to a man like Steve McRory how terrified she was? Damn him, she didn't want him probing into her inner doubts, her insecurities—they would only reflect on her credibility with him. She could feel his eyes on her as she twisted her napkin nervously.

"You don't trust me, do you?"

Leslie's own eyes widened with alarm at the unexpectedness of his comment and the brittleness in his voice. The feeling of anxiety expanded in her chest. How could she reveal her overwhelming feelings of inadequacy without seeming like an absolute idiot? She avoided looking at Steve as she chewed her bottom lip. The tension between them grew.

He watched her expressive face, his own a mask. Then he leaned back in his chair, his voice suffused with anger. "I see."

Leslie felt her face grow white as she forced herself to meet his granite glare. "You don't see, Steve." There was an air of despair about her as she pleaded with her eyes for him to understand. "I trust you—believe me, it isn't that." Her voice was so hollow she barely recognized it as her own.

He leaned forward and caught her clenched hands, in his. "Then why won't you tell me what's wrong?"

There was another long disturbing silence as Leslie tried to subdue the butterflies in her stomach. "I'm feeling totally overwhelmed and more than a little scared," she managed at last. "Ramco is prepared to invest millions of dollars on an exploration program based on my research."

She started to tremble as the fear became a gigantic wave rising within her. "Steve, what if I'm wrong?"

Steve's face suddenly relaxed into a warm smile and he squeezed her hands. "But, Dwarf, what if you're right?" He paused for a moment, studying her elfin face. "Your research is the most thorough

I've ever seen. You've put a thousand pieces together that others have overlooked or discounted, and you've presented us with a very positive picture.'' He reached across the small table and caught her chin in his hand. ''Something else, Les. In the oil patch, you have to be prepared to take risks. The only way you find gas or oil is by drilling for it. The companies that aren't sweating a little aren't taking any big chances—they're running in a comfortable rut without the challenges, without the excitement, without the element of risk.'' His voice was deep with sincerity.

She smiled weakly, her brow furrowed, her eyes dark with trepidation. ''That may be true, but the magnitude of this project still frightens me.''

Steve leaned forward and rested his arms on the table as he studied her. ''You really don't believe in your own ability, do you?''

Leslie shook her head, her face dominated by her wide dark eyes. ''But *do* I have any ability? Luther Denver felt this whole thing was insane.''

''He really did a number on you, didn't he?''

Leslie tensed as a new wave of uneasiness washed over her. What had ever possessed her to mention Luther? What would Steve think if he knew that the unscrupulous man was her stepfather?

Steve sensed her distress and squeezed her hands again. ''Leslie, would you tell me what actually happened when you quit Denver Oil?''

Leslie's mind raced. She was fairly certain that Ted had outlined the sequence of events that had led up to their joint resignations. There was no harm in telling Steve what had happened at her private meeting with

Luther, and what had transpired at the board meeting later. She was more certain now than ever that she didn't want him to know of the family ties.

In a subdued and slightly halting voice, she told him everything that had happened.

Steve's silent reaction seemed to be one of suppressed anger. He was still resting his arms on the table, but his thumbs idly caressed the backs of her hands as he scrutinized her face. "I see. Has your family been supportive during all this?"

Leslie felt as though some gigantic hand had squeezed every ounce of breath out of her. How could he have such keen perception where she was concerned? He seemed to be continually aware of her thoughts, leaving her few barriers for protection.

"Leslie, I don't like it when you won't answer me." His voice was soft and unthreatening, but there was more than a trace of determination in it.

Leslie sighed in defeat. She had never discussed her home situation with anyone. Strangely, she didn't mind telling Steve, but she didn't know how to phrase the facts without sounding petty.

She couldn't suppress the spasm of pain that quivered through her. It was not going to be an easy thing to do. "My family is not a close one. I'm illegitimate, and I'm afraid I was always an awkward and bitter reminder of a past my mother would have preferred to forget. She married when I was five, but my stepfather disliked children. I was never close to either of them."

She saw Steve's jaw flex, and his nostrils flared as he took a deep breath. "So you were alone."

"Except for my grandfather. My grandfather was

very special, Steve. He always had time for me. I missed him dreadfully when he died."

"How long ago was that?"

"Six years."

Steve said nothing for a moment, then he looked up at her, his eyes serious. "You once said that your career was very important to you. Why is that?"

"I need to know I have some value—that I can be productive and worthwhile, I guess."

There was a long silence as he continued to stroke her hand. Then Leslie went on, "I suppose that's the only way anyone can develop self-confidence, and self-confidence is a very real part of contentment. Maybe I'm wrong." There was a touch of panic in her voice as she added, "That's one of the reasons this project scares me so."

"Look, Leslie, I wasn't too certain that I was being particularly objective about this scheme," Steve said. "That's why I asked Uncle John to fly in and do an evaluation. I wanted his unbiased opinion. He feels that there is more than adequate evidence, supported by technical data, to go with it—so we go. It's my baby now."

Leslie grimaced, her voice dismal. "Then we'd better pray your baby is a gassy one, or we'll both get hung!"

Steve tipped his head back and laughed, then reached across the table and tousled her hair. "Don't worry, Dwarf, we can always outrun the posse!"

VERY LATE THAT NIGHT Leslie lay in bed, staring blankly at the blackness of the ceiling as she tried to rationalize her feelings for Steve. But there was no rationale, there was no logic; she loved him. There wasn't a shadow of a doubt in her mind that, like it or not, she was totally and unequivocally committed to this man.

She knew in her mind that someone like Steve McRory would never fall in love with a woman who wasn't self-possessed and mature. And she was still inexperienced in so many ways.

She knew, too, that no matter how hard she tried, there would be no way her mind could ever control her heart. She would just have to accept what the days ahead held in store for her. But she would continue to dream, for she loved him, and God, how she wanted him.

Leslie groaned and rolled over on her stomach, burying her face in her folded arms. It was frightening to admit that she had absolutely no resistance to his brand of magnetism, that she would willingly submit to any demands he made of her. There would be no limitations from her, for she could deny him nothing. If, by some twist of fate, they did become involved in an affair—and if she became pregnant— she wouldn't experience the intense regret her mother had. She would know pain and terrible loneliness, perhaps even guilt, but she would never, never regret it.

She knew all this to be cold truth, without embellishment, without coloration. She loved him totally, completely, unconditionally. She was his to do with as he chose. Her course was cast.

CHAPTER SIX

THE NEXT MORNING Leslie was sitting cross-legged on the map table, putting the finishing touches on the massive cross-section map of the Redwillow geologic structure. This map was the crucial one, for it identified the deep basin. The information had been gathered from a variety of sources—the electric well logs of other companies who had drilled unsuccessfully in the area; Leslie's own painstaking geological detective work; seismographic surveys.

Much time and a substantial amount of money had been saved by Steve's idea—of studying the data from old wells that had been drilled some twenty years before. At that time petroleum companies had been concerned only with discovering oil, and until now, no one had thought to use the records in a search for natural gas. Bits and pieces of the information had indeed come together like a massive jigsaw puzzle.

Leslie was so engrossed in her task that she was completely unaware Steve sat behind his desk, silently watching her. His brows were knitted in a frown as he toyed absently with a drafting pencil.

She had dark circles under her eyes that spoke clearly of a sleepless night, and there was an air of quiet resolve about her that he had never noticed before. It was obvious to him that she had come to terms with something that troubled her deeply.

He sighed heavily and tossed the pencil onto his desk, then stood up and walked over to the table. "Nearly done, Dwarf?"

Leslie nodded her head. "I should have it completed by this afternoon. It really was a stroke of genius, suggesting we dig up the records on those old wells—it's given us much more information to work with." She straightened up and stretched her cramped muscles as she smiled up at him. "Now if you can find that outcrop of beach conglomerate to support all this data, we'll be in business."

"You mean 'we.' "

Leslie's expression was quizzical as she studied his face. "We what?"

"We—you and I—are going to find that outcrop. We're flying to Grande Prairie tomorrow, and I have a helicopter booked for Saturday and Sunday."

Leslie's mouth dropped open in disbelief. "Me?"

"You."

She started to crawl off the table, taking particular care not to crease the map. Steve spanned her waist with his hands and lifted her off, then stood her before him. He draped his arms casually across her shoulders and grinned down into eyes wide with surprise.

"What's the matter, Dwarf?"

Leslie shook her head in confusion. "But why me? I thought— You said—"

Steve tipped his head to one side, his eyes dancing. "I said we'd use you for the preliminary research, and this is preliminary research."

Leslie looked into his piercing blue eyes, her
thoughts a whirl of confusion. To spend three days
with Steve would be heaven, but she had to be honest
with herself, as well as with him. "But Steve, I've
had no experience in this type of aerial survey. I
could miss something an experienced geologist would
spot. Don't you think...?"

His eyes narrowed, and his face became guarded as
he dropped his hands from her shoulders and sauntered back to his desk. His voice was casual. "Would
you rather not go?"

There was nothing in the whole world she wanted
more. She followed him and laid her hand on his
arm, her eyes dark with distress. "I want to more
than anything else, but I'm trying to be logical and
realistic. And I...." She halted, uncertain how to
express her other concern.

Steve turned to face her, his face unreadable.
"And what?" She glanced up at him, then lowered
her eyes, toying nervously with the buttons on her
jacket. Steve lifted her chin with his hand, forcing
her to look at him. "And what, Leslie?"

She shrugged, with a gesture that showed her embarrassment and shyness. "I don't want you to feel
obligated to take me...you know."

"No, I don't know."

"Well, I don't want you to think you have to give
me a big red balloon because I've been a good girl."
She fidgeted uncomfortably under Steve's unwavering gaze and a flush of acute embarrassment stained
her cheeks.

His eyes began to crinkle at the corners as a slow
smile softened his face. 'Well : never would have

looked at it from that exact perspective, but now that you've mentioned it...." His eyes were filled with warm amusement as he caressed her cheek with his knuckles. "But that's exactly why I want you to go. You've worked very hard on this and you've done an excellent job." He smiled again, his eyes gleaming. "So why shouldn't you have a red balloon for being such a good girl?"

Leslie had no idea how appealing she looked, her eyes wide with wonder, her face flushed with anticipation. Steve's gaze riveted on her moist parted lips, and slowly he lowered his head. Leslie swayed against him, then raised her mouth to meet his. It was a soft gentle kiss, but it aroused an aching desire in her that inflamed her senses.

She slipped her arms around his neck as he pressed her against him. His mouth moved against hers, slowly, sensuously searching; then he probed the recesses with his tongue. Her heart was pounding wildly and she was fighting for breath when he finally lifted his head and buried his face in her hair. Gathering her closer against his muscular frame, he held her with tenderness until the trembling in her body ceased. Leslie closed her eyes and savored the feel of him.

With a sigh, Steve slid his hands up her back and across her shoulders, then laid them around her neck, his fingers buried in her hair. Gently he eased her away and gave her another soft fleeting kiss. His eyes were glittering with desire and a touch of humor as he smiled down at her. "We could spend the rest of the afternoon rather involved in this most pleasant pastime, but if you want your red balloon tomorrow, that map has to be finished today."

Leslie smiled as she reluctantly withdrew her arms from around his neck. "Slave driver!" With an exaggerated sigh she climbed back on the table and began to transpose the data they had collected onto the map.

For a while Steve stood behind her with his hands rammed in the back pockets of his jeans, gazing at her reflectively. Finally he straightened and moved closer to her, sitting down on the edge of the table. "Why did you ever select geology, Leslie?"

Leslie looked up at him, a half smile on her face although her brow furrowed questioningly. Then suddenly she laughed. "Are you suggesting, indirectly, of course, that I should have made a living coloring maps?"

Steve grinned at her and flipped the end of her nose with the back of his forefinger. "Don't be impertinent!" Then he angled her a questioning look, his face serious. "No, really. Now that I know you better, it bewilders me that you could be wrapped up in something so cold and scientific."

Leslie's head shot up and her eyes widened with incredulity. "Oh, but it isn't that way at all! It isn't cold and scientific, it's...it's exciting and mysterious." She smoothed the map with her hand. "Look. You can stand on the most innocuous little knoll and see nothing but the surface. But then you begin studying what's three or five or fifteen thousand feet beneath you, and it's like opening up the most marvelous book. It's fascinating! You can discover what happened at that exact spot thousands of years before—and you can *see* what happened, what took place." Leslie's face was radiant, her eyes shining with excitement as she gestured at the map beneath her. "Look at this, Steve, just look at it. Because we know how to read it, the earth has revealed to us a secret that no one else knows about. It's so amazing...."

Leslie suddenly halted; she must sound absolutely ridiculous! She glanced up at Steve and found him watching her with an almost confounded look on his face. She could practically hear what he was thinking. Leslie dropped her head abruptly as a scarlet flush of mortification raced over her.

Here he was, prepared to sink millions of dollars into an exploration program, and she was rhapsodizing about the magic of geology like some half-wit. The familiar feeling that always swamped her after she had done something stupid pressed down on her.

Steve caught her face between his two strong hands and gently forced it upward. He winced slightly when he saw her expression. Smiling warmly he caressed her quivering lips with his thumbs. "Hey, Les, don't ever be ashamed because you see things differently. Your special vision probably gives you that extra insight that makes you so damned good at your job." The smile broadened into a devilish grin as he stated in a thick Irish brogue, "As Uncle John said, lass, ye are one of the enchantresses. One expects a wee bit of magic from them, the little people."

An indescribable warmth radiated through Leslie. If she hadn't loved Steve McRory before, she would have fallen in love with him then. She looked up at him and smiled shyly. Her voice was a faint whisper as she mimicked his Irish lilt. "I'll be thankin' ye, McRory, for believin' in the little people."

He bent over and kissed her, his breath warm against her lips as he whispered huskily, "You are most welcome, Dwarf."

His voice was tinged with some emotion that Leslie couldn't identify, but it didn't matter. He might not love her, but he was able to accept her as she was, and that gave Leslie's spirits a glorious lift.

LESLIE WOKE UP ABRUPTLY, jarred awake by a small sound that was alien, yet expected. It wasn't until a car door slammed outside that the haze of sleep cleared. She glanced at her bedside clock—six o'clock! That noise that had awakened her was Steve arriving to pick her up. Of all mornings to sleep in!

She bounced out of bed and grabbed up the red Chinese caftan laying on the foot of her bed. She slipped it over her head, shivering as the cold heavy silk slithered down her naked body, then raced down the hall. She nearly fell headlong down the stairs when she tripped on the hem.

Breathless and disheveled, she yanked open the front door just as Steve was reaching out to ring the doorbell. She made a grimace of apology as she motioned him in and closed the door softly behind him. "I slept in...."

He studied her attire, his eyes gleaming with speculation as he smiled at her in a way that made her breath catch. "I'm glad to hear that. For a moment I thought you were planning on wearing that on the plane." He leaned against the banister and let his gaze slide down her body with a thoroughness that left her feeling decidedly weak. "I must admit, you look spectacular, Leslie, but it would be most distracting for the pilot.''

Leslie blushed, then silently cursed that weakness for the millionth time. How could she ever appear poised and cool when she blushed like an adolescent?

She lifted her chin brazenly. ''Don't be ridiculous. I'm totally covered.''

''And most delectably, too.'' He reached out and combed his fingers through her tousled hair. ''You are so damned tempting, Leslie.'' His voice was a husky seductive lure, drawing her to him with a power that she could not defy. He kissed her softly, and his hands gently caressed the nape of her neck. Leslie whispered a soft protest as he drew his mouth away from hers.

''You don't have anything on under that, do you?''

She shook her head mutely as he stroked her lips with his fingertips. His voice was soft and provocative, but there was a warning note in it. ''Then, my lovely, I suggest you hie yourself up those stairs and get dressed very rapidly, or I won't hold myself accountable for my actions.''

Leslie stood transfixed, mesmerized by the smoldering look in Steve's eyes, a look that seemed to bind her to him. She reached up and softly touched the twitching muscle along his jaw.

Steve caught her hand and pressed her palm roughly against his mouth. Then with a muttered curse he pulled her to him, his arms crushing her in an embrace that seemed almost desperate. His mouth was hungry and demanding, and Leslie responded to his searching kiss with a fire of her own. Passion blazed up around them, consuming them in a fierce flame.

Abruptly, he pushed her away. "Damn it, Leslie, move." His voice was hoarse, but there was a ring of raw anger in it that snapped her out of her trance. His eyes were flashing blue fire.

Mortification seared through Leslie as she tore herself away from the warm haven of his arms and fled blindly up the stairs. She was trembling so badly that she had difficulty dressing. Now she had done it. She had made him angry.

She sighed heavily as she slipped into her sheepskin jacket, then reluctantly picked up a small canvas duffel bag and her camera case. He could unhinge her with a single look.

She wished she could remain in her room, but knew that was no solution. Briefly she toyed with the idea of making up an excuse so she wouldn't have to go. She had a job to do, however, and Steve was depending on her to do it. She would have to struggle through the best she could, even though the weekend had been ruined before it even began. With another sigh of resignation, Leslie left her room and slipped silently down the stairs.

Steve was sprawled in one of the big easy chairs in the living room, his head tilted back, his eyes closed. He stood up and stretched like a cat when he heard her approach. "Ready?"

Leslie nodded, her eyes downcast as he took the bag and camera case from her clammy hands. She had to force herself to keep from shying away as he opened the door for her. Stepping out into the cold

crisp air, she searched frantically for appropriate
words to phrase an apology, but her mind was blank.

Steve unlocked the passenger door of his four-
wheel drive and stowed her luggage in the back.
When he caught her elbow, Leslie thought he was going to help her into the high cab. Instead he swung
her around to face him.

Her eyes widened with uncertainty as he spanned
her jaw with his hand. "What's the matter, Les?"
The eerie glow from the streetlights cast long
shadows across his rugged face, cloaking his expression.

She shrugged her shoulders in a gesture of discomfiture. "I...I—" She closed her eyes briefly as a
tight knot in her throat prevented her from continuing.

Steve folded her stiff body in his arms. "Leslie,
I'm sorry that I snapped at you earlier. But things
were rapidly getting out of hand and believe me, I
didn't want that to happen—not like that." He
groaned as he molded her closer against him. "Oh,
Dwarf, you do play hell with my good intentions!"

The champagne of relief bubbled through Leslie,
intoxicating her. She felt a whisper of a kiss against
her temple, and she tipped her face up to look at him.
"I'm sorry, Steve. I didn't mean to...be like that."

He kissed her parted lips softly, then murmured,
"I know you don't. One of the things that's so
damned appealing about you is your innocence." He
kissed her again, then without warning scooped her
up in his arms and deposited her determinedly on the
truck seat. "In you go before we get sidelined again.
You could drive me crazy, Leslie Kairns!" He

slammed the door and strode around the front of the vehicle.

Suddenly the morning took on a new hue for Leslie. It was beautiful. The night sky was fading and the first light of dawn was tinting some fluffy cumulus clouds a shade of dusty mauve, heralding what promised to be a magnificent sunrise.

As they drove through the empty streets their conversation centered on what they hoped to find over the weekend. Leslie shivered when, once again, she thought of the magnitude of their project. The involuntary shudder didn't escape Steve's perceptive eyes. He reached over and drew her across the upholstered seat until she was snuggled firmly against him. "Still worrying about the project?"

Leslie rested her head against his leather-clad shoulder. "A little, but not nearly as much since we talked about it."

"Good. I don't want you getting in a 'twist' over it. I don't need a pretzel for a geologist."

He laughed as she punched him on the shoulder and lifted her nose imperiously. "What's wrong with that—pretzels are yummy."

He shot her a glance that made her skin tingle. "But they're also addictive. When you taste one, you can't stop." She couldn't even pretend to miss the insinuation, it was so pointed. Leslie turned pink, and his eyes sparkled with a roguish gleam as he laughed softly.

Steve swung off McKnight Boulevard onto a street that was unfamiliar to Leslie.

"Where are we going?"

"To the airport."

Leslie looked at him in puzzlement. "But this isn't the way."

"Really?"

"No, it isn't, and you know it!"

"Do I now?"

He was being deliberately obtuse. Leslie noticed the corner of his mouth twitch once as if he were holding back a smile. What was he up to? She was none the wiser when Steve wheeled into a darkened parking lot alongside a hangar. He switched off the ignition and the lights, then climbed out of the truck.

Walking around the vehicle, he opened Leslie's door and lifted her down. "Out you come, Dwarf. This is the end of the line." He set her on her feet, then reached into the back of the Blazer and hauled out their luggage. He handed Leslie her camera case, then slammed the door and locked it. "My admiration for you has shot up, Les. I didn't think there was a woman alive who could go away for three days and pack everything in one small bag."

Leslie slung the camera case over her shoulder and rammed her hands in her pockets as she fell into step with him. "That's a male-perpetrated myth, you know."

"It's no myth. I have three sisters who strip their closets bare whenever they go anywhere."

Leslie grinned and hitched up the shoulder strap of the case. Her voice was wistful as she said, "Three sisters. It must be great to come from a big family. Since I was an only child, I spent half my life wishing for brothers and sisters."

Steve laughed wryly. "It had it's moments, I can tell you. I'm sure there were times when mum and dad would have loved to drown the pack of us. I have two brothers as well. We'd fight like hell among ourselves, but heaven help the unsuspecting soul who tried to bother any one of us.''

Leslie laughed, warmed by the obvious affection Steve felt for his family. ''Where are they all, Steve?''

''They all live fairly close together. Mum and dad have a ranch west of High River. My youngest brother and sister are still at home.''

''And the others?''

''The middle brother and his wife live on the ranch, too. They've built a house right across from mum's and dad's. My two other sisters are married, one to a doctor in Okotoks and the other to an accountant in High River.'' Steve opened the side door into the hangar.

''You're the oldest?''

''Yes, worst luck.''

Leslie laughed as she followed him down the corridor and through another doorway. ''No wonder you're so impossible and bossy.''

''Watch it, woman.''

Leslie's answering retort was replaced by a gasp of surprise. The hangar housed several small aircraft, but the one that caught her eye was a sleek bright yellow plane that looked like it would have the speed of an arrow.

Her eyes were sparkling with delight and Steve grinned down at her. ''Have you ever flown in a small plane?''

''No, never—but I always wanted to.'' And she had. Her grandfather had traveled in his own Lear jet, and for shorter hops he'd always used a helicopter.

Steve approached the yellow plane, opened the door and swung the luggage inside.

"Is this yours?" Her voice was high pitched with astonishment.

"Yes. What do you think of her?"

"She's beautiful," breathed Leslie. She couldn't repress a little shiver of glee. "Oh, Steve, are we really going to be flying in this?"

"I guess we'll have to, unless you prefer to try out your red balloon," replied Steve, his voice heavy with dry humor.

Leslie stuck her tongue out at him, then ran her hand slowly along the tapered nose. "What is it?"

"A Beechcraft Baron. Why don't you hop in? I have to file a flight plan before we take off, but that'll only take me a few minutes."

Leslie nodded, her eyes sparkling, her face flushed with excitement. Steve's own expression sobered as he watched her, his eyes changing to a smokey blue. She glanced up at him, and that one look was enough for the attraction between them to catch them in its magnetic pull. Leslie's breathing became shallow and erratic as a swell of desire rose hotly within her, sending her blood pulsing through her veins like warm heady brandy. His eyes bewitched her, firing the longing he always awoke in her. As the tension mounted she unknowingly breathed his name.

With the grace of a panther he moved toward her and caught her roughly against him, his control gone. There was none of his usual tenderness in the demanding kiss, but instead, an unleashed hunger that searched for satiation as he devoured her lips. Leslie melted against him, denying him nothing, returning his passion in equal measure as her desire grew to a fierce ache. Her response ignited his own, and he moved his mouth against hers with an urgency that obliterated all rational thought. She clung to him, the only real thing in the unreal world of tempestuous longing. She had never experienced such a sweet eruptive turmoil before, and it left her helpless, mindless, totally at his mercy.

Leslie moaned as he dragged his mouth away and caught her face in his shaking hands. Without saying a word, he rested his forehead against hers, his breathing ragged.

After a long charged silence, he stepped gently back and kissed her softly. "Get in, Dwarf. I'll be right back."

Leslie heard a muttered curse as he strode around the plane. With trembling legs she climbed into the cockpit and sank weakly into the bucket seat. She tipped her head back and shut her eyes tightly as she tried to quell the stampeding emotions that churned inside her.

She was still sitting like that when Steve opened the door of the plane. She opened her eyes as he climbed into the pilot's seat. He slipped a clipboard into the pocket on the door, then turned to face her. His face became stern as he studied her tremulous mouth. There was a flash of remorse in his eyes, then he swore softly and reached across the cockpit to tenderly stroke her lips with his fingers.

He started to speak, but Leslie pressed her hand against his own mouth as she whispered, "Don't you dare apologize, Steve McRory. It was as much my fault as yours." A spark of humor glinted in her eyes. "I may be...inexperienced, but I'm not a china doll—I won't shatter." She traced the outline of his firm mouth, her eyes as soft as brown velvet. "If you keep it up though, I might melt."

A flicker of a smile played around Steve's mouth, dramatically softening the set lines of his face. "You're not safe with me, Leslie. You know that."

Leslie's expression was grave, her eyes earnest and unwavering. "But I *am* safe with you, Steve. *You* know that." A bubble burst within her, filling her with warm happiness. Steve would never deliberately hurt her.

"That's quite a vote of confidence, you know."

She flashed her dimples at him, her eyes teasing. "Will I spoil my ballot if I vote twice?"

Steve twisted around and reached across her, catching the harness of her seat belt. He carefully secured it around her, then he took her shoulders in his hands and shook her gently, teasingly. "I knew you were big trouble the minute I laid eyes on you," he laughed huskily.

Leslie grinned. "That is not true—I'm only a little trouble. Not even you can make a mountain out of a molehill."

He leaned forward and kissed the corner of her mouth. A current crackled around them like static electricity, and the power of attraction pulled Leslie into its field. A movement outside the plane caught her eye, however, and she struggled to maintain some equilibrium. "They've just opened the big hangar door," she whispered against his cheek.

"Does that mean they think we ought to leave?"

Steve hugged her hard, then settled back in the pilot's seat and fastened his own seat belt. His laugh was like a warm caress. "Ah—Dwarf, I think that was a very neat example of circuit breaking."

Leslie flashed back, her cheeks a telltale pink, "I think you're just procrastinating, Steve McRory. I don't think you really know how to fly this thing."

He slipped on his sunglasses and grinned. "There's that touch of defiance again. I'm beginning to think you like playing with fire."

Leslie was beginning to think so, too.

THE SUNRISE WAS INDEED BEAUTIFUL, beginning with a kiss of gold that touched the grayness of dawn, then fired the sky with oranges and purples and pinks. The clouds, now deep purple, were haloed with a rosy glow that covered the snow-capped mountains in a soft ethereal pink.

As the sun rose higher, the autumn colors of the landscape below took on the intensity of a van Gogh painting. From the awesome, rugged Rockies across the barren foothills to the sweep of flat checkered farmland, the colors were as vivid as an artist's palette. Over fields and villages, over lakes and forests they flew, and a panorama of beauty and color, of nature in its glory unfolded before them.

Leslie treasured those few hours. She spent each moment like a miser, as if it would be her last.

Steve had brought coffee and sandwiches, so they ate their lunch in flight. They talked, laughed, argued, and shared companionable silences. It was a perfect day.

A fierce band of regret tightened around Leslie's chest when at last they taxied down the gravel runway toward a single small hangar, which had Jansen's Air Service blazoned on it. The time had passed far too quickly, but she refused to acknowledge the remorse that threatened to spoil her happy mood.

Instead she turned her thoughts to other matters, and tried to recall everything Steve had told her about Bob Jansen. The two men had gone to high school together and had managed to maintain their friendship during the ensuing years. Steve had been best man at Bob's wedding, and it had been Bob who taught Steve how to fly.

A few years ago, Bob had sunk every cent he could lay his hands on into starting his air service. Now his thriving business boasted two twin Otters, a helicopter, and several small aircraft. It was from Bob that Steve was renting a helicopter for their search.

The plane rolled to a halt. Steve made some adjustments to the instruments in front of him, then turned to face Leslie. "Well, Dwarf, this is it. I suppose you're disappointed we didn't crash?"

Leslie laughed as he unclasped her seat belt. "I can't say I had a burning desire to crash, but I *did* think you were tempted to toss me out when we were arguing!"

"What! And spoil my fun? Never, especially when you always rise so beautifully to the bait." He reached out and ruffled her hair. "Come on. Let's see if we can catch Bob counting his money."

They were walking across the runway toward the hangar when a figure in blue coveralls came bounding out of the building. His face broke into a broad grin as he loped toward them. "When I saw that yellow lemon bouncing down the runway, I knew it had to be you. Still flying by the seat of your pants, I see!"

Steve laughed and clasped Bob's outstretched hand. "What do you expect when I had such a lousy flight instructor?"

"Well, he didn't have much to work with to begin with." He shook Steve's hand firmly. "It's damned good to see you, Steve. It's been a long time." Bob then turned to face Leslie and offered her his hand. "I'm Bob Jansen. Welcome to Grande Prairie."

Leslie, who was usually reticent with strangers, smiled back warmly, feeling completely at ease as Bob's big hand encased hers. She opened her mouth to answer, but Steve interjected, "This is Leslie Kairns, Bob. Leslie's my new geologist." There was something about his stress on the word "my" that caused a crazy little flutter in her breast.

Bob studied Leslie intently through squinted eyes, nodding his head approvingly. "Well, I'll be damned! Maybe there's hope for you yet, Steve. At least your taste in geologists has improved a hell of a lot!" He grabbed the luggage from Steve's hand and started striding toward a battered half-ton truck, which was parked beside the hangar. "Come on. Anne will have seen you land, and she'll be madder'n a hornet if we dawdle."

Leslie unobtrusively examined Bob Jansen. He was not as tall as Steve, but he was huskier. Whereas Steve had the long rippling muscles of a cat, Bob had the thick heavy build of a bull. There was the same rugged independence stamped on his tanned features, however, and his eyes possessed the same direct keenness. Yes, Bob and Steve were cut from the same fabric. She could see why they had remained such good friends.

Bob glanced down at her and grinned. "Well, what do you think, Miss Kairns? Will I pass?"

Leslie could feel herself turn scarlet. She met his level gaze with a sheepish grin. "I was just thinking that you must be made of stern stuff to have put up with Steve for so many years. You'll pass on that merit alone."

Bob gave a great shout of laughter. At the same time Steve shot Leslie a menacing leer. "Maybe I should have tossed you out after all."

Her eyes were sparkling with mischief, and she gave him a prim saccharine smile. "Before we took off or after?"

Steve's eyes narrowed dangerously as he caught her arm and marched her firmly around to the passenger side of the truck. He knew very well that she was making an oblique reference to the heated embraces they had shared in the Calgary hangar.

His voice was low and throaty as he reached out a finger and caressed her lips. "Little Leslie is playing with fire again, and little Leslie is going to get burned."

Leslie experienced the now-familiar sensation of drowning as his eyes held hers. She released her breath with a shaky sigh when his hand deliberately brushed her breast as he reached in front of her to open the door. They climbed into the cab, and she was acutely aware of the pressure of his body against hers, the weight of his arm on her shoulders when he'd stretched it along the back of the seat.

The thread of tension snapped when Bob gnashed the gears mercilessly. They roared off in a thick cloud of smoke and dust, the truck careering recklessly over the rutted gravel road.

Leslie looked up at Steve, her eyes wide with mock alarm. "And he thinks you fly by the seat of your pants!"

Steve winked at her and grinned as Bob protested, "Whose side are you on? There's nothing wrong with my driving—"

"If you have a strong death wish," Steve interrupted dryly. He rested his hand firmly on Leslie's shoulder and held her protectively against him as they bounced along.

CHAPTER SEVEN

IT DIDN'T TAKE LESLIE LONG to decide she genuinely
liked the entire Jansen family. Anne was a warm out-
going woman who put her at ease immediately. Then
there were the boys—three boisterous lovable scamps
who, to quote their father, could charm the rattles
off a snake. It was true, and Leslie fell in love with
each of them.

Robbie, who was five years old, and Steven, who
was three, flung themselves jubilantly at Steve, and
Leslie was filled with pride at his easy natural way
with them. Her feelings nearly smothered her when
he produced gaily wrapped gifts for each of the boys,
a very expensive bottle of perfume for Anne and
some twenty-year-old Scotch for Bob.

The constriction in Leslie's throat eased, however,
and a soft laugh rippled up when the baby, nine-
month-old Glen, refused to be charmed. He clung
shyly to his mother, rejecting the gift with a sharp
shake of his head. Steve handed the package to
Leslie, and when Glen came to her without hesitation
and buried his face against her neck, she was delighted.

At seven o'clock that evening Bob received a
phone call, informing him that some parts he needed
had arrived in Grande Prairie on the Greyhound bus.

"Steve, why don't you and Leslie drive in with me?" he offered. "It would give you a chance to have a look at our little city."

Leslie happened to glance across at Anne and saw a fleeting look of wistfulness in the other woman's eyes. With three small children, Anne would seldom have the opportunity to go out with her husband on the spur of the moment.

"Anne, why don't you go with them? I can tuck Steven and Robbie into bed, and besides, I'd like to have a shower." Leslie laughed, then grimaced. "I think I'm safer here anyway. I had the feeling your husband was trying to dispose of me with his wild driving."

Anne rolled her eyes and grinned. "I know. Isn't he a maniac behind the wheel?" She looked at Leslie hopefully. "Are you sure you don't mind?"

"No, in fact, I'd enjoy it." Just then the baby let out an angry yell and Anne automatically turned away.

Leslie jumped ahead of her. "You go on, Anne. I can settle him down." Without giving her an opportunity to argue, Leslie left the kitchen and walked down the hallway to the baby's room.

She was in the process of changing his soggy diaper when she heard the truck clatter down the road. She tucked Glen back in his crib, then rubbed his back until he drifted off to sleep.

When she returned to the spacious ranch-style kitchen, she was surprised to find Steve sitting at the table, helping the boys assemble a jigsaw puzzle.

"How come you didn't go with them?"

There was a twinkle in Steve's eyes as he looked u

at her. "I told Anne and Bob to make a night of it and that I'd stay here to make sure you guys don't burn the house down."

She made a face at him. "I love your confidence in us!"

"I thought you would."

Leslie busied herself tidying up the kitchen, keenly aware of the happy chatter of children's voices and the overwhelming presence of the man she loved. It would be so wonderful if— Abruptly she halted that dangerous avenue of thought. She must not allow herself the luxury of dreaming. She sighed pensively as she folded the tea towel and hung it up. Then she glanced at her watch; it was nearly bedtime.

She walked over to the table and tousled Robbie's shiny-clean hair. "Would you guys like some banana soup before you go to bed?" There was a ragged chorus of "Banana Soup" from them and Leslie laughed. "Sure. Do you want to try some?"

Robbie and Steven were willing to try anything, but Steve pulled a face of distaste. "Count me out. It sounds ghastly!"

"You don't know what you're missing."

"Oh, I think I do!"

Leslie personally thought the concoction was ghastly too, but it was a favorite of the kids in the hospital where she used to do volunteer work. She sliced bananas into two cereal bowls, sprinkled them liberally with crushed peanuts and added a dash of cinnamon. After pouring chocolate milk over the contents, she topped it off with a scoop of ice cream.

The boys enthusiastically rated it the best in bedtime treats, but Steve was not impressed. "That looks awful!"

"But Uncle Steve, it's dewicious," exclaimed Steven. "Wanna bite?"

"Lord, no!"

Robbie emptied the bowl and smacked his lips, then came to Leslie's defense. "I like it a lot, Auntie Leslie. You know what little boys like."

Steve grinned at Leslie, his eyes flashing boldly. "She knows what big boys like, too." Leslie shot him a tart look, and he laughed, his eyes sparkling.

"What do big boys like, Auntie Leslie?"

"Their own way!"

Robbie looked confused, but Steve tipped his head back and laughed. His shoulders were still shaking as he stood up and caught one boy in each arm. "You guys had better go to bed before this conversation gets right out of hand."

They squealed with delight as he started packing them off to their room. But little Steven reached out toward Leslie. "Tell us a stowy, Auntie Leslie."

Steve hitched him up. "No, Auntie Leslie wants to have a shower. Besides, I'll tell you a scary story guaranteed to give you nightmares." The boys thought that sounded just fine.

Leslie watched, an ache in her chest, as Steve bundled them off. She cleared the table and loaded the dirty dishes in the dishwasher. After making certain that the kitchen was in perfect order, she went down the hall and tiptoed into the baby's room, where she was going to sleep. Silently she stripped off her clothes, donned the Chinese robe, then slipped into the huge bathroom across the hall.

She felt refreshed after her quick shower. She had toweled her hair dry and was brushing it back when the door edged open and little Steven came in. "I wanna drink, prease."

Leslie swept him up in her arms and seated him on the vanity. She wiped the traces of the "soup" from his chubby little face, then gave him a drink.

He sneaked his arms around her neck and gave her a substantial hug. "Tuck me in?"

"I would love to, little man." She carried him into his bedroom, and tried to ignore the funny little skip of her heart at the sight of a long masculine body sprawled on Robbie's bed. She tucked Steven in, then kissed him good night.

Steve rolled to his feet and ruffled Robbie's hair. "Good night, sport."

"Good night, Uncle Steve." The boy looked at Leslie. "Will you tuck me in, too?"

Leslie nodded and tucked him in, then dropped a kiss on his forehead. "Good night, Robbie."

"Good night. You smell awful nice, Auntie Leslie."

"Why, thank you very much, kind sir." She switched off the overhead light and turned on the tiny night-light. "Sweet dreams."

There was the soft click of the door closing as Steve followed her out. Catching her from behind, he pulled her back against him. He bent his head and kissed her on the sensitive spot behind her ear. "Umm. You do smell good. I believe my godson is going to be a man of discernment and good taste."

Leslie managed a shaky laugh as Steve slowly released her and draped his arm around her, then led her down the hall to the large sunken living room. There he flipped on the light, motioning to the brick fireplace where wood and kindling had been arranged on the grate. "Why don't you light the fire, and I'll check out the stereo."

Leslie moved to the fireplace and knelt on the huge cushions piled in front of the hearth. She was aware of the click of a cassette being inserted into the tape deck as she held a flaming match to the paper. Her hand began to tremble when she heard the strains of soft music. The quivering flame caught and flared as Steve switched off the lamp, then sauntered toward her.

He reached down and pulled her to her feet, his low husky voice seducing her senses. "Dance with me."

Leslie tried unsuccessfully to free her hands. She lowered her head, her voice barely audible. "No."

"Why?"

She forced a feeble laugh. "I'd need stilts."

"What's the real reason?" There was the familiar ring of determination in his voice, and his grip tightened on her hands. She knew by his tone that the question couldn't be ignored. She glanced up at him. The flickering flames sent shadows dancing across his face, and she shivered. Just the thought of dancing with him started a curling tightness in her abdomen. "Because I don't think it's wise."

He drew her against him, ignoring her resistance. "I want to know why."

She rested her head weakly against his chest, struggling to stifle the magnified longings that tormented her.

He gave her an impatient little shake. "Answer me, Leslie."

She tried to be flippant, but her voice betrayed her by its husky tremor. "Because I don't want to put you in a 'twist.' Steve, I—"

He silenced her with a provoking kiss, at the same time running his fingers through her hair and gently caressing her ears with his thumbs. "Are you afraid of me, Leslie?"

She began to tremble against him. "No."

"Trust me?"

"Oh, Steve, you know I do. I just don't want—"

"Shh, sweetheart." He caught her to him and Leslie was lost. She melted against him and slipped her arms around his waist. The sensual music wove its web as they swayed to the throbbing rhythm, their bodies fused together. Leslie lost all awareness of time as she gave herself to the quiet intimacy that was theirs alone. As they danced, their movements became more and more languid, until they were practically motionless.

Steve lifted her up, his embrace tender, and carried her to the pile of pillows by the fireplace. Leslie hadn't expected the breathtaking sensation that galvanized her as Steve lay down beside her and gathered her against him. The feel of his body against hers was so beautiful that she uttered a little moan of pleasure. He sensed her reaction and held her more closely, soothing her with his strength, cocooning her in a wonderful serenity that gave her an incredible sense of belonging. She was safe and secure, protected from uncertainty and loneliness, from fear and pain. He seemed to surround her, and nothing, absolutely nothing, could touch her but him. His embrace never slackened as he held her for countless moments.

Then slowly, so slowly, he eased her away from him and with deliberate movements began to unfasten the gold frogs on the front of her robe. As he smoothed back the red silk, he raised himself on one elbow. Leslie heard him suck in his breath sharply as the firelight cast dancing shadows across her bare skin. His eyes lingered on her, drinking in the perfection of her body, the expressive beauty of her face.

Leslie felt no embarrassment or shame. She felt only a desperate need to know his body, to experience the feel of him. With trembling hands she reached up to caress his face, then trailed her fingers around his ears and down his neck to the buttons on his shirt. She undid them one by one, then slowly slipped her hands across his flat torso and up his muscled chest. She felt him shudder beneath her touch. His face darkened and his thickly lashed lids drooped. He was devouring her with his gaze; he caught her hands and held them in a possessive grip above her head. Their eyes met, communicating a need as old as mankind.

Leslie's body began to quiver as he laid his other hand on her cheek. With agonizing slowness he combed his hand through her hair, letting it wind around his fingers like strands of living silk. He trailed his fingers lightly down her face and traced the outline of her sweeping brows, then caressed her high cheekbones with his thumb as he drew his hand along her jaw. His touch became firmer as he explored her slim neck, his fingers lingering on the wildly beating pulse at the base of her throat. Leslie's eyes fluttered shut, and a spasm of desire shivered through her when Steve cupped her breast in his hand, tormenting her with a new surge of feeling. She trembled violently as he prolonged the sweet agony, continuing to touch her, to caress her like a master sculptor exploring the marble form of Venus.

Leslie struggled weakly to free her hands, but Steve's grasp tightened. His voice was thick with desire as he whispered, "You are so beautiful—God, so beautiful."

He lowered his head, his mouth hot and moist against hers. The ache in her grew as he dragged his mouth along her neck, leaving a trail of fire. She moaned again as his tongue probed her ear, sending chills of desire quivering through her body.

He had aroused her before, but nothing, nothing like this agonizing pleasure he was giving her now. He was lifting her to a pinnacle of longing that went far beyond sexual response, a height of passion that was sweeter, more tormenting than anything she could ever have imagined. As his mouth sought the rosy peak of her breast, Leslie involuntarily arched against him.

As he had come to know her body with his eyes and hands, now he came to know it with his searching mouth, arousing her until a storm of longing raged within her. She writhed beneath his ardent touch and he groaned hoarsely, releasing her hands and pulling her beneath him. As flesh fused against flesh, there was a tempestuous surge of mutual desire. He captured her yielding mouth with his; at the same time Leslie twisted beneath him, pleading with her tormented body for assuagement from the searing hunger. She slid her hands down his naked back to the waistband of his jeans, and with an urgent gesture, tugged on the barrier of clothing.

Steve released his powerful hold on her, allowing her space. But when her fingers fumbled with the buckle of his belt, he jerked away from her abruptly. Clenching his eyes shut, he rolled over on his back, his sweat-dampened body rigid with tension. Leslie slid her hand along his hard flat abdomen, but he grasped it tightly, then pulled her hot trembling body across his as he battled for control.

The heated turbulent charge that bound them together was shattered by the cold penetrating jangle of the phone. Steve swore softly, then released her, twisting out from beneath her and getting smoothly to his feet.

Leslie stiffened against the scalding ache of denied fulfillment. After a few moments, the turmoil abated, and she struggled weakly into a sitting position. The bracelet of her watch caught on the loosely woven fabric of one of the cushions, and with trembling fingers she unhooked the tangled thread. Automatically she glanced at the time and shook her head in disbelief. Ten o'clock! No wonder she was in such a state. For more than two hours she had been lost to the onslaught of Steve McRory's sexual magnetism—it was enough to rip any woman's composure to shreds.

She managed, with fumbling fingers, to fasten the front of her robe. Her mind was still swimming from the recent assault on her senses. Steve's lovemaking had led her down paths of desire of which she had been totally innocent. . . .

She sensed Steve's presence behind her immediately. Her uneasiness rapidly turned to panic; she felt so incapable of dealing with the situation. She had no experience on which to draw, and felt at an extreme disadvantage in that this wasn't a casual involvement for her. What could she say? What was he thinking? She had to get away from him, from his overpowering presence.

She started to rise, but Steve caught her from behind and hauled her back into his arms. "Where do you think you're going?"

She shook her head, her petite body tense and trembling as she refused to meet his eyes.

"Look at me, Leslie." His arms tightened around her, and Leslie was suddenly filled with dread at what she might see in his eyes. It cost her every ounce of courage she had to look up at him. What she saw caused her heart to constrict painfully in her chest.

The ravages of their tempestuous lovemaking had left a brand of torment on his rugged handsome face. He, too, had not escaped unscathed. There was a grim set to his jaw, but something lurking in the depths of his eyes allayed the spurt of dismay she experienced.

Hesitantly she reached up and laid her hand along his jaw, her fingers massaging the rigid muscles below his ear. He remained immobile for a moment, then with a soft groan caught her hand and ardently kissed her sensitive palm.

Leslie shivered, her eyes dark and soft as she whispered, "Don't be angry, Steve."

His eyes closed and Leslie could feel the muscles in

his face grow tense. When he opened his eyes, he gazed at her with a look that was so potent, so intimate that she could feel it burn through her. A little sob caught in her throat as she swayed. With a hoarse curse, he impatiently caught her against him, and sank back onto the cushions with her body molded tightly against his.

"I'm not angry, Les. There are times when you make me forget what an innocent you are. I forget that I've known you less than a month." His tone was dry and heavy with irony. "In fact, I forget damned near everything except how very much...." His kissed her tenderly.

Leslie would have given the world to know what he had been going to say. She sighed reluctantly when he lifted her into a sitting position and began to comb his fingers through her hair. She caught his hands and looked at him, her eyes very dark. "Steve, why did you...?"

He shook his head, his own eyes rueful. "You aren't ready for that kind of involvement, my darling. Not yet. Besides, that was Bob on the phone. They're at the hangar unloading the parts, and he phoned to tell me to have the coffee on. They'll be here in a few minutes."

Leslie felt a chill of apprehension when a withdrawn look settled on his face. He was pulling back, she could sense it. He was trying to tell her, in the kindest, most subtle way, that their relationship was getting too involved too quickly. She had known from the beginning that she wasn't the type of woman he would ever fall in love with, but the resurgence of that knowledge caused a pain around her heart that was nearly unbearable. She had to get away from him, from the spell he cast on her.

With a swift graceful movement, she twisted out of his arms and stood up, her back to him. "Please make my apologies to the Jansens. I'm really very tired, and I think I'll go to bed." With that, she fled from the room.

Leslie spent a tortured night trying to wrestle with the dilemma that faced her. She had lived with rejection all her life, and she'd thought she had developed an unbreachable psychological defense to protect herself. But Steve's discreet warning had wounded her deeper than any other rejection.

She couldn't fault him, for what he'd said was true. Their relationship was becoming too intense too quickly, and she was to blame. She had invested too much—her heart, her soul, her mind. She would pay for it with her future happiness and contentment. Yes, she would pay the price for loving him, and she would pay dearly.

Steve, on the other hand, had never considered having that intense an involvement. He looked on their association—outside their work, anyway—as a casual unfettered friendship. Unfortunately for him, the "casual attachment" was rapidly becoming cluttered with an intense physical attraction.

He liked her, but he didn't love her. And he had warned her in the most subtle way what his position was. She knew that somehow, some way, she had to get through the next two days without revealing to him the depths of her feelings. After Sunday there would be no logical reason for them to see each other again, for her work at Ramco would be completed.

Their contact would be severed, and she could disappear from his life as unobtrusively as possible. She didn't want to think about it. A future without Steve McRory in it was too dismal to contemplate.

Leslie felt as though she had just fallen asleep when she was awakened by sleepy grumbling from the crib. She forced her eyes open and flicked on the bedside lamp. Glen was hanging on the crib railing, scrutinizing her with solemn curiosity as he plucked distastefully at his thickly diapered bottom. His message was clear.

She glanced at her watch. It was only six o'clock, but perhaps this was his usual time for waking up. She changed him, then picked him up and cuddled him playfully against her. She was rewarded with a bright happy chuckle.

A convulsion of distress gripped her as a new realization penetrated the numbness that filled her. She had always wanted children of her own, but now.... She closed her eyes and buried her face in the baby's soft curls as she fought to stifle the empty ache.

Glen protested about being clutched so tightly, and Leslie laughed weakly. "Come on, little man. I don't think either one of us will be able to go back to sleep, so I may as well fix you breakfast." She hitched him onto her hip and carried him into the kitchen, where she strapped him into his high chair and gave him some toys to play with. Then she scrambled him two eggs and prepared some toast.

At first she tried to feed him, but he let her know with a grunt of indignation and a shake of his head that he was determined to feed himself. She handed him the spoon, which he immediately flung to the floor. Grabbing a handful of egg, he stuffed it in his mouth with obvious relish.

Leslie laughed and ruffled his hair. "Barbarian!" He gave her a messy grin as he mashed a wedge of toast into a gummy ball and offered her a bite. She grimaced back at him. "No, thanks. Gooey toast has never been one of my favorites. Now, what would you like to drink?"

Glen obligingly burbled back at her, punctuating his jabber with a wave of his sticky fist.

Leslie grinned. "Milk it is!"

"I think it was a wild guess on your part, or could you really translate that?"

The bottom dropped out of Leslie's stomach, and she had to fight to keep her voice level. "Of course I can translate—he speaks fluent scribble." She forced a bright smile as she turned to face Steve. He was lounging against the fridge, dressed in hip-hugging blue jeans and a fisherman-knit sweater that somehow exaggerated his masculinity and his size. His tawny hair was disheveled and slightly damp from the shower, and Leslie had a nearly irresistible urge to comb her fingers through it.

She experienced another twist of panic as he straightened and walked toward her. The feeling evaporated, replaced by a surge of love when he caught her face in his hands and kissed her softly on the mouth.

His eyes were partially concealed by his thick sweeping lashes as he narrowed his eyes laughingly at her. "Am I to believe you're a linguist of sorts?"

Leslie's mind was signaling "beware," but her heart betrayed her and she grinned back at him. She eased out of his embrace and brushed by him to get the milk out of the fridge. "Well, I suppose you could say that."

He swung the fridge door shut as she stepped away with the milk and a plastic bag filled with fruit in her hands. Then he straddled a chair and rested his arms across the back, watching her as she began to prepare a fruit salad for their breakfast. "You fascinate me, Miss Kairns. For an only child, you're particularly handy with kids."

"I did volunteer work in the children's ward of a hospital. I seriously considered going into medicine at one point, but...."

Steve was eyeing her closely, and he caught the flash of pain that flitted across her face. "But you couldn't stand the thought of ever losing a patient."

There was no need for Leslie to respond, for he had made a perceptive statement of fact. He was silent for a moment then he said, "You, Leslie Kairns, are quite a woman."

But not enough of a woman for you, Steve McRory, she thought. She shut her eyes when she recognized her bitterness, silently resolving she wouldn't let that wasted emotion taint her time with him. She would gladly pay the price—even though it was a soul-destroying one.

By late morning Leslie was nearly at the edge of her limit. Her lack of sleep the night before had prompted a violent headache, which had made her slightly nauseous. The erratic movement of the helicopter as they swooped over the rolling terrain had compounded both the headache and the churning of her stomach.

"What's the matter, Dwarf?"

Leslie managed a wan smile. "I just have a headache."

Steve studied her pale face, overwhelmed by her large black eyes, which were glassy with pain. "You're as white as a sheet." He glanced at his watch, then looked out the cockpit bubble. "There's a clearing off to the west. We'll set down there for a bit of a breather." With that, he banked the machine.

"Steve, don't do that. I'll be fine."

"Hush, Leslie. You look like you're ready to collapse."

She closed her eyes and swallowed hard. The concern in his voice nearly triggered her tears.

A few moments later there was a change in pitch from the engine, and Steve landed the craft. As the rotor blades whined to a stop he turned to face her and gently cradled her throbbing head in his hands. "Are you a little motion sick?"

"A little."

He stroked her high cheekbones with his thumbs, then kissed her forehead. "You sit here for a minute. Let me get things organized before you get out, okay?"

She nodded her head slightly, then closed her eyes. Steve climbed out of the helicopter, and Leslie was vaguely aware of the scrape of the picnic hamper Anne had sent being removed from the cargo compartment. There were sounds of additional rummaging, but Leslie concentrated on trying to ease the band of tension that encased her aching head.

When Steve opened her door, she swung her legs

around in an attempt to climb down. He slipped his arm under her, however, and carried her out into the bright impotent autumn sunshine. She shivered slightly as the cool brisk wind penetrated her clothing. A few yards away there was a rocky outcrop, and he gently placed her in the cocoon of eiderdown sleeping bags he had arranged there. He tucked one around her small frame as she looked up at him questioningly.

Steve smiled and explained, "Bob always has his aircraft equipped with survival equipment—the sleeping bags are part of the gear." He doubled the thickness behind her to form a comfortable pillow, then stood up.

"Steve—"

"Shh, Les. Just lie there quietly and I'll be right back."

Leslie closed her eyes and relaxed in the snug warmth that surrounded her. The huge boulders protected her from most of the wind, yet managed to capture what little warmth there was in the sun's ineffectual brightness. Her back was supported by a gently sloping slab of broken granite, which cradled her as comfortably as a hammock. The fresh crisp air eased her churning nausea, but she still felt unsettled.

The rattle of loose pebbles on the rocky face heralded Steve's approach. She opened her eyes as he crouched down beside her. First he handed her a plastic mug filled with steaming tea, then he held out his other hand, exposing two small pink pills. "These are Gravol, Les—they'll help the queasy stomach."

Leslie shook her head in weak refusal. "No, I don't think I'd better. Gravol knocks me out."

"Take them. Our schedule isn't so strict that we can't take a bit of a break."

Leslie reluctantly took the tablets from him, swallowing the bitter medicine with a shiver. Steve sat down beside her as she drank the rapidly cooling tea. He took the empty mug from her hand and placed it on a little ledge, then he drew back the sleeping bag and slipped his arm behind her shoulders. Gathering her against him, he nestled her throbbing head on his shoulder, then pulled the sleeping bag around both of them.

Leslie was feeling too miserable to protest. The last thing she remembered before she drifted off to sleep was the soothing comfort of his arms and his deep even breathing.

"Leslie."

It was so quietly spoken that for an unfocused moment she thought she imagined it. Steve's breath was warm against her cheek, and there was an imperceptible tightening of the strong arms that encircled her.

"Les."

Leslie stirred against him and sighed. She didn't want to leave the protective shelter of his arms, but she knew she must. She tried to sit up, but Steve continued to hold her firmly against him.

"Feeling better?"

"Much." And she was. Her headache had dulled and her queasiness had disappeared.

"Do you think you could manage some lunch?" Anne's packed enough to feed an army."

Leslie smiled against his jacket. "I think I could eat my way through most of it myself—I'm starved."

Steve shifted slightly and pressed her closer against

him as he twisted his arm so he could see his watch. "It's nearly one o'clock. We sacked out for over two hours."

"You too?"

"Like a rock." Steve continued to hold her, apparently in no hurry to move, and Leslie was more than content to stretch out the moments of intimacy as long as she could. He shifted his hold on her and slipped his hand to the back of her neck, and with his long strong fingers, began to massage the knot of tight muscles that were primarily responsible for her headache. Leslie relaxed under his ministrations and closed her eyes, acutely aware of the steady rhythm of his heart beneath her cheek.

"Why so tense, Leslie?"

Leslie's eyes flew open as she groped for a plausible answer. What could she say that would satisfy his shrewd mind?

"I'm—I don't know. Just tired, I suppose, and a little worried about the project."

Steve made no comment but caught her chin between his forefinger and thumb and tilted her head so he could see her face. His eyes were squinted against the glare of the sun. What was he thinking?

He pensively ran his thumb across her lips, his voice solemn. "I think I frighten you sometimes, little one—don't be."

Leslie felt her strength drain from her and a warm heady longing stir within her. She tried to still her racing pulse with a deep, tremulous breath. "I'm not frightened of you—I could never be frightened of you." It was no lie. She wasn't afraid of him, she was afraid of the way he made her feel.

That seemed to satisfy him, and he snuggled her against him and held her for another quarter of an hour. Finally he smiled at her and dropped a soft kiss on her upturned face.

He grinned wickedly, his voice suggestive. "Let's fly, my pretty."

Leslie grinned back at him as the last wisp of her blue mood was blown away by his teasing. "I think that means back to work, doesn't it?"

Steve nodded and sighed. "Unfortunately, that's exactly what I mean. Time's awasting!"

Leslie threw back the swaddling sleeping bag and stood up, then relished a long easy stretch. Suddenly the day held promise. Yes, Steve would be gone from her life very soon, but this day was still hers and she wasn't going to spoil it, or her measured time with him, by dwelling on the future. That would come all too soon.

They picnicked in the shelter of the rocks. After a second cup of coffee they loaded up the aircraft and embarked, once again in search of the elusive beach outcrop.

Leslie had trouble concentrating on the task before her. It had been an unusually long, unspoiled autumn, with the brilliantly colored leaves clinging persistently to their branches. The countryside was aflame with so much beauty that it made her ache inside.

The land was different from what she'd expected. She had always imagined the country around Grande Prairie to be heavily treed, but that wasn't the case at all. Rich rolling farmland swept off in a blaze of color to the eastern horizon. Huge farms with vast tracts of land could be seen from the air. Some fields were a muted gold from the stubble of harvest, some were black and rich with the fall plowing, and some were still green and lush, reluctant to give way to encroaching winter. Boundary lines flashed flamboyant oranges and reds as wild berry bushes rioted along the barbed wire fences. Ponds and lakes, bordered with the rust and bronze of wild grasses and bulrushes, glittered bright blue and silver in the brilliant sunshine. Farther west, agriculture and the forest industry went hand in hand, as fascinating as it was beautiful. The terrain became more rugged, more wild.

Up until then they had seen nothing that would correspond with the type of surface evidence they were looking for. They had begun their search at the southern rim of the basin and were working their way north by northwest. Leslie sighed. She was beginning to comprehend what a monumental task it would be. They could spend days searching.

An unusually sharp ridge came into view and Leslie experienced a flutter of expectation. "Steve, see that ridge off to the west? That looks promising."

"Okay—let's set down and check it out."

They hovered for a moment until Steve located a suitable landing site, then they dropped down. Leslie scrambled out and, crouching low to avoid the whirling blades, ran toward the ridge. Steve waited until the blades came to a complete halt, then jumped out and loped up the steep jagged slope to join Leslie.

She was inspecting the outcrop closely, determining the type of rock formation when he arrived. He watched her, his own face tense with anticipation as she hammered away some of the loose shale with her geologist's hammer.

Leslie pursed her lips and shook her head. "This formation is delta plain, Steve. This isn't it, that's for certain."

Steve shrugged and pulled her to her feet. "Well, we'll just have to keep looking."

And they did. Over and over and over again, they repeated the same routine with the same results. Not one of the outcrops bore any evidence of the beach conglomerate.

The sun was drifting lazily toward the western horizon when Steve glanced at his watch, then stretched his shoulders wearily. "I think we may as well head for home, Les. We haven't that much daylight left, and it's going to take us nearly an hour to get back to the airstrip."

Leslie slouched back in her seat, totally disgruntled by the lack of success. "I won't argue with you. I don't know how you feel, but I've looked at enough delta plain and river channel conglomerate to last me a lifetime!"

Steve chuckled. "A great geologist I have here! Don't get discouraged, Dwarf—we'll find it!"

Leslie smiled at him wryly. "This isn't exactly like looking for a prize in a box of popcorn, you know."

Steve's dancing eyes were masked by his sunglasses as he grinned at her. "But you have to admit, the element of suspense is somewhat greater."

"Who needs it?" she shot back.

He laughed, tipping his head back in what was now a very familiar and very dear mannerism. Leslie experienced a surge of awe as she watched him. His hair was tousled by the wind, and his tanned virile features were mellowed by his humor. Leslie refused to acknowledge the ache of despair that was nagging at her.

They were off at sunrise the following morning to continue their investigation, both of them buoyed by a good night's rest. As on the previous day, they checked every outcrop that remotely resembled what they were searching for.

As the day wore on, their high spirits gave way to quiet seriousness. Bit by bit, mile by mile, they were working their way in a northwesterly direction. Now they were flying over northern British Columbia. Leslie was beginning to feel extremely concerned, and she could tell by the chiseled set to his jaw that Steve was feeling the same way. They had found a lot more evidence of delta plain and river channel, but nothing that even hinted at a pebble beach conglomerate.

"Steve?"

"What?"

Leslie swallowed, reluctant to give voice to her doubts. "I think we either missed it, or it simply isn't here. We've extended our search miles beyond the bounds we had established when we did the mapping."

"I know." His chin jutted with determination.

Leslie frowned unhappily. Had this entire exercise been a monumental wild goose chase? She looked out the window, her face miserable. Damn, it had looked so promising.

The terrain was becoming more and more mountainous. They were flying over a ridge, and Leslie glanced back at some of the cliff formations that were flashing past. An odd sensation of premonition snaked through her. She turned in her seat and looked hard. They were different....

"Steve, can you find a place to land?" Her voice was brittle with tension.

Steve shot her a penetrating glance, then nodded. Leslie's face was taut as he put the helicopter down on a plateau just above the formation. Leslie was out of her seat before he had a chance to question her. She slipped and slid haphazardly on the loose shale as she clambered down the rocky slope.

Later she could never remember how she managed to arrive at the cliff. She scrambled up the rough face, a hard knot of expectation restricting her breathing. She was swinging her hammer almost frantically when Steve joined her, his own breathing labored.

The rock face gave way under her blows, and Leslie scooped up a handful of the rubble. She held it in her hands as though it was something fragile and precious and a wave of exhilaration and relief slammed into her. She could barely speak. "This is it! Steve, this is *it!*"

Steve knelt down on the ledge beside her and raked through the bits of rock in her hand. When he looked at her, his expression was fixed with excitement. Slowly he began to smile, as the realization finally penetrated. The smile changed to a dazzling grin as he caught her up in his arms and hugged her fiercely.

There was a peal of jubilant laughter. "We've got it. We've really got it!" He swung her around. "It's the old ocean bed! Listen, Les, just close your eyes and listen—you can damned near hear the surf crashing.''

It was crashing through aeons of time.

THE TRIP BACK to Grande Prairie was a blur for Leslie. The only thing she was really conscious of was the sharp bite of the rocks she still clutched in her hand. She was grinning so broadly her face had gone numb. They had found it! They had really found it!

"Leslie, do you realize—do you comprehend the magnitude of this? This discovery today extends the boundaries by miles. Dwarf, this damned field is huge—it covers hundreds of square miles!'' Steve gave a shout of elation and clenched his fist in exuberance. "Leslie, God bless you, you have discovered the largest field of natural gas in Canada!''

Leslie could only grin and clasp the pebbles tighter. She was beyond speech. She couldn't absorb it all.

Steve glanced across the cockpit at her and laughed, his fce alive with excitement. "You look like you don't quite believe it.''

"I don't...I can't.'' She turned to face him, suddenly frozen with doubt as her uncertainty came rushing back. "Oh, Steve, what if it's a low-volume field, or worse yet, what if there's no gas there at all?''

Steve reached across, caught her tight fist and squeezed it reassuringly. "There's gas and plenty of it—I know it!''

With a mixture of awe and fear Leslie opened her hand and looked at the pebbles lying in her palm. If only they could talk.

The rest of the afternoon was a rush of activity. Within half an hour of landing at the Jansen airstrip, Leslie and Steve were once again airborne in the yellow plane, this time destined for Calgary.

It was imperative that their well-planned strategy be put in motion immediately. Ramco had managed to acquire some key leases in the area, but now, since their discovery had extended the northwestern perimeter of the field, the company would want to expand their proposed land acquisitions dramatically. Steve wanted to contact his landman right away. All the precise map work they had done would now pay high dividends.

Leslie knew that Steve planned to obtain the surface rights through many different land brokers, thereby camouflaging Ramco's intentions from other exploration companies. No one would know that one company, and one company only, was going into Redwillow with a massive exploration program.

She also knew that he had three rigs and the support equipment on standby and ready to roll. They would move immediately onto leases already held by Ramco. The whole thing had to be done quickly and quietly. Word would be circulated that Ramco was drilling for oil, thereby diffusing any undue curiosity. The entire operation had the aura of a finely tuned commando raid. Time was of the essence, as was the element of surprise.

Leslie was still staggered by the find, but Steve was cool and competent, every inch an astute executive. He would be an imposing adversary, she realized.

It was late evening when they landed in Calgary. They went directly to McAllisters, and Ted was exultant at their news. Steve phoned John McRory, and with a nonchalance that astounded Leslie, he systematically activated the tactics he and Ted had so meticulously planned.

After the phone call, Ted and Steve discussed the operation, and blueprinted additional plans for the logistics support that would be required. Arranging for supplies, additional equipment and men to be on site at a specific date would be Ted's responsibility.

Leslie's head was swimming with a jumble of facts, figures and deadlines by the time Ted went to bed. Maggie had preceded him by an hour. She was on the sofa, staring into space, her feet propped on the coffee table. Sipping absently on a weak drink, she'd almost given up trying to marshal her thoughts when Steve sat down beside her.

He leaned back, his eyes hooded as he idly swirled his own drink. "I have a proposition for you, Leslie, one that I want you to consider very seriously."

A shiver of uncertainty ran through her. She clasped her hands tightly around her glass as she tipped her head questioningly. "What is it?"

He leaned forward and rested his arms on his knees, scrutinizing her from behind his thick lashes. "Would you consider coming on staff at Ramco as project geologist for the Redwillow program?"

Leslie stared at him, her expression registering her stunned confusion. She wasn't expecting this offer. She wasn't expecting it at all. Steve had hired her for the preliminary studies, and she had thought she'd get a friendly dismissal—more pointedly, the absence of Steve McRory in her life. Now this!

"But, you said— I thought—"

"I know what I said originally, but I've given it a great deal of consideration. You're aware of the scope of the program, and you're damned good at your job." He was watching her face with a steady, unnerving gaze. "It won't be easy for you, Les. You're going to be hassled by the rig hands, and other field personnel—and you're going to have to cope with it on your own. You're going to have responsibilities, and you have a lot to learn. You'll also have to deal with some very awkward situations simply because you're a woman in a man's environment. It won't be easy."

Leslie met his gaze directly. "Do you think I have the capability to handle it?" It wasn't an attempt to elicit flattery; it was a direct question, and Steve knew it.

"I wouldn't have asked you if I didn't."

Somewhere in her head, Leslie knew she should decline his offer and put as much distance as she could between herself and Steve McRory. But in her heart she longed to maintain some link with this man who had invaded her life and caused her such emotional chaos. It would have to be a strictly professional association, even if the circumstances between them had previously been romantic. There would have to be a detachment, a "hands-off policy" in the field. She had made a decision in Grande Prairie, but she was going to reverse it with this opportunity before her. She would do anything to postpone that dreaded moment when he walked out of her life forever.

She was aware of his eyes on her, and she looked up to meet his gaze. "I wasn't expecting this, Steve."

"I know."

"It's a little frightening."

"I know that, too."

Leslie toyed with her glass for a moment, then looked back at him, her face grave and thoughtful. "This decision of yours was influenced somewhat by the discussion we had about my lack of self-confidence, wasn't it?"

"Somewhat, but not entirely. I wouldn't consider asking you if your potential didn't outweigh the disadvantages. I think you know me well enough to realize that I don't pander to whims."

"Are you sure this isn't a whim of sorts? I'm not your responsibility."

For a split second, Leslie thought there was a hint of regret in his eyes, but she dismissed it as wishful thinking. "Steve, are you sure, are you truly certain that you want me there?"

Steve looked at her, his eyes enigmatic, his face inscrutable as he nodded his head. "Yes, Leslie, I want you there."

Fools rush in, thought Leslie. Aloud she said, "Then I'll go."

Had she been watching Steve's face, she would have wondered at the expression of angry dissatisfaction that flitted across it.

CHAPTER EIGHT

LESLIE FREQUENTLY DOUBTED HER SANITY during the days to come. She had committed herself to several weeks, or even months, of agonizing thoughts and feelings, but she couldn't turn back from the disturbing challenge that lay before her.

She would do her job to the very best of her ability, for she was determined to fulfill her obligations to Ramco Explorations. But she worried about how well she would handle the close association with Steve. Just being in the same room with him did strange things to her.

During her remaining days in Calgary, Leslie had to arrange for the geological equipment and supplies she would require. She also had to complete some research work. She felt very much alone, for Steve was out of town and Ted was frequently away.

She was now working with the engineering team at Ramco's main office complex, and she was not surprised to see the logistic requirements handled with the maximum of efficiency, the minimum amount of delays. To see the respect and loyalty Steve's employees openly displayed toward him filled her with a sense of pride. Luther Denver demanded subservience; the Ramco organization stressed teamwork. The attitude and morale at her new job was so totally different from the atmosphere at her old that Leslie sometimes caught herself wondering if she were really in the same business.

Leslie also made personal preparations. She was aware that the company would provide her with a vehicle once she was on location, but she'd told Ted that she wanted one her own size. He went with her to advise her in her purchase of one, and she came home with a bright red four-wheel-drive Toyota truck. It boasted wide chrome moldings, a black canopy on the back and smoked windows. It was flashy and certainly conspicuous, and Vivian Denver would have died if she had seen it. But Leslie loved it. Although Ted teased her unmercifully about it, she was impervious to his gibes.

She had heard nothing from Steve since the night he'd asked her to take on the Redwillow project. She missed him dreadfully, and spent many sleepless nights haunted by the intimate moments they had shared. She had one small secret solace though. She had furtively taken several pictures of him during their exploration trip, and two had been particularly good photos. One was taken the day they located the outcrop. Steve was standing on a massive boulder, his hands on his hips, his legs planted firmly apart as he stared out over a picturesque valley they had discovered. His head was thrown back, and he seemed to be challenging the rugged untamed land with his strength, his virility, his determination.

The second one had been taken at the Jansens'. Steve had adjusted the chain on Robbie's bike, and Robbie had thanked him with a quick hug before he sped off. Steve had watched him go, his eyes filled with amused affection. The gentleness, the warmth, the sensitivity of his personality were so poignantly evident that it caused a painful constriction in Leslie's chest every time she looked at it.

The other pictures of him were good, and she would treasure them always, but these two were superb; they were the essence of the man. Leslie had them enlarged and framed in a handsome leather and brassbound folder, then carefully slipped the three notes he'd written her behind the photos. She had the pebbles from the beach conglomerate encased in a glass cube and had a small silver plate attached to the base with the location and date engraved on it.

She kept the paperweight and the photos on her bedside table and chided herself for her futile gesture—only it wasn't really futile, for it did ease her solitary wretchedness.

Outwardly she appeared calm and composed about the challenges that lay before her, but inwardly she was agitated and terribly unsure. It was only by sheer will that she was able to accomplish anything. She became more and more anxious as the time marched on.

Too soon, it seemed, the day of departure arrived. It was five o'clock in the morning when Leslie went outside to start her truck and scrape the thick frost off the windows. As she sat on the fender waiting for Ted to say goodbye to Maggie, she watched the stars in the dark sky. It was hard to believe it was the first of November. There was no snow yet, and the days were unusually warm for this time of year, even though the nights were frosty.

Leslie slid off the fender and leaned against it as Ted left the house and came striding down the sidewalk toward her. He had a large duffel bag in one hand, and a beautifully tooled leather rifle case in the other.

Leslie felt a stab of grief when she recognized the case. It, and the custom-made rifle inside, had been bequeathed to Ted when Mac Kairns had died. Leslie knew it was Ted's most prized possession. Cherished memories came crowding back—her grandfather teaching her to shoot and his delight and pride in her deadly marksmanship; his amusement in her adamant refusal to shoot anything but impersonal targets and clay skeets. The long tramps they had taken through the woods, her grandfather with his rifle and she with her camera. His livid rage when Luther forbade her to continue competing in marksmanship competitions.... The memories were so special and she missed him still.

Ted raised the rifle as he approached Leslie. "I thought I'd bring this along. Big-game hunting should be really great in that country." He lifted up the canopy door and placed the duffel bag and rifle in the back of the truck. His face was angelically composed, but the devil was gleaming in his eyes. "Maybe you can come out with me one day, Leslie. I'd sure like it if you'd bring down a big bull moose for me."

Leslie defiantly stuck out her tongue at him. Ted had been a frequent companion on their hunting expeditions, and he was well aware of her aversion to taking an animal's life. Ted laughed, then pointed toward the cab of the truck. "Are you going to drive this peanut with wheels or am I?"

Leslie punched him on the shoulder, then opened the door and climbed into the driver's seat. "I'll drive my own rig, Ted McAllister. After a disparaging comment like that, I wouldn't trust you behind the wheel!''

"The feeling is mutual, girl. Mac should never have been allowed to teach you to drive—how he used to justify his own driving is beyond me!''

Leslie laughed. " 'Reckless caution mixed with aggressive speed,' '' she quoted.

"He used to scare the hell out of me—always made me feel like he was driving a fire truck. And you're just as bad.''

"Then you'd better do up your seat belt.'' With a broad grin and a touch of malice, Leslie revved the engine, threw the vehicle into gear and shot off in a hail of flying gravel.

THE DRIVE TOOK THEM NEARLY TWELVE HOURS. When it was beginning to get dark, Ted, who was now behind the wheel, told Leslie they had only a few miles to go before reaching camp.

She was feeling relatively relaxed, for Ted, in his casual, almost offhand way, was outlining the routine of oil-patch life.

"Oil companies don't always have their own rigs do the drilling. There are contractors who drill wells strictly on a contract basis. Our other two holes are being done by different companies, for example. One is a Challenger rig and the other is Hi-tower.''

"But it's Ramco's rig that's drilling the first wildcat well, right?''

"That's right. Companies number their drilling rigs, and the crews usually stay with the same rig no matter where it's drilling. This one is Ramco Two.''

"I didn't realize that the crews were always assigned to the same rig."

"It's the usual practice, but I don't think it's written in stone anywhere."

"What rotation will they be working?"

"Two weeks on and two weeks off, with 'twelve-hour towers' when they're in the field."

Leslie grinned to herself—another idiosyncrasy of the oil patch. Actually, shifts were called tours, but for some long-forgotten reason they were pronounced "towers." She glanced at Ted. "Which means that altogether there are four crews that rotate in and out?"

"Yeah, a crew each week. That makes a pile of men who go through camp every month."

"How many men does Ramco run on a crew?"

"Five—a driller, a derrickman, a motorman and two roughnecks."

Leslie laughed. "And in the proper order of rank, I noticed."

Ted grinned. "Every roughneck wants to be a driller someday, Les—a hand on the brake handle is the symbol of power and authority on a rig."

"Is it that, or the fact they don't have to wrestle drill pipe around anymore?"

Ted laughed as he nodded his head. "That, too—it's damned hard work. I do get a kick out of watching these young fellows. Years ago it took you fifteen years to make driller, but now, with the big push on for exploration, there're more rigs operating and the men get promoted faster. The young ones really strut. Now a roughneck can make motorman in a year, derrickman in two."

"The motorman works as a roughneck as well as looking after the motors, doesn't he?"

"Yeah. When they're tripping, he usually works the floor."

Tripping had to be the most grueling, demanding time on a rig, Leslie knew. "Tripping out" was when all of the drill stem was hoisted out of the hole, usually to change the bit or to add the core barrel. "Tripping in" meant reassembling the drill string stand by stand and lowering it back down the hole. The whole operation was referred to as a round trip—and it usually took several arduous hours.

Leslie could tell by Ted's expression that he was thinking about something that amused him. "What's so funny?"

"Oh, I was just recalling some of the incidents that have happened in the oil patch over the years. I have a book at home that you should read—it's called *Roughnecks and Wildcatters*, by Allan Anderson. He's collected a whole raft of short stories from the field. They portray the humor but also give you a fair amount of insight into the history of the industry."

"I'll read *anything* that will give me insight!"

Ted's face grew serious as he shifted the conversation into a slightly different vein. "You know, girl, some of these old rig hands are going to be a little put off having you around."

Leslie sighed. "I know, Ted—Steve already warned me."

"Well, don't let it get to you. Ramco hasn't had much of a turnover in staff over the years, for they've always treated their men very well. The fellows may be a little set in their ways, but basically they'll be decent and hardworking. Most of them have never seen women in the field before, with the exception of the camp staff. You know—cooks and camp attendants.''

"And I'm treading on sacred ground."

Ted chuckled as he switched on the headlights. "I don't know if the ground is sacred, or just that it's never been plowed before." He stroked his chin reflectively. "Perhaps this idea is a little out of step with the times, but I think that most of them feel women should remain in traditional women's roles, and that they shouldn't compete with men. They're bound to feel a little threatened by something they don't quite understand."

"Threatened?"

"Sure. It's something that they've never had to accept before, or adjust to—dealing with women in this capacity—and some of the older ones won't know how to handle it." Ted navigated around a large pothole, then glanced at Leslie. "Always try to put yourself in their shoes, girl. If you do, I know you'll be able to deal with their initial animosity."

"I hope so. This isn't exactly one of the high points in my life as far as courage goes."

"I know, honey. And I may as well warn you—it's going to be worse for you because you look half your age and you aren't exactly big. I've run across a few women geologists and engineers in my travels, and the majority of them have been big robust women who are a little rough around the edges. You're different, Les, so it's going to take them all some time to get used to you."

Ted was silent for a moment, and Leslie could

sense that he was considering something else. "Steve is really sticking his neck out by taking you on. I hope you realize that," he said finally.

"I know."

"He has a lot of confidence in you."

Leslie didn't answer. She didn't want to talk about Steve. She was in such a muddle as far as he was concerned. She ached to see him again, yet she dreaded it. One moment she would be filled with excitement about working so closely with him, and the next she would be apprehensive. All that remained constant were her feelings for him—those would never change.

"Leslie, there's something else you had better be on the alert for. Some of the guys are young pups, and I don't doubt for a moment that one or two of them are going to be a little persistent with their attentions."

"Don't be ridiculous, Ted."

"I'm not being ridiculous. Something like that could cause problems when there's a bunch of guys jammed together in a camp—and isolated to boot."

"I think you're way off base, but if it should happen, and I doubt that it will, you have my word that I'll deal with it."

"Don't be afraid to let me know if anyone is giving you any trouble."

"If I have to, I will, but that sort of situation is never going to happen."

Ted chuckled and shook his head slowly. "That's always amazed me—you don't have a vain bone in your body."

Leslie snorted, her cheeks flushed with embarrassment. "Not about my looks, maybe, but my driving skills are worth bragging about!"

"Ha! I'm glad you finally turned the wheel over to me when you did. I have this peculiar desire to live to a ripe old age."

Leslie pulled a face at him. She sat up straight and peered out the windshield as she glimpsed lights through the trees. "How much farther?"

"Just around the bend. We'll stop in at the rig before we go on to camp for supper, okay?"

"Okay." Leslie could feel herself grow pale. Here she was—miles from nowhere, going into a camp where nearly everyone would view her presence as an offense. Then there was the man who meant every-thing to her, who viewed her as . . . as what? She must be out of her mind. She closed her eyes and shud-dered. What had she gotten herself into this time? And could she get herself out of it in one piece?

The truck bounced to a halt and Leslie opened her eyes. A bombardment of impressions hit her; dark-ness falling like a curtain around the brightly lighted rig, a cacophony of noise that was muffled by the silence of the surrounding forest, a sense of purpose. This would be her home for many weeks. Could she ever fit in? She squared her shoulders as Ted switched off the ignition and turned off the lights.

He patted her arm. "One more thing, girl. If you ever need a shoulder to lean on or an ear to bend, I'm here."

She squeezed his hand, her heart filled with warm affection. "Thank you, Ted. You have no idea how much that means to me."

He gave a brief nod of satisfaction, then opened his door. "Let's go, girl. Everybody is likely curling up with curiosity over 'that woman.' "

Leslie laughed and hopped out of the truck, neatly catching the keys as Ted tossed them over the hood to her. He grinned as he thumped the fender. "I guess this vehicle of yours will pass, girl, considering it isn't a Ford."

Leslie narrowed her eyes at him. "What's so special about a Ford, Ted McAllister?"

Ted grinned. "Damned near every truck in the oil patch is a Ford, of one shape or another."

"Don't you think it's a little late to tell me that?"

"Where in hell did you get that oversized toy, Ted?"

Leslie experienced a nervous flurry when she recognized Steve's voice. She turned to face him, stuffing her hands into her jacket pockets in an effort to hide their trembling. She felt smothered by his irresistible smile, and her pulse raced when he came up to her. A warm weakness invaded her body as his eyes fixed on her for a breathless moment.

Ted's voice broke the spell. "It's Leslie's. She finally broke into her piggy bank."

"You two can cut out the cute remarks. I'm not going to stand here in this freezing wind just to listen to you slander my vehicle."

Ted motioned toward the rig. "Come on then. I'll give you the grand tour, Les." They walked across the uneven ground, which had been stripped of any growth. "How's everything going?"

"On schedule so far. We should spud sometime the day after tomorrow."

"Great! Is Frank Logan around?"

"Yeah. He's up in the doghouse."

Leslie's eyes ran up the towering, light-studded rig

to the small steel hut erected on the drilling platform, which was some thirty feet above the ground. The doghouse served as office, toolshed, lunchroom, and refuge from the weather for the drilling crew.

As they approached the rig, Steve touched Leslie's arm and pointed to a trailer. "That's the geologist's shack. Do you want to have a look?"

"Yes, I would. Did all the equipment arrive?"

"I think so, but you can check it out."

Ted veered away from them and called over his shoulder. "I'm going up to the floor to see how things are going. I'll catch you later."

Leslie felt abandoned as she was left alone with Steve. She wanted desperately to avoid any situation that might compromise the casual facade she was determined to present.

She followed him to the brick-red industrial trailer with definite misgivings. She was feeling strangely shy, and she really didn't know if she could maintain her mask of congeniality. Despite her uneasiness, however, she was keenly interested in the interior arrangements.

There was a tiny bedroom across one end, with an equally tiny bathroom next to it. A galley kitchen opened into a small living room. The living quarters were separated from the large lab area by a small hallway and a closet. The whole unit was compact and well planned, and Leslie could tell by the smell and the immaculate condition that it was new.

After touring the rooms she reentered the kitchen area, a delighted smile on her face. This would be the first place that was hers, and she felt a pleasant eddy of excitement.

Steve was leaning against the cabinet, a look of amused tolerance on his face. "The living quarters are small, but then you really don't take up much space, do you?"

Leslie slanted a look at him that was meant to be scathing, but her dimples gave her away. "You and Ted are beginning to sound like a broken record, you know."

He eased himself away from the cupboard and sauntered over to her, his eyes gleaming as he rested his hands on her shoulders. "Does that mean you think we're boring?"

Leslie looked up at him. Her breathing became suddenly shallow as a surge of anticipation awakened within her. There was a brazen challenge in his eyes; he was daring her to deny it.

Her voice was husky, but she forced herself to speak. "Don't try to back me into a corner...."

His arms came around her, and Leslie tried to steel herself as he slowly lowered his head. His breath was warm and tantalizing against her lips as he said, "You're already cornered, Leslie Kairns."

She tried to keep the kiss impersonal and light, but her willpower was decimated as he moved his moist mouth enticingly across hers, summoning a response that left her weak and helpless. He slipped his hand up her back, and then with an impatient gruff curse unzipped her jacket and opened it. With a muffled groan, he molded her tightly against his solid frame as his gentle kiss turned into a sensuous assault.

The aching desire that she had suppressed for so long came boiling out in a volcanic reaction that caught them in its searing flame. Steve's hands were moving over her back with passionate urgency, pressing her tighter and tighter against him, until Leslie felt their bodies would fuse together like two pieces of white-hot metal. He lifted her up until her hips were welded against his; the heat and the hardness of his touch drove her senses to a fever pitch. With every fervent movement of her body, with every impassioned caress, she was telling him that she wanted him.

And he needed her soft yielding body to satisfy his own rampaging hunger. Their famine had been long and desolate, one that had taxed their restraint to the limit. The need to appease their ravenous appetites was a frantic obsession that could be assuaged only by complete surrender.

Leslie shuddered against him, and the spasm echoed through Steve, who lifted her up until she was cradled in his arms. With a ragged groan, he dragged his mouth away from hers and started carrying her toward the bedroom. He had reached the doorway of the bathroom when a commotion of voices intruded into the trailer through the partially opened bathroom window.

Steve's arms tightened convulsively around her as he buried his face against her neck, his breathing hoarse and uneven. He grasped her tightly for a long moment, then slowly, reluctantly, set her on her feet. Supporting her with one arm around her waist, he spanned her chin with his hand and lifted her face. With a tenderness that made Leslie want to weep, he kissed her mouth.

Her lips trembled when he lifted his head and looked down at her, his eyes smokey with regret. "That's Ted and Frank coming in." He kissed her again, then with a heavy sigh squeezed her one last time. Easing his embrace, he stroked her hair. "I'm sorry, Leslie."

She stretched up and kissed his sensitive mouth once more, allowing her lips to linger briefly. Then, with a tremulous smile that camouflaged her inner turmoil, she slipped out of his arms and went into the bathroom, closing the door softly behind her. A bleak feeling closed around her as she stood staring at her reflection in the mirror above the sink. She shouldn't have come; she knew that as a certainty. She was only prolonging the agony.

Leslie had managed to corral some of her stampeding emotions by the time she heard the indistinct murmur of voices within the trailer. She sponged her face with a cold damp facecloth, then combed her fingers through her disheveled hair. With a deep breath she squared her shoulders and lifted her chin, then opened the door and walked out.

She found Ted, Steve and a burly heavyset man in the room that would be her lab. She was certain that this must be Frank Logan, the senior tool push for Ramco. Although nothing had been said specifically, she had a suspicion he would be the man who would most vehemently oppose her being on location. The tool push was responsible for drilling operations in the field, including the management of the drilling crews and the support staff. If she started out on the wrong foot with Frank Logan, her life at this rig would be a living hell. She was directly answerable to Steve, but Frank could, if he chose, make her job very difficult.

The three men were engrossed in a conversation.

Steve and Frank had their backs to her, but Ted was facing the door. She grimaced as she walked toward him but managed a grin when he winked at her. Steve and Frank turned to face her, and Leslie deliberately avoided looking at Steve as she stopped beside Ted.

He dropped his huge hand on her shoulder and squeezed it. The gesture telegraphed his confidence in her, and Leslie felt slightly fortified.

"Frank, I'd like you to meet Leslie Kairns, our project geologist. Leslie, this is Frank Logan, the tool push for this rig."

Leslie smiled and stretched out her hand. "Hello, Frank. I'm really looking forward to working with you."

Frank Logan ignored Leslie's offered hand and glared at Steve and Ted with a look of pure outrage. He looked back at Leslie in disdain and pointedly stuck his hands in his pockets. "You have to be kiddin'!"

Leslie knew now what the term "poker face" implied; Steve's face remained blank of any emotion when he answered, "Nobody is kidding, Frank."

The tool push looked like a man being strangled as his face turned dark with indignation. "I don't know where you found her, or why you hired her, but I can tell you right now, she ain't gonna last a week around here."

Leslie was shocked by the vehemence of his attack. She felt her temper flare at his unjustified assessment, but she had been warned that she would meet opposition. There was no hint of anger as she looked at Frank with a calmness that was borne of sheer determination.

"I can do my job, Frank."

"How in hell can you possibly do your job? This ain't no tea party, lady, and that's about all you could handle."

Ted interjected, "Leslie was the geologist who pinpointed this area, Frank. She knows what she's doing."

"I don't care if she pinpointed the Great Lakes. She ain't found nothin' till we drill into it." Frank snorted, his face contemptuous. "Knows what she's doin'—she knows what she's doin' all right! I'd like to know why she's here. Whose pocket is she in, anyway?"

Leslie had been watching Steve's face while Frank ranted, and she knew exactly what he was thinking. With that insinuating comment, Frank had effectively severed any association, other than a strictly professional one, between the two of them. Under no circumstances could she ever compromise Steve's position with any of his staff. He knew it, and she knew it, too.

"You're out of line, Frank." There was an icy warning in Steve's voice that frightened Leslie. She couldn't let him intervene on her behalf, or Frank would misconstrue his reasons.

Leslie placed her hands on her hips as she faced Frank, her expression determined. "I don't know what you're hinting at, Mr. Logan, but I've been hired to do a job, and that's what I intend on doing!"

Frank ignored Leslie and turned to Steve, his face red with rage. "Steve, my God, man, you ain't serious about this—you can't be! The oil patch ain't no place for anyone so frail."

"She stays, Frank. If you or Ted can show me evidence that she's not doing what she was hired to do, then she goes.'

"And who in hell is supposed to baby her through the hard work and rotten weather?"

Up until then, Leslie was considering backing down. But the suggestion that she was unsuitable because of her lack of physical stamina really infuriated her. One look at Steve's face told her he had doubts about that himself. He was obviously recalling his own initial assessment of her. Determination germinated within her, and her anger fertilized it until it flowered into sheer single-mindedness. He may never love her, but damn it, he would respect her or she would die trying!

Leslie glared at Frank and snapped, "I don't need any babying, Mr. Logan. I'm quite capable of looking after myself!"

Frank strode over to her, his manner menacing as he wagged his finger at her. Leslie realized he was trying to bully her into backing away from him, so she deliberately and defiantly held her ground.

His tone was heavy with sarcasm as he sneered at her, "I suppose everytime somethin' ain't goin' quite right for little Miss Geologist, you'll run cryin' to one of the bosses."

Leslie's eyes were blazing fire as her anger soared, but somehow she managed to keep her voice cool. "The only time I'll lodge any complaints, *Mr. Logan*, is if you or any of your men interfere with my duties as a geologist. Other than that, I said I can look after myself."

"Then, Miss Kairns, you do your job. Don't you

expect me or any of my hands to cater to you—and we'll just see how long you can hack it before you're weepin' on somebody's shoulder, whinin' about how mean we are. We'll just see!" He swept the trio with a look of indignant wrath and stomped out, slamming the door with such force that the entire trailer shook. A heavy silence settled over the room. The battle lines were drawn.

Leslie stood staring at the floor, frowning with annoyance. Just who did Frank Logan think he was, anyway? She glanced at Ted and saw an odd twitch at the corner of his mouth. If his expression wasn't so perfectly sober, she would have thought he was enjoying a private joke.

He looked at her somewhat apologetically. "Les...."

"Leave it, Ted," Steve said. "You'd better get out there and see if you can settle Logan down."

The older man shrugged, shot Leslie a perplexed beats-me look, then left the trailer. Leslie leaned against a cabinet and nervously toyed with a coil of pliable solder that was lying on the counter. She could tell by Steve's stance that he was both annoyed and disgusted by the recent confrontation.

"You shouldn't have challenged him, Leslie." His voice was controlled, but Leslie could detect the current of exasperation in it.

"I didn't challenge him; I merely defended myself. He had me hung, drawn and quartered before I ever opened my mouth." She turned to face him, her expression fixed. "You know that."

"Yes, I know that. That's precisely why you are going back to Calgary tomorrow."

Leslie felt as though he had slapped her. She stared at him, and her mouth dropped open in disbelief. "What exactly do you mean by that?"

"I've obviously made a mistake in bringing you out here. Frank Logan will go out of his way to make things difficult for you, and I don't think you're thick-skinned enough to handle it."

"Well, of all the ridiculous...." Leslie was seething. "The depth of my skin is *not* the issue! Just because someone likes or dislikes me has no bearing on how well I do my job."

"You are going home tomorrow." His voice was as cold as steel and just as hard. Steve walked toward the window and stood staring out at the brightly lighted rig, his arms folded across his chest.

Leslie felt the walls of the room closing in on her. His callous unjust dismissal of her really rankled. The hurt would come sometime later, but right now she felt nothing but a sickening distaste. She had to get away from him and the entire Redwillow project—it had brought her nothing but misery right from the beginning. She zipped up her jacket and headed for the door.

"I'll be gone at dawn. I really want to thank you for the confidence you've shown in me." Her caustic comment could not be misread. She had her hand on the door when Steve grabbed her by the arm and roughly whirled her around.

His eyes were like two blue chips of ice as he narrowed them angrily. "How in hell can you possibly cope with a camp of hostile men? They'll tear you to pieces in the first week, just like Logan said."

She was smoldering with an anger that barely suppressed her acute feeling of rejection. Leslie yanked her arm away and glared up at him as she spat back, "As if that would matter a damn to you! The only thing that concerns you right now are the ruffled feathers of your damned push. I can understand that, but what I can't understand is why you hired me in the first place. You must know him well enough to realize what his attitude would be. Under those circumstances, I can't understand why you bothered to haul me all the way up here just to send me back. That doesn't make any sense at all!"

"Right now, I'm questioning those reasons myself—and you wouldn't understand them even if I tried to explain them to you."

"Don't bother!"

"I had no intention!"

Leslie turned away. Her anger had spent itself, and an intense hurt was rushing in to fill the vacuum. She didn't dare stay a moment longer, or she would come apart in front of him.

She slammed out into the night and started running to her truck. She stumbled several times, unable to see where she was going. It was because it was dark, she told herself—it had nothing to do with the threatening tears. A sob caught in her throat as she yanked open the truck door and stumbled in. Through the blur she was trying to find the proper key for the ignition when the door was jerked open and the keys ripped from her hand.

"Where in hell do you think you're going?"

The fierce contraction in her throat made it nearly impossible to speak. Gripping the steering wheel in a desperate attempt to control her feelings, she managed to answer Steve with a husky whisper. "I've decided I'll drive back to Grande Prairie tonight."

"You aren't driving anywhere tonight." His voice was clipped and very abrupt. "Get over."

Leslie didn't have any resources left to argue with him, so she slid across the seat without protest.

Steve started the truck and rammed it into gear. The headlights flashed on, floodlighting the blackness that engulfed them. They drove to the geologist's shack in brittle silence, and he parked in front. Switching off the engine, he removed the keys and climbed out.

"You'll stay right here tonight," he snapped as he slammed the door and started to stride away.

Leslie nearly fell out of the truck in her haste to catch him. "May I have my keys, please?"

"No."

"But they're the only ones I have—"

"A small precaution. You're not driving on these lease roads at night. You'll get them back in the morning."

Leslie could tell by the inflexibility conveyed in his voice that it was pointless to argue. She turned and went back to the shack. Once inside she shut the door behind her, locked it, then leaned back against it and closed her eyes. She wished she could ease the strangling ache within her with a flood of tears, but she couldn't. She felt as though she was in some kind of trance as she wandered through the trailer to the living room and sank down on the sofa. An acute feeling of isolation spread within her as she sat there, alone in an impersonal room.

CHAPTER NINE

"Leslie."

Consciousness slowly but persistently infiltrated her mind. Feeling as though she was emerging from a cocoon of swirling fog, Leslie opened her eyes and blinked in bewilderment when she realized Steve was looming over her.

With a determined effort, she tried to straighten her legs, but her muscles were cramped and inflexible from the cold. Her thoughts snapped into gear when she realized she was huddling against the arm of the sofa, her legs drawn up, in an attempt to ward off the chill.

The recollection of the terrible scene the night before came flooding back, and she lowered her eyes in an attempt to avoid his gaze. He crouched down in front of her and reached out to take her icy hands in his, but she quickly stuffed them into the pockets of her jacket. His touch always rattled her, and she didn't want her thoughts any more confused than they already were. Swallowing nervously, she fixed her eyes on the floor.

"Leslie."

His tone warned her that he was in no mood for evasiveness. If she didn't meet his gaze, he would make her, and she was feeling far too vulnerable to cope with physical contact. She finally made herself look up at him. His face was a mask.

She drew her body into a tighter ball as she tried to think of something to say that would break the strained silence. "If you'd give me back my keys—"

"Look, Leslie, I was a bit riled last night...."

"Yes, I noticed." Her voice was uneven and very low, but there was a touch of cynicism in it even though she tried to ignore the feeling of despair that was sweeping over her.

"Leslie, listen to me...."

"Damn it, it's cold in here," bellowed Ted as he stomped in. "Didn't you turn up the heat last night?" He marched over to the thermostat on the wall and peered at it. After readjusting the setting he came back and dropped his big frame down on the sofa, nearly catapulting Leslie off into space. He totally ignored the scowl awarded him before Steve straightened up, went over to the window and stood staring out.

Ted looked at Leslie and ruffled her hair. "You're looking a little peaked this morning, girl. Didn't you sleep very well?"

"I slept fine, thank you." Leslie could feel an unexpected bubble of amusement rising within her. It was obvious that Steve was more than a little irritated by Ted's boisterous intrusion. It was also obvious that Ted was totally aware of Steve's vexation.

Ted thundered on, disregarding the tension in the room. "I talked to Frank Logan last night, Les. He's still not exactly thrilled to death about having a woman geologist here, but then Frank doesn't have much use for geologists, period. He thinks they're just excess baggage that tend to clutter up the works. Anyway, he finally admitted that you probably won't be much worse than most. He won't hinder you in any way—he won't help you much either, but then, maybe that's just as well. He said he wouldn't touch you with a forty-foot barge pole, so at least he won't get close enough to strangle you.''

Leslie sighed with relief. Trust Ted to take a direct approach to a problem and put everything back into perspective. Steve was glowering out the window, and he looked like nothing would please him more than strangling Ted. Ted knew, Leslie suspected, exactly what Steve was thinking, but he charged on anyway.

''I told Frank that you and I have always worked together as a team—''

''Ted, that's an outright lie!''

''Well, I don't know if it is. I never really specified that it was oil-patch work—anyway, let me finish what I was saying. I told him that we'd worked together a long time. . . .''

''That's another one!''

''It isn't really. When you work for someone like Luther Denver, two years *seems* like a long time. Now let me finish. I said that we had gotten to know each other pretty well and if I sat down and had a game of crib with you, he wasn't to get his nose out of joint because something might be going on.''

Leslie couldn't help it; she started laughing. She was beginning to feel slightly hysterical. Last night Steve had dismissed her; this morning Ted was talking as though she was here to stay. Steve was fuming and Ted was as pleased as punch. She didn't have a clue what was going on, and she was too tired, too cold and too hungry to care.

She looked from one man to the other as she wiped the tears of mirth from her eyes. "But, Ted, I'm not staying."

"Of course you're staying." It was a firm statement, delivered with absolute certainty, and it confirmed her suspicion that Ted had bulldozed Steve's objections out of the way. Ted's eyes were challenging her to stay and fight it out. When Leslie looked at him uncertainly, he clinched it with a slightly devious tactic. "The old man would have wanted you to, Leslie."

Leslie's eyes revealed the stab of sorrow she experienced at the mention of her grandfather. But the look was fleeting; Leslie lifted her chin stubbornly. Mac Kairns *would* have wanted her to stay. He had no patience with quitters.

"I'll stay," she said simply.

Steve glared at her, his face rigid. He flung her keys on the counter of the cupboard as though they were contaminated, then strode out of the room. Leslie watched him go, her heart wrung with a terrible sense of loss. Their mutual anger had driven a wedge between them, dashing any hope she had for even the most casual association. She was completely alienated from him now. From here on, it would be a very strained employer-employee relationship. Her stomach twisted into a tight ball as she fought down the frightening desire to cry.

EXHAUSTION WEIGHED HEAVILY UPON HER for the remainder of the day as she set about putting her trailer in order. First she unpacked all the supplies and equipment that she had had sent out and arranged it accordingly. When she had organized the work area to her satisfaction, she began on her living quarters. By the time she'd unpacked everything, no one would have recognized the barren little suite that it had been only hours before.

Most of her meals she would eat at the camp, but she had still decided to bring along ample provisions to stock her own kitchen. There would be times that she would prefer to remain in her own unit, and other times when she would be unable to leave the trailer because of security reasons.

Since Steve wanted to keep Ramco's drilling program confidential, this particular exploration, or wildcat well, would be classified as a tight hole. After a predetermined depth was reached, very rigorous security measures would be enforced to prevent other companies from scouting Ramco's operations. Traffic into the well site would be strictly controlled, and Tight Hole signs would be posted on the lease road and on the four corners of the lease property. Any unauthorized persons found on the lease could be legally prosecuted, but usually they were dealt with in a discreet but not too delicate fashion by the drilling crew.

Telephone conversations were transmitted by satellite to prevent oil scouts from intercepting confidential well data contained in the morning reports. The reassuring presence of the large dish antenna on the lease ensured reliable and secure communications with the outside world.

Ordinarily, a geologist was on site during only part of a drilling program. But since Leslie had taken a very extensive course in mud logging in Houston, Texas, Steve had asked her to closely supervise this aspect of the operation. A mudlogger was on site twenty-fours hours a day to monitor what was happening down hole as the drilling progressed. The geologist and the mudlogger were the only people who had ready access to the most crucial data concerning the type of formation and the underground pressures that were being encountered.

Because of this accumulation of information, the mudlogger's trailer and the geologist's shack would be locked when unattended, and all pertinent data would be kept under lock and key at all times.

Security was so rigid that only the geologist, the driller, the tool push and the "company man" were allowed on the rig floor when core samples of target formations were removed from the core barrels. The cores would then be crated and shipped, under guard, to the Calgary lab.

Since Ramco was still securing land rights in the area, it was essential that there should be no leaks. As the previous exploration in Redwillow had produced only low-volume finds, Ramco was still counting on the rest of the industry to disregard their wildcat venture.

Leslie's one big concern was that Luther Denver might find out she and Ted were employed by Ramco. If he did, he would surely realize that they had taken their theory to a rival company. And unfortunately, he still held extensive land rights in Redwillow. John McRory had been unperturbed by Leslie's concern when she'd shared it with him. He had assured her that Ramco's strategy was so well planned and so well camouflaged that Denver wouldn't realize what was going on until it was too late.

The afternoon was almost over when Leslie was finally satisfied that everything was where it should be. She was so tired she could barely stand, but there was only an hour before dinner and she knew if she lay down she would never wake up in time. Perhaps a walk around the lease would reenergize her.

Ted had recommended, with his usual bluntness that she stay off the rig until he could take her up, or Frank Logan might drown her in the mud tanks. With a certain amount of dry humor, she decided that Ted was probably right. But it should be acceptable for her to do a little exploring, as long as she stayed out of the tool push's way.

Leslie slipped into her jacket and slung her camera case over her shoulder. Opening the door, she shivered as an icy blast of wind caught her. Resolutely she stepped out into the bleak grayness of a dismal fall day and closed the door behind her. There were a few flakes of snow falling, and the wind held a warning of more to come. It didn't take her more than a few seconds to realize that the temperature was dropping. She turned up her collar and slipped her hands in her pockets as she slowly surveyed the scene around her.

A sharp pang of regret shot through her, for the heavy timber on the lease had been bulldozed away, leaving the drill site scarred and desolate. Ramco, she knew, had environmentalists on staff to carefully supervise the preparation of the lease and campsite, as well as the construction of the access road. They ensured that no unnecessary destruction took place, but Leslie felt a certain sadness that the untouched wilderness had to be razed for the development of energy resources.

She shrugged off the feeling and started walking toward the rig. Halfway there she looked back at the trailers—four of them—which were located on the extreme northern boundary of the lease. The dense bush had not been cleared behind them, so towering spruce and jack pine loomed above the brick-red units, which were lined up so precisely that they looked like a misplaced engineless train. The geologist's shack was to the west, then the tool push's shack, and then Ted's, as the drilling supervisor, or "company man." Ordinarily that would be all, but because of the magnitude of the program, Steve had elected to remain in the field. His trailer was located next to Ted's.

With a sigh Leslie turned back toward the rig, her gaze sweeping up the massive steel skeleton that was the derrick. She felt so small and insignificant. Everything was huge, powerful, exaggerated, magnified. No words could adequately describe it.

She took a wide-angle shot of the pipe racks, where thirty-foot lengths of drill pipe, drill collars and steel casing lay waiting for the drilling to begin. She took another shot of the drilling platform. It was crawling with men who were rigging up, but no one seemed to be paying any attention to her. She hesitated for a moment, then jogged across the stripped uneven ground, slowing to walk as she passed beneath the substructure and coming to a halt beside a rectangular boarded pit that was known as the cellar. In the center of the cellar was another hole lined with large diameter conductor pipe.

That was it. This was the beginning of the actual borehole. Very soon the drill pipe, with the attached bit, would be lowered into that hole, and the drilling of the well would begin.

Leslie felt awed as she stood staring down at the black hole. Thousands of feet beneath her might be the largest reservoir of natural gas ever discovered in Canada. She stood there a long time, totally motionless, as the realization of what this could mean broke over her. By the grace of God, they could discover enough natural gas to provide energy for the whole of Canada for decades to come. She felt overcome by the immensity of its potential.

After a while she walked back toward her trailer, scuffing her boots distractedly through the gray soil, totally absorbed in her thoughts.

"Leslie!"

She jerked her head up, her reverie shattered. Ted was standing by his truck, waving to her. She loped across the lease toward him, her camera clutched in her hand.

"Hi! I was just out poking around."

He leaned back against the fender of his truck and lit a cigarette. "Well, what do you think?"

Leslie slung her camera over her shoulder, then ran her fingers through her hair. "I think I should have been a teacher," she responded, her voice tinged with wry skepticism.

Ted straightened up and grinned as he walked toward the cab. "Don't get discouraged, girl. You'll get used to the grind." He yanked open the door and motioned her in. "Come on. I'll drive you over to camp—it's time for supper."

Leslie climbed in, laid her camera on the seat and slumped back. She hadn't been over to the camp yet, and she really dreaded going. One reason she had remained in her trailer all day was that she could avoid Frank and Steve. Now she would have to face them both, and she cowered at the thought. Frank would probably toss her out the door, and she was certain that Steve would ignore her completely. She wasn't sure which confrontation would be the worst, but she was so numb with exhaustion that she doubted if either one of them would have much effect on her tonight. In the last thirty-six hours she had had exactly two hours of sleep.

Sighing heavily, she rested her head against the back of the seat and stared out at the thick forest of spruce that was sliding past the truck window. She should have never taken on the job—she was completely out of her element.

As they pulled into the clearing where the camp was situated, she shrugged off her feeling of despondency and straightened up in her seat.

Having never been to a rig camp before, she surveyed the trailer complex with interest. She was fairly familiar with the layout of this particular camp because she had seen the blueprints for it when she'd been working in Ramco's operations department.

Provincial regulations stipulated that for safety reasons the camp must be located a certain distance from the rig. This site was several hundred yards farther back in the bush, however. The dense stand of trees that surrounded the location would not only provide excellent shelter from the wintry winds but would also muffle the noise from the rig.

Even to Leslie's inexperienced eyes the site seemed to have been carefully planned and laid out. A great deal of preparation had obviously been done before the units were trucked in. There was a thick base of gravel covering the entire clearing, and the area had been graded to provide good drainage away from the complex.

Ted parked beside the main door and glanced at Leslie. "Worried?"

She heaved a sigh. "It's too late for worrying."

"Don't get discouraged, girl."

"I'll try not to."

"That's the spirit. Come on—let's go see what Essie is going to fling at us."

"Essie's the cook, I take it?"

"She is—and a damned good one, too. She's a bit of a character, though—she has a reputation for picking favorites. Get on her good side and you'll be all set."

"I'm not exactly setting a record for that."

Ted grinned as he switched off the truck engine. "Maybe Frank Logan didn't exactly welcome you with hearts and flowers, but I have a hunch you could work your way around to his good side if you tried. He has a reputation for being a damned tough tool push to work for, but strangely enough, he always keeps his crews. He won't put up with any nonsense, and he runs a well-disciplined rig—his safety record speaks for itself on that account." Ted patted Leslie's shoulder reassuringly. "Don't be afraid to make the first move, Les—I don't think Logan is half as surly as he lets on."

Leslie frowned slightly as she considered Ted's

comments. Ted was seldom wrong in his observations concerning people—he had always been astute.

Ted squeezed her shoulder, then opened the door and swung out of the cab. "Come on—let's go put on the feed bag."

Leslie climbed out of the truck and followed him. If she had her choice, she would rather walk across a bed of red-hot coals than into the camp kitchen.

As it turned out, dinner wasn't the ordeal she had expected it to be. Frank Logan ignored her completely, and Steve wasn't there. She experienced a sharp pang of disappointment at his absence, but she had to admit to herself that it was just as well. Being around him would only make things more difficult and awkward—not that her situation could get much worse.

By the time she returned to her quarters, her misgivings were not quite so intense and unsettling. From her brief exposure to the men, she was able to assess the situation, and now she was able to determine for herself how she must relate to them. Leslie had a certain amount of confidence in her ability to cope in this male-dominated environment. She would do her job to the very best of her ability, she would be extremely careful not to ruffle any feathers unnecessarily, and she would be very cautious in her interactions with any of the men. She would prove to Steve that his initial confidence in her was *not* misplaced....

The next morning, Ted appeared in the lab, his face split with a broad grin. "Get your coat, girl, and let's go! They've finished dressing the rig and they're just about ready to start drilling."

Leslie's stomach lurched as she caught her jacket up from the back of a chair and slipped it on. With determined self-control, she managed to keep her voice steady when she turned to face Ted. "Do you mean I get to watch? Aren't you afraid Frank Logan will chuck me overboard?"

Ted laughed as he opened the door for her. "Old Frank will smoke, belch and rumble like an old volcano before he ever erupts. But before he does that, he's most likely going to sit there and steam for a while."

He placed the extra hard hat he had tucked under his arm on her head and tapped it firmly. "You have to wear this whenever you're around the rig, Les—it's mandatory safety equipment." He grinned again. "Frank would strangle you for sure if he caught you without it."

As they walked across the clearing the sun broke from behind a scattering of clouds. The air was fresh and crisp, but Leslie could still detect a hint of diesel fumes in the air. She hoped that the weather would hold for a while. Normally she looked forward to the first snowfall of the year, but now it would be an inconvenience they could do without.

The clamor from the rig was deafening as she followed Ted up the steep metal stairs. She was silently grateful for that, too—it made conversation nearly impossible. She needed time to try and clamp down the sickening nervous churning in the pit of her stomach. The burden of her accountability for this project was terrifying her. What if she was wrong?

She followed Ted into the doghouse, and her control was nearly shattered when she saw Steve lounging in the corner, a cup of steaming coffee in his hand.

He glanced at her, then looked away, his jaw fixed rigidly, his face taut. Leslie's mouth twisted into a grim smile when Frank Logan stood up and shifted his battered wooden chair, turning his back to her. Talk about cold shoulders.

She glanced up at Ted, and her smile became more genuine when she saw the glimmer of sheer devilry in his eyes.

"Morning, Steve—Frank. Great morning, isn't it?" There were murmurs of agreement, and Ted nodded his head, his face far too innocent. "I thought I'd bring Les up so she could see this project actually kick off. She's never been on a rig when we've spudded in, so I'm going to take her out on the floor and give her a running account of what's happening."

Frank's back stiffened, and Leslie could see a red stain creeping up the back of his neck.

Ted continued wickedly. "But I won't let her touch anything, of course."

With that, he caught Leslie's arm and hustled her through the door that led out onto the rig floor.

Leslie glared up at Ted, her eyes flashing. Why was he deliberately aggravating the situation? Was he doing it because of Steve, or Frank—or both? She didn't dare say anything, as she would have had to shout to make herself heard over the racket and the rig hands would have heard every word she said. Ted grinned down at her, his eyes dancing. He knew exactly what was racing through her mind.

Shielding her eyes from the glare of the sun, Leslie

tipped her head back and stared up at the gigantic
structure that towered overhead. This was no Tinker-
toy construction, but one that was massive and
strong.

Her eyes darkened with awe. The size, the power,
the immense weight was overwhelming, and she felt
smaller than ever. Lowering her head, she stared at a
splash of yellow sunshine that angled across the rig
floor. She had wanted to be a part of all this, and
now that she was she wished she were a million miles
away.

Taking a deep breath to quell the nervous flutter
inside her, Leslie glanced down at the draw works
control console. The driller was standing there, his
hand on the brake. He was the one actually responsible for making hole. The thousands of horsepower
required to drill were under his command.

She grinned when she saw him take a small flat can
from the breast pocket of his work shirt. Smoking
was strictly forbidden on the rig floor, so those who
had the habit either chewed tobacco or used snuff.
The driller was a snuff user, and Leslie watched the
ritual with fascination. He tapped the sides of the
container, then removed the lid and took out a pinch
of the ground moist tobacco. Deftly, he tucked the
tobacco inside his bottom lip, then replaced the flat
can in his shirt pocket. He shouted an instruction to
the rig hands as he turned back to the console.

Ted tapped her on the shoulder and pointed.
"Here we go, Les. They're lowering the traveling
block; they're going to pick up the kelly."

Leslie squinted as she looked up to watch the operation. With a feeling of grim inevitability, she saw a

roughneck guide the traveling block over to the rat-hole where the kelly was stored. If she had not re-sponded to Ted's challenge, she would now be on her way back to Calgary, safely removed from the horri-ble misgivings that were churning inside her. Why had she been so stubborn?

The roughnecks had swung the kelly over to the center of the floor and made up on the topmost joint of drill collar sticking up out of the rotary table. The drill collars, thirty feet long and weighing three tons each, were considerably heavier than drill pipe. Drill collars were used at the bottom of the drill string to put immense weight on the bit. The connection made, the driller picked up the kelly and two rough-necks, their muscles bulging, heaved the slips out of the table. The driller ran the kelly back down until the kelly bushing engaged the master bushing in the rotary table.

"Circle check!" bellowed the driller. The rig hands scattered to make the necessary checks; the driller waited, his hand on the power control. Thumbs up! The driller nodded, then turned on the power to the two mud pumps.

He cursed violently and switched off the power "The valve on the stand pipe's closed, damn it—open it."

A roughneck sprinted off as Ted rolled his eyes heavenward.

Again, thumbs up. Power on, half throttle. Leslie waited tensely, every muscle in her body rigid with suspense. They had to get the mud circulating before actual drilling could proceed, and normally it would only take a few seconds.

Full throttle.

Her stomach in a tight knot, she stood transfixed, as she watched the driller actuate the rotary table, and rotation began. He gradually released the draw works brake handle, and the traveling block inched down—slowly, so slowly, until the rotating bit touched bottom. This was it. They were making hole.

There was no flash of excitement, no burst of relief. Instead, Leslie's rationality was submerged by a rush of bone-chilling fear. Luther Denver's words kept rocketing around in her head, "Fairy tale, fairy tale, fairy tale." She turned away abruptly, unable to watch for another moment.

She felt like someone had knocked the wind out of her when she realized Steve was standing in the dog-house doorway watching her, the expression in his eyes obscured by the shadow from his hard hat. She had to get away.

Whirling around, she hurried down the stairs to a catwalk that ran along the mud tanks. When she reached ground level, she raced across the lease, her breathing harsh and uneven. Dashing into her trailer, she tossed her hard hat toward the sofa and grabbed her keys off the kitchen counter. Then she bolted from the trailer, banging the door shut behind her.

As she pulled away, her truck's wheels slinging loose gravel, she didn't see Steve sprinting across the lease toward her. She didn't see anything, except the rough dirt road that was her only avenue of escape.

CHAPTER TEN

LESLIE DIDN'T DRIVE very far. A few miles down the
lease road she spotted an overgrown trail that disappeared into heavy bush. Impulsively she turned onto
it and bumped along until she came upon a picturesque little ravine.

After climbing out of the truck she scrambled
down the bank, weaving her way through the spruce
and birch that shaded a chattering brook. She found
a sunny spot that was sheltered by a massive boulder
and sat down. Propping her back against the rock,
she stared at the sparkling sunbeams that danced
along the crystal-clear water.

Eventually the peace and solitude tranquilized the
fear that was pumping through her, and she was
finally able to look at her terror with objectivity.

Running solved nothing; she was behaving like an
idiot. As Steve had told her before, this project
was not solely her responsibility. Neither he nor Ted
nor John McRory were dummies, and they were involved, too. They had all thoroughly analyzed the
data, and each of them thought Redwillow had excellent possibilities. Yes, it was a gamble, but she
wasn't the only one throwing the dice. She was not
alone.

But if she wasn't alone, why was she feeling so

desperately lonely, a tiny inner voice kept asking. Leslie didn't dare think about the reason.

Nearly an hour had passed when, sighing heavily, she got to her feet, brushed the dried grass and twigs from her jeans, then climbed resolutely back up the steep slope. She returned to the rig site and parked the truck beside her trailer.

She was really at loose ends. There would be little for her to do until the rig had drilled a few hundred feet. Perhaps if she went over to Ted's, he would find something for her to work on.

She rapped on the door of his trailer and heard him bellow, "Come in!" As soon as she stepped inside, she regretted that she had. Steve was there.

Uncertainty assailed her as he turned around and their eyes met briefly. If it hadn't been for the formidable set of his face, Leslie would have sworn she saw a look of relief flash in his eyes.

Ted grinned at her and raised his hand in salute. "You've arrived just in the nick of time, girl. I'm dying for a cup of coffee, and the stuff I make tastes like rat poison."

Leslie returned his grin, then escaped into the kitchen, relieved to have an excuse to avoid Steve McRory. She was pouring the coffee into mugs when Ted entered the kitchen. "Only pour two, Les—Steve's gone over to the rig."

She put the extra cup away, then placed Ted's coffee before him as he settled himself at the table.

He took a sip, then glanced at her as she sat down opposite him. "What happened this morning, girl—get a little gun shy?"

Leslie grinned at him ruefully and nodded her

head. "Yes, I guess you could put it that way."

He leaned back in his chair and nodded his head knowingly. "It happens to all of us at one time or another." He winked when Leslie looked at him, her eyes wide with surprise. "The first time it happened to me was when Nick was born. I was standing at the nursery window, staring at my brand-new son, proud as anything, when it suddenly hit me—I was responsible for providing for that kid, responsible for his whole upbringing. It scared the hell out of me."

Leslie propped her chin on her hand, her eyes alive with affection and a touch of amusement. "You would have saved me a lot of agony if you'd told me about this sooner."

He shrugged his shoulders slightly, his expression apologetic. "I wanted to, girl, but that's a very real part of living, of maturing. Telling you about it doesn't really mean anything. You have to experience that sense of responsibility yourself."

Leslie slid her finger around the rim of her mug, her face reflective. Then she looked up and smiled. "Well, I certainly did experience it!"

Ted patted her hand, his eyes crinkling with amusement. "I know." He folded his arms across his massive chest and studied her face. "Are you going to be able to hack it, girl?"

She smiled again, wryly this time. "Yes, I can hack it." Ted nodded his head in approval.

There was a brief silence, then Leslie changed the subject. "Ted, do you have anything for me to do? I'd sure like to have something to keep me busy."

Ted drained his mug and slid it across the table as he stood up. "You're in luck. I just happen to have a little task awaiting. All the paperwork for this program has to be taken out of the shipping boxes and filed.''

Following him into the office area, Leslie grimaced when he motioned to the incredible clutter of schedules, drilling manuals, parts catalogs and boxes of files. ''Go to it, girl. That should take care of your spare time for a while.''

Leslie shook her head dubiously. ''This might take forever.''

Ted laughed. ''Might at that!'' Putting on his jacket, he picked up his hard hat from the desk, then started for the door. ''I have to go over to the rig. Frank Logan's having problems with the welder. He's almost ready to run him off.''

He opened the door and stepped out, then came back in, shaking his head. ''Hell, I nearly forgot. Leslie, don't go wandering off in the bush by yourself. A Mountie stopped in while you were gone. Apparently there's a badly wounded grizzly in the area. Some hunters reported it to the game warden, who's trying to track it down—he lost the trail just a little way from camp.''

Leslie set her chin angrily, her eyes flashing. ''I suppose someone was using him for target practice.''

''Sounds like it.''

He grinned as he opened the door again. ''I'll escape before you get wound up on the subject. I haven't recovered from the last lecture I got from you.''

Leslie looked a little sheepish, then laughed and waved him off. But after he left she grew serious again. She had had an uncomfortable premonition about that wounded bear, when Ted mentioned it, but she shrugged it off as an irrational concern.

It was two days later that the premonition became a bleak ugly reality. Leslie doubted if she would ever forget the sickening horror of the incident.

She and Ted were returning to camp after he had completed an inspection of the other two drilling locations. One section of the newly constructed lease road ran along the bank of the rushing Redwillow River, and the scenery was spectacular. Leslie was gazing out the window, lazily enjoying the rugged unspoiled wilderness that swept up to a rocky ridge on the opposite bank of the river when Ted said, "Wonder what's going on up there?"

She shifted her gaze. Frank Logan's truck was parked at the side of the road, and he and two other men from the rig were staring at something on the far side of the river.

Ted pulled up beside them and rolled down his window. "Is something wrong?"

Frank came over to the truck and rested his elbow on the open window as he motioned to a clump of gnarled shrubs just below the ridge. "There's a bear up there—looks like a grizzly. It's actin' kinda peculiar, and we was wonderin' if he might be the one the game warden's after."

Ted motioned to the glove compartment. "Get my binoculars, girl, and have a look."

Leslie located the glasses, took them out of the leather case and removed the lens covers. Scrambling out of the vehicle, she raised them to her eyes and focused on the top of the ridge. She scanned the rise slowly, then she froze, her face suddenly pale. Wordlessly she handed the binoculars to Ted.

He frowned slightly and took them from her. When he located the animal, he swore softly as he dropped his arms. ''God, what a hell of a mess!''

Frank Logan took the glasses from Ted's hand and swept the outcrop in turn. When he spoke, his voice was ragged with anger. ''Somebody would have to be dummer'n sackful of hammers to do somethin' like that. I wonder what ammunition they was usin'?''

Leslie wondered, too. One side of the bear's face had been blasted off, there were gaping wounds in its shoulder and one front paw was badly mutilated. The pain-racked animal was swinging its head in agony.

Ted didn't say anything, but opened the truck door and lifted the leather rifle case from behind the seat. Leslie watched numbly as he removed the weapon and began loading it.

''Hell, Ted—you can't get that bear from here,'' interjected Frank. ''That's an impossible shot!''

''Well, he sure in hell can't get across the river to get any closer,'' argued one of the other men.

Ted didn't say anything but continued to load the rifle. He finished the task, then methodically wiped the lens of the telescope with the tail of his shirt.

It was a nearly impossible shot, but Ted was an excellent marksman. An awful cold clamminess crawled down her spine as Ted looked at her, his eyes unwavering. Yes, Ted was an excellent shot—but Leslie was better, and they both knew it.

Leslie was unaware of the sound of an approaching vehicle as Ted came toward her. The sun glinted ominously off the barrel of the rifle he held in his hand—her grandfather's rifle.

"You have to put that animal out of his misery, Les. You know that."

Leslie looked up at him, her eyes dark, her face tight with despair. Without saying a word she reached out and took the rifle from him.

There was a murmur of incredulity behind her as Leslie walked over to a flat boulder and stretched out on it. With icy calmness she made the necessary mental calculations, judging the distance and the wind factor. Beads of perspiration appeared on her brow as she squinted through the telescopic sight. She wanted to be sick as the bear swung his mutilated head around and the full extent of its injuries was visible. She swallowed hard, then squeezed the trigger.

She fired three rounds before the beast finally staggered and collapsed, its massive body crumpling like a rag doll. Leslie closed her eyes for a moment, her tense body motionless, then somehow she found the strength to get to her feet. She forced herself to smile at the stunned admiration and the words of congratulations that greeted her. Handing the rifle to Ted, she deliberately avoided his eyes. When somebody took her arm, she looked up numbly.

Steve's grip tightened as he felt her stumble slightly. "I'd like you to ride back to camp with me, Les. There's a couple of things I want to talk to you about."

Leslie nodded her head, and somehow managed to climb into the truck unassisted. Leaning her head back against the seat, she clenched her teeth together and closed her eyes. She would not be sick. She just would not.

Nothing was said as Steve started the truck and waited for the other two vehicles to pull out ahead of him. They hadn't gone very far when Leslie opened her eyes. The ordeal wasn't over yet. She started to shiver violently, and she ground her teeth together as she tried to stifle a strangling surge of nausea.

Steve glanced at her, then braked abruptly. He reached across the cab, but Leslie sprang out of the truck and bolted blindly into the underbrush. The brittle naked branches snagged her clothes and clawed at her hair, but she stumbled on until her enervated legs collapsed beneath her. She staggered against a tree and sank to her knees as the convulsions of retching sapped the rest of her strength.

Steve's arm encircled her chest, supporting her slight frame, and his other hand held her forehead as spasm after spasm racked her body. When the turbulent heaving finally subsided, he eased her back against him. "Are you going to be okay?"

When she nodded mutely, Steve lifted her in his arms. He carried her over to a huge old birch tree and sat down, his back braced against the trunk. Pulling a handkerchief out of his jacket pocket, he gently wiped her mouth, then brushed her hair back from her damp face. She could feel his breath against her temple as he nestled her body firmly across his lap. He pressed her face against the rough wool of his jacket, his arms cradling her securely against him.

A shudder of revulsion rippled through Leslie, and the pressure of Steve's arms tightened more firmly around her. She was so drained, so spent, she could hardly speak. "Steve...."

"Hush, Les. We'll talk about it later when you're

feeling a little stronger." His voice was quiet and soothing, and Leslie finally allowed her trembling body to relax against his. The security and strength she was drawing from him eased the horror that had debilitated her. The smell of his pipe tobacco clung to his coat, and for some strange reason its aroma had a calming effect on her; she allowed herself to think of nothing else. She closed her eyes as the pressure of his arms increased.

It was quite some time later that Steve spoke, his voice husky. "Leslie, I've got to get back to camp—I'm expecting an important call from Calgary, and I have to be there when it comes."

Leslie didn't want to leave the secure warm cocoon of his embrace, but he had other more pressing responsibilities to deal with. It took every ounce of willpower she had to disengage herself from his vitalizing strength and stumble to her feet.

She had started to brush some dried leaves from her sleeve when her head began to swim again in a sickening gray swirling fog. She reached out in an attempt to catch herself as her legs gave way, but Steve caught her before she hit the ground. He swore softly as he forced her head down between her knees.

"I didn't faint, Steve. My legs just—"

Her weak protest was cut off abruptly. "Just sit like that and don't argue. You went as white as a sheet."

Leslie sat there until the fog cleared. "I'm okay now. Really," she said at last. Steve watched as she slowly lifted her head and took several steadying breaths. She focused her gaze on a moss-covered rock until she was certain everything wasn't going to go into another spin.

"I guess I'll have to try that again." She made a motion to stand.

Steve's voice was oddly gruff as he caught her up in his arms. "I guess you won't. I don't think you have the strength to crawl out of here, let alone walk." His arms tightened around her protectively as he started walking back toward the truck, carefully avoiding low-hanging branches. The only sound was his even breathing and the crunch of crisp leaves and dried twigs beneath his feet.

On the drive back to camp, he was remote and silent, his face an unreadable mask. It wasn't until they were a short distance from the rig that he finally spoke, his voice low. "That was excellent marksmanship, Leslie."

"Thank you," she responded stiffly. She had no pride in what she had done. She had hated having to kill the beast—hated it.

"You did what you had to do, even when it was distasteful to you. To do something like that takes courage."

Looking out the window, she shook her head, her voice low and dispassionate. "It doesn't take courage; it takes skill."

"Sometimes it takes courage to use that skill."

"It was an act of mercy. If you could have seen how dreadfully it was wounded...." Her voice broke treacherously and she swallowed hard.

"I did see, Les—I had Ted's binoculars."

"It was so awful...."

"You've never shot anything before, have you?"

"No, only targets." Only targets. She had just shot something other than a target—and some of her innocence had died the minute she squeezed the trigger.

Steve reached across the seat and caught her hand in his, his grip firm and reassuring. Suddenly things didn't seem quite so bleak. She looked at him and smiled weakly. "Thank you for playing nursemaid."

He glanced at her, his eyes softening as he smiled back. "It was my pleasure."

He released her hand as he wheeled into the parking space beside his trailer. He switched off the ignition, then turned to face her. He looked at her seriously for a moment, then took both her hands in his, his voice husky. "Leslie, I need to talk to you—"

The truck door was yanked open and Ted stuck his head in. "Steve, John's on the phone—he says it's important."

Steve squeezed Leslie's hands before he swung out of the cab. Leslie watched him follow Ted into the trailer, her thoughts in a muddle. When she climbed out of the truck, she slammed the door somewhat harder than necessary behind her. Damn it, she wanted to know what he'd been going to say. She sighed again as she walked toward the geologist's shack. Well, at least he was talking to her.

She clenched her hands as she recalled the feel of his arms as he carried her out of the bush. Yes, he was talking to her—but she wanted so much more than that.

LESLIE LAY IN HER BED, vaguely aware of the steady throbbing of the rig as it drilled on during the darkness of the night. She blocked out the noise and instead focused her hearing on the wind that was whining desolately through the spruce trees outside her window.

She had been in camp for ten days now, and day by day her job was falling into a comfortable routine. There had been a definite shift in the men's attitude toward her since the episode with the bear. She smiled to herself. There had even been a change in Frank Logan—he didn't grumble and mutter when she went over to the rig. Ted had teased her, saying that she might have lost the initial battle with Frank, but she had won the war when she shot the grizzly.

She didn't know if it was the change in attitude, or if she was simply getting over her case of stage fright. In any case she was feeling more and more at home. Bit by bit, she was making her own space.

Her own space—her own empty space.

She sighed and rolled over on her stomach as she thought about Steve. She never had found out what he wanted to talk to her about. The call from John must have been very important, for Steve had left for Calgary immediately. And he still wasn't back.

A concerned frown creased her brow. She had an uncomfortable conviction that something was wrong. Why had he gone to Calgary in such a rush? Ted was aware of what was going on, she suspected, but he had been very evasive when she had questioned him about it.

Then there was the question of the other two rigs. They had been contracted from Alberta-based drilling companies, for Ramco's own rigs were involved in drilling programs elsewhere. From the timetable Ted and Steve had drafted, they should have been on location by now. Roads had been cleared into the sites, and the leases had been prepared, but no rigs had appeared. That puzzled Leslie. She didn't like the uneasy feeling that was nagging away at her. She didn't like it at all.

She rolled over again as restlessness plagued her. Damn it, but she had to block the thoughts that were flooding through her mind or she would never get to sleep. Glancing at the luminous numbers of her digital clock radio, she groaned and raked her fingers through her hair. Ted was going back to Calgary the next morning, and he'd said he had strict orders from Steve that she was to take some time off now before the work load picked up. They were to leave first thing in the morning, and she would never wake up in time if she didn't get to sleep soon.

As though drawn by a magnet, Leslie's gaze focused on the pictures of Steve that were sitting on the night table. She closed her eyes and concentrated on taking deep breaths, but her mind played tricks with her and memories of him came crowding in, igniting a warm yet empty ache within her. Those special memories would keep the loneliness at bay—at least for a little while.

Leslie did sleep in the next morning, and she had to rush to be ready by the prearranged time. Finally, with her shoulder bag in one hand, her suitcase in the other and her jacket slung over her arm, she tore out of the trailer. She nearly dropped them all when she saw Steve's Blazer parked next to Ted's truck. He was back!

And she was leaving—damn! As she walked over to Ted's, her mind was scrambling to come up with some logical reason why she couldn't go. There wasn't one single excuse—not one!

As soon as Leslie entered Ted's cluttered office, she could feel the tension in the air. Steve sat straddling a chair, his arms draped across the back, his head resting on his arms. He was terribly concerned about something; that was obvious. She cringed inwardly when she considered how much responsibility he shouldered, and how everyone took for granted his ability to deal with a broad spectrum of problems. He was everyone's rock.

Steve lifted his head and caught her watching him. For a moment their eyes locked and Leslie felt powerless beneath his spell. With a supreme effort she tore her gaze away from his, but the ache in her didn't abate as she felt his eyes linger on her. She felt so flustered when she was physically close to him, and she clenched her hands tightly in an effort to suppress the tingling sensation that was vibrating in her.

Walking to the window, she stood staring out at the lights on the rig, which stabbed the early-morning darkness with piercing intensity. How would he react to her now, she wondered bleakly. He had been so gentle after she'd shot the bear, but that didn't necessarily mean he had forgiven her.

There was a murmur of subdued conversation as Ted and Steve continued to talk. Leslie's stomach dropped when Steve finally stood up and moved toward the door. *Please don't ignore me,* she pleaded silently. *Please don't.*

He stopped beside her and laid his hand on her shoulder, his tired face softening as he smiled down at her. "Have a good trip, Dwarf—and don't forget to come back."

Relief flooded through her as she smiled back at him, her voice slightly breathless. "I'll be back."

He slipped his hand along her shoulder, his warm touch exciting her. "Good." Swiftly and unexpectedly, he bent over and kissed her, then turned and left.

Leslie was cemented to the spot as a warm glow grew within her. She took a deep breath to ease the suffocating tightness in her throat, then turned to face Ted.

He was staring unseeingly at the jumble of papers on his desk, his face creased with a troubled frown.

"What's the matter, Ted?"

He raised his head and ran his fingers through his hair. "Nothing that concerns you, girl."

She walked over to the desk and picked up a pen, twisting it between her fingers. Her face was contemplative. "It's obvious that something is very wrong. Steve looks like he's under tremendous pressure, and since I *know* there're no major problems with the drilling program here, it has to be something else." Ted remained silent and Leslie stared at him, her eyes narrowed, as she continued to toy with the pen. "Why aren't the other two rigs on site, Ted?"

As she watched him, she tried to pick up a clue in his expression. Almost immediately a cold unpleasant speculation forced all other thoughts from her mind. She continued to watch Ted closely as she played her hunch. "It has something to do with Denver, doesn't it?"

His head jerked up and he stared at her, obviously confounded at her unanticipated question. His reaction was a total giveaway. Alarmed, Leslie sank down onto the chair Steve had vacated, her knees suddenly weak. So Luther was up to his old tricks. She tossed the pen on the desk angrily and locked her entwined fingers around her raised knee.

"I think perhaps this *does* concern me, Ted. After all, Luther is more my affair than anyone else's."

Ted shook his head slowly, and he heaved a weary sigh of resignation. "Luther found out, one way or another, that Ramco has bought up the leases in this area. He made a public announcement a couple of days ago stating that Denver Oil released all of its landholdings in this area because their extensive exploration program here was completely nonproductive."

"But that isn't true. Denver didn't have an 'extensive exploration program' here. They only drilled four wells and they weren't even looking for gas...."

"I know. I know, Les, but Luther isn't exactly honest. We both know that. Besides, he's always had a grudge against Ramco—that's why he was so damned anxious to take them to the cleaners in South America. He'll do anything he can to make them look bad."

"How can he have any impact on this project? He can't touch them now."

"Not directly, maybe. But indirectly he's managed to box them in a corner. He's put out the word that anyone investing in a wildcat operation here would lose their shirt."

Leslie's alarm turned into a cold sinking feeling. It didn't take a genius to figure out what had happened.

Her voice was flat and clipped with controlled wrath. "Ramco overextended its budget for this project by purchasing rights for all that additional land. Because of Luther's underhanded scheme, Ramco can't secure the extra financial backing they need to carry out the exploration program—that's the picture, isn't it? That's why the other rigs aren't on site, right?''

"In a nutshell.''

Leslie felt sick. Luther Denver had deviously outmaneuvered them with his usual subterfuge. His vendetta seemed so pointless, too. Yet there had to be a reason; there was always a specific motive behind everything he did.

The only thing that possibly made sense was that Luther was trying to force Ramco into releasing some of its landholdings. And the only reason he would do that was if he had changed his mind about the potential for Redwillow. Yes, that reasoning would definitely explain Luther Denver's scheming—he wanted back in.

Leslie's eyes narrowed in concentration as she mulled over her rationale again, trying to find a flaw in her logic. But there wasn't any.

"He wants in here, Ted.'' Her voice was strong with certainty. "For some reason, he's changed his mind about the deep-basin theory, and he's trying to force Ramco into selling off some of the leases. He's trying to muscle his way back in here.''

Ted pursed his lips and frowned, then scraped back his chair and stood up. He began pacing back and forth, his arms folded across his chest, his head bent in concentration as he considered Leslie's theory.

He stopped in front of her and slowly nodded his

head as he stroked his chin reflectively. "That would certainly explain everything. I thought he was just being a miserable bastard, but I think you're right. He's trying to force Ramco's hand." Ted flipped his jacket off the hook by the door and put it on. "I'm going to talk to Steve about it—"

"No!" Leslie jumped up from her chair and caught his arm. "No, Ted, don't. Just listen for a minute. Why don't you see what gossip you can pick up on the grapevine while you're in Calgary? You have contacts everywhere, so you should be able to dig up some information that would make this an explanation instead of speculation. We could be a mile off base." Leslie knew they weren't; she had never been more certain about anything in her life. She had to stall Ted, however. There was an idea developing in her mind, and she needed time to think about it.

Ted looked at her for a long agonizing moment, then nodded his head. "A few more days aren't going to make much difference—and you're right. We could be a mile off base, but I doubt it."

Leslie let out her breath slowly as the moment of uncertainty passed. She was going to have to be very careful. If Ted discovered what she was considering, he would go straight to Steve. And Steve McRory must not find out about her plan until it was in place. He would probably strangle her when he did, she thought wryly.

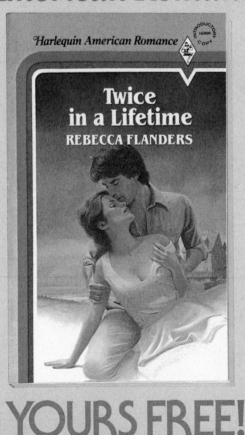

GET THIS BOOK FREE!

Experience *Harlequin American Romance*...

with this special introductory FREE book offer.

◀ SEE EXCITING
DETAILS INSIDE

Send no money. Mail this card
and receive this new, full-length
Harlequin American Romance
novel absolutely FREE.

CHAPTER ELEVEN

TWO DAYS LATER, a very sophisticated Leslie Kairns was sitting in the sumptuous outer offices of Kaidon Industries. She had arrived in Vancouver the evening before, and had lain awake most of the night, carefully planning how she would neutralize Luther's corrupt dealings. There were some very powerful resources at her disposal, and she was going to employ them to the maximum.

She felt a small twinge of guilt when she thought of the elaborate network of lies she had told Ted and Maggie to conceal her destination, and her reasons for going. She really hated lying to them, but this was so important—and she had to keep it a secret.

"Miss Kairns, Mr. Donner will see you now."

Leslie followed the immaculately groomed secretary and murmured her thanks to the older woman as she was ushered into a grand and magnificent office.

"Leslie!"

A short, stout, elderly man stepped from behind his desk and extended his hands in a warm gesture of welcome as he bustled toward her. She smiled at him fondly as she placed her hands in his and kissed his wrinkled cheek.

"Hello, Gordon. It's good to see you."

Gordon Donner stepped back and studied her, his

round face creased by a broad smile. "You certainly have become a splendid young woman, dear." He squeezed her hands firmly, then shook them in mild rebuke. "It's been a long time since I saw you last—your graduation from university, I think."

"It was."

He released her hands and motioned her into one of the massive, brass-studded leather armchairs that faced his desk. "Constance and I have sorely missed your visits since you've started working." His face grew solemn with concern as he lowered himself into the comfortably battered high-back chair behind his desk. "I must admit, I could never understand why Mac encouraged you to develop a career. It seemed rather pointless, under the circumstances."

Leslie smiled, her eyes dancing with amusement as Gordon continued to digress into his favorite dialogue—his bewilderment with one Leslie Kairns. Gordon had been her grandfather's partner and trusted friend for many years. He had always been baffled by Mac Kairns's insistance that Leslie not be coddled because of his wealth. Mac firmly believed that an overabundance of luxury could smother a person's initiative and drain them of the will to succeed, and he had deliberately encouraged Leslie to be independent. She had often held part-time volunteer jobs, and her schools had been selected because of their academic excellence rather than for their ability to cater to the idle and frivolous rich. Mac detested most of the young people who frequented his exclusive country club. He felt that a good number of them were drifting purposelessly through life, relying on family wealth to provide for their whims.

Because of Luther's cold reluctance to acknowledge Leslie's existence, and because of Mac's adamant stance that she be equipped with an adequate education to provide for herself, Leslie had grown up completely isolated from the plastic society that Mac loathed.

On her grandfather's death, Leslie had been shocked to find out the extent of his immense wealth. He had left her a sizable trust fund, a very valuable art collection, some properties and all his personal effects.

His two closest cronies had been left property for which they had a personal attachment. Mac gave Ted his hunting lodge, a sizable sum of money and the rifle; he left Gordon his vacation properties in Hawaii, a sixty-foot yacht and the onyx chess set they had spent many hours huddled over. He had remembered everyone else who was close to him, from his secretary, to the accountant who had been with him for forty years.

Several of his favorite charities had received handsome bequeathals, and he had initiated scholarships in a number of universities. The remainder of his personal fortune had gone to Vivian.

It had stunned Leslie and absolutely enraged Luther when Mac left her his entire block of controlling stock in Kaidon Industries. The company had extensive international holdings in lumber, mining and diversified manufacturing ventures. Mac had expected that Luther would be incensed, so he had cunningly drawn up the will so it could not be contested.

After the paralyzing shock had worn off, Leslie had treated the issue with casual indifference. Wealth and power meant nothing to her—her grandfather's death was too heavy a price.

"You know, Leslie, you don't have to persist with this ridiculous and misplaced commitment to Luther Denver. If you insist on working, why don't you go to work for a mining company? Heaven knows, you own enough of them!"

Leslie laughed, her eyes sparkling. "I'm not working for Luther anymore, Gordon."

"Thank God for that! Luther always made my skin crawl!"

Leslie grinned as she settled back in her chair and crossed her legs. Resting her elbows on the well-padded arms of the chair, she said quietly, "Gordon, I think it's time that Kaidon Industries expanded its interests and took a serious look at the petroleum industry."

Gordon seemed completely taken aback, but she continued, "I've had the opportunity to be involved in an exploration program that has all the indications of developing into one of the largest natural gas finds in Canada." Her eyes sparkled as she tipped her head to one side. She was also an experienced fisherman—she knew how to wiggle the bait.

Gordon took it, hook, line and sinker. He hunched over and rested his arms on his desk, his eyes keen with interest. He smiled as he narrowed his eyes. "Don't sit there looking smug, Leslie Kairns—let's have the goods!"

Leslie curled up in the chair and grinned. "I thought you might be interested." Her face became sober as she went on. "I'll detail the operation for you later, but I'll give you a brief profile of what has happened so far. Ramco Exploration has acquired very significant landholdings in northwestern Alberta.''

Gordon's busy eyebrows shot up and a strange look flitted across his face. ''I take it that you are now employed by Ramco Exploration?''

''Yes, I am.''

''Good company—I've heard a bit about them.'' He waved her on. ''Do continue.''

''Well, the bottom line is that because of some unethical machinations by Denver Oil, Ramco cannot raise sufficient capital to cover the cost of the exploration program. I think Luther is trying to force Ramco into raising the necessary capital by liquidating some of their landholdings in this particular area. Denver can pick up the leases and cash in on the bonanza.''

Gordon Donner leaned back in his chair and studied the young woman in front of him, a reminiscent smile tugging at the corners of his mouth. He didn't say anything for the longest time, then he reached over and pressed the button on his intercom.

''Cathy, hold all my calls and cancel all my appointments for the remainder of the day. Oh, and phone my wife and tell her I'm bringing Miss Kairns home for dinner.'' He leaned back again and pressed his fingers together in a steeple. ''Now, Mac Kairns's granddaughter, let's hear it from the beginning.''

Leslie slipped off her shoes and snuggled deeper into the comfortable chair, and in a clear steady voice she told Gordon Donner the whole story. She eliminated no detail, except, of course, her personal feelings for Steve McRory.

When she finished relating the sequence of events, Gordon studied her through hooded eyes. Then he rammed a partially smoked cigar in his mouth and lit it. He puffed on it reflectively for a moment, then held it between his thumb and forefinger as the blue smoke eddied around his head in a gentle swirl.

"This Steve McRory means a great deal to you, doesn't he?" He was contemplating the tip of his cigar, a look of contrived innocence upon his face.

She didn't even try to prevaricate—it wouldn't work with Gordon anyway. Her eyes were sober and dark as she answered, "Yes, he does."

"And how does he feel about you?"

Leslie looked down at her clasped hands and tried to keep her voice from exposing the twist of pain that stirred within her. "He sees me as a capable geologist."

"Does he know you're here?"

Leslie's head shot up, her eyes registering her alarm. "Heavens, no! He has no idea who I am—he doesn't even know that Luther is my stepfather. Gordon, he must never find out about my... my involvement with Kaidon Industries!"

Gordon snorted. "My dear, you and I *are* Kaidon Industries!"

"I know, but—"

"Would that influence his attitude toward you in any way?" It was a pointed question, and Leslie knew exactly what Gordon was hinting at.

She shook her head in a gesture of deprecation. "Do you mean, would he suddenly view me differently if he knew about my wealth?"

Gordon nodded.

Leslie smiled dryly. "Yes, he would view me very differently. If he had any idea what I was doing right now, he would fire me so fast that I wouldn't know what hit me. He doesn't like schemers. And he definitely isn't the type who would fall all over a woman simply because she had money coming out of her ears!"

Gordon chuckled. "I see. I do believe I detect a note of disgruntlement!" He rubbed the bridge of his nose as he digested the information she had divulged. There was an electric silence, then he stood up, walked over to the wall and pressed a button. A door slid open, revealing a built-in bar. He poured a glass of Perrier water, then raised the glass, his bushy eyebrows questioning. Leslie nodded her acceptance. He poured a second glass and splashed ice cubes in both drinks. Handing her one, he seated himself behind his desk again.

"I take it Ted has no knowledge of your little scheme?"

Leslie looked only slightly sheepish. "No—I lied. He and Maggie think I've gone skiing in Banff."

"Why didn't you confide in him?"

"Because I knew as soon as he found out I was coming to see you, he would go straight to Steve. I had a hard enough time convincing him not to say anything about Luther being my stepfather."

"Ted's going to find out sooner or later, you know."

"I know, but I want to postpone the day of reckoning for as long as I can."

Gordon smiled, his eyes twinkling. "You have a touch of deviousness in you, you know." He rubbed his nose reflectively. "When will you be back at Red-willow?"

"We should get there about noon on Thursday. We're flying to Grande Prairie that morning."

"Hmm. So...you would prefer to have Kaidon make its financial commitment before Ted finds out what you're up to?"

"Yes."

"He's been very supportive, I take it?"

"Very. He's been an absolute brick—I wouldn't have had the courage to go on with this after I left Denver if it hadn't been for him."

"How do you see this investment being arranged?"

"I'm sure some sort of legal arrangement can be made whereby only my shares in Kaidon are used as collateral for the venture."

Gordon stared at her, his solemn expression masking the sparkle in his eyes. "So it would be a no-risk venture for me?"

"Yes."

He rubbed his nose again, then sighed with mock despair. "Leslie, Leslie! Would you deny an old man some excitement in his sunset years?"

Leslie experienced a surge of emotion as she studied his face, trying to find some indication that he was joking. He chuckled at her intent look, then picked up the phone.

"How do I get in touch with this paragon of yours?"

Her face came alive with a mixture of relief and elation, and her voice was choked with emotion as she gave Gordon Steve's phone number at the Redwillow drilling location. She held her breath as the older man dialed, silently praying that Steve would be at his trailer.

He was.

"Mr. McRory, this is Gordon Donner of Kaidon Industries in Vancouver speaking. I understand you are trying to arrange the financial backing for a petroleum exploration program in Alberta. Is that correct?"

Steve's response was acknowledged by several nods of Gordon's bald head.

"I see. Mr. McRory, Kaidon is always interested in participating in new ventures, and we would certainly consider this type of investment. Would it be possible for you to come to Vancouver immediately so that we could explore the possibility of a joint venture?" There was another long pause.

"Friday morning would be fine. It might expedite matters if you could arrange to have your legal people here as well." Gordon winked at Leslie. "Fine! Fine! We'll see you the first thing Friday morning, Mr. McRory."

Gordon Donner barely had time to hang up the phone before Leslie pounced on him and hugged him soundly. He patted her cheek awkwardly, unused to open displays of affection.

There was a reminiscent look in his eyes when he finally spoke. "I do believe that Old Mac knew what he was doing after all. I believe he did."

IT WASN'T UNTIL THE TRIP BACK to Grande Prairie that Ted had a chance to tell Leslie what he had found out about Luther Denver while he was in Calgary.

"You were right, Les. Luther does want to get back into Redwillow."

"How did you find out?"

There was a twinkle in Ted's eyes when he answered her. "I took Willie Thompson to lunch."

Leslie laughed. Willie Thompson was a drilling engineer for Denver Oil, and was probably the biggest gossip in the industry. "So what did Willie have to say?"

"Well, it seems that Luther hired some hotshot geologist from the States who has a big reputation as a finder. He had a look at the research you did, and to make a long story short, he told Luther that Redwillow was the hottest geological prospect he'd seen in a long time."

"You're kidding."

"No—hell, no! I guess the fellow didn't know Luther had sold off his land position in that area."

Leslie's eyes were wide with anticipation. "What did Luther do?"

Ted chuckled. "Willie said Luther went into a rage—he tried to lay the blame everywhere except on his own doorstep."

There was a flash of anger in Leslie's voice. "That's Luther for you."

"That's not the whole story. The geologist figured that the basin might be several miles larger than you projected, so Luther had a helicopter fly this guy in to see if he could find the beach outcrop."

"And did he?"

"Yeah, he did—it took him two weeks, but he found it. Luther did some scrambling and tried to pick up the rights to the land on the northwest edge.

When he found out that Ramco had those, too, I guess he nearly tore the building down.''

''I'll bet he did!'' Leslie nodded her head, her mouth set in a firm line. So Luther was caught in his own trap. Her face became sober as she thought about the outcome of Luther's discovery. ''I suppose that was when he started undermining Ramco?''

''That's right.''

''Are you going to tell Steve?''

''Yeah, he has a right to know—not that it will do him any good.''

Leslie wanted so badly to tell Ted about her intervention on Ramco's behalf, but she simply had to keep Kaidon's involvement a secret until the plans for the joint venture had been ratified. If Ted found out what she had done, he'd go directly to Steve, and Steve, she was certain, would refuse to deal with Kaidon—and with Leslie Kairns.

She was feeling really edgy about the whole thing. If luck was with her, Ted wouldn't find out who was negotiating the deal. There was the very real risk that Steve would confide in Ted about the offer, however. She wished she could come up with some scheme to keep them apart until Steve left for Vancouver. And if, by some incredible miracle, her luck held, there was a chance that Steve would never find out about her part ownership of Kaidon. There was a chance, a very slim chance. . . .

''Leslie, did you hear what I said?''

She'd been so deep in her thoughts that she wasn't aware Ted had said anything. ''I'm sorry, Ted, I'm afraid I wasn't listening.''

''I said, apparently this geologist graduated from

university with Steve, and he told Luther that Steve was the best damned geologist in the class. Apparently he has a sixth sense—''

"Steve's a geologist?'' Leslie's voice registered her shock. A geologist—no, it couldn't be! "But he told me he had his degree in petroleum engineering!''

"He does, but he took geology first. He's pinpointed some large finds for Ramco.''

Leslie's brow creased with a puzzled frown, and she chewed her bottom lip. Why? Why had he never told her he was a geologist? Why had he hired her, for that matter? He certainly didn't need her, even for the preliminary work. He could have done that himself once he knew where the basin was located, and Ted had given him that almost immediately. Why? It didn't make any sense. . . .

TED AND LESLIE ARRIVED back at Redwillow just in time for lunch. They went into the kitchen together, but Ted paused at the door as he scanned the room. Then he turned to go.

"Aren't you going to have anything to eat?''

He shook his head. "No. I want to talk to Steve right away and tell him what I found out.''

If Leslie could have been granted one wish right then, she would have had Ted locked in a closet until Steve left for Vancouver. She had a strong hunch that Steve would say nothing about the possibility of a joint venture with Kaidon until the negotiations were finalized, but she didn't know for sure. Steve had to leave sometime today to be there early the next morning, so there was only a matter of hours that she had to worry about. Her eyes were dark with apprehension as she watched Ted walk out of the kitchen—damn it, nothing could go wrong now. It just couldn't! But she didn't do a very good job of convincing herself.

Leslie caught a ride back to the rig with the camp attendant, who was taking lunch over to the men on shift. She had planned on walking, but it was so cold outside that she changed her mind. Winter was here, even if it hadn't snowed yet. It was strange, but as they approached the rig, she felt like she was coming home—and she hadn't felt like she ever had a home since her grandfather had died. The noise of the rig, the racks of drill pipe, the smell of diesel fuel were now a familiar and somehow reassuring part of her existence, her life. This was all so real, so exciting, so worthwhile. Yes, it was good to be back.

In her office there was a succinct memo from Steve lying on the counter. It brought her up to date on the depth and the type of formation they were drilling through. She read it carefully, then tossed it back on the counter—there was nothing unexpected in it. They would have to drill several thousand feet before things started to get interesting.

She glanced around. Apart from unpacking her bags, there was not one thing for her to do. Even the last sample taken from the shale shaker had been logged.

Leslie picked up the report and read it again, her mind wandering. Why hadn't Steve told her that he was a geologist? It was almost as though he'd deliberately omitted telling her that fact. There had been countless opportunities for him to mention it....

"Doesn't it meet your approval? The way you're

frowning, I would have to assume you've found some glaring error.''

Leslie jumped, her muscles stiffening as Steve's voice intruded sharply into her confused thoughts. Laying the paper on the counter, she turned and forced herself to meet his gaze.

There was a strange guarded tension emanating from him that made her feel very uneasy. Had Ted unwittingly given her secret away?

Swallowing against a knot of nervousness she tried to keep her voice natural, but it quavered revealingly. ''I was just wondering why you never said anything to me about your being a geologist, that's all.''

His eyes narrowed with a piercing look as he sauntered across the room and stood beside her. He picked up one of the vials that held a sample of rock cuttings and rolled it slowly between his long fingers.

''Ted just asked me the same question. What difference does it make?'' There was an evasiveness about him that she found bewildering. He was hedging. . . but why?

Her uncertainty made her cautious, anxious. ''I can't understand your reasons for hiring me. You certainly didn't need me—''

''I never said I didn't need you, Leslie.'' His abrupt low tone *was* concealing something. What if Ted had given her away?

''I'm leaving for Vancouver today,'' he said.

Leslie had one fearful suspended moment of horror when she nearly answered, ''I know.'' Somehow, in an effort to appear casually indifferent, she managed to keep her face expressionless, but her voice betrayed her. ''Will you be gone long?''

Steve stared down at her. "Why, do I detect a slight note of concern?"

She lowered her eyes, her long lashes fanning her cheeks as she toyed nervously with the pencil she picked up.

"No answer, Leslie? I must have been wrong."

He tossed the vial back onto the counter and started to walk away. A rush of dismay swept through her, and she knocked over a stool in her haste to reach him before he opened the door. She couldn't let him leave with this odd remoteness left hanging between them.

He turned to face her as she caught his arm. His eyes were like shafts of blue steel, his mouth a grim line, his nostrils flaring.

"Steve, I—" he frightened her to death when he looked at her like that, but she dredged up her rapid ly dwindling courage "—I do care, and...and I hope you have a good trip."

She dropped her hand and turned away, suddenly regretting her impulsive action. Her knees nearly gave way beneath her when he caught her by the shoulders and spun her around. She staggered against him as the force of his action threw her off balance, and automatically reached out to steady herself. Her hand came in contact with the hard wall of his chest, and a treacherous weakness overcame her. She shut her eyes against the hot tightness that turned her insides to jelly. Steve's arm came around her. He buried his hand in her hair, and pulled her head back. She didn't dare look at him.

"Dwarf?"

There was something about his softly spoken

query, his use of his nickname for her, that dissolved what little resistance she had left. She looked up at him, her eyes dark and pensive with despair. He was watching her with a fixed gaze that seemed strangely uncertain. She swayed against him, her senses bewitched by the spell his eyes cast on her. They stood transfixed, mesmerized by a fascination so overwhelming that it bound them together with an unrestrained power.

The spell was shattered by the sound of someone stomping up the steps. With an infuriated curse, Steve dropped his arms and stepped away. When Frank Logan burst into the trailer, a distance of several feet separated Leslie and Steve.

Leslie deliberately kept her back to the two men as she moved over to the counter and needlessly rearranged some of the written reports. If she'd been granted a second wish that day, she thought ironically, she would have locked Frank Logan in the closet, too.

"Steve, how soon are you leaving? That Jim kid has split his arm pretty bad, and he's going to need stitches—I thought maybe you could take him to Grande Prairie when you go."

Steve's voice was slightly clipped and very controlled. "I can be gone in ten minutes. Where is he?"

"He's at camp in the first-aid room."

"Get him ready to go. I'll have to pick up my luggage from my trailer first, then I'll be right over."

Frank nodded curtly and slammed out. Leslie turned to face Steve.

He was standing with his hands on his hips, an expression of angry frustration on his face. "Damn it anyway!'' But when he came toward Leslie and took her face in his hands, his touch was tender. "Leslie, damn it, I have to go." He looked down at her, his eyes filled with regret. Then with a groan, he pulled her against him in a crushing embrace.

"I'll be getting back from Vancouver next week. As soon as I do, you and I are going to have a long talk." He bent his head and kissed her, his mouth moist and gentle against hers. When he lifted his head, the message in his eyes filled her with a beautiful warmth. He shut his eyes briefly, then with fixed resolve, he reluctantly did up his jacket.

Leslie smiled softly as she turned up his collar. She let her hand rest lightly against his jaw, her voice a husky whisper. "Take care, Steve."

Her touch acted like a catalyst that destroyed his self-restraint. He covered her hand with his and held her palm against his mouth, kissing it with a passion that turned Leslie's bones to water. Her breath caught sharply, and she closed her eyes as the hollow hunger he always aroused in her throbbed within her. Her surrender was instantaneous when he pulled her roughly against him and covered her yielding mouth in an urgent searing kiss. She whispered his name when he tore his mouth away again and molded her fiercely against him.

He held her tightly for a moment, then relaxed his arms and kissed her again. His breath was warm against her lips as he whispered, "You take care, too, Leslie."

Obviously unwilling to let her go, he brushed a wisp of hair from her face with trembling fingers, then held her face in his hands. "If this trip wasn't so damned important, I'd say to hell with it." He kissed her softly on the temple, his hands cradling the back of her head. "Promise me, Les, that we'll talk the minute I get back."

She gazed up at him, her eyes large and solemn. "I promise." She reached up and touched his cheek, not caring that her feelings for him were so apparent. It didn't matter. She threw all caution to the wind as she murmured, "I'll miss you so, Steve."

He inhaled sharply, then caught her against him once again, pressing her hard to his chest. "I'll miss you—God, how I'll miss you. These last two weeks have been hell...." He held her for a moment, then eased his grip as he sighed heavily. "I have to go, Les.."

She pressed her fingers against his lips, trying to blink back the tears of happiness that were glistening in her eyes. "I know you do."

He bent his head and kissed her again, then released her. Pausing at the door, he stared at her for a spellbinding moment, then with a muttered oath, he turned and hurried down the stairs.

Leslie stood at the window and watched him go, vaguely aware that snowflakes were spiraling down from the leaden sky.

CHAPTER TWELVE

IT WAS STILL SNOWING Friday morning, and by noon the ground was covered with several inches of snow. Leslie stood looking out the window, her face bathed in awe. It was fascinating how in a matter of hours, a bleak, desolate landscape could be transformed into a wintery-white fairyland.

She glanced at her watch. If she left now, she would have time to walk over to the camp for lunch. If anyone saw her, of course, they'd really think she was out of her mind. Even Ted, who could cover miles of rough terrain without breathing hard, always drove over to the camp for meals.

Leslie took a deep breath as she stepped outside. Everything smelled so clean and fresh. The snow squeaked beneath her leather boots as she started walking—she loved wintertime, especially after a fresh fall of snow.

She paused for a moment and let the huge delicate flakes settle undisturbed on the navy blue fabric of her parka. Each snowflake had its own perfectly symmetrical design and Leslie was always fascinated by the fragile intricate patterns. A snowflake had to be one of the most beautiful creations of nature.

Leslie sighed with satisfaction and started to walk. After a minute she pushed the hood of her parka off her head and stuffed her gloves in her pocket—it was funny how warm the air always seemed during a heavy snowfall. And how hushed. There wasn't a whisper of wind through the snow-ladened spruce boughs, and even the steady drone of the rig seemed to be muffled.

The snow piled up beneath the trees with bridal-satin smoothness, marred only by the occasional rock or stump. The pine and towering spruce that crowded both sides of the road made a Christmas-card picture, their branches covered with a thick fluffy frosting. Some saskatoon bushes, which had been bleak brittle skeletons a few hours before, were now crystal coated as they reached gracefully to the sky. While Leslie watched, a blue jay landed on one of the branches, and the gentle movement sent the diamond dusting of snow showering to the ground.

Her absorbed fascination was abruptly shattered when a truck pulled up beside her. Frank Logan reached across the cab, swung open the passenger door and barked at her, "How come you're walkin'? Wouldn't your truck start?"

Leslie's first impulse was to make a sharp retort, but she stifled the urge. Instead she gave him a forced smile and lied. "I didn't feel like cleaning it off so I decided to walk. Besides, it isn't that cold." Logan was not the type of person to be empathetic toward someone who thought snow was beautiful.

"Get in—I'll give you a lift."

Leslie didn't want to get in—she wanted to walk. But she didn't want to give Frank the impression that she was avoiding him. After all, this was the first time he had spoken to her without being forced into it. She climbed in.

He put the truck in gear and started off. There was an awkward heavy silence that made Leslie nearly cringe in the corner.

"Do you do much huntin'?" he asked abruptly.

For a moment she didn't know what he was talking about; then she realized he'd been thinking about the episode with the bear. "No, I don't do any, really. I used to go often with my grandfather, though."

"You're a damned good shot."

Leslie looked at him with dumbfounded amazement. She wouldn't have been any more shocked if he had leaned across and kissed her. Her mouth was still hanging open when he continued, "Don't like killin' animals, I take it."

"No...no, I...I don't." Good grief, now he had her stammering like an idiot!

"Can't see the sport in it myself."

His words were gruff and staccato, and his face looked like it was chiseled out of granite, but there was something...something in his manner that was oddly approachable.

"I suppose all this snow is going to make it difficult at the rig?"

Frank shrugged. "The men grouse and grumble, but with the rig floor closed in, it ain't so bad. Besides, it's kinda pretty." He braked sharply as a rabbit darted across the road in front of them. Leslie looked at him, her brow lined with surprise, her eyes slightly squinted as she considered the man behind the wheel.

This Frank Logan was out of character, not the same person she *thought* he was. Maybe, just maybe....

This is getting to be a habit, she thought as she threw caution to the wind. "It is pretty—that's one reason I decided to walk. You don't see things the same way when you're driving."

"Nope, you don't. I like snowshoein' in weather like this. It's, well...relaxin'.''

Leslie looked at him as he parked beside the steps that led into the camp complex. This time her smile was a genuine one. "Thank you for giving me a ride." She would have liked to have said more, but she wisely left it at that. She didn't want to put him off, just when things were beginning to look up.

Leslie had to struggle to keep from laughing at the look of disbelief that swept across Ted's face as he came into the kitchen and saw Frank Logan sitting across the table from her. When he finally sat down beside her, his expression was sphinx-like and in-scrutable, but Leslie knew him too well to miss the wicked twinkle in his eyes.

He greeted them both, then looked directly at Frank. "I heard this morning that you've given Ernie his notice." Ernie was one of the mudloggers, but he wasn't Ramco staff. Several members of the support staff were contracted from independent companies— water haulers, casing and cementing crews, and mud-loggers.

Frank nodded his head. "Yep, I did."

"What happened?"

"He was drunk on shift last night. I'm runnin' him off the minute I can get a replacement for him."

"With this weather, it's going to be a while before we can get someone else out."

"Yeah, I know." Frank didn't sound too happy

about that. He looked at Ted, his eyes like cold steel. "He was drunk once before on shift, and I told him then it was the last time. We're gettin' into a formation where we're bound to hit pockets of gas. I ain't riskin' a kick that could blow the rig apart and my men with it because some ass—some damned fool can't get his head together."

Leslie looked at Frank and silently scored up a point for him. He had given the man a second chance, even though he could have lost his own job over it. Leslie had the feeling that Frank Logan didn't much like "running people off," but he would do it in a second if it jeopardized the safe operation of the rig.

Drinking on the job was no minor offense. In fact, the crews weren't allowed to have any liquor with them while they were in camp. Ramco ran "dry camps" for two reasons—the first, because it was dangerous. Anyone working on the rig who was not in total command of his senses could be the victim of a serious accident, or the cause of one. Secondly, it kept the brawling to a minimum. Leslie had heard several stories about parties getting out of hand, the ensuing ruckus leaving the camp half destroyed.

Leslie looked at Frank, and hoped she wasn't doing something impulsively stupid, when she said, "I've had a course on mud logging, Frank. If you want, I could cover Ernie's shift until you find a replacement. You're right about the formation—it could be risky."

Ted looked at Leslie as though she had just taken leave of her senses. Frank himself said nothing, but kept on eating, seemingly deaf to her suggestion. He carefully cleaned off his plate with a crust of bread, then pushed it away from him. Finally he looked at Leslie and shook his head. "Nope—a twelve-hour shift of mudloggin', plus your own work—it's no good."

Leslie was disappointed that he had refused her offer; it had been her way of extending a peace offering. Frank drained his coffee cup, then set it down on the table with a gesture of finality. "But I was thinkin' that you, Ted and me could split the shift."

Ted looked like someone had just hit him in the stomach, while Leslie grinned broadly. "Essie just brought out some blueberry pies," she said. "I'll go snag one for us."

LESLIE WAS GLAD to have the extra work. It filled her time, leaving her little time to think. Her thoughts were a jumble, and the more she tried to sort out the confusion, the worse it became.

There were times when she was so filled with elation that her spirits soared; then there were other times that she was coldly aware of the impossibility of anything permanent developing between Steve and herself. She had purposely avoided telling him the whole truth, and he would despise her for that.

How he would react to the fact that Luther Denver was her stepfather was questionable. She had *no* illusions about how he would react when he found out she was the major shareholder in the company that was financing the exploration program for Redwillow. He would be furious about the deception, and she couldn't blame him for that because she loathed duplicity herself. What frightened her more than his anger was the nagging suspicion that he would have nothing more to do with her when, and if, he found out.

Her doubts were further compounded after she screwed up enough courage to tell Ted what she had done. He had been deeply concerned about her decision not to tell Steve that she was, in fact, the major shareholder of Kaidon Industries. After much reasoning, however, she had convinced him that there was no other way.

Ted's weathered face had set in a worried frown as he slowly shook his head. "Steve's going to feel like you've bought him, Les. As sure as hell, that's how he's going to feel."

Leslie had never looked at it from that point of view, and Ted's observation haunted her. Because of that, she made one definite decision—she was going to keep her identity a secret for as long as she could. And if her anonymity was threatened, she would be the one to tell Steve the truth. He would not find out the facts from someone else—she owed him that.

By Sunday the snow was deep and drifting. A grader, fitted with a large V-plow, had cleared the twenty miles of company road, but by suppertime the wind had picked up momentum. When Frank came to relieve Leslie in the mud-logging shack at midnight, he confided to her that he expected the road to be impassable by morning.

He had sent Ernie out that day, but now he didn't know when a replacement would arrive. Leslie had told him not to worry about it, but with a humph Frank had said that "a little thing like her couldn't go without sleep.'' Leslie couldn't help but smile. Frank was still equating size with stamina, but she was beginning to have a sneaking hunch that he believed women should be coddled.

The conditions outside were awful. Leslie squinted, her long lashes shielding her eyes from the driving snow that whipped against her face. It was drifting so badly that she could barely see the indistinct outline of the trailer units through the ominous whirlwind. Bending her head against the freezing, slicing wind, she watched the silver crystals slither along the ground, creating the illusion that the earth was shifting beneath her feet.

By the time she was inside and had closed the door of her trailer, her cheeks were stinging from the freezing wind. The temperature had dropped that morning, but now the windchill factor plunged the temperature even lower. She didn't envy the men working on the rig. The canvas skirt that protected the rig floor helped to break the wind, and there was a fair amount of heat generated by the equipment, but it would still be terribly cold.

She had a warm shower, then made herself a cup of hot chocolate. The wind was beginning to moan with a melancholy lament that left her feeling strangely sad. It seemed to compound her feeling of apprehension about the future.

She was still awake, thinking dismal thoughts, when she heard a soft knocking at her door. She glanced at her clock radio as she slipped into a fluffy pink housecoat. One-thirty. There must be trouble at the rig.

A blast of arctic air swirled around her when she

opened the door. Steve McRory, his face shadowed by the hood of his parka, was standing before her.

"Steve!"

"I saw your light on, so I thought you might still be up."

Leslie caught his arm and pulled him inside, shivering as she closed the door against the blinding blizzard. Steve took off his parka and hung it on the hook by the door, then slipped out of his boots.

Her eyes registered her alarm as he turned to face her. He looked nearly frozen and ready to drop from exhaustion, but he never gave her a chance to speak. Whispering her name, he pulled her against him, holding her like he would never let her go.

He was shivering violently, and she could feel the cold and fatigue radiating from him as she wrapped her arms around his waist. Easing herself slightly away from him, she looked up at him in concern. "You're nearly frozen, Steve."

He closed his eyes and rested his forehead against hers, his arms tightening around her. "I had to walk the last couple of miles. The road was blocked solid." He sighed wearily and he cradled her against his chest. "I had to get back tonight. With that wind, I knew it might be days before they could clear the road, and I'd have gone crazy waiting."

Alarm filled her. Walking that distance in weather conditions like these was a risky dangerous move. No wonder he was shivering so—he was probably suffering from hypothermia.

"Come on, you're not standing out here in this drafty hallway." Her chin was set with determination as she led him through the kitchen and into her bedroom. "You are going to get into bed and I'm going to make you something hot to drink."

"Les, I can go back to my own—"

"Shut up, Steve."

He tried to smother a smile at the firmness in her voice, then shrugged slightly, his voice filled with suppressed amusement. "Yes, mother."

She grinned at him, then brushed past him and straightened the covers on the bed. "Would you like some soup?"

He gave her a very dry look. "As long as it isn't banana soup."

She laughed and made a face at him, then left the room. When she returned, Steve was in bed, his eyes closed. She could tell that he was trying to control his shivering. She set the tray on the bedside table, then sat down on the edge of the bed and tenderly smoothed his tousled hair.

He opened his eyes and smiled at her. "Are you mothering me, Miss Kairns?"

"Of course—for the time being." She bent over and gave him a light fleeting kiss. Before he could respond, she lifted her head and handed him a steaming mug. "The only canned soup I had in my Mother Hubbard's cupboard was tomato."

She could tell that his normal reserve of energy was nearly spent. He had to struggle into a sitting position and wearily ease himself back against the pillows. Leslie placed the tray across his lap. "And I made you a toasted tuna-salad sandwich that would make Essie cringe in horror."

Steve laughed. "I'm so cold and hungry I'd eat dog food right now."

Leslie grinned at him as she reached across him and tucked the comforter around his naked shoulder. Curling up beside him, she remained silent while he ate. He looked so tired.... She chewed her bottom lip anxiously as she wondered if something had gone wrong.

When he had finished the sandwich she lifted the tray and set it on the floor. Her eyes were solemn, reflecting her concern. "Steve, has something gone wrong? You look like you haven't slept for a week."

He took another sip of soup, then shook his head. "No—all our problems have been miraculously solved. We'd lost the financial backing that we thought was solid, and it was really worrying me. Another company in Vancouver is coming in now, though." He wrapped his hands around the mug and smiled ruefully. "If I didn't know better, I'd start believing that I had acquired a fairy godmother."

Leslie suddenly felt like something was caught in her throat, but she somehow managed to suppress the urge to cough. She didn't even want to *think* about what Steve's reaction would be if he realized he was in his good fairy's bed. She clasped her hands in her lap and stared at them, preoccupied with her uneasy thoughts.

She didn't look up when Steve leaned over and placed the empty mug on the night table. When she finally lifted her head, she felt as though someone had pulled the plug on her world. Steve was holding the leather folder that framed his photographs. The damned pictures! She hadn't even thought of them when she'd brought him into her bedroom. Disconcerted, she closed her eyes and bowed her head.

Damn! Damn! Damn! Why hadn't she thought of them...?

His hand caught her chin and forced her head up. "Leslie, look at me."

She made herself meet his gaze, her eyes filled with distress, her face ashen. He laid the folder on the bed beside him, then separated her tightly interlaced fingers with his hand. His voice was low and husky when he spoke.

"You said I look like I haven't slept for a week— that's not far from the truth." He carried her hand to his lips and kissed it softly, then looked at her, his eyes deadly serious. "Ever since I left here on Friday, I've had one hell of a time focusing my attention on anything. All I could think about was getting back to you. As soon as Uncle John arrived in Vancouver to take over the business negotiations, I bolted for Red-willow."

Releasing his grasp on her hands, he picked up the photographs and studied them. "Leslie?" he asked at last.

There was such a warm irresistible tenderness in his voice that it brought tears to her eyes, and a fierce ache of longing swelled in her breast, unleashing her secret dreams. Maybe he cared for her more than she thought. *Please let it be so,* she pleaded silently. *Please let it be so.*

She swallowed, her voice a tremulous whisper. "Steve, I—I don't know where to begin."

He set the pictures back on the table, then took her hands in his again, his touch reassuring, his words gentle and encouraging. "Why don't you start at the beginning?"

She took a deep shaky breath as she tried to blink away the tears that were suspended on her lashes. She was risking everything. "I...I didn't know what hit me after I met you...I didn't know what was happening to me. I was so...so awed, so overwhelmed by you. Then after that day in the park...." Leslie closed her eyes as she fought to control the frightening immobilizing need to cry. She looked at Steve, her mouth trembling, her eyes beseeching as tears coursed down her cheeks.

Steve whispered her name as he pulled back the covers and drew her down beside him. A warm weakness invaded her when she realized he was completely naked except for his white cotton briefs. He groaned hoarsely as he molded her body tightly against his, holding her in an embrace that was as protective as it was powerful, as tender as it was fierce. "Oh, Leslie, it feels so good to hold you—to feel your body warm and soft against mine. There have been so many times that I ached to hold you like this. I feel so damned empty when I'm away from you."

He caught her by the back of the head and pressed her face against the curve of his shoulder. The painful contraction in Leslie's throat eased a little, and she closed her eyes as she savored the beautiful sense of security that enveloped her. Nothing could harm her when he was holding her; nothing mattered except that he cared.

He held her until the raw emotions in her ebbed, then he eased her beneath him. Raising himself on one elbow, he captured her face with his hand. With infinite gentleness he covered her mouth with his, his kiss warm and vital as he cradled her against him.

Her heart was racing and her breathing labored when he finally lifted his head and softly kissed her eyes.

He took a deep measured breath as he combed his fingers through her hair. "Leslie, I need you to talk to me. I want you to tell me what happened after that day in the park."

There was an aura of uncertainty about her as she touched his face with her fingertips, her eyes soft and luminous. Her voice was tremulous as she whispered, "I had to admit to myself that I was in love with you, Steve. I didn't know how to cope with the intensity of my feelings. . . and it frightened me."

His arms tightened around her, and he trailed his mouth down her neck, his lips moist and tormenting as he murmured, "Why did it frighten you?"

Shivers of excitement coursed through her as he caressed the sensitive hollow beneath her ear with his tongue. He bracketed her face with his hands and looked at her with gentle questioning. "Why were you so frightened?"

She closed her eyes and took a deep shaky breath. "You devastated all my emotional barricades with that first casual kiss. I felt so vulnerable. . . ."

His voice was low and provocative. "Leslie, that first kiss was anything *but* casual."

She glanced up at him and flushed. "But I thought it was intended to be. . . that."

He caressed her lips with a tormenting feathery touch, then laughed huskily. "Not even remotely. You had one hell of an impact on me the minute I laid eyes on you—then you smiled, and I was completely lost."

She stared at him with amused skepticism. "You

acted like you wanted to strangle me when I left the restaurant that day, Steve McRory, and you know it!''

He grinned. ''Am I really that transparent?'' He shook his head and smiled wryly. ''I did feel like strangling you. I wanted you to stay. But you were so aloof when you refused. I was so certain that I would never see you again if I let you get away from me. You gave me some very bad moments, you know.''

''I didn't.''

''You did. That night I asked you to do the preliminary research for Redwillow. You were suddenly so remote. . . .''

''Oh, Steve. . . I wasn't remote. I was so horrified, so appalled by what you had told me about Luther Denver.''

''I realized that later, but I sure in hell didn't at the time. Then, when you stormed out of the office that day, I really thought I had blown it for good.''

Leslie couldn't help but laugh at the rueful tone in his voice. ''Poor Steve.''

''Yes, poor Steve—you had me going in circles.'' His face sobered abruptly, his eyes changing to a smokey gray. ''Why did you run from me that night at Bob's and Anne's? I put in one rotten night, trying to figure out what had happened. Did I frighten you?''

She shook her head as she took his face in her hands, her eyes dark and solemn. ''No. . . well, yes. . . in a way. I never dreamed that I could respond the way I did. It scared me that I was so. . . so out of control. But that isn't the reason I left. I thought you were trying to warn me not to get involved. . . .''

Steve lightly covered her mouth with his fingers. "I *was* warning you, my love. I'd known you less than a month, but I knew what my feelings were toward you. I was afraid that I was rushing you too fast, and I wanted to give you some time."

Leslie slipped her arms around his neck and closed her eyes as he kissed the curve of her shoulder. He gathered her against him as he turned onto his back and snuggled her closer. She smiled contentedly as he pulled the covers over her and held her close.

"Steve, why didn't you tell me you were a geologist?"

There was a slight pause, then he heaved a sigh. "I didn't want you to find out about that. I could have strangled Ted when he told you."

"Why didn't you want me to know?"

He sighed again before he answered her. "Because I thought you'd start questioning my reasons for offering you the job as project geologist."

Leslie smiled and smoothed her hand across his bare chest. "And what were your reasons?"

Steve gave a throaty laugh as he squeezed her against him. "Are you sure you really want to know?"

"Yes."

"Are you going to get in a 'twist' if I tell you?"

She laughed. "I promise I won't."

"All right, the prime reason I hired you was that I didn't want to leave you behind in Calgary. I didn't think I could stand not seeing you for weeks on end."

Leslie struggled free of his embrace and stared down at him. "Steve McRory, how can you put *that* on an employee evaluation report?"

He laughed and drew her back down against him.

"I don't know. But I can honestly say that you're efficient, conscientious, dependable...."

"Stop! That sounds far too businesslike and very boring. Personally, I liked the first reason better."

She felt him smile against her forehead as he ran his hand slowly up her back. "It's true, though—and that's the second reason I took you on staff. You're a fine geologist, but you didn't have much confidence in your ability. I was certain that you only needed some field experience to gain that. You made a comment once, that confidence is a very real part of contentment. That really stopped me in my tracks and made me think, I can tell you. I wanted you to be happy, Les—and I realized then that I had to give you some time. I had to give you a chance."

"And you regretted that the minute that Frank Logan and I collided."

Steve groaned. "I wanted to punch Frank, and shake you...."

"Yes, I know."

He shifted slightly so he could see her face, his eyes grave. "I was angry because Frank's comments were too close to the truth. I was feeling so guilty about exposing you to such a rough, harsh existence just because I was selfish enough to want you here with me. Then after you and Frank clashed, I realized that I would have to stay away from you completely or he would make your life miserable. That's why I wanted you to go back to Calgary. But Ted talked me out of that."

He closed his eyes, his jaw rigid as a spasm of pain flitted across his face. "That was the worst ordeal I've ever experienced in my whole life. I hated having that rift between us; I hated watching you struggle along on your own. But I knew if I went near you even once, I would never be able to stay away." He opened his eyes and looked at her with such burning intensity that Leslie felt as though she had been drawn into a whirlpool.

"I love you, Leslie...and I need you like I've never needed anything or anybody before in my life."

For a suspended moment of time, Leslie's heart stopped beating. Then a golden bubble of joy burst within her, filling her with the most glorious happiness she had ever known. All the love that she had kept locked away in her heart came pouring out with a power that was almost frightening with its force.

Steve took her face in his hands, his own expression twisted by a grimace of anguish. "I love you, Leslie, and I want you. And heaven knows, I need you—I need you so damned much." He crushed her against him as he captured her mouth with a scorching kiss, one that sent her senses reeling as their mutual desire became a fierce all-consuming flame.

Leslie was tossed into a tumultuous sea of emotions, was burned by a scalding agonizing hunger. Steve's mouth was savagely seductive as it ravished hers, his embrace paralyzing as he held her closer and closer against him. He moved his body against hers as if he were trying to absorb her, to fuse their two beings into one. Her yielding was complete, an impassioned surrender.

He groaned as he caught her hair and tugged her head back, then buried his face against her neck, his breathing ragged. He shuddered as Leslie clung to him, her own body trembling uncontrollably. There was such a storm of denied desire within her that she could barely breathe, but the heated weight of Steve's body on top of hers soothed the throbbing ache.

With a massive effort, Steve reluctantly eased his weight from her. Her arms tightened around him as she whispered tremulously, "Don't, Steve. Please don't go...."

She heard him grind his teeth together as his body tensed; he was fighting for control. He supported his weight on his elbow and grasped her face in his shaking hands. His eyes were smoldering as he gazed down at her, his face taut. Then, gently, he brushed back a wisp of hair that was clinging to her cheek, his voice low and tortured. "I can't be trusted around you."

Tenderly she combed her fingers through his hair, her own voice husky with a deep longing. "I want you, Steve...I want you to love me."

His breathing was rough and labored as he continued to gaze down at her, his desire blazing in his eyes, drawing her beneath him in a desperate embrace.

With a low groan he raised his head and covered her moist parted lips with his mouth, and Leslie felt as though every cell in her body was aroused by the molten surge of passion that pulsated through her.

She felt the muscles in his back bunch beneath her hands as he raised his weight and fumbled with the tie at her waist. A tremor quivered through her as he brushed back the folds of her housecoat, his touch like fire against her sensitized skin.

He slid his hand beneath her hips, binding her body against his in an embrace that was unrelenting.

Their skin was soldered together, Leslie's breasts flattened against Steve's chest as he pressed his naked muscled thighs between hers. His tongue plundered her yielding mouth, and his body moved against her with an agonizing deliberate slowness that drove her into a realm of blistering sensation, robbing her of coherent thought. Every detail of his aroused masculine form was imprinted on hers with a heated desire, so wild, so intense, so beautiful that it lifted her beyond reality.

Her virginal body responded to the rhythm of his, the molten tension building within her, carrying her toward the sunburst of sexual discovery. She slipped her hand beneath the waistband of his briefs in a desperate, almost frantic attempt to remove that last barrier between them.

Steve tore his mouth away from hers and caught her hand in a crushing grip. "No...Leslie, no." He buried his face in her hair, his body trembling, his breathing harsh as he whispered, "Help me...God help me, Leslie. I want you so badly...I don't want to stop."

The tortured desperation of his plea penetrated the rampaging desire that stormed within her. She cradled his head against the curve of her neck, while a feeling of fierce protectiveness swept through her.

Tears slipped from beneath her closed eyelids as she held him with all the strength she possessed, the awful empty ache of denial burning within her. Her breathing came in ragged gasps as they clung to each other, their sweat-dampened bodies molded fiercely together.

Opening her eyes, she gazed into Steve's smoldering ones as he softly wiped away the traces of tears with shaking fingers. There was such an anguished impassioned tenderness burning in his eyes that it brought more tears to her own.

"Oh, Steve..." she murmured brokenly.

He kissed her, his mouth moving against hers with a lingering gentleness.

Sighing softly, he captured her face between his hands as he reluctantly raised his head. His voice was low and sensual, and his breath feathered against her lips. "When I'm away from you, I swear to myself that I'm going to make love to you, to possess you... but when I have you in my arms, I can't let myself."

He slowly stroked her cheek with the back of his hand, his face solemn. "I can't violate your trust in me." She could feel his heart beating wildly against hers, but his touch remained tender and undemanding. "I can't treat this like a casual affair. I need you, Leslie. I want you to be my wife."

Leslie's eyes were radiant through her glistening tears and her heart burst with a happiness that tore her apart inside. She was moved to such depths that she couldn't speak, but her answer was shining in her eyes. A sob caught in her throat as she felt him tremble beneath her touch when she smoothed her hands up his naked back.

Once again he whispered her name, wrapping his arms around her and holding her in an embrace that was fierce and possessive. His breathing was still tortured as he struggled to restrain himself.

She caught his head in her hands, and a soft moan was wrung from her when she recognized the naked curbed hunger that was burning in his eyes. Raising her head, she kissed him, her mouth moist and inviting as she trailed her tongue across his bottom lip.

His arms crushed her tighter as he responded to the liquid fire that was boiling through her. Holding her immobile in his powerful embrace, he raised his head and took several deep breaths.

He shuddered against her, his voice so low and tormented that she could barely hear him. "You scare the hell out of me, Leslie. You're like a fragile wisp of magic—and I'm so afraid I'll hurt you." Desperation radiated from him as he murmured, "I want you so badly...."

Leslie could barely breathe for the hot throbbing ache that was growing within her. "You can't hurt me when you're loving me," she whispered back, her mouth trembling.

Steve clenched his eyes shut and raggedly sucked in his breath as he fought a battle for control. But his desire sliced through the bonds of restraint when she twisted beneath him, silently pleading with him to quench the fire of passion that was consuming her.

His hands on her naked body were compelling, intimate, arousing her to such incredible heights. Leslie became oblivious to all else except the sound of their labored breathing and the hot liquid tide of desire that was surging within her.

His body was filmed with sweat when he finally took her, their bodies fusing together, then moving with a primitive hypnotic rhythm. The tide of their love kept building and building until it was a flood, and as it crested, Leslie was suspended briefly on the verge of magnificent revelation. Then waves of release slammed through her.

Steve ground his body against her, and a tortured cry was wrung from him as he shuddered violently, his arms tightening around her savagely.

They clung together for a long time as the flood waters of their stormy consummation ebbed and a drifting state of contented tranquility enveloped them. It was in the aftermath of spent passion that Leslie realized her face was wet.

Supporting his weight on his elbows, Steve eased away slightly, then took her face in his hands and tenderly wiped away the traces of tears with his thumbs. With a deep satisfied sigh, he lowered his head and kissed her, his mouth soft, pliant and so very gentle.

He braced his body to roll away, but her arms tightened around him. "Don't go, Steve," she whispered huskily. "It's so beautiful to be able to hold you like this."

He caressed her face with his fingertips, and there was such warmth in his eyes that it made her heart catch. His breath was warm against her mouth as he murmured. "I'm too heavy for you, little one."

Her hold on him was firm, unrelenting. "No, you're not. I don't want you to go."

He sighed softly as he gazed down at her, his eyes filled with love. He reached out and switched off the bedside lamp, then he slipped his arms around her, their naked bodies merging together in the darkness.

CHAPTER THIRTEEN

LESLIE AWOKE THE NEXT MORNING still securely cradled in Steve's embrace, his head nestled firmly against her breast. To wake up safe and warm in his arms mesmerized her with a beautiful heady feeling of contentment.

Last night he had carried her through a scalding passion to a fiery climax that went far beyond her wildest dreams, his love surrounding her, giving her the most secure sense of belonging that she had ever known.

Steve stirred slightly, and Leslie rested her hand lightly on the back of his head. She didn't want to wake him if she could help it; he so desperately needed to sleep. She glanced at the clock radio and sighed with resignation.

She hated to leave the warm haven of his arms, but it was time to get up. When Ted was on site, he usually picked her up for breakfast, and she wanted to move Steve's parka and boots before he arrived.

Ted would have to be told that Steve was back at Redwillow in case a crew was sent out to clear the road and discovered his empty truck. Perhaps she was being ridiculous, but she didn't want him to know that Steve had spent the night with her.

Ted would take it in his stride, and he would certainly never make any reference to it, but those hours were so special and so intimate that she didn't want anyone else to know about them.

She closed her eyes and quietly savored the weight of Steve's body against hers for a few more moments, then, reluctantly, she eased away from him.

"No, don't go," he murmured, pulling her firmly against him and rolling onto his back.

She smiled as she gazed down at him, marveling again at the long thick lashes that fanned across his cheeks. She smoothed his tousled hair, then tried a second time to ease out of his embrace without disturbing him. But his hold on her was unrelenting.

His breathing remained even and regular as he continued to hold her. Les couldn't resist the temptation, and she kissed him, her mouth pliant and moist against his parted lips. The pressure of his arms increased as he responded to the tender provocative caress, and his hands began to roam seductively across her hips as he pressed her closer against him. His touch fanned the flame of desire that was rapidly spreading through her whole body.

She took his face in her hands, his jaw rough from a day's growth of beard, and took a deep unsteady breath as she unwillingly lifted her head. In a husky whisper she said, "Steve, you have to let me go."

"No, I don't."

She laughed softly as she gave his head a gentle shake. "Steve McRory, you big fake. I thought you were asleep."

He slowly opened his eyes, which were soft with slumber, and smiled at her lazily. "I'm not letting you leave this bed."

Her own eyes dancing with mischief, she grinned at him. "If you don't want Ted and Frank Logan stomping in here looking for me, you'd better let me go."

"I'll fire them both if they set one foot inside this bedroom."

She laughed, "And wouldn't that create a marvelous scandal!"

Steve closed his eyes and grinned, then caught her head and nestled it against his shoulder. "I could hold you forever, Les—it feels so good to have you here with me."

Leslie was filled with such an overwhelming surge of emotion that she couldn't speak. Tears of happiness blurred her vision as she snuggled closer against him, her hand pressed against his cheek. His arms tightened around her as he sighed softly, then kissed the top of her head.

Serene contentment enveloped them as they lay wrapped in each other's arms. Several peaceful moments passed before Steve's hold on her relaxed slightly, and Leslie knew he had drifted back to sleep.

Very carefully she eased out of his arms, his hands trailing across her hips as she moved away. She tucked the quilt around him and dropped a kiss on his temple, then smiled softly as she watched his breathing become deep and regular.

She gazed at his rugged virile face. How she loved him! And the miracle was that he loved her in return.

Her features became solemn as she watched him sleep. Would his love survive the shock of finding out the truth about her? She pushed aside the bleak chilling thought and refused to allow herself to consider the answer. Her happiness was based on a moment-to-moment existence, and she would not risk one second of that until she absolutely had to.

She had trouble concentrating on her work that morning. She was keenly aware that Steve was sleeping in her bed, and her thoughts were persistently invaded by intoxicating recollections of the hours she had spent in his arms. She finally gave up trying to work as a lost cause, and let her mind wander at will until it was time for lunch.

As soon as she returned to the trailer, she slipped into the bedroom to check on Steve. She found him sprawled across the bed on his stomach, still dead to the world. He had on his jeans, so obviously he had been up while she was gone.

She had pulled the blanket from under his legs and was bending over to cover him up when his hand shot out. Catching her wrist, he tumbled her onto the bed beside him.

He opened his eyes and grinned at her as he rolled her beneath him. "Do you know that you have a strong maternal instinct, Miss Kairns?"

She wound her arms around his neck and grinned at him. "Does that alarm you?"

"Not at all. We'll just have to have a pack of kids to keep you happy."

She nuzzled her face against his neck and kissed the pulse that was throbbing in the curve of his shoulder. "There are a few other things you do that make me happy, you know."

He inhaled abruptly, his chest crushing the soft curves of her breasts. His arms tightened around her almost fiercely, then he laughed softly as he climbed off the bed and pulled her up with him.

"Don't be a torment, or I'll send you back to Calgary after all." He let one hand rest on her hip as he leaned over and swept his shirt off the chair. When he slipped it on, Leslie brushed his hands aside and started doing up the buttons for him.

"Would you now?"

He laughed as he hooked his arms around her waist. "Not on your life. You're here for the duration, whether you like it or not."

She did up the last button and let her hands linger on his chest as she smiled up at him, her eyes dancing. "I like it."

He kissed her soundly, then propelled her firmly out of the bedroom. "I think," he said tightly, "that you'll drive me to distraction."

She laughed up at him as she hugged him hard. "I'll feed you before I do that." She stretched up and kissed his chin, then slipped out of his arms. "Essie sent over a dinner for you—I put it in the oven to keep warm."

Steve ran his hand through his hair, then grimaced. "Could it keep for another half hour? I'd like to get cleaned up first. I feel like a derelict."

As it turned out, that afternoon was theirs alone. The wind howled around the trailer, secluding them inside with blinding blowing snow. No one would venture into the bitter cold unless they absolutely had to, but to discourage unexpected visitors, Steve locked the door when he returned from his own trailer.

After he finished eating, he carried Leslie back to the bedroom and dumped her in the middle of the bed. He sprawled out beside her and laughed as he gathered her against him. "We're going to make the most of this rotten weather. We may not have another chance to be alone for days."

Leslie snuggled against him and draped her leg across his. "I think you're trying to tell me in a tactful way that we're going to have to be very discreet, Steve McRory."

He laughed, then acceded to her comment with a sigh. "We *are* going to have to be discreet, Les."

"I know—but it's better than not seeing you at all."

"Leslie, what's the story on your family? You've never mentioned them since that night we talked in Calgary."

His question was totally unexpected, and Leslie went suddenly cold. For a fleeting instant she was tempted to tell him about Luther Denver, but she rejected the impulse almost immediately. If he knew that Luther was her stepfather, it would open the door to him discovering her connection with Kaidon Industries. No—she had to keep those facts hidden for as long as she could.

"What is it, Les? I could feel you tense up as soon as I mentioned it."

She told him a half truth instead of the whole. "It's a difficult thing for me to discuss, Steve. I moved away from home the same day I quit at Denver, you see. There would have been ugly repercussions at home because of what I had done. If I hadn't left, I would have been told to leave." She closed her eyes against the remembered pain of that day. "I'll never go back. Never."

"Do you have any relations other than your mother?"

"No, mother was an only child. There are no living relatives of my grandparents, either. There's no one else except the McAllisters."

"Have you ever thought about trying to trace your father?"

"I used to, but I haven't one clue to his identity. Grandfather couldn't tell me, and my mother wouldn't—and there is no one else who would know."

"What about Ted?"

"I asked him right after grandfather died, but he doesn't know anything, either. It was a closely guarded secret, for some reason."

Steve didn't say anything for a long time as he stroked her back with slow movements. She finally raised her head and looked at him, her eyes painfully serious. "I want to talk to you about it, Steve, but I just can't...not yet."

He smiled at her with understanding as he trailed his finger down her nose. "I know that, my love." He pressed her head back down to his shoulder and cuddled her closer against him, then continued caressing her back. "I very much want you to come home with me for Christmas and meet my family. I was concerned that there might be someone else you'd rather spend it with, that's all."

"There's no one on earth I'd rather spend Christmas with than you."

His laugh was throaty as he hugged her. "You're doing it again. You get that husky little tremor in your voice, and I want to seduce you and say to hell with the consequences."

She twisted in his arms so that she could see his

face, then she smiled at him enticingly. "What's stopping you?"

The gleam of amusement died in Steve's eyes and was replaced with a look of very sober concern. "Your innocence is stopping me, Les. You never once considered what the outcome could be." He cradled her face tenderly in his hands. "We're playing with fire—and I don't want to expose you to any more risk. When we have a family, I want it to be because we've planned for it, not because I can't control myself."

A constricting ache developed around her heart when she witnessed the tormented look in his eyes. She laid her fingers across his mouth to silence him. She loved him far too much to allow him to hold himself in self-contempt.

"I love you, Steve...so much," she whispered brokenly, her eyes dark and solemn. "I could never deny you anything. Never." She took a deep shaky breath in an attempt to control the swell of raw emotion that surged inside her. "You created such a turmoil in me when you—you made love to me last night." She softly caressed his lips with her fingertips. "To know that you care enough about me to protect me—that's such a special feeling, and I love you all the more because of it." Tears were gathering in her eyes, and she tried to blink them away. "We may be playing with fire—but I don't care. I'll take that chance."

Steve inhaled sharply. Then, his body rigid with constraint, he kissed her very softly. With a deep sigh he cradled her head against his shoulder and began to comb his fingers through her hair. "I love you so much, Leslie—more than I ever imagined I would love anyone." He hesitated for a moment, as though searching for adequate words to express his feelings. "You've filled an emptiness in me. You've given my life a whole new dimension." He laid his cheek on top of her head as he buried his hand in her hair. "Because of how I feel about you, you arouse a passion in me that I didn't know I was capable of."

He tilted her head back and looked at her, his gaze so serious, yet so tender that it brought new tears to Leslie's eyes. "Your virginity...well, you don't know how honored I felt last night. I value your love, I value your trust. I value every single thing about you."

Leslie was so touched, so overwhelmed by his words that she couldn't respond. With tempered ardor he kissed away the tears that spilled from her eyes, then nestled her against him in a protective possessive embrace.

"Last night was so very special," he murmured. "I woke up once during the night and you were so warm and trusting as you slept in my arms. It was so beautiful. I've never experienced such a feeling of total contentment ever before."

His sincerity, his candidness ignited a warmth in Leslie, filling her with an impassioned longing to give him the kind of contentment, the feeling of completeness that they had both experienced the night before. She shifted her head and kissed the curve of his neck, her lips lingering against his smooth warm skin.

Catching her face in his hands, Steve turned toward her, his eyes smoldering with a fevered look. "Leslie—don't."

She smoothed her trembling fingers across his soft sensuous mouth. "I love you, Steve. Nothing matters but you." She stroked his lips as a light flush colored her cheeks. "And you don't have to worry about there being any risk—not right now."

He gritted his teeth and drew in a deep breath before he spoke. "You are so hard to resist...you arouse feelings in me I can't control."

With tantalizing lightness she caressed the tense muscles along his jaw, her voice low with a meaningful intimacy. "I want to lose myself to you. Like I did when you were loving me...when you were in me."

Steve crushed her against him with unbridled passion. "Ah, Leslie, you cause such a storm in me." His mouth covered hers in a deep searching kiss as he molded her hot yielding softness against him.

His breathing was labored when he tore his mouth away from hers. "I need you. God, how I need you." When he pulled her on top of him, she melted against his aroused body like hot wax as he reclaimed her mouth.

There would be no denial, no restraint this time, for the fire of desire was raging out of control, and it could only be quenched by the pounding waves of total fulfillment.

THAT CLANDESTINE AFTERNOON and their intimate hours together turned out to be a special gift from the gods. From the following day on, it seemed as though there was a conspiracy against them.

The other two rigs arrived in Grande Prairie, but the foul weather and the heavy snowfalls seriously hampered their transportation to the drill sites. Nearly 120 loads of equipment, twenty-five tons each, had to be hauled in by enormous diesel trucks. It was a constant battle to try and keep the rig roads clear, and on more than one occasion a powerful D-6 Caterpillar tractor was used to drag a truck, load and all, through miles of packed drifts.

Consequently, Leslie rarely saw Steve during the next week, and when she did, it was usually very briefly at mealtimes.

Then problems developed with the mud-logging equipment, and that meant a heavier work load for Leslie. The additional work brought with it an unexpected bonus, though. Steve and Ted were practically never at Ramco Two, and Leslie found herself relying more and more on Frank Logan's vast practical experience. The more time she spent with the gruff tool push, the more she liked him. He possessed a droll sense of humor that delighted her, and though he was not formally educated, he was unquestionably an expert in his field.

At first Frank viewed her interest cautiously, but when he realized that Leslie was truly anxious to learn all she could, his attitude toward her relaxed. He took her under his wing and Leslie's field education began in earnest.

She sometimes had the uncomfortable feeling that Frank viewed her with the ill-disguised pride of a father watching his firstborn learning to walk. In spite of that, however, a solid friendship developed between them.

Steve was unaware of how the professional relationship between Frank and Leslie had flourished. He assumed that there was still a guarded restraint between them, and it wasn't until one day during dinner that he discovered how wrong he was.

They were sitting at the table, finishing their dessert, when he casually mentioned that since the other two rigs were finally on site, he would have more time to spend at Ramco Two. Since he would be on location more regularly, he would be able to look after the problems with the mud logging.

Frank stared at Steve, then growled, "Les, ain't a dummy, you know. She knows what she's doin'."

The stunned look on Steve's face was something to behold, and Leslie had all she could do to maintain a straight face.

When Frank continued with, "Me and Les can manage jest fine," Leslie had to excuse herself and leave the kitchen.

As Christmas came closer, her uneasiness over her possible exposure was overshadowed by her nervousness about meeting Steve's family. She desperately wanted them to like her, but she was so shy and reserved with strangers that she was terrified they would see her as aloof. She was totally at ease when she and Steve visited the Jansens, and she was now casually and unquestionably accepted as one of the team at Redwillow. The thought of facing Steve's family left her quaking inside, however.

Leslie's personal worries were compounded by added demands at work. They had drilled into the Cardium formation and encountered severe underground pressures. The crisis was further complicated when the mud man, a contractor, fouled up the weight of the mud, and the drilling fluid was too light to counteract the formation pressure. There were several tense hours while a gas bubble was circulated up and safely flared. By the time the nerve-racking ordeal was over, Leslie was exhausted and edgy.

It was very late in the evening when Steve arrived at the geologist's shack and found Leslie still hunched over her work counter, her face pale and drawn.

"I thought I told you to go to bed," he said quietly, removing his parka and boots.

Leslie shrugged wearily as she slipped down from the stool and came toward him. "I just had a couple of samples to log, that's all. Would you like a coffee?"

He took her face in his hands and tipped her head back so he could study her. "No, I don't want a coffee, and neither do you. You're going straight to bed before you drop in your tracks." He combed his fingers slowly through her hair, then kissed her tenderly on the forehead. "Go on, Les—off you go. I'll shut off the lights and lock up for you."

Slipping her arms around his waist, she rested her head on his chest and blinked back the tears of weariness that were burning her eyes. Just this once she wished he could stay, that she could seclude herself in the insulating safety and comfort of his arms.

Steve hooked his knuckles under her chin and lifted her face. Their eyes met and held, his steady gaze penetrating the barrier of her silence.

There was a very husky tremor in his voice when he murmured, "Go on—get into bed, and I'll be there in a minute."

When Steve finally appeared at the bedroom door, Leslie was sitting in the middle of the bed brushing her hair, unaware that he stood silently watching her. She had on a charming old-fashioned nightgown that was delicately patterned with dainty pink rosebuds, the collar, cuffs and yoke liberally trimmed with lace. She looked very young, very innocent, and so very fragile.

He breathed her name and she turned to face him. A heady excitement percolated through her as she stared at him, her wide dark eyes revealing her innermost emotions.

He had taken a shower, and his long, powerful naked body gleamed bronze in the soft light, the beads of water on his shoulders glimmering like jewels. There was a charged enchantment radiating between them, and their surroundings seemed to fade away into nothingness, leaving only the two of them caught in a web of magic.

Slowly he came toward her, his eyes never leaving hers as he took the brush from her nerveless fingers and tossed it on the floor.

Sitting down on the edge of the bed, he began undoing the buttons at her throat, his touch like a current of electricity, sensitizing her, arousing her.

Leslie closed her eyes, her breathing suddenly labored as she tired to draw air past the golden heaviness that was unfolding in her chest. His hands were tender, awakening, as he slipped them up her body, stripping the garment from her. A low moan was wrung from her, and she swayed toward him as he gently cupped her breasts in his hands.

"Look at me, Leslie," he whispered huskily. Taking a deep shaky breath, she opened her eyes. Immediately the fever that she witnessed in his gaze invaded her body. He eased over on the bed until his back was firmly propped against the pile of pillows, his legs stretched out before him. The muscles across his shoulders and chest rippled as he grasped her and lifted her on top of him, her legs straddling his. The profound intimacy of the embrace sent desire coursing through her like hot liquid, dissolving her thoughts, her strength, her will, paralyzing her with a need so fierce that she was helpless against it.

She raked her fingers roughly through his thick hair and clutched his head against her as his warm moist mouth captured her breast. An ache grew deep within her, throbbing through her with an erotic pulse.

Her hands became urgent as she caressed his shoulders, his back, her body moving sensuously against his as he continued to torment her.

A spasm shot through her as he slowly entered her and a feeling of frantic helplessness filled her when he grasped her hips, preventing her from moving to the turbulent tempo that was pounding through her blood.

His arm came around her and held her immobile as he pressed her head down, his lips tantalizingly light against hers. "We have the whole night, love—the whole night," he whispered roughly.

Her arms tightened around him, her voice tremulous with suppressed passion as she murmured against his lips. "I don't think I'll last the whole night."

He slid his mouth down her neck, his tongue leaving an agonizing trail against her heated skin. "I'm going to make love to you until neither of us can stand it any longer."

His words were like a spark in dry tinder, and she was caught in the blaze. She melted against him, her body twisting seductively as she settled her weight on top of his.

She felt him tremble as he crushed her against him, his voice low and ragged. "Oh, Leslie, Leslie—you don't know how I want you." He covered her mouth with a flaming hungry kiss that engulfed her with an ardent obsession, fusing their bodies together in its white-hot heat.

It was a long time later that they lay together, their passion spent, the embers of contentment glowing within them. Leslie was still sprawled on top of Steve, their arms around each other, their legs intertwined.

He slipped his hands up her back, pressing her closer against him as he sighed, "It's going to be so good to get away from here for a while. I'm counting the hours until we leave for Christmas. We both need some time together without trying to maintain a distance all the time."

The qualms about meeting his family assailed Leslie, and she tensed against the apprehension that chilled her.

Steve caught her shoulders and eased her away from him, his eyes questioning as he looked up at her. "You aren't worrying about that, are you?"

As usual, his perceptiveness caught her off guard and Leslie lowered her eyes as she tried to think of a way to evade his question.

He spanned her jaw with his hand and lifted her face. "What's the matter, Les? I want you to tell me."

She made a disconcerted little grimace as she looked at him with solemn eyes. "I know it sounds totally ridiculous, but I'm scared stiff to meet your family. It's so important that they like me, and I know I'll be struck dumb with shyness."

"So, what's wrong with being shy?"

"Nothing, I suppose. It's just that . . . ."

Steve raised his head and kissed her parted lips, then smiled up at her, his eyes dancing. "First of all, my sweet, it's not one damned bit important if my family likes you or not. What *is* important is that I like you." His own smile broadened as he saw the beginning of a grin tugging at Leslie's mouth. "Furthermore, I think I should give you a preview of what's happening at home right now. My mother is in a fluster about your coming, worried silly that everyone will act like uncivilized barbarians while you're there. She will have scoured the house from stem to stern and baked everything imaginable, hoping that she'll have prepared at least one thing that's your favorite. Then there's the trauma of deciding whether you'll be more comfortable upstairs in Donna's old room, or in the guest room on the main floor."

A sparkle of amusement had been growing in Leslie's eyes at Steve's account, and her fears fell away as laughter bubbled up. "I think you're making this up, Steve McRory!"

He grinned. "It's the truth—every word."

"Are you sure?"

"Positive. Would I lie to you?"

"I don't know. Would you?"

"Never." The humorous gleam in his eyes softened into a warm irresistible look that made Leslie weak inside. "And here's another little-known truth for you." He laid his hand on her cheek, his touch caressing. "Do you know that I've discovered I have a definite weakness for dimples? Every time you smile at me, I want to drag you off and kiss you senseless."

A blush colored Leslie's cheeks. Steve laughed softly as he wrapped his arms around her and held her close. She glanced down at him; then with an impish challenge that could not be misconstrued, she gave him a slow provocative smile that deliberately flaunted her dimples.

Steve's expression changed abruptly, and the sparkling blue of his eyes changed to a smokey gray as he stared at her. Leslie's breathing became erratic when he caught the back of her head and gave her a deep searching kiss.

Leslie clung to him, her body infused by a tingling weightlessness as she became acutely aware of the virile masculine body beneath hers. A shiver trembled through her as the potency of his kiss kindled a heated response within her.

With a muffled oath, Steve pulled his head away and pressed her face roughly against his neck. "Oh, Les—you do drive me crazy. I don't know how in hell I'm going to keep my hands off you when we're at home."

Leslie hadn't even considered that aspect, and sighing softly, she raised her head and gazed down at him. "I hadn't even thought of that."

He smiled wryly, his eyes filled with regret. "But you do understand why, don't you?"

She ran her fingers through the thick matting of hair on his chest, then slipped her hand along his neck. Her eyes were solemn as she nodded. "We'll be in your parents' home, and we have their values to respect. And then there's your kid sister...we'll be setting an example for her."

He sighed as he nestled her against him, and buried his hand in her hair. "That's right. So for heaven's sake, don't give me any kind of encouragement. It's going to be tough enough as it is."

"I don't think I'm going to be very good at this, Steve—having to do one thing when I want to do the exact opposite."

He laughed then, his voice rich with amusement. "I do believe, Leslie Kairns, that I detect a hint of rebellion in that statement." He stroked her head, then whispered huskily in her ear, "But it does do wonders for my male ego to know that you aren't exactly reluctant to come to my bed."

Leslie shivered, but not from cold, and her body was infused with a familiar warmth as she felt his arousal beneath her.

"I love you, Steve...so much," she whispered brokenly.

His eyes were smoldering as he turned her face so he could look at her. "It seems like such an incredible miracle that you do. I can't quite believe it." He claimed her mouth with a kiss that was searing in its intensity, and Leslie responded—but not before the cold reality of her deception focused in her mind. Her passion was fed by her fear.

Please believe it, she pleaded silently as she moved against him. *When you find out the truth about me, please believe that I love you, above all else.*

CHAPTER FOURTEEN

LESLIE STOOD BEFORE THE WINDOW in her lab, a cup of steaming coffee in her hand, surveying the rig site. There had been several heavy snowfalls over Christmas, and now enormous mountains of dirt-pocked snow were piled along the boundaries of the lease. A thick sparkling crust of hoarfrost covered everything, and the brilliant sunlight fired the crystals with icy fire. It was so beautiful.

She rested her head pensively against the frame of the window, her eyes suddenly blind to the outside world. She was feeling oddly disjointed this morning.

On the one hand, she was really glad to be back at Redwillow, back in the swing of things. But on the other, she was feeling despondent that her delightful carefree interlude with Steve was over.

The ten days she'd spent at the McRory ranch had been fantastic. Never had she experienced such warmth, such complete happiness in her whole life.

They had arrived on the Sunday before Christmas, and Leslie had been petrified when she was unexpectedly confronted with Steve's entire family— grandparents, parents, brothers, sisters, nieces and nephews.

Her knees had wobbled uncontrollably, and there was a quaver in her voice when Steve introduced her to everyone. The warm security of his arm around her shoulders insulated her from the acute terror she expected to feel, however.

By the time they sat down for Sunday dinner, Leslie was feeling a little less timid, but her self-confidence was still very shaky. Then two things happened that swept away her shyness.

One of Steve's nephews was a handsome little three year old. Jeff was very tired and cranky during dinner, and absolutely nothing his mother did could pacify him. With exasperated weariness, Donna finally lifted her son out of his high chair and turned him loose in the hope that he would find something to amuse himself with. But Jeff wasn't satisfied with that, either. He stood at the fringe of the group, a sullen look on his face as he glowered at everyone.

No one else took much notice of the sulky little boy, but Leslie's heart went out to him. Quietly and unobtrusively, she set about to charm the little fellow out of his dark mood, and it didn't take her long to worm a reluctant smile out of him. Step by step he edged closer to her. When Leslie motioned to him, Jeff hesitated only a second before he came to her and willingly scrambled onto her lap.

No one else was aware of the little byplay except Steve, and he had a warm knowing grin on his face as Leslie cuddled the little boy against her.

He leaned over and whispered in her ear, "It's a good thing he's too young to appreciate *all* your charms, Leslie Kairns."

Leslie blushed and tried to smother a smile. She glanced up to find Steve's father, Hal McRory, watching them, a broad grin on his face.

"You've a bad pair there, Leslie," drawled the rancher. "Steve and Jeff are both bullheaded and inclined to want their own way. I hope you can manage the two of them."

Without thinking, Leslie responded, "I think I can."

Hal laughed heartily and nodded his head. "Yes, I think you can." There was such a wealth of amusement and approval in his voice that Leslie suddenly felt very much at ease, even though she was embarrassed.

The other incident happened a short time later. Steve's mother, Doris, had listed off a selection of pies that she had prepared for dessert. One of them was pecan—and pecan pie was Leslie's absolute favorite. When she stated her preference, everyone at the table could tell by her tone of voice that Doris had indeed made a hit. The delighted smile on the woman's face as she handed Leslie a large helping confirmed Steve's prediction. Leslie had a terrible time to keep from laughing when she glanced at him and saw the wicked sparkle in his eyes. So he had been telling the truth.

Steve read her thoughts and gave her a look that said clearly, "See, I told you so."

The holidays had been wonderful from then on....

Sighing, Leslie straightened up and took a sip of her coffee. Yes, she was really sorry the holidays were over, but at least Steve was here with her.

She combed her hand through her hair, a worried look on her face. It would be so perfect...if only this deception over Kaidon was out in the open. Damn!

She and Steve had decided not to set a date for their wedding until they knew the outcome at Redwillow, and Leslie was foolishly hoping some miracle would happen that would solve all her problems. The thought of losing Steve was too awful to contemplate.

With another deep sigh, she turned from the window and walked across the room. Setting her cup on the counter, she glanced at her watch, then picked up her jacket. Steve would be back from breakfast by now, and after all her dismal thoughts, she needed the reassurance of his warm welcoming smile.

When she entered his office a minute later, however, she felt as though she had walked off a cliff into thin air. A horrible feeling of vertigo swam over her as she stared dumbly at the scene before her.

Gordon Donner, her partner from Kaidon Industries, was sitting on the sofa across from Steve's desk, puffing on a cigar, his bald head shining like a smooth melon beneath the glare of the light.

No! It couldn't be. But it was.

By a supreme effort of self-discipline, Leslie rigidly braced her weak sagging body. Somehow she managed to compose her face before Steve realized what an awful shock she had just received.

Both men looked up as she closed the door. Steve smiled, his eyes lighting up with love when he saw her. "Good morning, Leslie. I didn't expect to see you for at least two hours."

She smiled back at him, and for an instant, as their eyes locked with a silent intimate message, she forgot the crisis at hand. He could turn her to putty with one glance.

She lowered her eyes as she felt a blush color her cheeks. "Good morning."

Gordon stood up and Steve introduced him. "Leslie, I'd like you to meet Gordon Donner, president and chief executive officer of Kaidon Industries. Kaidon is the company that has entered into an exploration agreement with us for Redwillow. Gordon, this is Leslie Kairns, our project geologist. It was she who initially identified Redwillow as having the potential of a major gas field."

Gordon's face was perfectly calm, but his eyes were sparkling with a devilish glitter as he took Leslie's outstretched hand. "Well, well, I must admit I didn't expect the geologist to be a charming young lady, Miss Kairns. Steve's told me a great deal about his fantastic geologist, but I must apologize, I was expecting a man."

The lies you tell, she thought, then laughed, partly out of sheer relief and partly out of genuine amusement. Here she was, being introduced to her own business partner. And there was Gordon, acting like he had never seen her before in his life. He was being very cautious about protecting her identity, and she loved him for it. Her secret was safe—for the time being.

"I think Steve deliberately avoids making any reference to my gender. He seems to take a fiendish delight in springing me on the unsuspecting."

The gleam in Gordon's eyes intensified. "Yes, my dear, I can understand his delight—you certainly are unexpected. But that may backfire on him someday, mighten it?"

Leslie's eyes widened with alarm. Would Steve catch the subtle innuendo in Gordon's remark?

She let out her breath in a low controlled sigh when Steve laughed, "It has already, Gordon. Believe me, it has already!" He was looking at Leslie with an eloquently suggestive stare.

After a breathless moment of eye-to-eye contact, she lowered her own eyes shyly. The color in her cheeks deepened as he laughed softly. He could rattle her so easily!

Later in the day, Leslie found out that Steve had invited Gordon to Redwillow to see the Ramco operation firsthand. Leslie gave a silent heartfelt thanks for Ted's absence. When he returned from his time off, she hoped Gordon would be gone. Separately they were bad enough, but together, the chances of a slip were multiplied. The two men had known each other for such a long time that one of them would be bound to make an innocent slip, exposing their comfortable relationship. It would simply be too big a risk.

John McRory arrived in Redwillow the following evening, and he, Gordon and Steve spent the best part of the next day closeted in Steve's trailer.

That afternoon Frank Logan and Leslie went over to the camp for a coffee. They were sitting in the kitchen, indulging in Essie's fresh cinnamon buns when Leslie laughingly suggested that John, Steve and Gordon were probably planning a takeover of one of the major oil companies.

Frank's voice was clipped with puzzled amazement as he reached for another roll. "Didn't Steve tell you about what happened while you were gone?"

"He said that there were some problems, but that you had them under control. What did happen?"

"Well, let's see now—I'll have to think on it to get it in the right order. First of all a new mud man showed up here, one I ain't ever seen before. Never thought much about it—these contract guys are always changin'. Anyhow, we lost circulation right after. I was madder 'n hell, but that ain't uncommon—mudmen can screw up the mud without even tryin'. Most of the time we're better off if they stay in camp and play gin rummy. Let the derrickman look after the mud."

Frank stuffed half a roll into his mouth, and Leslie could have screamed in frustration. But she managed to keep quiet as she waited for him to wash it down with a gulp of coffee. "What happened next?"

"Well, we had to suspend drillin' and start weightin' up the mud, addin' barite until we finally got circulation back. Could've been dangerous.

"That was the first thing, but I didn't get suspicious until a bunch of the hands went into town for a few beers one night. A couple of gents came over to the table and started askin' them a bunch of nosey questions. How deep was the hole, what formation we was in—stuff like that. Course, the rig hands don't know a hell of a lot about what's goin' on, except that it's bloody cold work and they get fed three times a day...."

"What about the two men in the bar?" It was a blatant attempt to get him back on track.

"Oh, yeah. Well, one of these gents told the crew they were looking for experienced rig hands, and they offered them wages that was just plain ridiculous, they was so high. The hands told me—'n I straightened 'em out on *that*." Frank stuffed the rest of the roll into his mouth, and Leslie had to clench her hands into fists to keep from pounding him. She gritted her teeth together as he reached for another roll.

Suddenly he grinned a little sheepishly. "I guess I'm kinda prolongin' the agony, ain't I?"

Leslie felt the exasperation dissolve in her and she laughed. "You certainly are. Here I am, hanging on to the edge of my seat, and you keep eating those damned cinnamon buns!"

"Good, ain't they?"

"Frank—!" It was a suppressed squeal of irritation.

He cast a wistful look at the tray of rolls, then heaved a resigned sigh. "Well, I figured somethin' was up, so I started keepin' a close eye on things. There used to be a lot of dirty dealings in the oil patch, and I figured somethin' pretty dirty was cookin' here. Real late one night I caught two scouts—they turned out to be the same two from the bar—snoopin' around under the shale shaker, tryin' to catch a sample. Mark was with me and we hung a good lickin' on 'em and run 'em off."

Leslie burst out laughing. Mark was about six foot four, and two hundred and some pounds of solid muscle; Frank was as tough and as strong as drill pipe. If he said a "good lickin'," then he meant a "good lickin'."

The amusement in Leslie's eyes died abruptly, and a very familiar uneasiness climbed up her spine with icy fingers. Luther was up to his old tricks. She stared at her coffee cup, her mind in such a turmoil that she never even noticed as Frank ate two more cinnamon buns.

When she finally looked at him, her face was very grave. "Have there been any other incidents?"

"Nope. We got a couple of extra men in to patrol. I imagine that Steve and John and that Donner gent are tryin' to figure out whose behind it."

No, they aren't, thought Leslie, *because they already know.* What they were trying to figure out was how they were going to stop him. Her uneasiness turned to dread. She knew how, but there would be an element of risk for her.

By the time she returned to the lease, she had decided what she was going to do. She was sticking her neck out, but she had no other choice. Gordon wouldn't do it unless the suggestion came from her.

With her stomach in a knot, she walked over to Steve's trailer and went in. Gordon was seated at one end of the sofa and John McRory at the other, his arms folded across his chest.

Steve was sitting at his desk, his hands clasped behind his head. He smiled at Leslie. "Hi. Where have you been—over to the kitchen pigging out on Essie's cinnamon buns?"

For an instant Leslie looked like a small child who'd been caught red-handed, then she grinned ruefully. "I hate it when you do that, Steve McRory!"

He laughed, then gave her a menacing look. "At least you could have been decent about it and brought us some."

Taking off her jacket, she sat down in the chair by his desk and stretched out her legs, her smile one of unmerciful satisfaction. "I *would* have, but Frank ate them all."

John grinned and shook his head. "If Frank

wasn't the best tool push in the country, I'd run him off for that!''

Leslie smiled faded. When she looked at Steve her face was solemn, her voice quiet. "Frank was in a talkative mood. He told me what happened over Christmas."

Steve sighed and ran his hands through his hair. "I hoped you wouldn't find out about that. It isn't your concern."

"It is my concern." Leslie was aware that Gordon's eyes were suddenly riveted on her with a guarded alertness, but she continued in a steady voice. "It's one of Luther Denver's contrivances, and we all know it. It's obvious that he doesn't know Kaidon Industries is supporting the program financially, and he's still attempting to box you in a corner. He would do anything to get his hands on some land in Redwillow, including sabotage."

John stood up and went to the window. "We realize that, Leslie. We just aren't too sure what's the best way to stop him."

Leslie looked intently at Gordon, her eyes questioning. He gave her an imperceptible nod and she inhaled slowly. "If he knew Ramco had very secure financial backing, he'd realize his scheme is a futile one."

There was a flash of admiration in Gordon's eyes as he laced his fingers across his chest and nodded his head. "You're right, Leslie—I'm sure of it. And I would be more than willing to publicly acknowledge Kaidon's investment in Redwillow."

Steve shook his head, his face concerned. "I'd rather not publicize it, Gordon. If the size of this venture ever hit the papers, it would create a rash of speculation in the Grande Prairie area. People would naturally start investing in businesses and land in the hope that the area would boom. If the basin is productive, there would be no damage done. But if it's nonproductive, they could lose their life savings.''

Gordon rubbed his nose and pursed his lips. ''You have a good point, Steve.'' He was reflective for a moment, then said, ''Then I'll contact Mr. Denver personally. He certainly isn't going to make a public statement, especially when Denver Oil ignored the potential of Redwillow.''

Steve looked at John. ''What do you think?''

''I think it's our only recourse. We can't allow this to continue.''

Leslie knew he was thinking of Nora's death. She stared at her hands for a moment, then she glanced at Steve. ''There's one thing I don't understand. Why does Luther have such a grudge against Ramco? It seems like he won't be satisfied until he destroys the company. What drives him—why is he so vindictive?''

John McRory exchanged an intent look with Gordon Donner, and Leslie experienced a stab of uneasiness when neither of them would meet her questioning gaze. John turned and stared out the window again, his bearing tense. Obviously both men were avoiding her question.

Steve seemed to be unaware of the stifled atmosphere as he rubbed the back of his neck wearily. ''There is a vendetta, Leslie—over something that happened years ago.''

She tried to ignore the uncomfortable edginess that

was nagging at her as her attention focused on Steve. "What happened?"

He sighed and rocked back in his chair, balancing his weight on the two hind legs as he once again laced his hands behind his head. "When Uncle John started Ramco, he had a partner by the name of L.J. Owens. Early in the developmental stage of the company, a wealthy industrialist was brought in as a financial backer for one of their larger projects. This fellow had a daughter who happened to be engaged to Luther Denver. To make a long story short, she jilted Luther, and she and L.J. planned to be married."

Leslie could feel the blood drain from her face as her stomach shrank and a cold feeling of foreboding settled upon her. Her eyes locked on Steve, her breathing shallow and rapid. "And . . . ?"

Steve reached forward and rested his arms on the desk, his head lowered as he abstractedly toyed with a magnetized pile of paper clips. "Unfortunately, L.J. was killed in an accident the week before he was to be married. There was a bad kick at one of the locations and the rig caught fire."

Leslie could hear the dull throb of her pulse as it echoed in her head, and it seemed like her voice was coming from a long way away. "Did Luther eventually marry this girl?"

Steve shrugged. "I have no idea. All I do know is that Luther has been trying to even the score ever since."

Leslie's lips were stiff, her body rigid as she turned toward John McRory. "John, did he . . . did he eventually marry the girl?"

John slowly turned to face her, his face very grave.

He stared at Leslie fixedly, then sighed heavily and reluctantly nodded his head. "Yes...yes, he did, Leslie."

Steve looked at Leslie, suddenly bewildered. "Les, what's wrong?"

Leslie was trembling violently, and she clenched her hands into white-knuckled fists to control their shaking as she whispered hoarsely, "L.J.'s name—what was his name, John?"

John looked at Gordon, his eyes bleak, then looked back at Leslie and answered with a gruff clipped voice. "Leslie Jordan Owens."

Leslie buried her face in her hands and moaned in anguish, "Oh, my God!"

Steve stared at her, then at John. Suddenly his face went white with incredulity as the facts began to register. His reaction was instantaneous. He sprang to his feet and threw the chair out of his path as he strode toward Leslie, pulling her rigid body into his arms. His eyes flashed blue fire as he cradled her protectively against him and pressed her stricken face against his chest.

His voice was like a rapier, piercing and edged with cold steel. "What in hell were you thinking of, John? She didn't know—my God, she didn't even know who her father was, and she had to find out like that! How bloody damned insensitive can you be? Why in hell didn't you tell me the whole story?"

Leslie was totally unaware of what was happening around her—she was oblivious to Steve's seething rage, to the distorted conversation that was echoing around her, to the worried looks that Gordon and John exchanged.

She had her eyes clenched shut, and she was frighteningly pale as she clamped her teeth together in an attempt to control the convulsive shaking that possessed her. She felt as if she was frozen. Her muscles were stiff and unresponsive, and she was cold, so cold.

Though her body was numbed by the awful shock, her mind was a jumble of frenzied thoughts. Her father...no wonder Luther had despised her! No wonder he was so ruthlessly determined to annihilate Ramco.

Eventually, through the confusion, a new terrifying realization dawned. The tragedy had come full circle. The grim history was being interwoven with the lives of father and daughter. In a way, in an indirect way, she had unwittingly inherited his place with Ramco. Her father....

She looked up, her eyes dark with shock. "Steve...."

"Shh." He eased her away from him and guided her over to the sofa, where he sat her down. "I'll be right back." His voice was gruff with concern as he touched her white face with his fingers.

It wasn't until he walked away from her that Leslie realized that, except for them, the office was empty. She huddled on the sofa, her face buried in her hands as the horrible reality of what she had just discovered kept churning around and around in her mind.

This explained everything—her mother's remoteness, her emotional fragility. It even explained the peculiar look that had flitted across Gordon's face when she told him about Ramco. It was so obvious that both he and John knew the whole story...but it was also obvious that Steve didn't.

"Leslie, can you sit up a bit?" She lifted her head as Steve slipped his arm around her shoulders. "I want you to drink some of this."

He held the glass to her lips and Leslie took a swallow, then grimaced with distaste. It was straight Scotch. She gulped down the contents of the glass, then shuddered. She hated Scotch.

She tried to smile at Steve. "I thought this was supposed to be a dry camp," she whispered weakly.

His smile didn't reach his eyes as he sat down beside her. "Strictly medicinal." He gathered her into his arms and lay down on the sofa, her trembling form nestled protectively against his. The heat from his body eventually penetrated the iciness that encased her, and she was finally able to relax. The liquor acted as a sedative, and her body seemed uncommonly heavy as she shifted slightly so she could look at Steve's face.

She stared at him, her pupils dilated, her eyes dulled with shock, her voice husky with an inner anguish. "Don't be angry," she whispered.

His arms tightened around her; then he tenderly smoothed his hand across her cheek and cradled her head against his shoulder. "I can't help being angry. That was one hell of a cruel way for you to find out."

She took a deep shaky breath and closed her eyes. "Not that.... Don't be angry because I didn't tell you Luther was my stepfather."

He had been stroking her hair, but abruptly he stopped, and Leslie felt him stiffen. That fact had obviously not registered before.

The tone of his voice frightened her. "Why didn't you tell me?"

Her mouth was so dry that she had to swallow several times before she could answer him. "I didn't think you'd have anything to do with me if you knew. I was so afraid that you would mistrust me and question my motives if you found out. In the very beginning I didn't want you to know because it might jeopardize the project. Then, later, I thought you might loathe me because of it."

Steve didn't reply for a long time and Leslie knew he was seriously considering what she had said. Finally he kissed her forehead softly and his embrace tightened. "If I had found out right away, I probably would have been incredibly suspicious." He kissed her again, his voice a gentle reprimand. "But did you think that I valued you so little that I wouldn't understand?"

Leslie pressed her face against him as she whispered, "I didn't know what you'd think. What Luther had done was so unforgivable."

Laying his hand on her head, he buried his fingers in her hair. He was silent for a moment, but when he finally spoke there was an edge to his voice that was slicing. "To think you had to survive in an environment like that incenses me. I could break his neck...."

Her arms tightened around him convulsively, and she pressed her face against his shoulder. "Don't, Steve. It doesn't matter now."

"It *does* matter—he's victimized you all your life and you didn't even know why."

Leslie raised herself on one elbow, then took his rigid face in her hands, her voice soft. "He can't hurt me anymore. He can only hurt me through you—by making you doubt me."

Steve stared at her briefly; then his face relaxed and became immeasurably tender. "I care too much about you to ever hurt you intentionally, Leslie. You are the most incredible thing that's ever happened to me." Her eyes filled with tears and his arms tightened around her fiercely, his voice resolute and sure as he murmured gruffly, "I love you so much."

Their solitude was marred by the crunch of footsteps outside the trailer. "Damn it," muttered Steve, kissing her softly before he lifted her into a sitting position. He was standing up when the knock sounded at the door.

It was John. "Frank wants you over at the rig. They're having trouble with the mud pumps."

Steve exhaled sharply, then glanced at Leslie, his eyes intense with regret. He snatched up his parka and slipped it on, then picked up his hard hat. "I won't be long, Les."

She managed to smile at him before he went out the door.

John stared out the window, watching his nephew walk across the lease. He appeared to be preoccupied by thoughts that concerned him deeply, however. Leslie wondered what he was thinking about.

She brushed back the lock of hair that was clinging to her face and tipped her head back slowly. She was so dizzy.

John turned and focused his attention on her. "You look a little out of it. What did Steve give you, anyway?"

"Medicinal Scotch," she retorted dryly.

He smiled. "I'm sure it was." He stretched out on a chair, then folded his arms across his chest.

Leslie raked her fingers through her hair, her eyes somberly reflective as she stared into space. A singsong verse from her childhood popped into her mind: "A time has come, the walrus said, to talk of many things." But the talk would not be "of shoes and ships and sealing wax, of cabbages and kings." She opened her eyes and looked at John, her voice low with resignation. "So. . .it's time to talk."

John nodded, his face solemn. "Yes, I guess it is."

She closed her eyes briefly as a feeling of total hopelessness settled upon her. This was the beginning of the end. Then she rubbed her forehead with a defeated gesture. "You knew my grandfather?"

John gazed at her for a moment, then sighed and nodded his head. "Yes, I did. It was actually through your father that I met him."

"When did you realize who I was?"

He leaned back in the chair and stretched his legs out in front of him. "Right from the beginning. I had a hunch when Steve told me about you on the phone before I came to Calgary, but I wanted to find out for sure before I said anything to him. I don't know if you remember, but Ted called you 'Leslie Jordan Kairns' when he caught you standing on the map. I knew then, but I must admit I got one hell of a shock when I saw you. You resemble your father very much, Leslie—it's uncanny."

"Why didn't you tell Steve then?"

"I probably would have if you hadn't been so much your father's daughter. When I started questioning you about Redwillow, it was as though I was watching him in action. You have so many of the same mannerisms—the way you lift your chin when you're being pressured, the way you chew your bottom lip when you're thinking about something. I felt I owed you a chance to prove yourself. Since I knew who you were, and your relationship to Luther, there would be little risk in playing a waiting game.''

"Why didn't you confront me?"

"I intended to. But when Steve phoned and told me that Kaidon Industries had contacted him about financing the exploration program here, I realized you were depending on your identity remaining a secret. After Steve left Vancouver, I confronted Gordon and asked him what in hell was going on. He leveled with me. And when I realized how you felt about Steve, I decided it would be best if I kept my nose out of it.''

Leslie's face was a study of misery as she mulled over everything that John had told her. When she finally spoke, her voice was devoid of expression. "Does Ted know the whole story?"

John shook his head. "The only one who knew outside the family was Gordon Donner.''

Leslie closed her eyes. Her game was over. Her anonymity was no more.

"Why didn't you tell Steve at the beginning, Leslie? What made you decide to keep your identity a secret?''

She made a helpless gesture with her hands as she looked at him. "When Ted first went to Ramco about Redwillow, I was sure that Steve would be suspicious about the scheme if he knew I was Luther Denver's stepdaughter.''

John frowned as he considered her explanation, then nodded his head slowly. "Under the circumstances, you were probably assuming correctly." He pursed his lips, and his brow creased with consternation. "Did you know what had happened in South America then?"

"No, Ted and I didn't find out about that until a little later—after Steve decided that Redwillow had potential. After he told me the whole horrible story, I was determined that he wouldn't find out about Luther until my theory was proven."

"Why didn't you tell him who your grandfather was?"

"It wasn't pertinent at the time. My wealth had nothing to do with my being involved at Redwillow."

"Until we had our financial backing yanked out from under us."

Leslie rubbed her forehead again with a gesture of weary dejection. "That's right. I couldn't just sit there and watch the program collapse because of a lack of money."

A heavy silence filled the room, permeated only by the monotonous drumming of the rig. Leslie thought about Steve, and how he was going to react when he heard the whole story. She had no choice—she had to tell him now. That was the grim unalterable reality.

"You love my nephew very much, don't you?"

The pain was nearly intolerable as she whispered, "So very much."

John stood up and leaned on the desk, not facing Leslie. "You're going to have to tell him the truth about you and Kaidon. He's bound to find out sooner or later. Too many people know now, and someone will make a slip...and Steve isn't stupid.

He's apt to put the whole story together himself if he ever stops to think about it.''

"I know I have to tell him, but I also know how he's going to react.''

John turned to face her, his features creased into a perplexed frown. "He's going to be furious, all right, but perhaps he'll come around.''

Leslie closed her eyes against the hollow feeling of impending doom. She knew that Steve would be furious, but she had no illusions about what the outcome would be. He would be angry about the deception, true. But the insurmountable barrier was the fact that Kaidon, and more specifically, Leslie Kairns, was supporting Ramco's extensive drilling program with millions of dollars. Steve's pride and independence would not permit him to accept that kind of assistance from his future wife. He would avoid her like poison after he found out. And now she was going to have to tell him.

"You have every right to be involved with Ramco, Leslie. It was your father's driving energy that established this company in the first place. This was your birthright, your legacy, right from the beginning.''

Leslie opened her eyes and looked at John, her eyes dark with wretchedness. "Steve could accept that line of thought, providing the Kairnses' millions hadn't floated this operation. As Ted said when he found out what I had done, 'He's going to feel like you bought him, Leslie'—and I know it's true. He'll never forgive me for deceiving him.''

John didn't argue. He couldn't; what Leslie said was the truth. He shook his head sadly. It was too damned bad.

Fate had dealt her a nasty hand: a father who had died before he could protect his child with the honor of his name; a stepfather who despised her because she was the living proof of his wife's love for another man. Then her grandfather, the only member of the family she was close to in her life, had died, leaving her an immense fortune that was going to bring her nothing but heartache and loneliness. He'd felt sick when Gordon Donner had told him the whole story.

He studied Leslie as she sat on the sofa, staring blindly at her clenched hands. She certainly wasn't helpless, but she was so very vulnerable. Her obscurity would be blown to bits, and she would suffer the exposure of harsh and brutal publicity. For someone as shy as she was, that would be an agonizing ordeal. She wouldn't be able to breathe without the fact being documented by the press. Yes, the media would have a field day with her—young, enchanting, single...and rich. He smiled wryly. Rich was a weak word to describe her immense wealth. She would definitely be marketable news, and Leslie Jordan Kairns would shrink away from it all, just as some blossoms fold and close at darkness.

She would build a wall, a fortification around herself. John could see her eventually secluding herself away in some remote part of the world, her privacy protected by high fences, guard dogs and security police. And she would wither up and die.

John turned and stared out the window, his face grim. Steve would be so enraged that he would never consider this aspect of Leslie's life. He would walk out on her and leave her to the wolves.

Yet John couldn't condemn Steve, either. Had he,

John McRory, been faced with the same circumstances when he was thirty-two years old, he would have felt exactly the same way—that he had been betrayed. But he had suffered a terrible loss when Nora died, and the experience had given him a different perspective on life. Some things, like money, didn't really matter a bit if you had to live your life alone.

He rubbed his hand wearily across his face and sighed. It was one hell of a mess, and he didn't know if he could do anything to help sort it out.

He turned and walked over to the sofa, then sat down beside Leslie and took her cold hands in his. "You don't have to tell him immediately, Leslie."

She looked at him and nodded her head weakly. "Yes, I do. He leaves on Thursday for the Independent Petroleum Association of Canada convention. I'll have to tell him before he goes. Luther might be there, and if he ever suspected that Steve knows nothing about grandfather or about my ties with him, he would use that knowledge—you know he would. There's always the possibility that he may have pieced the truth together by now—Luther, I mean. You can never underestimate a man like him. We're being watched, and since the program is obviously continuing, he has to be suspicious about the financial backing."

John studied Leslie, his eyes narrowed with concentration. "That IPAC convention—that's not until the day after tomorrow. I could make arrangements to go in Steve's place."

Leslie smiled wanly as she withdrew her hands. "Thank you, John, but you know I can't keep putting it off. I have to tell him."

"I'm so sorry about this, Leslie."

Her voice was tinged with bitterness. "So am I."

What could he say? She had said it all.

"What was he like... my father?"

He smiled warmly as he caught her under the chin. "You are so much like him—in the way you think, the way you do things. He was a geologist, too, and loved his work as much as you do. And then there's the physical resemblance—your coloring, your eyes, the same smile. He'd be so proud of you, Leslie. As proud as anything, and you would have been proud of him...."

As John told her about his old friend, some of the pain in Leslie eased a little. Her father was no longer a faceless question mark, but a living breathing human being. If it hadn't been for her consuming dread about facing Steve, she would have found solace and consolation from her newfound knowledge. At least she was no longer a fatherless child. It was a heartbreaking trade-off, she thought dully. She was gaining the reality of her dead father and losing the man she loved.

She glanced up and her eyes darkened. Steve was standing in the doorway, his somber gaze fixed on her with a look that spoke of his very real concern. She shivered. She didn't know how she would survive without him beside her.

He moved across the room and crouched down in front of her, tenderly taking her pinched face in his hands. John stood up and murmured something, then left them alone.

Steve studied her, his eyes filled with anxiety.

Then, with a soft curse, he gathered her up in his arms and cradled her against him. He eased her down on the sofa beside him.

Leslie closed her eyes, wrapping her arms around him with a desperate terrified strength that transmitted her despair. The time for her and Steve was running out.

His arms tightened around her protectively. "What is it, little one? You're trembling and you looked so frightened."

Her breath caught on a stifled sob as she whispered brokenly. "Oh, Steve—I need you so."

"Leslie, what's wrong?" Concern sharpened his voice, and he tried to ease her away from him.

"Just hold me, Steve, hold me. Please... I need you so much and I'm so scared."

His arms tightened around her and she clung to him, hanging onto these last precious minutes. As she lay in Steve's secure embrace, she suddenly understood what breed of desperation had driven Nora to take her own life. That alternative felt far more tolerable than the tortured and empty life that faced Leslie. Numbness settled over her, and she felt like her soul was withering and dying within her. She could put if off no longer; the truth that would destroy must be told.

Without looking at Steve, she eased out of his arms and slipped off the sofa. He gazed at her questioningly, his face worried. She was deathly pale, and there was an agony of pain in her eyes that he'd never seen before.

"Leslie, for God's sake, what's wrong?"

She touched his lips with her trembling fingers.

"No, Steve, don't. I have something to tell you, and when I do, you're going to despise me."

She turned from him and moved to the window, her body stiffly erect. "But before I tell you the truth about myself, I want you to know that you are the most special, the most important person who will ever touch my life."

"Leslie...." He rose to his feet and started to come toward her.

"Please, Steve—don't touch me or I'll lose the will to do what I have to do. It's going to be the most difficult thing I've ever done." Then, with no excuses, no embellishments, she told him the whole story. She omitted nothing.

When she finished, there was a heavy frightening silence. Steve finally shattered it, his voice like brittle ice.

"Get out."

CHAPTER FIFTEEN

WHEN GORDON DONNER went into the geologist's shack the next morning, he was shocked by Leslie's appearance. She had dark hollows under her eyes, her face was stricken and pale, and there was a frightening set to her mouth. But what alarmed him more than anything was her eyes—there was no sparkle of life in them at all.

He hurried over to her and took her clammy hands in his. "Leslie, what happened?"

"I had to tell Steve everything, Gordon."

God, he thought, *her voice is the same as her eyes.* Out loud he said, "I see." He studied her for a moment, then released her hands and stuffed his in his pocket, sensing that she didn't want him to touch her. He took a slow measured breath before he spoke. "Under those circumstances, I think you'd better come back to Vancouver with me."

"Yes, I think so."

"The Lear jet is in Grande Prairie. I'll phone that Bob Jansen and have him pick us up in a helicopter. How soon can you be ready to go?"

"Now. My clothes are packed." She picked up a vial of rock cuttings and stared at it. "The financing stays in place, Gordon."

He rubbed his nose, then nodded. "Yes, of

course." He turned toward the door. "I'll have John make the necessary arrangements."

"You'd better tell him what happened. It could be awkward for him."

"Very well, if that's what you want."

Gordon shook his head as he went out the door. It was almost frightening. There wasn't a flicker of emotion in her eyes, or in her voice. He had been with Leslie after Mac had died, and she had been devastated by the loss—but nothing, nothing like this.

After Gordon left, Leslie set the vial back on the counter and walked stiffly over to the window. She folded her arms in front of her and stared across the lease to the rig. It was such a towering giant of a thing—mechanical slave to man, impaled on its massive substructure, its innards relentlessly drilling into the bowels of the earth, unthinking, unfeeling.... Leslie shivered and turned away from the window. Oh, God, how could she ever learn to stand it—this awful pain?

The door of the trailer was yanked open and Steve strode in, his face white with rage. He slammed the door behind him, then approached her with the menacing grace of a stalking cat.

His voice was an icy sneer. "So, Miss Kaidon Industries, I hear that you are planning to dump the whole project and go running off to Vancouver. It must be nice to be able to walk out on your responsibilities."

Leslie turned to face him squarely, her face a waxen mask, her body unnaturally stiff. "Kaidon is not withdrawing its financing, so the project is not in danger." Her hands gripped her forearms convulsively. "You told me to get out, so I'm getting out." For a brief moment, Leslie thought he was going to strike her.

He clenched and unclenched his hands, then snarled, "You used me...you used me to even your score with Luther." He gritted his teeth, his eyes narrow and threatening, his body rigid with barely controlled fury. "The minute you walk out of here, this joint venture with your company is finished, Miss Kairns, and we won't drill another inch. Since you're now a partner, you'd better damned well start acting like one. If Ramco has to sell off some of its acreage to cover its own financing, you know bloody well that Denver Oil is going to move in. Is that what you want, Miss Kairns?"

Nothing showed on the plastic facade of her face, but in her mind, there was a soul-shattering moan of protest. *Don't do this to me, Steve—don't do this.*

He grabbed her shoulders and shook her roughly. "Is that what you want?"

"No."

"Then," he seethed through clenched teeth, "you had better tell Gordon Donner you *won't* be going with him, because if you don't...."

He was blackmailing her in the most unforgivable way, but he wasn't finished with her yet. He stood glaring down at her, his hands on his hips. "Your father started this damned company—your grandfather financed it. Now you don't even have the guts to stick out one project."

If anything could have penetrated Leslie's numbness, that reference to her father and grandfather was it. A convulsive spasm bolted through her, and she turned away abruptly. There was a stifling silence and then she spoke, her lifeless voice only slightly uneven. "I'll stay."

Some of the edge was gone from Steve's anger, but his voice was still cold and harsh. "And you *will* stay, until I say you can go."

"Yes." Silently she was thinking, *until you have taken your pound of flesh.*

"Since you are now a partner in this venture, you'll attend the IPAC conference in Edmonton with me. We'll leave here Wednesday afternoon."

Leslie heard the door open behind her and she assumed it was Steve leaving. But it was Gordon.

"Leslie won't be returning to Vancouver with you, Gordon. She's going to be staying."

The businessman's eyes shifted from Steve's grim, unrelenting face to Leslie's rigid back. "Is that right, Leslie?"

"Yes."

Gordon pursed his lips, and his face creased with a worried frown. "Are you sure that's what you want?"

Leslie turned to face him. "Yes."

He glanced at Steve again, then walked over to Leslie and took her hands in his. "You know that Constance and I would love to have you any time you decide to come."

She forced a tight-lipped smile and nodded. "I know that." A cold chill feathered down Gordon's spine. Leslie had the exact same look on her face as Vivian Denver did. He had always thought that Leslie's mother was cold and dispassionate. Perhaps, unthinkingly and a little unkindly, he had misjudged the woman.

LESLIE SAT STARING OUT THE WINDOW of the plane with unseeing eyes. The last four days had seemed like an eerie suspended nightmare for her. Somehow she had managed to do her work with automated precision; somehow she'd maintained the tight control on her reactions. She'd been relieved that Ted had been sent to the east coast to do some troubleshooting for Ramco. If he'd arrived in camp and said one kind word to her, she knew she would have come apart.

Steve had flown to Calgary the same day Gordon had left Redwillow. Before he'd left, he had warned Leslie that if she tried to avoid the conference in Edmonton, he would come get her and drag her there by her hair if he had to. She didn't doubt him for a minute.

She leaned her head back against the headrest, then glanced at John McRory. He was sitting in the seat beside her, a sheaf of papers spread out on the top of his briefcase. He looked as exhausted as she felt. He had been very understanding—but then, he understood better than anyone how she was feeling. He never mentioned Steve, but frequently talked to her about her father. Leslie felt as though she had really come to know her dead parent, and that had provided her with some inner peace. John had given her a photo of him, and every time she looked at it she had the most peculiar feeling. Even she could see the remarkable resemblance.

John glanced at his watch, gathered together his

papers and, with a deep sigh, lifted the lid of his briefcase and slipped them inside. He snapped the locks closed, then slid the case under the seat in front of him.

He smiled ruefully at Leslie as he dropped his pen into the inside breast pocket of his suit jacket. "I'm afraid I haven't been very good company for you on this flight, Leslie."

She returned the smile. "You were excellent company, John. I was too tired to talk anyway."

"Yes, I know you were." He patted her hand. "I was wondering if you would do me the honor of having dinner with me this evening?"

"I'd like that . . . very much, thank you."

"Good." He glanced at his watch again. "I hope it doesn't take forever to arrange for the car rental."

It didn't, in fact, but getting to the hotel took a while. From the airport they had to drive into the center of the city, and traffic was exceptionally heavy. By the time they arrived at the Westin Hotel, Leslie was developing a throbbing headache. It was caused, she knew, from a combination of exhaustion, lack of food, and a buildup of anxiety. She felt somewhat more secure when she realized that John's room was across the hall from hers. She felt safe with John.

After sleeping soundly for nearly two hours, Leslie had a long shower. She felt obliged to take some pains with her makeup and hair, but she did it with little enthusiasm. She had just finished dressing when there was a knock at the door.

Without looking in the mirror, Leslie picked up her silver evening bag and went to answer it. She felt the blood drain from her face as a constricting band of tension squeezed her chest. It wasn't John. It was Steve.

He braced his arm against the doorframe as he silently studied her with narrowed eyes. Leslie felt like she had been frozen into immobility by his look, and she felt every muscle in her contract against the awful ache that suddenly encased her.

He looked so handsome—and so very remote. The awareness seemed to stretch between them like a silent scream, and Leslie felt her control falter. Those blue eyes that could be so warm with love and laughter were now ice cold with anger and distaste.

The door behind Steve opened, and Leslie felt a nearly hysterical sense of relief when John McRory stepped into the hallway. His voice was calm and assured. "Steve—I didn't know that you had arrived. Leslie and I were just going down to dinner." He smiled at Leslie as he adroitly maneuvered past his nephew and drew her into the corridor. "You look lovely, Leslie." He tucked her arm firmly through his and squeezed her hand reassuringly. Leslie was so grateful for his tactful intervention that she felt weak.

John nodded toward Steve. "Why don't you join us? You can bring me up to date on what's happening with our operating agreement on the east coast."

Please say no, she thought wildly. *Please say no.*

"Sounds like a good idea," said Steve as he fell into step with them.

The dinner wasn't the ordeal that she'd expected. After two goblets of very good wine, Leslie felt less jumpy, and she could tell by her inner warmth that the wine had put some color back into her cheeks.

John and Steve talked business, and that suited her perfectly. She found it interesting, and she didn't have to say anything.

It was about nine o'clock when they finally left the dining room. They were walking through the lobby toward the elevators when John and Steve paused to speak with an old acquaintance. Leslie wanted to avoid introductions and explanations, so she walked ahead a few paces, then stopped to read the notices on the bulletin board concerning the conference.

A cold shiver rippled down her spine and her skin shrank with revulsion as a voice, a very familiar, sneering voice snapped out behind her. "Well, I see little Leslie has finally had her professional coming out. How nice."

Leslie turned to face Luther Denver with an icy calmness. She suddenly realized that she was no longer afraid of this man. "Good evening, Luther. I didn't think snakes came out at night."

Her open disdain and her haughty bearing caught him completely off guard—but only for a moment.

"Well, well, the whimpering mouse has turned into a cat with claws. You surprise me...I didn't think you had it in you."

"You never had any idea what I was capable of, Luther. But then, you were never particularly astute at reading people."

Fury blazed in his eyes and he took a threatening step toward her, his voice shaking as he ground out, "There's a rumor that you threw the Kaidon fortune behind Ramco. Who were you buying, Leslie—the company or the man? I hear you and Steve McRory are an item."

Leslie shrank neither from him nor from his sneering comment, but determinedly held her ground. "The joint venture was indirectly arranged by you—did you know that, Luther? After you machinated a lack of financial confidence in Redwillow, I had no choice but to back them financially."

"But I'm certain Steve McRory was only too delighted to see all that money dumped into his project."

"He didn't even know. Steve McRory isn't the type of man anyone can buy—he isn't like you."

Luther's hand jerked at his side, and Leslie unconsciously braced herself for a blow, but he restrained himself. He was livid with rage, and his eyes bulged as he flexed his hand threateningly. "If you had swung Kaidon Industries behind Denver Oil.... You owed it to me—all that money—and you took it to Ramco."

It was then that Leslie realized how his irrational jealousy was like an insidious sickness within him. She stared at him scornfully. "Owed you, Luther? I owed you nothing. You despised my father, and you treated me like garbage because of it. If there's anybody I owe, its Ramco—especially after what you did to them in South America."

"You filthy little bitch!" He would have struck her then, but John McRory stepped in front of Leslie and grabbed Luther's arm. His face white with controlled fury, his voice slicing, John growled, "Touch her, Luther, and so help me, I'll kill you. It would give me supreme pleasure to break your goddamned neck."

Luther stared at John for a second, then he yanked his arm away, swearing violently as he turned and strode away.

Leslie started to shake, and for one awful second she thought her knees would collapse beneath her, but John slipped his arm around her waist. His face was still etched with anger, but his voice was gentle. "Come on, Leslie, I think both of us need a good stiff drink."

She glanced up at him, her face bloodless, her lips so stiff she could barely speak. "I think we do." She looked away, and her stomach plummeted as a sick feeling rose within her. Steve had obviously witnessed the whole ugly encounter, and the look on his face was savage. But strangely enough, she sensed that this time his white-hot rage was not directed at her. Without uttering a word he turned away and strode rapidly across the lobby toward the main doors.

Leslie tipped her head back and took a deep shaky breath. "How much did he hear?"

"Every word." Unexpectedly, John chuckled. "You pack a verbal wallop, my dear. It did my heart a world of good when you called him a snake."

Leslie had an uneasy feeling. "He'll try to even the score, John."

John grinned down at her, his eyes sparkling with amusement and admiration. "Perhaps, but he's an idiot if he tries to tangle with you, Leslie Jordan Kairns, and he probably knows it. If you wanted to, you could ruin him."

Leslie didn't say anything—she was feeling too apprehensive. Luther would attempt a retaliation; she knew it in her bones.

By the next morning, Leslie felt as though she had driven herself to the extreme limit. She had slept very little during the night. The incident with Luther had shaken her, adding to the already formidable pressure she was under. She desperately wanted to go back to Redwillow, but she was certain that Steve would never permit it. Somehow she had to find the energy and strength to get through the next two days. But she simply couldn't take much more.

She was in a banquet hall, seated between John and Steve, trying to concentrate on the speaker. But she had another blinding headache that was beginning to make her feel ill. She pressed her hands to her temples in an attempt to dull the pounding in her skull.

Steve leaned over, his voice indifferent. "Is something wrong?"

She looked at him, her eyes glassy. "I have a bad headache. Would you mind if I went up to my room?"

For an instant she thought he was going to ignore her request, but finally he nodded and swung his knees into the aisle so she could pass.

The banquet hall was on the second floor of the hotel, and as she walked across the large reception area toward the elevators, she heard someone yell behind her, "There she is!"

Suddenly she was surrounded by reporters shoving mikes in her face, and a claustrophobic panic gripped her as flashbulbs exploded around her, blinding her with sunburst brilliance.

"Miss Kairns, are you now prepared to take up the reins of Kaidon Industries—our source tells us that was Mac Kairns's intention."

"Miss Kairns, what exactly motivated your involvement with Ramco Exploration?"

"Miss Kairns, would you look this way and smile?"

"Miss Kairns, Miss Kairns, Miss Kairns," reverberated in her head like a burst of machine-gun fire, and her panic grew into paralyzing terror when she realized she was hemmed in, totally unable to escape.

Then Steve was beside her, his arm around her shoulders. With a seething oath he knocked the camera out of the hands of one photographer who was blocking their way and roughly pushed him aside. There was a confusion of shoving and a commotion of loud voices, then a respite of silence.

Leslie realized numbly that they were in an elevator. The door slid open, and a silent angry Steve caught her arm and propelled her swiftly down the corridor. He paused outside his door, and Leslie was jarred out of her numbness when she realized he was searching his pockets for his room key.

A new feeling of panic rose within her. She didn't dare go into that room with him. She was just too raw and exposed to cope with him alone.

She retrieved her key from her purse and quickly unlocked her own door. She never had the chance to shut him out, however. Steve pushed his way into the room behind her and quickly closed the door and set the dead bolt.

Leslie shivered when she heard loud voices approaching down the corridor. "Can they get in here?"

His voice wasn't unkind when he answered, "No, they can't get in here." Then she heard him mutter under his breath, "I'd like to see them try."

She collapsed into one of the easy chairs, her hands

clasped into white-knuckled fists as she made a conscious effort to stop shaking.

Steve walked over to the window and stood staring out, his hands jammed into his pockets. ''I'd like to know how in hell they found out.''

Taking a deep breath to try and calm herself, Leslie answered him, her voice wavering, ''It has all the markings of one of Luther's stunts. I expected him to retaliate—and he knows how I'd hate publicity.''

Steve turned around, his shoulders set with anger. ''Luther is turning into a monumental pain in the ass. I talked with Frank this morning, and he said that someone tried to break into my office last night. Then the water hauler told him that those two scouts were seen on the lease road earlier.''

Leslie didn't respond, but her mind was in turmoil. One thought kept occurring over and over again, and Leslie's face became fixed with resolve.

This vindictiveness of Luther's had to be stopped before there was another tragedy. John had been right—she could ruin Luther if she wanted to, and that gave her a sense of power she had never experienced before. Yes, she would have to be the one to deal with Luther Denver.

A sharp pang of unbearable loneliness stabbed through her as she glanced at Steve's back. This nerve-racking exposure would be tolerable only if he could forgive her, but she realized it was a fruitless thought. She bowed her head and blinked back the tears that were scalding her eyes as Steve strode to the door.

''I'm going down to have a talk with the management about security. You be sure and lock the door after me.''

She nodded her head, unaware that he was watching her with a bleak look on his face. The door clicked shut, and wiping the tears from her eyes, she moved across the room to secure the lock.

She remained motionless for a moment, then, with a set look on her face, went to the phone and dialed. After a brief silence she said, her voice decisive, "I'd like to place a person-to-person call to Mr. Gordon Donner at Kaidon Industries in Vancouver, please."

It was early evening when John McRory went across the hall and knocked on Leslie's door. Steve had told him about the episode that morning, and he wanted to check on her before he went down to the banquet. It would have been very traumatic for Leslie, and he was certain she was nearly at the end of her endurance.

The door opened, and the stunned surprise John felt registered immediately on his face.

Leslie gave him a brittle smile. "If I'm going to face the consequences, I'm going to face them in style."

He whistled. She had on a flame orange silk dress with a high rolled collar. The cut was startlingly simple, but absolutely stunning.

John shook his head when she turned around to pull the door shut behind him. The entire back was cut away. It was not a dress for a shy reserved woman—but then, there was something about her tonight that was anything but shy and reserved. She looked spectacular . . . and she also looked very determined.

"I didn't think you'd feel up to the banquet."

"Oh, I feel up to it."

John scrutinized her face. There was a tone in her voice that made him slightly suspicious and definitely uneasy.

"There will probably be a horde of reporters downstairs," he cautioned. "They become very tenacious about a story like this."

"I realize that." She started walking down the corridor. "Let's get this over with, shall we?"

They rode in silence down to the reception area. The elevator stopped, and before the doors opened, Leslie squared her shoulders and lifted her chin. She was gathering her resolve around her like a suit of armor.

Steve was standing in the foyer, talking to a group of men. He glanced up and his whole body stiffened when he saw Leslie there with John. Excusing himself, he left the group and came striding toward them, anger flashing in his eyes.

"I don't think it was very wise for you to bring her down," he snapped at John.

John gave him a level stare. "I didn't *bring* her down," he responded pointedly.

Leslie ignored their conversation as she studied the people milling about in the reception area. "How long until dinner?" she asked in a tightly controlled voice.

John and Steve exchanged troubled looks, then John answered. "Not for another hour. They always have cocktails first—it gives the delegates an opportunity to mingle."

"Then we'd better mingle, hadn't we?"

As time progressed, John's expression became more and more concerned. This was a new Leslie. She was poised and charming, and an aura of tenacity radiated from her. She was up to something, but what? She reminded him of L.J. when he was determined to have his own way. The poise and the charm were simply a smoke screen for single-mindedness.

He wasn't the only one who was feeling uneasy. Steve kept watching Leslie through hooded eyes, his face enigmatic. But there was a tension in him, as though he was poised for action.

Leslie didn't allow John's very obvious concern to penetrate her veneer of control. Gordon Donner had called her again just before she'd come down, and now she was secure in knowing that she had the weapons at her disposal to stop Luther once and for all.

Before long a member of the press spotted her among the crowd; after that it was like iron filings clustering around a powerful magnet. In a flash she was hemmed in by reporters, and the questions began to fly.

A cold inflexibility grew in her, giving her a strength she hadn't known she possessed. Not one person there could have guessed what a terrifying ordeal it was for her. She answered each question with a calmness that belied the acute nervousness churning inside her.

They hammered at her with rapid-fire queries for some time before she was able to manipulate the tenor of the interview. She smiled a tight little smile when one reporter finally asked the question she was waiting to hear.

"Miss Kairns, is it true that Kaidon Industries became involved with Ramco because of the prospects of a big find?"

Now, thought Leslie with grim amusement, *I have them aimed in the direction I want them to go.* She neatly skirted the issue of Redwillow by throwing them a more tempting bone. "Naturally any company exploring for petroleum has hopes for a big find, but my involvement with Ramco really stems back to my father. He was one of the original owners when Ramco started its operations a number of years ago."

This *was* news and there was a babble of questions, drowned out by one reporter who raised his voice above the clamor. "Your existence was a very well-kept secret, Miss Kairns, and we haven't been able to find out much about you. For instance, who was your father?"

"L.J. Owens. Unfortunately, he was killed in a rig mishap before I was born."

"You were raised by your grandfather?"

"My grandfather had a tremendous impact on my life, but I lived with my mother and stepfather."

"And who are they?"

"My mother," explained Leslie with dry amusement in her voice, "is, of course, my grandfather's daughter." There was a ripple of laughter and then she continued, "My stepfather is Luther Denver from Denver Oil."

More big news. She was giving them a headline story, and the newsmen were scrambling for more.

"Is Kaidon Industries involved in any way with Denver Oil?"

There was an unflinching purposefulness in her response. "Not yet." Then her tone softened, and all the mesmerizing charm she had displayed throughout the entire interview was back as she smiled. "Now, gentlemen, would you please excuse me?"

There was something about how she said it that made every reporter there realize the interview was over, and that they wouldn't get another word out of her no matter how much they pressed her. She smiled again, then with regal dignity walked away from the cluster of microphones. The only indication of the tremendous strain she was under was her pallor.

Steve caught her roughly by the arm just as she entered the banquet hall. "You've made your point, Leslie. Now I want you to get the hell out of here. I'll deal with Luther Denver."

She looked up at him, her face drawn and very white. "You accused me once of running out on my responsibilities. Well, I'm not running anymore." With an abrupt, desperate movement she jerked her arm free of his grasp. "Just leave me alone, Steve. For God's sake, leave me alone." Her voice broke treacherously and she whirled away, but not before he saw the glimmer of tears in her eyes.

It took every ounce of willpower she had to compose herself as she walked away from him, fighting a battle to suppress the panic that was threatening to demolish her control. She had to hang on for just a while longer. . . .

"You look like you could use this." Leslie turned

to find John McRory standing beside her, a drink in his hand.

She took the glass of amber liquid from him, then smiled ruefully. "Am I that readable?"

He took a long drag on his cigarette, then exhaled slowly as he solemnly studied her through the haze of smoke. Finally he shook his head, a touch of irony in his smile. "No, you aren't that readable—not anymore. In fact, I'm beginning to realize that you aren't even predictable." His face sobered and his voice was very earnest. "Don't tangle with him, Les."

She looked away and gave a derisive little laugh. "I think it's time we stopped playing games."

John sighed heavily. "Yes, I suppose it is." There was a heavy silence, then John rested his hand on the small of her back. "Let's go find a table," he suggested.

Leslie looked down as she ran her finger pensively around the rim of her glass. Then she glanced up at him, her expression deceptively passive. "Thank you, but no. I'm planning on dining with my stepfather."

Sucking in his breath sharply, John stared at her for a moment. Very slowly he grinned, a look of admiration dawning in his eyes. "Would you mind if I tagged along?"

"Not at all."

Actually, it was far easier than Leslie anticipated; it just took a little audacity. Behaving as though her presence was expected, she and John joined the small group of men to whom Luther was talking.

She waited for a lull in the conversation, then spoke with relaxed familiarity. "Hello, Luther.

Didn't mother come with you?" It was such a commonplace question that it caught Luther completely off guard.

Dumbfounded, he stared at her for a split second; then his features became rigid as he answered stiffly, "No, she didn't."

"Denver, you sly dog," interjected the man standing beside him. "If I hadn't eavesdropped on the press session with this little lady, I still wouldn't have known she was your daughter."

Luther's cheek twitched as his hand tightened around the drink he was holding. "She's my stepdaughter," he corrected, his voice cool.

The man acted as though he hadn't heard Luther as he addressed Leslie. "You'll just have to join us for dinner, young lady, and give us the scoop on old Luther here."

Leslie felt a spurt of adrenaline tingle through her as she gave him an engaging smile. "Well, thank you very much. I'd like that." *Wouldn't I just love,* she thought wryly, *to give you the real scoop on old Luther here.*

The man stretched his hand toward her. "The name is George Hartley—Hartley Drilling."

With a smile glued on like wallpaper, Leslie shook his hand, then included John. "This is John McRory, president of Ramco Exploration." The two men shook hands; then Hartley introduced them to the other men.

Sensing that she had Luther effectively cornered, she pressed her advantage. "You remember John, don't you, Luther? I believe you were in South America together, weren't you?"

His face was like white granite as he snapped coldly, "Yes, we were." For an instant Leslie expected him to crush the glass he held in his hand.

They were just about to sit down at the table when Steve joined them. John introduced him to the other four men, and Leslie felt her stomach contract into a hard knot when Steve pulled out her chair for her, then sat down beside her. His closeness was so painfully unsettling that she had the overwhelming desire to bolt. Forcing herself to remain seated, she tried to cope with the choking claustrophobia that was pressing down on her. She felt as though she were caught in a trap, and the presence of Steve, his face looking like it had been hacked out of stone, nearly shattered her resolve. He was there because he was suspicious of her motives, because he didn't trust her.

She swallowed, then stiffened her back. Somehow she had to dredge up the strength to get through this next hour. Somehow.

As she'd expected, the situation turned out to be a taxing experience. The entire conversation during dinner focused on the granddaughter of the very wealthy, powerful Mac Kairns. Hartley made certain that the others became aware of who Leslie was and how vast a fortune she commanded. She felt as though her life was like a pile of garments on a rummage-sale table—pawed through, mauled over, and left crumpled and disorderly after it had been exposed to curious, probing eyes. It was a frightening sensation, but she managed to restrain her fear and present the image of a poised and confident young businesswoman. She *had* to—she couldn't falter now.

Leslie was well aware that Luther's fury was becoming volcanic as she answered an endless string of questions. Slowly she was backing him into a corner and he knew it, and she experienced a certain amount of grim satisfaction. Yet she almost had to admire the man—he had an iron control that was unbreachable, and a cunning mind. He would not go down without a battle.

"Well," said George Hartley as he set down his empty wineglass. "I must confess I envy you, John. For an exploration company that has the financial resources you do, the sky's the limit right now. It takes big bucks to go wildcatting."

John chuckled. "I won't argue that point, believe me. Our financial arrangement with Kaidon kept us on our feet."

"Yes," reiterated Hartley, "you're a damned lucky man to have a huge corporation like Kaidon behind you."

John glanced at Leslie, a look of approval in his eyes. "Well, George, that's true, but I think our luck really peaked when we hired Leslie. Something she didn't tell you was that she's our project geologist. This girl is a natural finder, and there aren't many of those around. You can have all the financing in the world behind you, but unless you produce, it isn't worth a damn."

"So," said one of the other men, his eyes gleaming with speculation, "I take it you're onto something big?"

"Possibly."

"I don't suppose there's a chance in hell that you'd let us in on the secret?"

"Not a chance," laughed John.

Hartley looked at Luther, a droll grin on his face. "Heavens, man, why didn't you snap her up? Or did you think we'd all say you were after her money?" There was a ripple of laughter that turned into embarrassed silence when Luther didn't respond.

"I did work for Luther for two years before I went to Ramco. We both felt it would be best if I left."

There was an awkward lull and George, realizing that something was going on that he didn't grasp, tried to shift the conversation to a safer topic.

"Kaidon has never been involved in the petroleum industry before, has it?"

A feeling of anticipation slithered down Leslie's spine. The trap was being set; now all she had to do was bait it. "No. There are several mining companies within the corporate structure, but up until now the petroleum industry has been overlooked. We're reevaluating our potential in this area now, though."

George Hartley grinned knowingly. "In other words, you're ready to jump in with both feet."

"As a matter of fact, Gordon Donner and I have been considering just such a possibility. There is an Alberta-based company that we're interested in." Leslie paused, then continued, "Gordon was discussing a possible merger with a number of the major stockholders today. He phoned me with the results of those discussions just before I came down this evening. They're very anxious to do business with him, especially since he made them a very attractive offer."

Leslie felt Steve grow tense, his eyes riveted on her

as the next question came. "Why is this company so attractive to Kaidon?"

"It isn't attractive," responded Leslie, her voice very controlled. She deliberately fixed her eyes on Luther, her message to him acutely clear. "The president of the company is trying to manipulate one of our other interests. Since the man refused to be rational, it seems logical to simply eliminate the problem."

The reaction around the table was electric, but Leslie was isolated from it. Her whole attention focused on her stepfather. Luther's body jerked as the implication of her statement hit home. He stared at her, his jaw tightening, his hands doubled into fists, and an intense loathing burned in his eyes.

"Is the takeover imminent?" questioned one of the men.

Leslie's eyes never left Luther's face. "That really depends on the disposition of one man and what he decides to do."

She laid her napkin on the table and pushed her chair back. "It's been a very long day. Would you excuse me, please?"

With her heart racing and her hands clammy, Leslie left by the side door. There was another small reception area outside the banquet room, which had large windows overlooking the street below. She walked over to them, but her attention was welded on the door behind her. She took a deep breath and braced herself as it swung open and Luther came toward her, his face menacing.

"What in hell do you think your doing? You'll never get away with a takeover of Denver Oil."

"But I can—and I will if you don't call off your dogs, Luther."

He faced her, his voice seething with fury. "You," he sneered maliciously, "don't know what in hell you're talking about."

Her voice was quiet, but it had a ring of finality to it that was chilling. "Try me, Luther—just try me," she challenged, her eyes flashing. "If you don't back off, and back off *now*, I'll use every cent I have to bring you down. I'll break you, Luther—I'll wipe you out. And you know I have the resources to do it."

He took a step toward her, crazed with rage, his face contorted. "What makes you think you can call the shots? Who in hell do you think you are, you sniveling little bastard?"

She never moved, she never flinched, but drove the last barb home with a calm icy voice. "I'm my father's child and don't you forget it."

The taunt was too much for Luther, and he slapped her across the face, then caught her with a brutal backhand. He never had the chance to strike her the third time, for he was suddenly spun around by a hand that had his shoulder in an iron grip. A hard right hook to Luther's jaw sent him sprawling. Steve McRory yanked him to his feet, and Leslie realized that he was going to hit him again.

She caught his arm and held it. "Don't—he isn't worth it." Her head was still ringing from Luther's blows, and she could taste blood in her mouth, but her rigid composure protected her like a shield as she gazed at her stepfather. "Remember what I said, Luther. I meant every word." With that she turned and walked away.

She was nearly at the elevators when Steve called her name. That shattered the dam of her emotions, and all the fear, hurt and unhappiness came boiling through, stripping away her defenses. She sprinted toward the elevator, a panicky phrase running through her head. *You have your pound of flesh, Steve McRory. My God, you have your pound of flesh!*

She felt his fingertips brush her shoulder, and with the desperation of a hunted animal she managed to squeeze through the closing door of an elevator. For one brief terrifying instant, she thought the door would reopen, but it stayed closed. As the elevator rose with agonizing slowness, Leslie felt the panic rising in her.

Her heart was pounding frantically in her chest, the pulse echoing in her head, as she slammed the door to her room behind her and, with fumbling fingers, set the dead bolt. Then she closed her eyes and leaned weakly against the door, her breathing raw and labored. She was safe—for a few hours, she was safe. No one could reach her here.

She was frozen with a new wave of fear when she heard footsteps outside her door, and she jumped away as though she had been scalded when someone tried the doorknob.

"Leslie, let me in."

She backed into the room, her eyes widening as though she expected Steve to come bursting through. As he called out to her again, she covered her ears with her hands. Her legs were no longer able to support her, and she collapsed on the bed and began to shake.

She jumped when the phone jangled shrilly by her elbow, and without thinking, she picked up the receiver. Staring at it dully, she was about to hang it up when she recognized John's voice vibrating hollowly from the instrument.

"Leslie—don't hang up! Just listen to me for a minute—please, Les, don't hang up." She continued to stare at the receiver she held in her hand. "Leslie, are you listening?"

She closed her eyes and put the receiver to her ear. "Yes."

"Are you all right?"

"Yes."

"Leslie, please unlock the door! Let me...."

"No!" Her voice was a tormented whisper. "No, please don't. I just want to be left alone...please, John. I can't handle any more tonight."

"Leslie...." There was a long pause, then it was Steve's voice. "Unlock the door, Les—I want to talk to you."

With a helpless little moan she pressed the button on the phone and cut him off, then dropped the receiver on the bed.

She had no awareness of time as she huddled there. It seemed like hours had passed when she finally stood up, her muscles stiff and cramped, and walked to the window to stare out at the silent street.

A web of destruction had been woven through their lives. A curse...and they were all victims, even Luther.

His passionate obsession for a woman who couldn't respond to his adoration had warped his life, crippling him with jealousy, and he had become twisted and sick because of it. There could be no respite from the consuming bitterness for him. Every single day he had to endure the gut-twisting emasculation of Leslie's existence, a living breathing reminder of his wife's liaison with another man. Another man who had experienced the hot-blooded passionate response that he thirsted for, while he had been left with the remote unyielding shell.

For Luther, Vivian's personal tragedy was a destructive torment. He had lived a famished man, denied the ever present but untouchable feast, and his life had become a ceaseless hell.

Leslie felt a sudden unexpected compassion for her stepfather, whose unsatisfied passion must be fermenting inside him like poison. Her own barren life would be preferable to his tortured existence. At least she had known joy so pure, so electrifying that she would never forget it, no matter how many empty endless days she had to face.

She sighed deeply. An eternity of grief and loneliness stretched darkly before her—day after day after day. As the eastern sky lightened, heralding yet another agonizing day, Leslie longed to reach out and hold back the dawn. . . .

A knock at her door jarred her from her trance, and she glanced dully at her watch as she went to the door. It was morning. She felt totally devoid of feeling as she opened the door.

Steve was standing there, his arm braced against the doorframe, his face ashen and lined with tension. He looked away, his expression unsteady but detached. "I think it might be best if John took you back to Redwillow today."

Her daze of exhaustion was penetrated by a vague feeling of perplexity. The anger was gone from his voice. His attitude was strangely bewildering, and she felt very confused. She rubbed her forehead with an uncertain gesture.

Not looking at him, she turned around and walked back into the room. "Yes, it probably would be best."

It was only then that it registered—she was still wearing the flame-colored dress.

FEBRUARY ARRIVED and with it came milder weather. There had not been another incident at the rig since Leslie's confrontation with Luther, and now there was an air of untroubled anticipation at Redwillow. They were getting close to the geological formation that made up the beach conglomerate. Anytime now they would know—and the waiting would be over.

There had been a dramatic change in Leslie since her return from the ill-fated conference in Edmonton. She had a quiet confidence about her that had never been there before. Unfortunately, her effervescent zest for life appeared to be the price she'd paid for it. There was no brightness left in her; instead there was a dispassionate air of resignation.

She kept all her associations on a strictly professional basis, with the exception of Ted McAllister and, to a lesser degree, Frank Logan. The only time she seemed to relax her guard was when both men were in camp...and Steve was away.

She had somehow managed to tell Ted the whole painful story, then had asked him never to bring it up again. And Ted, with the compassionate insight of an old friend, complied.

Frank, on the other hand, had become her self-appointed bodyguard. On more than one occasion he had forcefully dragged nosey reporters away from the camp. His protective attitude stirred a certain amount of wry amusement in Leslie, but she had to admit to herself that she slept better knowing that no one would get within a five-mile radius of her unless she wanted it. It helped a little, having the two of them there.

So the days marched relentlessly on. And the pressure intensified for Leslie. Not only did she have the extra work load of the other two rigs that were now drilling, but she was once again experiencing the same old feeling of doubt about the project. What if she had been wrong? What if, on top of everything else, the beach conglomerate was dry? What if. . .?

She had asked Frank to have samples of the cuttings from the shale shaker gathered hourly, and during the day she processed them immediately. Frequently she got up at three o'clock in the morning to do an analysis of the samples gathered from midnight on. She wanted to know the minute they penetrated the Falher formation. She also monitored the mud-logging operation closely. If the gas units started to increase rapidly, she immediately wanted to know that information as well. She was nearly dropping from exhaustion, and her nerves were taxed to the limit, but she kept pushing herself on.

She found the three o'clock shifts the most difficult, and tonight was no exception. Her wretched loneliness closed in on her, suffocating her as memories of Steve seeped through her barrier of determination, haunting her with disturbing clearness.

She closed her eyes and rubbed her forehead wearily, then with a heavy sigh squared her shoulders and placed the cuttings under her microscope. She studied the chips, then intensified the magnification. She straightened up, her face suddenly drawn as she sat transfixed, her hands clasped tightly together.

Maybe she was wrong. She looked through the microscope again and shifted the chips with a probe. The cuttings displayed a high-porosity factor. It was the beach conglomerate—the Falher zone.

She pushed the microscope aside and rested her head on her arms as the reality of what lay on the slide washed over her. This was it—and she was scared.

She didn't move for a long time, then she pushed herself to her feet and picked up her parka and put it on. Once outside, she never noticed the clearness of the night sky or the brightness of the stars. She walked directly to Ted's trailer, her mind oblivious to anything except that in the next few hours the waiting would finally be over.

She had to knock several times before Ted finally came to the door, his hair rumpled, his eyes cloudy with sleep. She stepped in and shut the door behind her.

"Leslie, what—"

"Do we core now, or do we wait until morning?"

He stared at her dumbly for a split second, then a look of alertness swept across his face. His voice was decisive. "We core now. Go get Frank up and I'll meet you at the rig." He started to turn away, then he grasped her shoulders, his voice laced with humor as he reassured her. "Don't look so scared, girl. If it's a duster, what the hell! It's your money we're spending, and you never wanted the damned stuff in the first place."

For the first time in weeks, Leslie's grin was spontaneous and genuine. "Your logic might be weird, but it certainly does take the edge off things."

He grinned back at her. "Go get Frank."

Coring was a long drawn-out affair. They had to trip out to change the bit for the core barrel, then trip in and drill sixty feet, then trip out again to retrieve the sample. It would be a very long night.

Frank and Ted were in the doghouse, calmly playing a game of crib. Leslie shook her head and smiled ruefully as she went in. They were old hands at this waiting game, and she envied them their seeming unconcern. She was anything but calm. God, but she wished it didn't take so long!

Ted looked up at her and grinned. "Damn it, girl, quit your fidgeting and pacing—you'll give us all ulcers." He nodded toward the electric kettle on the folding table. "Why don't you make us an instant coffee?"

"Okay." Leslie plugged the kettle in, then opened the door of the little cabinet behind the table to get the jar of coffee and the powered cream. She winced as a powerful smell hit her, and she warily looked inside. The cupboard was revolting. There was an open can of pineapple juice that was fermenting away in undisturbed splendor, the top of it an unhealthy green; a dried-up wedge of cheddar cheese that was measled with mold; a jar of mustard without a top, the contents dried and cracked. The object that intrigued her most, however, was a plastic bag that contained some black oozing mush. It looked and smelled suspiciously like rotten onions.

Her expression was one of amused aversion as she looked at Frank. "Would you mind if I cleaned this out?"

He nodded his head in assent. "Was hopin' you'd volunteer. It's beginnin' to smell a mite."

A mite! That was an understatement.

Leslie dragged the metal garbage container over, opened up the green garbage bag inside and started pitching. At the very back of the cupboard she found a coffee cup filled with a spectacular growth of blue furry mold. *A chemistry teacher would sell his soul for a culture like that,* she thought. With a grimace she tossed cup and all into the garbage can. She wiped out the inside of the cupboard with a questionable rag, then placed everything that was usable back inside. She tied the top of the garbage bag firmly in a vain attempt to contain the host of smells, then straightened up and brushed her hands off on her jeans.

When she turned around, her stomach dropped like a rock. Steve was leaning against the first-aid cabinet, watching her through narrowed eyes. She felt like a butterfly impaled by his piercing stare; she was trapped by it, unable to move, unable to look away. She saw the muscle twitching in his jaw, and she desperately wanted to reach out and smooth away the stern lines around his senuous mouth.

He seemed to read her thoughts, and he sucked in

his breath, then jerked away. She heard him swear as he yanked open the door and strode out onto the rig floor.

She felt like her whole body had been immersed in freezing water. With trembling hands she picked up her parka and bolted for the door.

"Hey, what about our coffee?"

She never answered as she fled into the night. She couldn't.

She had never expected that. She had expected anger, loathing, cold remoteness, but she had not been prepared to see the pain. It had been in his eyes—that awful, unrelenting agony that twisted one's insides into an aching knot. She had never meant to hurt him, but she had. She had hurt him to the core.

CHAPTER SIXTEEN

WAITING. It seemed to stretch on forever. Leslie felt like there was a big coiled spring inside her that was driving her on like a mechanical doll.

John had said that they should have the results by midafternoon of the following day, and as that deadline drew closer, Leslie became more and more on edge. She was with Ted in his office, waiting for the phone call from John that would tell them what the lab had found. It was obvious that she had at last infected Ted with her nervous restlessness, for he was pacing back and forth. The air was blue with smoke; he had chain-smoked his way through half a pack of cigarettes.

He butted another one in the overflowing ashtray, then put on his hard hat and picked up his jacket. "Hell, Leslie, I can't stand this any longer. I'm going over to the rig for a while. Why don't you come with me? You're apt to die from smoke inhalation if you stay in here for very long."

"I think I'd more likely die from suspense if I left the phone."

"Well, if you change your mind, come on over. We can start an argument with Frank to take our minds off this damned waiting."

"*You* start an argument with Frank—I'm not leaving the phone."

It was about two hours later when Leslie's endurance reached its limit. She was just putting on her parka when the phone rang. The sharp sound startled her, and her heart was pounding against her ribs as she scrambled for it. She swore when she tripped over the garbage can in her haste to reach it. Sprawling across the desk, she caught it on the second ring.

"Ramco Two."

"Hello, Ramco Two. What were you doing, Leslie—sitting on the desk waiting for the phone to ring?"

It was John. Leslie struggled into an upright position and brushed her hair back from her face. "You're close...." She felt like she was poised on a high pinnacle from which she was going to be pushed. There was a chance that she would fly, but there was also a chance that she would crash to the ground. Her insides churned with fearful anticipation as she asked the inevitable question. "What did the analysis say?"

There was a hair-raising silence before he answered. "What do you think?"

"John McRory, this is not the time to play guessing games. What was the report?"

He laughed, and she could hear the exhilaration in his voice. "Hell, Leslie, it's even better than we hoped for. A conservative estimate based on the results of this well and on the projected size of the field, would be fifty trillion cubic feet of natural gas. But I wouldn't be at all surprised to see it go as high as two hundred trillion. It's a humdinger of a find."

Leslie's knees caved in beneath her and she sank

weakly into the chair, totally stunned by John's news. She felt such a wave of relief that it made her feel narcotized. *Trillion*—a thousand billion—a million million. The immensity, the volume absolutely staggered her. She could barely grasp it!

"Leslie, what happened? Did you faint?"

She took a deep breath and tried to focus her mind. "Nearly...it's a bit overwhelming."

John laughed again. "I wish I was there to help celebrate—it's so damned exciting! Have Steve call me as soon as he can."

"I will. I wish you were here, too—it won't seem quite right without you."

"Bless you, Les. Take care and we'll talk to you later."

"You too, John. Goodbye."

Leslie hung up the phone; she was still in a trance. Two hundred trillion. *Two hundred trillion.* . . . The reality finally penetrated, and Leslie sent the chair flying as she let out a shout of exuberance. She bolted from the trailer, and her feet had wings as she flew across the lease. They'd done it—they had really done it!

She had never experienced this kind of incredible high before in her life. She took the stairs up the doghouse two at a time and barged in, slamming the door open. Ted sprang to his feet the moment she burst in, and he caught her as she threw herself into his arms. She felt like her lungs were going to explode, and she gasped for air as she blurted out the news.

"Ted...John said...at least...fifty trillion...cubic feet. Trillions! I can't...believe it!"

Ted let out a shout as he gave her a mighty bear hug that nearly collapsed her laboring lungs. "Hell, that's fantastic." He gave Leslie another crushing hug, then more or less dropped her. She staggered to catch her balance as he slammed open the door to the rig floor and bellowed for Steve.

There was an outbreak of noisy jubilation. This find would put Redwillow on the map. It was the largest gas find ever in Canada.

Twenty minutes later Leslie was still flying high, her face flushed, her eyes shining with excitement. Suddenly Steve turned to her, his face expressionless, his voice like a razor. "Well, Leslie, I guess you've got what you wanted. This is going to be a very profitable venture for Kaidon Industries."

Leslie felt as if he had hit her in the stomach. With those cruel cold words, he burst her bubble of elation, and an agony of unhappiness exploded within her with a rending pain. The color drained from her face, and without uttering a word she turned and fled from the doghouse, her vision blurred by scalding tears.

She groped blindly for the handrail, but her momentum carried her forward and she missed her footing. Her last rational thought was that she was falling; then there was an excruciating ripping in her shoulder as she tumbled down the steel stairs.

She lay at the bottom, battered and stunned, as the racking pain from her shoulder shot through her like the red-hot blade of a knife. The pain immobilized her for several agonizing moments, but eventually she was able to struggle weakly into a sitting position, carefully cradling her right arm against her as shafts of fire pierced through her. She bit back a moan and closed her eyes against the dizzy sickening gray fog that threatened to rob her of consciousness. The pain was a familiar one—she had experienced it once before when she had taken a bad fall during a high-school gymnastics class. She had dislocated her damned shoulder again.

Struggling to her knees, she took a deep shaky breath as the mist swirled in her pounding head. Leslie reached up to touch a bruised throbbing lump in her hair, and swore under her breath when she saw that her fingers were covered in blood.

"What happened, Leslie?" She moved her head cautiously and saw Frank Logan hurrying down the steps toward her, his face creased with concern.

"I fell down the stairs." She swallowed hard and took several deep breaths. She still felt like she was going to faint.

He knelt down beside her and gently touched her head. "From the top?"

"Yes."

"My God...." He reached out to pick her up, but she caught his hand before he could touch her. "Frank, I...I've dislocated my shoulder...."

He swore again and stood up. "I'm goin' for the stretcher—"

"No!" She closed her eyes and waited for a fierce contraction of pain to ease. "No, don't Frank—please...I don't want a scene."

He crouched down beside her and steadied her with his hand. "Can you get up?"

She nodded her head weakly. "If you'll just help me a little." He slipped his arms around her and

watched her face intently as he carefully tightened his
hold and lifted her up in his arms. She clenched her
eyes shut and gritted her teeth together as another
spasm of pain shot through her, robbing her of her
breath. With infinite care Frank carried her across
the windswept lease. Every jarring step he took sent
the awful pain piercing through her, and she could
feel beads of perspiration forming on her cold
clammy skin.

Once inside her trailer Frank set her gently on the
sofa, his movements slow and gentle as he carefully
eased his arms from around her.

"I'm goin' to leave you just for a minute, Les—I
want to send Gus out to check the road and see if it's
open so we can get you into Grande Prairie to the
hospital."

Leslie closed her eyes in assent. "Please don't tell
anyone what happened, Frank—not even Ted."

He stared at her deadly white face, marred by a
trickle of blood oozing down her temple. There was a
grim look on his face as he growled, "I won't tell Ted
or McRory you're hurt, but I'll have to tell them I'm
leavin' the lease. And I'm goin' to have to get Mike—
he can strap you up so the pain ain't so bad. It's goin'
to be a hell of a trip over them damn rough roads."

Leslie looked at Frank, her eyes pleading. "Just
Mike, Frank—no one else." Mike was the medic for
the camp, and Leslie knew if Frank told him to keep
his mouth shut, he would keep his mouth shut. Frank
stared at her for a brief second longer, then he shook
his head and stomped out, slamming the door behind
him.

Leslie eased her head back until it rested against

the back of the sofa. She hurt all over—her hip, her knees, her head, her ribs. She felt like she had broken every bone in her body, but that was to be expected after bouncing down thirty feet of stairs.

Opening her eyes, she stared blankly at the cupboards. The sharp scalding pain was finally easing into a steady intense ache. Gingerly she eased herself forward until she could stand up. She steadied herself against the wall when dizziness swept over her. Creeping over to the sink, she turned on the tap and dampened the end of the towel under the cold water. She was just about to wipe the dried blood and perspiration from her face when the door crashed open behind her.

"What in hell is this crap about Frank Logan taking you to Grande Prairie today? I made it very clear you weren't leaving here until I said you could go!"

Leslie's hand tightened on the rim of the sink, and she began to tremble violently. She was in no condition to cope with another burst of Steve's anger.

"Damn it, Leslie, don't turn your back on me when I'm talking to you!"

Leslie heard Frank shout as Steve grabbed her injured arm and spun her around. An awful searing pain shot through her, and the bolt of fire in her shoulder drove her to her knees. The room began to turn in a sickening spin, and she fought to hold on to a thread of consciousness as she felt herself sway. Strong arms caught her and held her firmly before she could crumple to the floor.

Frank Logan's voice was loud and strangely distorted as she rested her head feebly against his shoulder. "Hell, man—what in blazes do you think you're doin'? Can't you see the girl's been hurt?'' Frank's big hand caught her firmly by her good shoulder as he carefully eased her back. ''Are you okay, Les?''

''Yes.'' Her voice was barely audible.

Steve's voice sounded oddly strangled as he crouched down beside her. ''What happened to her?''

''She lost her footin' and fell down them damn rig stairs. She says her shoulder's dislocated.''

''She *what*?''

''I said. . . .''

''Never mind—I heard you.'' She felt Steve's hand on her hair, and she wondered dully why it was shaking. ''Leslie?''

With a massive effort she lifted her head and looked at him, her eyes dark and glassy. He was very pale, and his expression was one of bitter self-reproach. Leslie forced a ghost of a smile.

He sucked in his breath sharply and jerked his head back. He'd reacted as though she had slapped him.

''I sent Gus out to check the road. If it's clear, I'm drivin' her into Grande Prairie to the doctor.''

There was an edge to Steve's voice that Leslie had never heard before. ''It isn't open. Mark radioed in about an hour ago. The main road is clear, but the rig road is drifted in solid, so he had to go back to Grande Prairie.'' Steve reached out and gently traced the dried trickle of blood back up to the throbbing lump on her head. He tenderly parted her hair with his fingers, then swore softly as he slipped his arm around her waist. ''Let me help you up, Les—you can't stay down here on this cold floor.''

She swayed against him as she stumbled to her feet, and his arm tightened around her as he held her against him. There was a tense silence, and when he finally spoke his voice was strained. "We can't get you out of here today, and we can't leave your shoulder like that." There was a heavy pause, then he continued, "I'm going to have to reset it for you."

She glanced up at him and experienced a different kind of pain when she saw the gut-twisting distress in his eyes. She didn't trust her voice, so she only nodded.

"Do you want me to fetch Mike?" asked Frank.

Steve looked down at Leslie, and she shook her head in response to his silent question. She knew Steve had had an extensive course in industrial first aid, and she would rather that he did it.

"No, but you could see what he has in the way of medication in the drug cabinet...and you could bring back one of those good slings."

"Right—an' I'll get someone goin' on that road. Mebbe we can have it open by mornin'."

Frank turned to go, and Leslie reached out and touched his arm. "Thank you, Frank."

The tool push nodded self-consciously. "Was nothin'—I'll be back in a flash."

As soon as he left, Leslie looked up at Steve, her face taut with pain as she whispered hoarsely, "Let's get this over with."

Steve's jaw flexed stiffly, then he sighed as he glanced down at her, his eyes unreadable. "Yes, I guess we'd better."

He kept his arm around her as he guided her into the bedroom, where he turned her toward him, his face set in unyielding lines. "I have to take your parka off, Les, and it's probably going to hurt like hell when I do."

"I think I'll sit down." Her shaking legs wouldn't support her much longer.

"Do you want to wait until we can give you something to dull the pain?"

She shook her head.

Steve swung the chair around and Leslie sat down. He crouched in front of her and unzipped her parka, then carefully slipped her left arm out of the sleeve. She grasped on to the seat of the chair as he tucked the bulk of the coat behind her back. Glancing at her pale rigid face, he took a deep breath as he gently began to ease the right sleeve down her arm.

Leslie clenched her teeth against the searing pain. Steve's fingers were trembling as he undid the buttons of her plaid flannel shirt, but it was the only indication that he was affected. With the same gentle care, he removed her shirt, then pressed his hands forcefully against his thighs.

It was only then that Leslie noticed the beads of perspiration on his forehead. She reached out and wiped his brow with the palm of her left hand. Her heart was filled with compassion when he rested his head against her knees.

He didn't move for a minute, then, silently, removed her boots and socks. "Can you stand up for a second? The snow has melted on your jeans and they're damp."

His arm supported her as he unbuckled her belt, undid her zipper and stripped her pants off carefully. She heard him swear and she glanced down. There was an ugly purple bruise spreading from her hip to just above her right knee.

He raked his fingers through his hair, then stood up, his face pale. His voice was clipped and hoarse. "You have to lie down, little one—close to the edge of the bed."

She did as he asked. The pain was far worse when she was lying down, and she closed her eyes and turned her face away from him. His fingers probed her shoulder and she sucked in her breath. Then she felt him grasp her arm and brace his knee high up on her ribs.

A bolt of white-hot electricity ripped through her with such a devastating force that it left her shaking violently from the shock. Her jaws were locked together, her muscles rigid and she fought down the churning nausea in her stomach. She felt Steve check her shoulder, then he caught her face in his hands.

"Leslie?"

She opened her eyes and stared at him. He looked so haggard and drained. He smoothed her hair back from her damp forehead, then covered her with the comforter. "I'll be right back, Leslie—Frank just came in."

She was shaking so badly that she couldn't unclench her teeth to answer him. She closed her eyes and tried to stop shivering, but she was so cold. At least that ordeal was over.

She opened her eyes when Steve came back into the bedroom. He set a bottle of capsules and a glass of water on the night table, then started unwrapping a length of gauze.

Leslie eased herself over on her left side and tried

to struggle into a sitting position. Steve slipped his arm around her back and supported her uninjured shoulder. He folded the sling, then quickly and efficiently bound her arm snugly against her breast, in such a way that there was little pressure on her shoulder.

He opened the bottle of capsules and shook two into his palm. "These are pretty potent, so they should help the pain. It will likely take half an hour before they start working, though."

Leslie put them in her mouth, took a sip from the glass of water that Steve had handed her and swallowed the capsules. He took the glass from her shaking hand and set it on the table, then said, "You'd better lie down; you look like you're ready to collapse."

She shook her head. "I'd rather sit up. Everything starts spinning when I lie down." She wouldn't be able to stand the pain when she was laying flat—not until the pills started working.

"In other words, your shoulder is less painful when you sit up."

Her eyes flew to his face, her wide-eyed expression registering her surprise. His smile was stiff as he stared down at her. "I can see right through your little deceptions now, Leslie."

An overwhelming feeling of remorse shot through her and she bent her head, trying to blink back her scalding tears. She felt so miserable and isolated, and she wanted nothing except to be left alone with her physical pain and emotional despair.

Steve caught her chin with his hand and tilted her head up, but she couldn't look at him. She couldn't bear to witness his icy disdain. "I'm sorry, Leslie—that was very cruel."

She looked at him then, her eyes blurred with unshed tears. "I don't blame you for feeling how you do about me."

He gently wrapped the comforter around her shaking body, then sat down beside her, his arm braced behind her, supporting her back. "How do you think I feel about you?" His voice was flat and expressionless.

She stared at her hand, which was clenched in her lap. "I think you wish you'd never laid eyes on me."

"Do you really believe that?"

She nodded her head as she wiped away the tears with her fingertips. "Yes."

"How did you fall down the stairs? They weren't icy."

It was a totally unexpected question, and it left her feeling particularly vulnerable. "I was careless."

He spanned her chin with his hand and forced her to meet his unwavering stare. "You were crying, weren't you?"

She didn't answer him—there was no need. "You're going home as soon as we can get you out of here," he said.

Home, she thought bleakly. *I don't have a home.* Releasing his grip, Steve stood up and walked out of the room. So the end had finally come. Leslie pressed her hand over her face as she was stricken by a soul-shattering grief for the loss of what might have been. She sat huddled on the bed, her endurance broken. He had just walked out of her life, and she could no longer bear the pent-up agony that clawed at her. The tears began to fall, and raw racking sobs ripped through her as she finally broke down and wept violently. Her inner dam had finally shattered with the stress.

Strong arms encircled her, and her head was cradled firmly against a broad chest. Nothing else registered as all the loneliness, fear and anguish she had locked away for so long raged forth in a stormy tempest terrible to witness.

Steve drew her across his lap and rested his cheek on her head as his arms tightened around her. His face was a gray tormented mask; he said nothing, but instead let her purge her pain with the unrelenting tears.

Leslie didn't remember much after that. The medication cocooned her in a drifting ethereal numbness, leaving her with only vague impressions. She had become a functioning robot.

She remembered Steve dressing her the next morning, and she recalled some of the trip to Grande Prairie; she also remembered boarding a commercial flight, and changing planes in Edmonton. But it wasn't until they had been in the air some time that the drugged disjointed sensation cleared and she became aware of what was happening. She felt vaguely alarmed when she realized it was dark out. She had lost an entire day, and she remembered practically nothing of it, except that Steve had been with her constantly.

She glanced at the man beside her. He was slouched in the seat, his head tipped back against the headrest, his fingers laced across his chest. For an instant she thought he was sleeping, but then he blinked and she realized his eyes weren't completely closed. He was obviously thinking about something very deeply. He looked haggard, his face lined with tension and fatigue.

He must have sensed she was watching him and he turned to look at her. "Are you feeling uncomfortable?"

She shook her head. "No, just numb."

He checked the sling to make sure it was snug, and he saw her try to swallow. "Is your mouth dry?"

"A little."

"It's the medication that's doing it." He signaled to the flight attendant, then turned to her again. "Would you like a glass of juice?"

"Yes, please."

Steve murmured something to the stewardess, then glanced at his watch. Leslie didn't have the energy or strength to check her own. It didn't matter anymore; her time had run out.

"Here's your juice, Les. We're only a few minutes from touchdown."

She nodded her head as she took the glass from him. She hadn't realized how thirsty she was until she began to drink, and never had apple juice tasted so good. She drained the glass and handed it back to him.

He passed the empty glass to the waiting attendant, then adjusted Leslie's seat into an upright position and checked her seat belt. She heard the jet engines change pitch, and the Fasten Seat Belt sign flashed on. Pressing her head back against the headrest, she closed her eyes. She hoped the landing was a smooth one so it wouldn't jar her shoulder and start it aching again. She wanted to maintain this disconnected feeling for as long as she could.

The landing was smooth, but Leslie didn't open her eyes until the plane taxied up to the terminal and stopped. She unbuckled her seat belt and watched the other passengers as they clamored out of their seats and gathered their belongings from the overhead compartments.

She glanced at Steve and wondered why he wasn't moving. In response to her questioning look, he said, "We'll wait until the plane empties. You don't need someone bumping into that shoulder."

She dispassionately wondered what he was going to do with her when they did deplane. He wouldn't abandon her—Steve wouldn't do that—but she hoped that he wouldn't come with her to the McAllisters'. She would much rather that he simply put her into a cab and send her on her way with a minimum of fuss.

A terrible ache grew in her breast, and tears hovered dangerously close to the surface. She had to hang on to herself until he was gone—she desperately did not want to create another scene.

Steve stood up and grasped her elbow as he helped her out of her seat. Her legs felt like rubber, and she staggered slightly as she slipped into the aisle. He steadied her, then retrieved their coats from the overhead compartment. He held Leslie's as she slipped her left arm into the sleeve, then he draped the coat carefully over her injured shoulder and handed her her shoulder bag.

The aisle of the plane seemed ten miles long as Leslie started toward the exit. She wanted to get off the plane, out of the terminal and away from Steve McRory as fast as she could. She had to get away from him before she came unglued. She had no resources left with which to fight the terrifying panic that was growing inside her.

She stumbled as she stepped onto the enclosed ramp, and Steve grabbed her arm and held on to it firmly as he guided her through the ramp corridor and down the stairs.

As they walked through the door to the arrival area, Steve scanned the crowd as though he was looking for someone. He altered their course and Leslie felt a cold knot of dread when she recognized Steve's father standing on the outskirts of the crowd gathered along the luggage conveyor belt.

She came to an abrupt halt, her face very pale. How could she possibly face a member of Steve's family?

Glancing up at Steve, her mouth trembling, she nervously grasped her shoulder bag against her. "Steve, I can take a cab to the McAllisters'...."

He turned toward her, his features suddenly inflexible, his eyes piercing her like blue shafts of steel. "What in hell are you talking about?"

She felt confused and uncertain. "You said...you said you were taking me home...."

He scrutinized her with an odd unreadable stare, then slipped his hand up the side of her neck and captured her chin in his hand, his voice low and determined. "I *am* taking you home, Leslie—and home has never been the McAllisters'."

"I don't understand—"

"This isn't the time or place for a discussion," he said tautly. "Come on. Dad's waiting for us."

He never gave her an opportunity to respond, but gripped her elbow and piloted her over to his father. 'Hi, dad.''

"Hello, son." Hal McRory smiled warmly down at Leslie. "Hope that trip wasn't too hard on you, Leslie. Steve said you took quite a fall."

She glanced up at Steve, then gestured self-consciously as she looked at his father. "I'm just bruised a little."

Steve snorted, and Leslie could feel herself flush as he spoke to his father. "Where's the car, dad?"

Mr. McRory motioned to the glass doors just behind him and grinned. "It's right outside, parked in a No Parking zone."

Steve gave his father a rueful amused look, then glanced down at Leslie. "Why don't you take Leslie to the car, and I'll get the luggage."

Hal nodded. "Sure thing."

"Make certain no one jars her shoulder—and help her when she gets into the car—and you'd better put her in the back seat." Steve turned away.

Hal grinned down at Leslie, a wicked sparkle in his eyes. "I hope I have all his orders straight—he's sure turned into a bossy cuss."

Leslie couldn't help but smile back at him. Hal put his arm around her, his massive frame shielding her from the jostling crowd as he guided her out of the terminal. The blue Cadillac was right outside the door, parked in the crosswalk, its hazard lights flashing defiantly. Leslie shook her head wryly. The McRorys seemed to make their own rules.

By the time she was settled in the car, her shoulder was throbbing mercilessly and her bruised leg was aching. She leaned her head back against the seat and closed her eyes. It had been several hours since Steve had given her any medication, and it was obvious the numbing effects of the drug had worn off.

Hal McRory got out of the car when Steve came from the terminal and helped him stow their suitcases in the trunk. Steve walked around to the passenger side, but instead of getting into the front seat, he climbed into the back beside Leslie.

He took the bottle of capsules from his jacket pocket and handed two to her. "Will you be able to swallow them without water?"

She nodded her head and put them one at a time in her mouth. Then her eyes widened as Steve eased her onto his lap. Ignoring her bewilderment, he tucked her uninjured arm around his neck, then cradled her head against his shoulder, holding her in a firm comfortable position.

"Are you ready to roll?" came Hal's inquiry from the front seat.

There was no humor in Steve's voice when he answered his father. "Yes—and you can break the speed limit if you want." He stroked Leslie's hair as he whispered huskily, "I know you've just about had it, Leslie, but this is the last leg. Try to sleep."

Leslie couldn't answer him. The tenderness in his voice was nearly her undoing, and she closed her eyes against the sting of threatening tears.

By the time they hit the outskirts of Calgary, the turmoil of her confused thoughts had fallen victim to a deep drug-induced slumber, and she slept, safe and secure, in Steve's arms.

She didn't wake up until they arrived at the Mc-

Rory ranch, where the cold crisp winter air brought her around to a state of semiconsciousness as Steve carried her from the car to the house. Steve and his mother had her settled comfortably in bed in a matter of minutes, and Leslie fell asleep immediately, her hand clasped firmly in Steve's as he watched over her.

CHAPTER SEVENTEEN

WHEN LESLIE AWOKE the next morning, she felt groggy and oddly displaced until she recognized the dainty old-fashioned wallpaper that covered the walls of the tiny bedroom.

It was then that the fog disappeared abruptly, and was replaced with a feeling of confused desperation. Why? Why had Steve brought her here? She closed her eyes as a sense of acute hopelessness swept over her. She couldn't take much more of the hostility that had radiated from him the last few weeks. She was too battered and bruised, both emotionally and physically. She just wanted to disappear and hide away—from everything and everybody.

She sighed, then cautiously shifted her body, biting back a groan as a shaft of pain shot through her. She was so stiff and sore that she could barely move, but somehow she managed to ease out of bed and creep to the window.

Brushing back the curtains, she squinted against the sharp brightness of sunshine reflecting off the brilliant white snow. She stared out unseeingly at the rolling land, her small face drawn and pale, her eyes dark with an inner torment. Steve had done her no favor by bringing her here. Too many memories from the happy days they had spent at Christmas crowded in on her, smothering her with a terrible ache.

She let the curtains fall across the window when she heard the door open behind her. "Good morning, dear. I thought I heard you stirring."

Leslie forced herself to smile at Doris McRory. "Good morning. By the look of the sun, I would guess that the morning is nearly over, though."

"It's going on eleven. Steve said you would probably sleep late. I think perhaps my son had a heavy hand with the drugs he was giving you." Mrs. McRory smiled warmly. "He had to go into Calgary today, but he left some very specific orders about you. I don't think he trusts us on our own."

It isn't you he doesn't trust, Leslie thought grimly.

"We have an appointment in the city to have your shoulder X-rayed early this afternoon, so we should leave here by twelve-thirty." She began to straighten the bed. "Would you like a hot bath, dear? I'm sure you must be aching all over. You certainly have some nasty bruises."

Leslie heaved a sigh of appreciation. "There's nothing I would like better."

Doris pursed her lips with motherly concern. "Steve said I was to be sure and help you, and that I mustn't leave you alone."

Leslie's smile was slightly fixed as a spurt of anger colored her cheeks. She didn't know why he was so concerned—she certainly wasn't going to drown herself in his damned tub!

The bath was the most wonderful one Leslie ever had, the heat soaking away the stiffness and soothing her aching muscles. Her shoulder was badly bruised, but the intense pain had definitely eased; unfortunately her ribs and hip were still extremely sore. Mrs. McRory shampooed her hair and blew it dry for her, so by the time Leslie was dressed, she was feeling almost human. Almost.

By the time they arrived back at the ranch, she was so exhausted that she could hardly drag herself up the stairs. The technician hadn't been particularly gentle in positioning her shoulder for the required X-rays, so it was aching badly again. The doctor had insisted on X-rays of her hip and ribs as well, and she felt as though she'd been thoroughly mauled. Her hipbone was bruised, it turned out, and she had hairline fractures in three ribs, but fortunately no permanent damage had been done to her shoulder. After suffering through the countless X-rays, however, Leslie felt as though someone had tossed her down another flight of stairs.

Mrs. McRory helped her undress and get into a loose nightgown. With relief, Leslie took the medication the doctor had prescribed and eased herself into bed. She stared unhappily at the ceiling as she waited for the drug to carry her off into oblivion, to block out the thoughts and images that were tormenting her. But unconsciousness did not arrive before the tears of anguish. When she finally fell asleep, her thick eyelashes were tangled and wet, and only in slumber did her tight fists relax. She slept deeply, so she didn't hear the door open, nor did she hear the scrape of the chair as it was drawn closer to the bed.

THE OLD-FASHIONED FRINGED LAMP on the bureau in the corner cast a dusky amber glow in the room, patterning it with soft murky shadows. Leslie's eyelids were still heavy with sleep as she gazed around. The gentle light was oddly reassuring as it dispelled the darkness.

Her vision blurred suddenly as a haunting misery welled up inside her. A desperate little sob escaped her lips when the reality of her loneliness fragmented that brief tranquility. She covered her face with her left hand, struggling to stifle the sobs of panic that were choking her.

There was a whisper of a sound, then a masculine hand caught her wrist. Steve's voice was strained as he whispered, "Don't cry, Leslie—please, don't cry." He slipped his arm beneath her as he sat down on the bed beside her.

Leslie looked at him, her tear-glazed eyes wide with uncertainty at this unexpected change in him. The anger was gone. Her mouth was trembling when she spoke, her voice low and shaky. "Steve. . .?"

"Shh, Leslie—just let me hold you for a little while." With profound tenderness he lay down beside her and gathered her against him. Leslie clenched her eyes shut as she struggled to swallow the sobs of overpowering relief that assaulted her. Steve silently nestled her shaking body closer to his as he softly stroked her hair.

It took a long time for the fierce battle of raw emotions to subside in Leslie, but finally, harbored safely within his arms, she was able to relax weakly against him. She didn't try to fathom the change in his attitude toward her; instead, she savored the warmth and closeness of him. He was no longer angry, he was holding her with gentleness, and that was all that mattered.

She opened her eyes as Steve's hand spanned her chin. A shudder quivered through him as he kissed her, his lips warm and undemanding. There was a restrained hunger in him that moved her deeply, and Leslie responded to him, yielding to his every touch, offering him the comfort that he was searching for with his sweet poignant kiss.

He lifted his head and with trembling fingers touched her cheek; then he sucked in his breath and pressed her face against his neck. His eyes were revealing his inner pain, and there was a feeling of desperation radiating from him. An ache twisted around Leslie's heart, an ache that was nearly unbearable. She had not been the only one to suffer agony, and she was filled with a wretched sense of guilt. She had never meant to hurt him as she had.

She swallowed hard against the tightness in her throat, then murmured huskily, "Please forgive me, Steve. I never meant to hurt you...."

He covered her mouth with his fingers, then looked down at her, his eyes haunted, his face pale and grave. His voice was a tortured whisper when he said, "After all that I've done to you, can *you* forgive *me*? I love you, Leslie—so very much. And I need you so badly."

Fervent hope rose in Leslie as she stared at him, her expressive elfin face registering her disbelief. There was a moment of electric silence, then she whispered tremulously, "Are you sure you still want me?"

"Yes! God, yes! I want you and I need you...." There was such anguish in his voice that it hurt Leslie to hear it. He buried his face in her hair as he groaned, "I can't imagine my life without you. Nothing would mean anything to me unless I have you."

Leslie slipped her uninjured arm around his shoulders as happiness burst within her. The cold aching emptiness was shattered, leaving her filled with a beautiful warmth and fierce protective love. Tears of relief streamed down her face as she clung to him with all the strength she possessed.

"Oh, Steve, I've been so terrified. I didn't know how I would survive without you. I felt like I was dying inside."

"I've been such a bastard, Leslie. When you told me about Kaidon Industries, I couldn't think rationally. All I could see was all that damned money, and I felt like you'd bought me. To me, it seemed as though you'd deliberately trampled my pride and my sense of independence. It damned near destroyed me to know that you didn't need me as much as I thought you did."

Easing away from him, she laid her hand on his cheek, her face solemn. "But I do need you—in so many ways. I need your strength, your love. I need the sense of security only you can give me." She smoothed her hand across his tense face, her eyes willing him to understand. "You saw the money—all I see is the awesome responsibility. Someday Gordon isn't going to be there to give direction, and that frightens me to death. Thousands of people around the world depend on Kaidon Industries for a livelihood, and someday the decisions for running that company are going to be mine. It terrifies me. I know I can't handle it alone." She caught his hand and laced her fingers through his, her grip transmit-

ting her fear. "I don't need you to support me financially, Steve, but I desperately need you to support me
in so many other ways. I need you...far more than
you need me." Tears were glistening in her thick
lashes and her voice was shaking with an urgency to
make him understand.

Steve stared at her for a moment, then pulled her
against him and pressed his face against her neck, his
breath warm against her skin. "Ah, Leslie—I feel like
such a heel for hurting you so. I've been so blind."

She closed her eyes and pressed her cheek against
his. "I love you, Steve McRory. You have no idea
how safe I feel when you hold me."

With tender care, he eased her onto her back and
gazed down at her as he bracketed her face with his
hands, his eyes filled with regret. "There have been
so many times I've loathed myself for how I was
treating you. Your deception drove me to retaliation.
I deliberately set you up so that you'd have to face
Luther Denver, and then there was that ugly incident.
I felt so damned responsible, but it was too late to
undo the damage. When you locked yourself in your
room and refused to talk to me, I felt so rotten—you
were so alone." His face contorted with a grimace of
remembered agony. "And when I grabbed you so
brutally after your fall...and I hurt you so...."

Leslie smoothed her fingers along his cheek, her
eyes dark with tenderness and compassion. "Don't
Steve—please don't torture yourself thinking about
the past. It doesn't matter anymore. What matters is
this very moment." She caught the back of his head
and pulled it down. She kissed him softly, her mouth
pliant, warm and inviting.

Steve groaned and twisted his mouth away, his body trembling. "Leslie...ah, Leslie, don't tempt me. My control is shot to hell and I want you so badly."

"Steve...."

He covered her parted lips with his fingers, his eyes smokey and haunted. "I have to leave in a couple of hours. I have to catch the last airbus from Calgary to Edmonton so I can meet Bob Jansen early tomorrow morning—he's flying me back to Redwillow." He closed his eyes, his face lined with regret. "I don't want to go—God, I don't want to go." He looked at her, and Leslie could see the misery that was tearing at him. "Six more rigs will be moving into Redwillow in the next few weeks, Leslie, and I have to be there."

Leslie tenderly combed her fingers through his tawny hair, her eyes soft with understanding. "I know you do."

"I don't want to leave you."

"I know that, too."

His face softened as he tenderly caressed her slender neck, his touch feather soft, sending shivers of pleasure tingling down her spine. "I'll be back in four weeks, Les, and we should be able to manage a few days to ourselves. If you don't mind not having a big wedding, we could be married...."

Her eyes were shining with happiness and unshed tears as she hugged him tightly against her. "Oh, Steve, I don't *want* a big wedding. I just want you, and the sooner the better!"

Steve laughed huskily, his eyes kindling with a mesmerizing warmth. "I do like that kind of enthusiasm."

She smiled at him softly, her dimples flashing. "Do you now?"

"Yes, I do...and you know it." He kissed her soundly, then released his hold on her and sat up. "Come on, we'd better get the hell out of this bedroom. The situation could get out of hand pretty fast."

Leslie slanted a provocative look at him. "I'm sure you could handle it."

"Leslie...." Behind the laughter was a warning note that she recognized, and she smiled.

"Cheek." He laughed as he carefully helped her off the bed. "We'd better go down and talk this over with mom and dad. But knowing my mother, she probably has everything planned already."

He kissed her again, his mouth lingering for a breathtaking moment. Then with a shaky sigh, he took her hand firmly in his and led her from the room.

Steve paused on the little landing halfway down the stairs. He whispered her name, and Leslie looked up at him, her bubble of happiness giving way to a familiar heart-stirring warmth when she saw the smoldering look in his eyes. She buried her fingers in his tawny hair as he bent his head, his mouth covering hers in a demanding kiss that rocketed them into a dimension of passion filled with naked hunger.

His mouth was hot and moist as his tongue probed the sweetness of her mouth, with a desperate urgency that sent her senses wildly spinning. Desire licked through her blood like wildfire, robbing her of every coherent thought except the need to hold Steve in her arms, to experience the soaring release of love. She gave a low moan of protest when he jerked his mouth away, his breathing ragged, his heart pounding frantically as he nestled her against him.

"These next four weeks are going to be the longest weeks of my life. God, but I'm going to miss you."

LESLIE DISCOVERED FOR HERSELF that Steve's prediction was all too accurate. The days crawled by with agonizing slowness, and the nights were tortured and never ending. Her longings left her sleepless and aching for his touch. The only thing that kept her sane was Steve's nightly phone calls, but even those were tainted by the knowledge that they were hundreds of miles apart.

Doris McRory, in her warm, perceptive way, offered Leslie the understanding that had been denied to the young woman all her life. During the following days, a strong bond of friendship developed between the two, and Leslie cherished the sense of belonging that filled her with such deep contentment.

The plans for the wedding seemed simple enough initially. There was to be an informal church wedding, followed by an open house at the McRory ranch. Leslie had felt guilty about involving Doris in so much extra work, but she wisely sensed that the McRorys' would be offended if she had hired caterers for the reception. Steve's sisters enthusiastically pitched in to help, all of them delighted that their big brother had finally decided to marry, especially since they all so thoroughly approved of Leslie.

However the preparations soon turned into a community event, and more than once Leslie was moved to the brink of tears by the warm generosity of the people in the district.

And the days did pass, one by one. Steve was to arrive home late Thursday night, and Leslie was counting the hours. By Wednesday she felt like the clock had stopped. She was restless and edgy, her nerves stretched taut by the endless waiting. To make matters worse, Steve's call that night was very brief, and for Leslie, very unsatisfactory.

When she finally went to bed, she tossed and turned fitfully, unable to sleep. Steve would be home tomorrow, and the thought filled her with excitement and eager anticipation. She felt exactly like a child who was fidgeting her way through the unremitting eternity of Christmas Eve.

Finally, climbing out of bed, she went to the window and stared out at the snow-covered landscape, which was bathed in the silver glow of a full moon. She closed her eyes and rested her forehead against the cool windowpane, able to think of nothing but that moment when they'd finally be alone. An aching fever curled inside her as she thought about that moment when their bodies would be welded together as one....

Gripping the window ledge, she tried to suppress the awful emptiness that was gnawing at her. She had to stop this or she would go mad!

She sighed and opened her eyes, starting to turn away from the window. The gleam of headlights through the dense stand of bare trees beside the house arrested her. The lights went out; then there was a slam of a vehicle door. She glanced at the luminous face of the clock by her bed. It was two o'clock in the morning. Who...?

Expectation tingled through her, and with her pulse racing, Leslie slipped from the room and ran silently down the stairs. The light in the kitchen was switched on as she flew through the living room.

"Steve!"

He whirled around, the exhaustion in his eyes giving way to delight as she catapulted into his outstretched arms.

Laughing through her tears, she hugged him fiercely. "Why didn't you tell me you were coming home tonight?"

His embrace was like a vise as he crushed her against him. "Because I wasn't sure until the last minute if I could get away. Besides, I wanted to surprise you."

"I'm so glad you're home. It's been so long...."

"God, I know." His voice was suddenly gripped with a surge of emotion. "I've been driving myself crazy thinking about you. Oh, Leslie," he groaned, then bent his head and kissed her with an unchained urgency, his mouth moving against hers with a searching hunger that sent a hot current through her.

She strained against him, aching for them to be reunited totally. Sensing her fervor, he lifted her body up until her hips were welded against his, and the intoxicating feeling of their aroused bodies molded so tightly together fragmented her consciousness with a ground swell of desire. His powerful body seemed to envelop her as he buried his face in the hollow of her shoulder. Shivers of erotic pleasure coursed through her as his moist tongue savored the taste of her skin, her flesh agonizingly sensitized by his touch. Slowly he trailed his mouth up her neck, and a low sob escaped her when he explored the recesses of her ear.

She clung to him, her body trembling as he whispered, "I want you, Les. I want to touch you, to feel your skin against mine." His embrace was desperate as he pressed her closer, his heart beating wildly against hers.

Leslie felt like she was drowning in a fever of feelings. "Don't stop," she breathed, her voice quavering with the storm of sensation that was bombarding her. "I don't want you to stop."

She felt him shudder as he claimed her mouth with an abandon that was devastating.

"Steve, is that you?"

Steve jerked as though he had been shot, and Leslie felt as though someone had just immersed her in ice water. His chest heaving as he fought for breath, Steve slowly let Leslie down, then protectively cradled her against him.

It seemed to take a massive effort for him to answer. "Yes, it is, dad."

"Does Leslie know you're home?"

"Do you know I'm home?" he whispered gruffly against her hair.

Leslie detected a hint of amusement in his voice, and she managed a tremulous smile as she looked up at him. "I know you're home. I can tell by the state I'm in."

Steve tipped back his head and laughed as he hugged her. There was still laughter in his voice when he called up to his father, "She's already down here."

"Tell her to start the coffee. I'll throw some clothes on."

"Okay." Steve stood gazing down at Leslie, his sapphire eyes like blue magic, then kissed her with such tempered longing that it made her ache. With immeasurable tenderness, he took her face in his hands and gave her a slow provocative smile. "Damn him. He's putting on his clothes just when I was ready to tear yours off." He kissed her softly, then in a very low voice said, "There's no justice in this world."

Leslie didn't say anything, but smiled up at him, her eyes soft and misty with love.

His hands tightened on her face as he drew in his breath quickly. "Don't look at me like that," he sighed, his eyes smokey and compelling. "It makes it so hard for me to let you go."

Leslie slipped her arms around his waist and snuggled against him. "The waiting is almost over, love. Just three more days."

He kissed the top of her head, then tunneled his hand in her hair. "It's not over by a long shot. I know these next three days are going to be the longest and the most difficult ones I've ever spent."

As LESLIE PREPARED FOR BED Friday night, she reflected on that comment of Steve's. The past days had been long and very difficult. An electric tension crackled between them, and their sexual awareness of each other had continued to grow until they were prowling restlessly like two caged cats. The only time they could relax their guard was when there were others around to act as a buffer between them. But even then it didn't always help.

The strain was affecting both of them, and there were moments when it was intolerable. There had been a situation that night after the wedding rehearsal that had sent questioning looks flying from one family member to the other.

Steve had been leaning against the fireplace, a drink in his hand, while Leslie had been sitting beside Doris on the sofa across the room from him. She had laughed at something Hal had said, and then she'd glanced across at Steve, her eyes sparkling, her face flushed. He was watching her, his face impassive, his jaw set. Anyone else might have thought he was angry, but Leslie could see the tightly leashed passion that was smoldering in his piercing blue eyes.

She could feel the raw hunger in that look as she stared at him, her eyes darkening, her breathing uneven as her body responded to his silent message as if it had been a physical caress. Their eyes had locked and held for a paralyzing moment; then with a muttered oath, Steve had slammed his drink down on the mantel and strode out of the room.

There had been an awkward silence. Leslie was keenly aware of what was wrong, but it wasn't something you could very well explain to the family.

She sighed wearily and slipped into her housecoat. There would be a nerve-grating tension gnawing at them tomorrow. In fact, if they made it through the ceremony without snapping at each other it would be a miracle. She closed her eyes and clenched her hands at her side as she suddenly felt like weeping. If only. . . .

"Are you still awake, dear?"

Taking a deep breath, Leslie turned and smiled at Mrs. McRory. "Yes, I am. Come in."

Doris slipped into the room and closed the door softly behind her as Leslie sat down on the edge of the bed. The older woman sat down and put her arm around Leslie's shoulders, her voice gentle with concern. "Is something wrong, Les? You were so quiet after Steve huffed out. Have you had a quarrel?"

Leslie glanced up, then lowered her eyes. "No, we haven't quarreled—it's nothing like that. It's...it's the waiting."

Mrs. McRory patted Leslie's hand sympathetically, then nodded her head, her eyes warm with understanding. "I see." She didn't say anything for a moment, then she patted Leslie's hand again. "When you go down to Steve, mind the third step—it creaks something fierce."

Leslie's eyes widened, her expression one of stunned bemusement, and then she blushed hotly. Doris smoothed Leslie's hair, then hugged her, her eyes brimming with tears. "I'm so happy, Leslie. You're exactly the kind of wife I've always wanted for Steve. I love him very much and I know you're going to make him very happy."

Leslie hugged her back. "I'm going to try very hard to do just that."

"I know you will." She kissed Leslie on the forehead. "God bless you, darling."

For a long time after Doris left, Leslie remained motionless, overwhelmed by the poignant happiness that filled her. Not only was she marrying a man whom she loved beyond reason, she was also acquiring a very special family.

With trembling fingers, she brushed the tears from

her eyes, then she went to her suitcase and removed a wispy mauve negligee set.

A few moments later she was standing outside the guest-room door. She took a deep breath in an attempt to steady her vibrating nerves, then knocked softly. It startled her when Steve opened the door almost immediately.

Wordlessly they stood staring at each other; then he stepped aside and motioned her in. He closed the door behind her, then walked across the room to the window and stood staring out, his hands resting on his hips. He was so distant that a cold knot of uncertainty tightened in her stomach.

He loosened his tie before he spoke, his voice strained. "Is there something wrong, Leslie?"

She clasped her hands together and swallowed against the nervous flutter in her midriff. "Your mother just came to see me."

"And...?"

She swallowed again, then whispered, her voice faltering. "She said...." Leslie had to take a deep breath before she could go on. "She said to...to mind the third stair when I came down to see you."

There was an odd edge to his voice, and his back stiffened. "Did she?"

Leslie suddenly realized it was a mistake to have come, and she turned to go. She had just opened the door when Steve's arm shot in front of her and pushed it shut.

Catching her by the shoulders, he turned her to face him. There was a low evocative tenor to his question. "Did you?"

Leslie couldn't look at him, and she twisted her fingers together nervously. "Did I what?"

Slipping his hand under her chin, he gently lifted her face. "Did you miss the third step?"

She stared at him numbly for a split second, then dimpled up at him, her cheeks pink. "Yes."

Steve's intoxicating smile seduced her, and Leslie gazed up at him, completely captivated by the warm intimate look in his eyes. There was a long silent interchange between them; then she reached up and slowly undid Steve's loosened tie.

He never touched her, but his jaw tensed, and the warmth in his eyes kindled into a flame of desire as Leslie unbuttoned his shirt and slipped it off his shoulders. There was a heavy breathlessness in her as she smoothed her trembling hands up his naked torso and across his chest. Steve's breathing became more labored as she slowly explored his body with inquisitive hands.

When she undid the buckle of his belt, his face twisted in a tormented grimace and he hauled her into his arms. He crushed her against him, his voice hoarse.

"Leslie...oh, Leslie, you don't know what you do to me when you touch me like that."

His mouth sought hers, and her lips parted willingly as she surrendered to him the moist sweetness of her mouth. Like a parched man, he seemed to drink all the love she offered him, his lips moving thirstily against hers.

Leslie was aware of his belt buckle pressing against her and of the layers of chiffon that slithered between them as she pressed her breasts against his chest. Slipping her hand up his rib cage, she savored the feel of his warm skin beneath her touch. A compelling need to have his naked body against her own rose within her, and she slid her hand beneath the waistband of his slacks.

Steve murmured her name raggedly, then eased her away from him and with trembling hands, brushed the negligee from her shoulders. He kissed the curve of her shoulder, his mouth hot against her skin. With tormenting slowness, he slid the straps of her nightgown down over her shoulders, exposing her breasts.

An exquisite fever of anticipation flamed through Leslie as he slowly smoothed the mauve silk from her body. For hot hypnotizing moments, he looked at her, his gaze like an erotic embrace; then he reached out and tenderly cupped her breast in his hand. He lowered his head, and a bolt of heat scorched through Leslie as his mouth covered the rosy peak.

A sweet fermenting weakness invaded her body, and her strength dissolved with his arousing caress. She swayed against him, her bones melting like warm honey, and sensing her helplessness, he gathered her up in his arms and carried her to the bed.

Her heart pounded wildly, her blood like mulled wine as she watched him undress. As he came to her, she whispered his name. It was as if two white-hot halves were forged together as one when he finally gathered her naked body against the length of his.

They held each other until the tempest abated, and their passion scorched through to another dimension—a dimension of intoxicating pleasure. One hot rich sensation after another flooded them. Steve's exploring mouth slowly and entreatingly awakened every nerve in Leslie's body until she was trembling beneath his unrelenting assault. There was a throbbing swell growing within her, inundating her with feelings so profound, so evocative, that she felt as though she was going to drown in them.

Wanting him to know the exquisite ache pulsing through her, Leslie trailed her mouth down his neck to his chest, her tongue inscribing moist circles on his salty skin. His hands grasped her head, his fingers thrust in her hair, and she felt his muscles grow taut beneath her mouth as she stoked the fire in him.

Savoring the taste of him, the texture of his skin, she continued to arouse him, her moist mouth searching and provocative. Lower and lower she went, until her tongue probed the recesses of his navel. She slipped her hand up the inside of his thigh, her touch agonizingly light as she began to stroke him.

A shudder shot through him, and a low tortured cry was torn from him as he grabbed her wrist and yanked her hand away. "Leslie, no more," he ground out hoarsely. "I can't stand any more."

He lifted her on top of him and with a muffled groan, he took her, his body penetrating the heat of hers with an excruciating slowness that was nearly unbearable. Leslie felt like she was suffocating as searing desire ripped through her like a flash fire.

Cupping her face in his hands, Steve whispered, his voice compelling, "Open your eyes, Leslie. I want you to look at me."

A sob caught in her throat as she gazed down into the blue fire of his eyes, eyes that were drugged with desire.

With a deliberate measured pace, he moved beneath her, transporting her to the very brink of rapture—then he paused. She hung onto him with a desperation that seemed to wring at her very soul. A floodgate had been released, and her immeasurable feelings for him came boiling out with the force of wild white water—rampaging, uncontrollable and with such untamed beauty. Leslie could feel the storm rising in Steve, as well, as two violent torrents merged into one, flinging them into the turbulence. Their gaze was fused by their mutual need, and Leslie was immobilized by the unendurable longing that raged in her.

Over and over again he brought her to the very point of no return, until the flood tide could no longer be denied. A low moan was wrenched from her lips, and with an unleashed desperation, Steve pulled her down to him, his mouth possessing hers with a frantic hunger. Like a solar flare, their passion erupted as fire met fire and their bodies merged into one glorious flame.

A very long time later, the fire of passion had finally diminished to the glowing embers of perfect serenity, and they lay wrapped in each other's arms, fulfilled and complete. Steve gently combed his fingers through Leslie's tousled hair as she pressed her face against the curve of his neck.

His arms tightened around her in a tender sheltering embrace as he sighed contentedly. "Thank heaven I came to my senses when I did! I can't imagine my life without you."

Leslie kissed the pulse at the base of his neck, then lifted her head and looked down at him. She caressed his bottom lip with her fingertips, the huskiness of her voice touched with uncertainty. "I hope you never regret it, Steve. Our life together is always going to be so public, so scrutinized."

Smiling softly, he brushed back a wisp of hair that was clinging to her cheek. "I know that—and I know it's going to put tremendous pressure on us." There was such a poignant warmth in his gaze that it brought tears to her eyes. "But I also know that all of it will be bearable as long as you're beside me."

Her mouth trembled as she whispered, "I'll be there."

Steve wiped away the tears that were clinging to her lashes. "In a few more hours you'll be my wife," he said, his face growing sober and his eyes smokey. "I love you, Leslie. For the rest of my life, I'll love you."

Leslie was so moved that she was unable to speak, but she responded to him wordlessly, giving him all her boundless love with a pliant passionate kiss.

With a soft groan, Steve's arms tightened around her, and he held her like he would never let her go.

THE WEDDING PARTY CONTINUED long after Steve and Leslie left on Saturday night.

The younger people had, by sheer numbers and noise, driven the older ones out of the living room and into the seclusion of the kitchen.

The McAllisters, the Donners, the Logans, Steve's parents and John McRory were all gathered around the huge kitchen table, enjoying some of Doris's delicious pastries.

"Well, Ted, I'll wager you never expected a wedding to be the outcome when you went to Steve with the Redwillow proposal,'' declared John McRory as he added cream to his coffee.

Maggie McAllister laughed and shook her head. ''Then you don't know my husband as well as you think you do, John. Ted's an old matchmaker from away back. I knew exactly what his scheme was the very first time he invited Steve over to the house.''

Gordon Donner laughed heartily, his round belly trembling. ''No wonder you looked so pleased with yourself when you gave the toast to the bride. You looked like the cat who drank all the cream.''

''Well, I figured I was allowed to feel a little smug,'' said Ted. ''But you have no room to talk, you old scoundrel. You looked like you were about to pop a few buttons off your vest when you gave Les away. You'd have thought you'd arranged the whole thing all by yourself.''

There was a ripple of laughter, then a brief lull that was jarred by the racket from the other room.

''I ain't seen such a pretty bride since we was married, Amy,'' commented Frank Logan, patting his wife's hand affectionately. ''When she came down that aisle, she looked like there was a bright light glowin' in her. And when she looked up at Steve with them big eyes shinin' and filled with them big tears, I had to do some heavy swallerin', I tell you.''

Ted and John exchanged looks of amazement. Big, rough, tough Frank Logan...?

Constance Donner blew her nose, then sighed with deep feeling. ''I know exactly how you felt, Frank. Steve watched Leslie come down that aisle as though she was the only person in the whole world. Then he came to meet her with that look on his face...and he took her hand in his and kissed it...well I cried like a baby.'' She tried to mop away her overflow of tears with a very damp hankie. ''They acted like there wasn't another soul within miles of them. It was so beautiful.''

Laughing shakily, Doris McRory also wiped her eyes. ''If you keep this up, Constance, you'll have us all crying again.''

Hal McRory smiled kindly at his wife and patted her shoulder. ''There's nothing wrong with tears of happiness. It's so wonderful to see two people who are as happy as Leslie and Steve.'' He sighed and nodded his head with satisfaction. ''It sure has been a very special day.''

Many miles away, in a darkened hotel room, two very contented people lay wrapped in each other's arms, happiness eddying around them like a sun-dappled brook.

For them it had indeed been a special day, a day of love and laughter and the heartfelt good wishes of family and friends. It had been filled with the joy and expectations of a new beginning—a beginning that held all the splendor and beauty of a fresh spring dawn.

A Harlequin

ROBERTA LEIGH

Collector's Edition

A specially designed collection of six exciting love stories by one of the world's favorite romance writers—Roberta Leigh, author of more than 60 bestselling novels!

1 **Love in Store**   4 **The Savage Aristocrat**
2 **Night of Love**   5 **The Facts of Love**
3 **Flower of the Desert** 6 **Too Young to Love**

Available in August wherever paperback books are sold, or available through Harlequin Reader Service. Simply complete and mail the coupon below.

What readers say about SUPERROMANCE